Ginny Gall

Ginny Gall

A NOVEL

Charlie Smith

HARPER PERENNIAL

NEW YORK • LONDON • TORONTO • SYDNEY • NEW DELHI • AUCKLAND

A hardcover edition of this book was published in 2016 by HarperCollins Publishers.

HarperCollins books may be purchased for educational, business, or sales promotional use. For information, please e-mail the Special Markets Department at SPsales @harpercollins.com.

FIRST HARPER PERENNIAL EDITION PUBLISHED 2017.

Designed by Sunil Manchikanti

Library of Congress Cataloging-in-Publication Data has been applied for.

ISBN 978-0-06-243496-8 (pbk.)

17 18 19 20 21   OV/LSC   10 9 8 7 6 5 4 3 2 1

One always thinks there's a landing place coming. But there aint.

—VIRGINIA WOOLF

BOOK ONE

In front of the Celestial Theater sat an old africano woman who covered her long bald pate with a yellow scarf that trailed down her back like a tail. Each morning she washed the scarf in the Collosso Fountain in Mecklenburg Square and put it on again, wet, over her brown, speckled head. Across the city she pulled a small cart stacked with books, every page of which was crossed out in heavy charcoal strokes. She sang church songs to herself and lived on pieces of fruit and chunks of stale bread she picked up behind groceries. On her arm she carried a basket filled with worked-over letters she'd written to her daughter who had died years before of the Spanish flu. An old black man with a leg stump worn white as snow hailed her every day from the courthouse steps but she would not speak to him. The old man begged pennies from passersby and ate raisins one by one from a paper sack. Down the street at the old stone jail an aged white lady in clothes made of rice sacks waited for her son to be let out but her son had been burned up in the jailhouse fire years before. A deaf man who passed her every day yelled at everyone he passed that it was too late to save themselves, from what he never said. He carried a sleek black duck under his arm. A young girl sold conjuries from a bucket. She gave the money she received to her father who got drunk and crawled on all fours before her begging forgiveness. An old man in a nappy top hat, an ex-opera singer whose voice one night on stage disappeared like a raccoon into a thicket, tried in a whisper to explain to a skinny man looking for his no 'count son that time would embellish and modify all things. "The Executioner," as he was called, a remittance man from the Maritime Provinces, condemned everyone he met to a gruesome death. He prided himself on never sentencing anyone to the same death twice (he was mistaken about this because he easily lost count and didn't remember *who was who). He carried on his belt a noose that was blackened with years of grimy handling. He pressed the drunks and streetwalkers he passed not to hurry, for the Reaper, he said, was the only one at home. An old man each evening tried drunkenly to sell his mule a hat. His friend, with a face pop-eyed like a victim of strangulation, also drunk, explained to any who asked that the mule was an old friend from childhood. In the lobby of the Peacock Hotel the goldfinches sang their tinny songs. Each was attached to the perch with a thin silver chain. An old woman, sad for years, stared into her hands. In those days we were all birthed into a world of make-believe, so profoundly and intricately conceived that we took it for real, and lived accordingly.*

1

He was born on the shaded back porch of the board and batten house, cabin really, that smelled in every room of pork fat and greens and of Miss Mamie's Coconut Oil Soap his mother used to wash down the floorboards. The back porch because that was as far as his mother got on the hot July day in 1913 exactly fifty years after the final day of the Battle of Gettysburg, a day uncelebrated in Chattanooga. His mother, Capable Florence, called Cappie, a good-time gal who worked sometimes as a domestic but hated the work and made most of her money processing one of the back rooms at the Emporium—former slave quarters of the old grocery exchange, then a cookshop and hotel for negro folks passing through Chattanooga, and now the city's main brothel—in a big narrow vestibule divided by curtains into a half dozen smaller rooms that could be rented for two dollars an hour.

When her water broke as she was coming through the backyard carrying a sack of oranges given to her by a oldtime customer, her children had tried to help, but the gushing stinking swirling unexpected secret waters of her body—her agony and the way her eyes momentarily rolled back in her head—had scared them near to death. As she hauled herself up the back steps they stood out in the yard screeching. Cappie didn't have time or the inclination to tend to them. As she staggered on the first step, feeling the animate, resolute, massacree push of her own body ejecting itself or attempting to, experiencing in this moment the extremity of panic as her body told her—shouted—that such crudesence was in fact *impossible*, followed immediately by the give in her muscles that let her know *that was a lie*, the gummy little bushy-haired head poked forth. She was still climbing the steps as the baby's shoulders jimmied their way through, yelling as she came (while Coolmist yelled *Git down! git down!* and the twins crouched at the base of the little chinaberry tree, clasping hands around the trunk), not willing anything but surrendering to some power in herself that compelled her, or allowed her, she said later, to raise herself, like a wreck being raised off the floor of the Tennessee river, some old wedding cake of a riverboat, lifted streaming and creaking—and *bellering*, her daughter said later—and keeping her feet like a woman wading through biting snakes, crouched, bowlegged, staggering on the sides of her delicate high-arched feet, making the top step, her trailing leg weighing suddenly a thousand pounds so that she felt as if the cradle of her hips was cracking as she raised her foot and lurched forward, attempting to make it to the big rocker—why was it leaned face-first against the side of the house with its skinny legs sticking up like an old man praying?—yelling at Coolmist to pull the God almighty chair out, that she never made it to, at least not before the full compact bundled body of her fourth child squirted out, falling not straight down but in a slant off to the side but not so quickly that she wasn't with one hand able to catch the baby by the arm and keep it from hitting the floor, which at the time was the most important thing.

As for Delvin, though he didn't remember this episode until they told it to him, first his sister Coolmist and then the twins and then his mother when he came crying to her, he always had a sensation of falling or of being about to, an emptiness in his gut as if he had just let go or been let go of. The little twitch that comes to everyone just at the border of sleep and wakefulness, the start or jump, was for him a powerful kick; he felt himself thrown backwards from a height, falling into a deep pit that had no happiness at the bottom of it; and he lashed out from it; he fought back.

"Shoo, it was just this world snatching at ye," the old man John William Heberson, called J W, told him, clucking his stony laugh, speaking of the fall from his mother's womb. "But she cotched ye, didn't she?" he'd add, his eyes sparkling. J W was the old africano storekeeper down the road who paid his mother to visit him, every Saturday evening after he closed up. "Yessir," he said, "she cotched ye."

And she did, Delvin would think, marveling. He liked to walk off by himself along the grassy ravine that separated Red Row from white town. The ravine or gully was deep and craggy with outcroppings of gray mica-flecked granite. At the bottom flowed a constant stream that ran thin and rusty in dry times and heavy, clumsy and milky with mountain runoff, after a rain. The ravine ran up through neighborhood and woods until it folded itself back into the mountains where among the sassafras and laurel slicks Delvin liked to lie down and dream about his life. His mother read to him from a book of French kings—another customer gift—and he saw himself not as one of them exactly but as one of their company, a gallant lieutenant of kings, the one sent out into the wilderness to find a place for people to settle, some sweet land that had grapevines and wild strawberries and blueberry bushes growing in clumps and sweet apple trees you could pick little striped apples from and carry around in your pockets to munch on. In the dusk of a summer afternoon he would walk down the center of the street carrying a stalk of sugar cane or a bottle of buttermilk given to him by Mr. J W for his mama and he would caper as if the street was a rope he was balancing on—he was always teaching himself how to stay upright, keep from falling—and he didn't want to tell his mother that the good things he brought her were gifts from somebody else.

All around him was a world intricate and rich with smells and sounds that fascinated him. He loved the look and feel of the rusty dust kicked up out in the street whenever an automobile passed and he loved the smell of the mules parked with their wagons in front of Bynum's and he loved to sit on the wooden bench out in the yard in front of the Azalea Bethany church on Slocum street to listen to hymns being sung and he loved the smell of baking in Miss Consolia Dikens's outdoor oven that was big as a little cabin and stoked with wood from a pile that smelled of apples and he loved the swaying of the bulrush cane down in the gully and he loved the other kind of cane, sugar cane, that was stacked like broom handles in the big wooden barrel outside Heberson's and liked to buy a stalk for a penny and strip the snakegreen hide off with his teeth and gnaw off a chunk and chew the sweet iron-tasting juice into his mouth. He loved the sound of the little girls' voices as they passed on their way to school and even liked the way they mocked him as he sat in his tiny yellow rocking chair on the little front porch. Four years old and rocking up a storm and telling his little two-year-old neighbor about how French kings lived in the hills up the gully and kept great castles and palaces stocked with fresh fish and sweet potato pudding and big jars of strawberry soda.

"What's the difference between a castle and a palace?" his older brother Whistler asked, laughing at him.

He was teaching himself to read from the funnypapers he got from stacks at the back of Heberson's store, getting old J W first to read them to him then again while he moved his fingers through the words. After that he could read the panels himself.

"He's got em learnt by heart," J W said to Cappie, who was sitting beside Delvin on the plank back steps of the store eating canned oysters out of a little white china dish, giving every fourth one to Delvin who didn't care for them and surreptitiously put each one in his pocket. She was fascinated by what her chappie could do, even if he was reciting. Reciting was even better than reading. Any fool could read—she could read and wasn't a fool, but many others were—but how many got the natural head power to keep all those words in order inside his brain?

"He's a wonderanemous child," she said licking the small plump body of an oyster before forking it into her mouth.

Not that time, but three times later, reading the adventures of the Katzenjammer Kids, he told his mother what was true—that he really was reading. He went more slowly and his mother at first didn't like it—she liked better the zippy way he had when he memorized the words—but he explained to her that now he could take a piece of paper with writing on it and didn't have to have somebody read it to him first before he could tell her what was there. "It's like I can tell the secrets now," he told her. She lay in her bed late at night after she came in from the Emporium thinking about this. She had long believed that life was a secret thing, built on secrets, most of which she had no idea how to learn. That boy's building him a key, she thought. He's going to establish hisself.

Just beyond the crossing of Bynam and Adams streets was the oakwood bridge that led to the world of the white folks. Huge and ponderous, all powerful, it squatted over there.

"Like a big old hog," Cappie told her children. "It'll eat you up—unless you're quick. And eat anything else it takes a mind to," she said, her dark yellow eyes burning. "You got to be mindful every minute," she told them. "You got to study their ways and not slip up. Or they'll get you."

But Delvin felt called to the territory on the other side of the gully bridge. He was sure he could make his way.

One day he sneaked out of the yard and crossed over—he could see the bridge from the house, and see the church steeples and the big square commercial buildings and the indecipherable flags on top of the Courtney Hotel—and made his way along Adams street past the Sinclair station and the printing plant and the big white stone post office that looked like a fortress and past the other buildings of stone and brick masonry with their big glass front windows behind which were potbellied washing machines and silver tubs and birchwood iceboxes with big silver handles and couches like the ones over at the Emporium except without the gold tassels and buckets and dynamic-looking water pumps and big glass-covered pictures of people riding horses.

What particularly drew him was a store he came on that had spangly colorful dresses in the front window, dresses that were buttoned onto dummy bodies with small painted white women's heads on them. These dresses were yellow like sunshine and sky blue and honeydew green and had tiny colorful stones sewn into them. The stones were like the precious gems in the stories of kings, the booty and priceless possessions of kings and queens right here in this mar-

velous place just over the bridge that after all was like a bridge in
the story of great King Charlemagne that he had to cross in the Alp
mountains to get to the terrible vandals who were demeaning the
empire, and here *he* was, nearly five years old and feeling fine, looking right at such preciousness.

Though he could hear his mother's voice saying no, he could not
keep himself from climbing the two white marble steps and ducking
into the store.

He headed straight for the dresses and knew no better than to
scramble up the little wooden step into the window. He began to
run his fingers over the jewels. One of them, a green shiny wonder
he hadn't even noticed from outside, the size of his thumbnail, came
off in his hand. He slipped it into his pocket. There were so many
who could mind? He ran his hands over the soft fabric. It made a
faint hissing sound under his fingers. He would like to take this dress
home to his mama. Maybe there was some way. But then there were
jewels on this other cascade of smooth green cloth, jewels of dark
yellow like his mother's eyes, red jewels and a few that were clear—
diamonds he knew they were called, the most precious of all, though
not the prettiest. He began to pick the stones like berries and put
them in his pockets.

He thought his heart might give out. It was hard to draw breath.
His body tingled. But he was a brave boy and would not falter. He
believed he had strength in him.

He slid to his left, eyes on the glitter of the brightest of the yellow
stones, a stone that caught light of different colors in its depths.
He rustled through dresses that very well could be the dresses of
magnificent royalty, the shimmery fabric hissing and whispering
as he brushed by until he was able to reach his small hand out and
nearly . . .

At that moment he felt a sharp pain in his back. At the same time
he heard a voice shout out, a white voice.

"You damn little dickens!"

He was snatched up into the air by his shirt, hauled out of the
window and flung down onto the carpeted floor of the shop. He was

dazed and couldn't place himself. Loud white voices filled the air. Through a haze he saw contorted white faces glaring down at him. Ugly faces, sickly red and furrowed, with misshapen noses and tiny nostrils clotted with snot. Demons. He shrunk from them, or would have if he'd been allowed to, but he was held down by a foot on his chest.

"You quit squirming, you pickaninny booger."

He was hit again, this time with the flat of a broom. His mother had once hit him with a broom. He began to cry, he couldn't help it. He was jerked to his feet, but he didn't have the strength to hold himself up. He fell to the floor.

"Look at that," a voice cried, "look what that little sneak's got in his hand."

"Oh, don't touch it!"

"Open your hand, you little pirate."

The yellow jewel fell from his fingers. He could hear the soft noise it made when it hit the floor. Was it a dream? He was pulled back to his feet and held while the broom was applied to his buttocks, four, five, he lost count how many times. He was sobbing now, and no longer knew where he was. He had never known, he guessed.

Pulled by the shirt, his favorite, pale green, worn for the occasion, that had torn all the way down one side, he was lifted and carried as one would carry a shot animal by the tail, and deposited in the street. An automobile blew a blast on its horn. He heard the shuffling of a mule and then its sneeze and a string of mucus blew over him, wetting his face.

Voices were speaking to him, but he could not tell who they were, which of the white folks addressed him.

He pulled himself to his feet as a car honked a long squealing blast. He staggered to the curb, shakily climbed the speckled granite rim and was swept back into the street. Above his head the leaves of a large beech tree shivered and rushed in the breeze. He got to his feet, and, startling himself and maybe the white people who still squeaked and blatted around him, he began to run.

"You better run, you little africanis!"

He didn't quit running until he was on the Red Row side of the bridge. Dodging behind a big loquat bush, he stopped, bent over and began to draw back his breath. Those blaring, crumpled, pink-and-red-mottled faces. He'd seen angry colored faces among them too.

Cappie found him that afternoon sitting in his little yellow rocking chair with tears streaming down his face, still wearing the green cotton shirt. His sister had pinned the halves of the shirt together because he would not take it off. Coolmist told Cappie what had happened. She had heard it from Miss Maylene Watts, who was employed by the Minor family over on Covington street. Miss Maylene had been accompanying Mrs. Watts downtown to carry packages for her when she saw the boy tossed into the street. Mr. Jimmy Coolidge, who janitored for the Atwell Appliance store across the street from the Miss and Mrs. Style Shop, had filled her in on the details. According to the story Delvin had been thrashed in the street by Mr. Billy Hammock, the assistant manager of Cooper Drugs on Main street.

A hot gushing rage filled Cappie's body, almost blinding her. She couldn't hear what her daughter was saying. A stiff, bony purpose rose in her. She rushed out of the house and down Adams street. At the intersection she stepped on the meaty half of an apple lying in the dirt, slipped and fell to her knees. She pushed herself up and as she did so she saw the white underflesh of her knee and inside it a crescent-shaped slice of blood. A nausea filled her but she made herself start out again, limping onto the bridge.

Mr. Dominion Baskrell, a one-eyed negro barber just passing by, stopped her by grabbing her arm.

"Where you going now?" he said. "Git down. You aint goin to rile the white folks."

"Get off me," she cried, pulling her arm. Her voice that she thought should be loud was only a whisper. She felt a feathery faintness. Blood ran down her shin, a thin stream. "I got to go," she said and started on, but before she got all the way across the bridge a suffocating tiredness came over her. Poor child. My poor child. She began to weep. The tears felt like cold water. Why aren't they hot? she wondered.

Just beyond the bridge she stopped in a field where a market was held every Saturday. Some white boys were throwing a ragged ball around. A couple of them stopped to look at her. Shame crawled her. She was wearing her work clothes, a shiny, ruffled purple dress cut halfway up her thigh, and she carried her black patent leather pocketbook. The buildings of the city, up a slight incline from where she stood, seemed the ramparts of a fortress reared up before her. The heaviness in her body weighed her down. She couldn't go forward. She began to walk, angling off to the other side of the street where a solitary house stood. She couldn't tell quite where she was. She seemed to be sliding backwards down a slope. She bent and picked a purple thistle flower.

She still had this twirl of silky filament in her hand when she reached the bar at the Emporium.

Later that evening she appeared at the back door of Mr. Louis Miller's clothing shop on Ducat street. She slipped inside the little boxlike back entry and yelled up the stairs for him to come down. She visited him on Wednesday nights after his store closed. He was an old flat-faced white man who had lived forty years in the town. Miller poked his head out of his door. He saw a drunken familiar woman with her hair all spriggy and spiraled around her head. He had always liked the darkest women; black as Africa, he thought of them as, but Cappie was blacker than that. She shouted that he had broke her child.

He tried to calm her and was able to for a while. He was frightened and wondered if she had a knife on her. But he was a kind man and was saddened by the trouble she described. That little boy—like many very young colored children—was a pretty little thing. Miller had brought her in behind the closed back door, but he didn't take her upstairs. As she came close to him he smelled the rich rank odor that he associated with the jungles of Africa, a smell of the untamed and unknowable world that both taunted and fascinated him, the smell that was her mix of pomade and junk perfume and bad food and fear sweat blended with the whole combination of dust and wash water and hog grease and happiness and terror and fealty and love juice and sooty lantern wicks and coal oil and hallelujahs and the sweet stink of old aunties bending down to kiss little boys on the mouth and the half worn away miseries in the heart of a woman with no stake but pride and humility in such a world as this. And in Cappie's case too the ashy smell of lye soap and the sour tokay wine she used like a tonic. An assortment added to his own characteristic sour smells, smell of new clothes and worry and pickles and dryness of soul and lingering stinks of exclusion and distemper and forlornness and milk and stale bitter cheese. Both of them were attracted by the smell of the other.

Miller felt in his groin the customary stirring he thought of as soundness of spirit and life-giving and he was afraid he would wither and die without. But he was scared. He talked to her in a steady and precise way that only infuriated her further, choking her heart until in frustration and despair she struck him hard in the head with her stiff laminated purse—once and then more than once—and left him lying on the warped wooden floor of his back hall.

She was picked up for drunk later on the street outside the dress shop where Delvin had received his instruction.

In the jail she screamed and threatened, banging her hands on the doors until the jailer, a man because the woman who usually tended to the drunk or fighting negro women was home sick with influenza, until this man, Shorty Burke, a dreamer who in seven months would be stabbed in the neck and killed by a woman he'd been in love with since the second grade, threw buckets of cold pump water four times at Cappie until she stopped yelling and slunk off to a corner where she sat holding her wounded knee, crying, and fitfully sleeping, until the shift change at first light when through the high windows of the old stone cell the eastern light, in a trick of play that neither the architect or the builder or the police chief himself had considered, at this time of year threw a single beam of radiant pale yellow light against the bars, making them shine like silver rods and crosses marking some heavenly spot on earth.

She was let out—she had the money to pay her fine—and was able to make her way home in the emollient, fribbly sunshine to see her child. He still sat in his little chair. He had slept in the chair but only after fatigue pulled him reluctantly down. Through the afternoon and evening, even as his sister fed him from a bowl of fried grits, forking the crisp bits of corn mash into his mouth with a stained fork as she liked to do, pretending that he was her baby, he hardly noticed anything. Through the meal and then through the lengthening twilight into evening with its hoots of men walking in the street and its soft calls of young women walking arm in arm wearing their loose shawls and then into the cries of pain and loss that marked the late hours, he stayed fixated, turning in his fingers the two small gems shaped like cat eyes, one clear as clear water and the other deep yellow, almost brown, that he had kept, and had polished that afternoon with the Astoria polish his mother used on her treasure of six silver spoons she kept in a wooden case that had once held a silver Colt pistol. These gems in the faint light from the kerosene lamp set on the floor beside him shone with an artificiality that drew him, a strangeness and allure that even as he stared at them he felt haunted by as if he was already stranded off in some country where the light of such delicate beauty never reached. They were part, he knew, of the stories his mother had told him and read to him of kings and treasures and palaces in far lands—lands that these jewels proved were so close, so nearby, that if he only thought hard enough he could somehow, without knowing any other key or possibility, get himself to.

Delvin waked to his mother kissing his face. She smelled of wine and of the jailhouse, a familiar combo; not one he liked. But he really liked the kiss. He was almost gone to five years old now and still he believed his mother was a woman who would belong to him for the rest of his life. It amazed him that a woman so big and filled with rich smells and talk could belong to someone like him. It gave him a sense of the possibilities in the world and a belief in his own strength and in the power of desire. The kissing was fine. A rough happiness roared in his body. He trembled and his hands shook as she snatched him up and squeezed him against her. The husked raw ache began to melt away against her lean hard maternal creatureliness. She set him on his feet and looked him in the face.

"Don't worry about none of that," she said, her voice hoarse and creaky but filled with an insistence he couldn't turn away from. Her eyes seemed black as pitch. "None of that meanness," she said, "has a thing to do with you, boy. Not one speck of it. You know what I am talking about?"

He only half did, and it was that half that brought tears to his eyes.

"Weep you should, little child," she said, running her hand harshly and lovingly over his springy hair. She felt bound by chains to this earth. Chains running back into the white world and down into pits and wells she was terrified of being pulled into. Yet in her life was much happiness. She was not ashamed of how she lived. Her children fascinated her. The two men she helped along—Mr. Miller and old Heberson—were dear to her, in a way. She was scared of them and she appreciated the gifts they gave her. She wondered about Mr. Miller and hoped he was all right. Maybe she ought to go see about him, but she wanted to tend to her child first.

She walked him across the yard to the little open shed where the washing took place and cleaned him up, recleaned him. Delvin stood in the washtub as she bathed his body, which she at first warmed by the fire in the open kitchen. Coolmist had already built a fire of fat lighter and alder sticks. A mockingbird darted in and out of the angle of brush fence separating their yard from the alley and the cottage next door. Across the way a woman called "Cora . . . Cora, I can't find the mat . . ." in an expressionless voice. The mockingbird flicked up into the slim maple tree and began to set out a little song like a peddler rolling out a sleeve of silver watches. Delvin, who had not complained and had hardly spoken since he came home, began to shiver. The water was warm but he couldn't stop. He trembled and shook, teeth chattering. He cringed from a dream of mule snot and hard paving stones and yellow leaves of a beech tree like tiny grabbing hands reaching out for him. The hands of those white people like claws grabbing him. Cappie remembered times she'd lain in bed shaking from the disharmonies of life. The boy, sturdy, sleek, his perfect little black seal body, skin as smooth as polished wood, made her heart break. He jerked like a man with the quakes, tears streaming down his face. As the quavering gradually trailed away he shut his eyes and leaned back in her arms. A trance, she thought. Alarmed, she wondered if he might never come free of it. But he was in a heavenly state. She was about to shake him back into the world when she realized he was asleep. Just a little boy, tired out. She wrapped him in the big square of soft toweling Mr. Miller had given her for Christmas, carried him into the house and set him down on her bed.

Delvin didn't wake when in the blank foreshadow of morning the police came in three cars to get his mother. Before the white men even got in the house Cappie had slipped out the back. She ran up the alley, crossed Tremaine, zipped around the corner onto Van Buren, leapt a collapsing syringa hedge, skinnied down into the gully and was on her way into the mountains. She was barefoot and wore an old flower print blue dress she liked to sleep in out on the rocking chair on the back porch in the afternoon sunlight. She ran leaping from rock to rock up the valley until she was far enough ahead of the police to cut into the woods. She had been partially raised in the woods, in her auntie's cabin back in a hollow across the mountain, and she knew how to go on through the laurel scrub and sourberry thickets. No police could keep up.

Back at the house they rounded the children up and took them to the juvenile center over on Wilson street where they were kept in the africano section and looked after by Miss Pearl Foster who was subscribed a pittance by the city to mind destitute, deserted and wayward negro children. It wasn't until the next day when Curtis Wunkle, an eleven-year-old wandering boy notorious for stealing shiny objects of little value, showed up that Delvin and his three siblings were told of his mother's predicament.

"She's wanted for a killing," Curtis said, smirking at the thought. He knew what their mother was known for over at the Emporium. And now she had come home with blood staining the hem of her purple satin party dress. It was Curtis's auntie Belle Campion who, herself fresh from the jail, had informed the child of the Cappie Florence plight (Florence wasn't even her real name, they said). "She done coldbraced that old jewman up Ducat street," he said to the fourteen other child habitués of the city establishment.

"You mean murdered?" Winston Morgred said. He was a small albino child of six whose parents had been killed in the Homefield warehouse fire. Winston (called the Ghost) had skin that was a pasty white and his hair was orange. ("Like a negative of a africur," the owner of the office supply store where his mother had swept up, said.)

"Murdered?" Curtis laughed. "I *mean* murdered. Left that old man lying in a pool of his own blood in the back of his own store. Knocked him down with a car jack the size of a locust log—that's what my auntie said."

"None of that's true," the twins cried, but they were shouted down by the excited children.

Delvin slid around to the side of the testimony crowd, slipped through, and before anybody could stop him caught Curtis with a punch in the mouth. The surprised boy fell back squealing. A fight broke out. All the boys including Delvin socked and swatted at each other like something out of the funnypapers, the sadpapers. Miss Pearl rushed from her office where she had been working out the youngsters' documents, poor things, and swinging a big torn felt hat beat the hooligans into submission. It was time for supper.

The children were marched into a small room lit by kerosene lamps. A long table wrapped in tin sheeting with squared-away corners. The regulars, the long-termers, led the way to a back window of the same kitchen that served the white children in the larger, electrically lit hall on the other side. Into a tin bowl was scooped grits, stew beans with gravy and a chunk of cornbread hard as a schoolbook.

Back at the table they ate with spoons attached by thin lengths of chain to an iron firedog screwed into the tabletop. It was the oldest child's job to sort out the chains and pass the spoons to the children. They were supposed to sit quietly, but this quiet was almost impossible to maintain.

During the week Miss Pearl read to them at meals from the Bible. This was Delvin's first experience with the famous old legends and tales. As time passed he found himself enthralled with the stories, especially the ones concerning wars and killing. The story of Joshua, who stopped the sun and knocked down the walls of Jericho with a bugle shout, was his favorite. He daydreamed of great victories won by obscure means such as horns and freakish powers. He was impressed with the Lord. The French lords were familiar to him from his home study. The lord the old Israelites called upon seemed mighty capable though he liked mostly to hang back in the shadows. This appealed to Delvin, who liked to lay low himself.

He mentioned to Miss Pearl that when he grew up he wanted to go after the Lord's job.

"That job's not for us human beings," she told him, with no smile in her hard black eyes. "All we can do is follow him."

"I'd like to get up close to him."

Misunderstanding, she was pleased with the little boy.

At night the children trooped into a long high-ceilinged room behind the dining room. Two wide low platforms ran the length of the room on either side. Canvas mattresses filled with hay were laid widthwise on these platforms, one side for the boys, the other for the girls. A ragged green curtain ran down the middle partway, giving a little privacy. Delvin and his brothers and sister arrived on the day the mattresses had just been stuffed with fresh timothy hay, a hygienic procedure that took place every month or so if the guardians thought of it and if there was any hay available (donated). The timothy was newly cured and smelled spicy and welcoming. At home he slept on a cotton tick on the floor of the second bedroom when his mother wouldn't let him into her bed.

He missed the house, missed its smells of rich perfume and

cornmeal and grease and silver polish—missed the streets of Red
Row that smelled of dreaminess and stewed collards and deep green
shade and mica and ashes and kerosene and a hundred kinds of
panbread—but mostly he missed his mother. At supper, listening to
the little orange-haired boy, Winston, he had experienced the sinking, falling sensation in his chest. His whole body tingled and what
was usually compact and strong inside him began to dissolve. He
drank water and ate the hard bread in an attempt to replace it. If his
mother had been there he would have thrown himself into her arms
and made her hold him tight. Every day at home, sometime during
the day, maybe more than once, she would grab him up and squeeze
so tight he couldn't take a breath. In her arms there was no need to
breathe.

He got out of his bed and ducked under the curtain and got into
his sister Coolmist's bed. Coolmist was crying and at first seeing her
little brother made her ashamed of her tears. But she couldn't stop
and she liked anyway to have little Delvin to snuggle in with her.
They clasped each other in their arms. Down the row the twins were
hugging each other. Miss Pearl as she walked the rows saw this and
left the lamp burning longer than usual. Whimpering and moaning
and sobbing, even yells, shrill cries and yips, were a common feature
of foundling home nights.

The room smelled like a field in the country. Delvin was on his back
on his own pallet. He heard a small chirping sound—a cricket—and
stayed still, listening. The cricket was nearby. He raised himself and
waited in the half-lit dark. The cricket chirped at the edge of his mattress. It was caught inside, in the fresh timothy hay stuffing, near the
top that was closed with two big Bakelite buttons. Delvin couldn't
undo the buttons but he could still reach his hand inside. He lay
quietly waiting for the cricket. When it chirped again he had its location. He slipped his hand under the canvas and caught the insect.
It was a shiny black handsome creature with a swashbuckling set of
feelers.

"Hidy, bug."

He wished he had something to keep the cricket in, but there was nothing, not even in the little bundle of clothes he had been allowed to bring with him from the house ("What the hell you wearing?" one policeman said). He held the cricket loosely in his hand. His face scrunched with worry. "I'm sorry I caught you."

Despite himself he was getting sleepy.

"All right," he said.

He put the cricket in the pocket of the frilly dress shirt he had taken off to get into the coarse nightshirt the home made all the children wear. He lay down but almost immediately raised up to check on the cricket. It was already gone, sailed off into the dark. Delvin felt a pang in his heart.

"Oh me," he said and lay back. "Mama," he said into the dark, his lips barely moving, "where are you?"

On his back, looking up into the dark that was dimly lit by high long narrow windows, he felt the tears start, brim, spill and trail down his cheeks. He didn't think to wipe them away. I wonder how tall I am, he thought. Wonder how tall Mama is. And then he was asleep.

Cappie did not reappear, and after the pumping of informants and interviews of the girls over at the Emporium and a few neighborhood householders and the personal searches and tracking expeditions into the woods and bulletins issued to surrounding states, the police department decided they probably wouldn't find her. Delvin, if anybody had looked for him, spent the next year and a half living the orphan's life, first in the local foundlings home and then out in the Homeless African House in Tullawa where he spent mornings at school and afternoons working in the apple orchards pining springlings. Despite his willingness to prove he could he was informed that he did not know how to read and was forced to learn all over following the confusing Boatwright method taught at the time in Tennessee schools. He chafed but went along and relearned or overlearned first his ABCs and then the puny words and pitiful sentences printed under the pictures of white children in the books passed out each afternoon by Moneen Butler, a cinnamon-colored girl originally from the high mountains in east Tennessee.

He fell in love with Moneen and was smartly rebuffed and ministered his heartbreak by zipping through the little brown biographies of famous americans he got from the school library. He discovered books, real books, as rideable transports into habitable territory. He tried to enter the town library but was turned away. He tried to enroll in the regular colored primary school, walking two miles along Fallin street under the long line of oaks and sycamore trees and past the garages and metal shops and appliance stores, but he was turned away there too; he had no parent or guardian except the state, which paid him little mind, other than being the ready agent of preventing little homeless darkies from getting too fresh. Nobody at either school recognized him as the son of the infamous murderer Cappie Florence, though her crime and flight were an oft-told tale in the negro and white communities.

On the day he showed up at the public school dusty and barefoot carrying in his pocket a case dollar folded small as a quarter, a bill he'd lifted from a drawer in the back office of the Muster General Goods store, and was turned away hurt in his heart, instead of returning to the orphanage he crossed town and walked along Overlook street, the north boundary of Red Row. There, beyond its edge, white enterprise dribbled along past the meatpacking plant and the old deserted fertilizer plant on Supline road to the dusty red-earthed pebbly field used for traveling circuses and revivals. This day the field was occupied by the Clyde Beatty circus. Delvin paid ten cents of his dollar to sit in the africano section, a bank of seats high up under the eaves and far from the band. He was just beginning to enjoy the performance, especially the midgets on unicycles, when the clown parade began. As they began their sniggery stroll, waving and juking and shooting at each other with flower pistols, he grew agitated. He was far away from the sawdust rings, but not too far to see, underneath the clowns' ribald paint, the faces of watchful, unamused white men. This sight frightened him in a way that made him sick to his stomach. He jumped up and fled the swooping gray tent.

The circus was in the big field across the street from the Constitution Funeral Home, the leading negro funeral home in Chattanooga. Cornelius Oliver, mortician and the proprietor of the Home, the richest africano man in town, a man who even during the Great War bought a new Cadillac every year, which he rode in driven by his chauffeur Willie Burt Collins—Mr. Oliver to the community, Ollie to the white folks—was sitting in his side room speaking in a genial but uncompromising voice to his assistant secretary, Polly, about the perfidy of white folks, and especially the white folks in city government who had promised him that the circus would be moved to a lot on the other side of the quarter, when he caught sight of Delvin in his cropped overalls and the navy sweater he'd pulled off the pile at the H(omeless) A(fricano) house.

"Who is that little boy walking down the middle of the street?" he said. "Come look out here."

Delvin was trying (unsuccessfully) to light a kitchen match with his thumbnail as he walked.

"Hey you, boy," Oliver called, but Delvin ignored him. "Run get that boy," he said to Polly.

A fast runner herself and a girl who hoped every day for something different from yesterday, she set down the pitcher she was using to water the fading begonias and leapt out through the open study window.

"My lord, child," Mr. Oliver said, but Polly didn't hear him. She was already sprinting across the narrow patch of close-cropped lawn to intercept Delvin, who saw her coming and veered over to the other side of the unpaved red clay street.

"You, boy!" Polly cried. She had no trouble catching him. It was the holding of him that was difficult. "I got something for you," she said.

"Many's spoke of such as that," Delvin said, "but few's delivered. Let me go."

"This is something good. Mr. Oliver wants to speak to you."

"That your name for the devil?"

"You dumb little clodhopper, don't—"

"I aint no farmer, I'm from . . ." He couldn't remember the name of his street.

"Don't you know who Mr. Oliver is?" She was dragging him by the arm across the street. Down the way a breeze shuffled leaves in a big beech tree. A white man in a large straw hat pushed an automobile with a small boy behind the wheel. "Like I said, the devil uses many a false appellation." This last word he'd picked up from a book he'd found back at the HA house. Or maybe he'd heard it in the street. He was a sharp one for listening in.

She continued to drag him back to the funeral home.

"You taking me into that place—that undertaker's?"

"Mr. Oliver is a funeral director."

"Whoo, you looking to bury me?"

"I might, but Mr. Oliver wants you for his charity work, I expect."

"I don't need no charity."

"No, I reckon you are beyond anything charity could do."

She reset her grip and dragged him into the house, which was cooler than outside and dim and hushed. The last few steps he had gone along with her, curious to see what a bonecracker was up to. Down a hallway paved in soft red carpet she knocked on the paneled white door of Mr. Oliver's study and was invited by a grave tenor voice to enter. The big room with its vast oak desk with inlaid green felt top, its green leather couch and rug-upholstered armchairs, its tables with fresh flowers in clear vases and assorted mementoes from Mr. Oliver's customers, its painting on the wall between the two tall windows of Wolfe Dying at Quebec, its rugs in painted patterns of red and green, was the fanciest room Delvin had ever been in . . . if he set aside the front parlor of the Emporium. Recalling the fancy swags and silk bunting, the mural of the Queen of Sheba dancing for the enthralled King David—or was it Solomon—and the rose settees with the working ladies lounging on them like perfumed cats, a pang of longing for his mother touched Delvin.

Oliver, a discerning man, voluminous in his physical being and not without concern for others, said, "Boy, you've suffered a loss, haven't you?"

Delvin didn't want to discuss this with a stranger. "I'm doing fine," he said.

"Why were you running?"

"To get away from that circus."

"Rightly so, my young man."

This made Delvin feel a little better. It troubled him that he would be frightened of the clowns, especially when no one else appeared to be. "What was it you wanted?" he said.

"I need an errand boy and a helper," Mr. Oliver said.

"How much you pay?"

"Two dollars a week and keep."

Delvin liked being in the room. He liked Mr. Oliver's round fat face. Except for Long Dog Wilkins, The Negro Giant, Mr. Oliver was the largest man he had ever seen.

"Who's your mama and daddy?" Mr. O inquired.

"I got none."

"You're on your own, son?"

"Been since I was near to five."

Mr. Oliver laughed, a bubbly, analgesic laugh. "How old are you now?"

"Six and a half."

"Where do you live?"

"At the Bell Home."

"Oh, of course."

Oliver contacted the home and made the arrangements for Delvin to stay at the mortuary. He had done this before, following a vague impulse to help little boys. He himself had been a little boy set out on the streets of Montgomery, Alabama. At eight he had hoboed a train from Montgomery to Chattanooga where he had been pushed off a boxcar ladder, breaking his ankle on a switch tie. An old yard worker had come on him crying and taken him home and with the neighborhood healerwoman's help straightened his ankle and put it in a poplarwood boxsplint. He stayed with this gentleman and his wife

for three years before he began working for Mr. Duluth Mathis, the
former owner of the funeral home. Mathis, who had no children, had
eventually passed the business on to him. A bachelor, he looked now
for other little boys he might fling a lifeline to. It loops back around
to me, he would think as he sat in the big tub in his tile bathroom,
feeling not so lonely, not so lost.

Delvin accepted the job and went to work, uneasily at first, fetching
items from the pantry, doing light cleaning, digging in the garden and
watering the flowers, hauling out trash and burning it in the metal
drum out back, picking up pecans and bringing them in a yellow
enameled bowl he wondered if stolen from kings, and staying close to
Mrs. Parker, the cook, and to Polly, in case they needed a quick boy
for anything. It offended him to work in such a place, and scared him
and made him sad in a way he didn't quite understand, but they fed
him copiously at the big pine table in the kitchen where with the
sidemen and the maids he had his meals, and he liked sleeping out
in the little barn or shed behind the house, in a room beside the
stalls that smelled of sweet hay and leather (that is, before he moved
into the house to a small square bedroom off Mr. O's big bedroom).

He was not shown the working areas right off. Oliver's experience
led him to believe that the living so feared and hated death that only
a special sort of person was fit to work in a funeral parlor. The first
time he brought Delvin into the viewing room where the embalmed
corpse of Mrs. Fretwell Jenkins lay in repose in double-ruffled collars, the boy cursed and ran out of the room. They did not have that
many departed put on view. People usually kept their deceased at
home after the embalming. Only the very poor, or those who for private reasons did not want the body in the house—some of those reasons being superstition, panic, hatred, flaunting of wealth, neglect or
simple grief—left the deceased entirely to Mr. Oliver. If the truth be

known, he liked to keep the dead close by him. Taking the body in hand, like a prodigal returned, he pampered and coddled the former person, bringing him or her into the gentleness and beauty that most lacked in their living lives. He wished for them to remain with him as long as possible. It hurt him to have to release them to the rocky soil of the Appalachians.

This affinity made Mr. Oliver one of the most effective mourners a departed soul could wish for and was one reason he had been able to build up the business so well after Mr. Mathis's demise. He himself had handled the embalming of the not so old man, who had died of a stroke as he sat at the kitchen table eating a slice of vinegar pie. A tenderness had flooded him as he intimately handled the remains. Mr. Mathis's sloped shoulders, saggy breasts, spindly hairless legs, horny toes, big speckled belly, his crisp private hair and tiny genitalia had fascinated him. He sat in a white kitchen chair alone in the embalming room beside the corpse as a son might sit beside his father waiting for him to wake. Oliver had no illusions about the dead awakening, but he felt in his vigil a sense of the enormity of death that was subsumed usually in his experience of loss when the embalmed and dressed-up carcass was taken from him. He placed his hand on Mr. Mathis's cold hairless breast and did not move it for half an hour. He knew what meat came to, but he knew too that this heap of flesh was the last of what he could look to in memory. It was like a faint echo, fading gradually as he listened. As he had done for no other dead person in his life, he leaned over the plumped-out, yellow-skinned face and kissed his benefactor gently on the lips, thinking as he did how he loved him and also that the corpse needed a little more solution.

He had dressed Mr. Mathis in the suit he wore to direct funerals, an off-the-rack black broadcloth suit purchased by mail from Brooks Brothers in New York City. In the pockets he had placed the small gilt-framed picture of his mother that Mr. Mathis kept by his bed, a silver penknife, a small blue marble he had carried since childhood, a tiny gold medallion presented to him by the Negro Benevolent Society for his service to the community, a paperbound copy of Shelley's poems marked with a small red bookmark at Mr. Mathis's favorite poem, "Ode to Dejection," and an ivory locket containing a photograph of a fair-haired young white woman, the secret love of Mr. Mathis's life, unrequited. Mr. Mathis had been buried out of the Mother Holiness church over on Barlow street and it had taken all of Oliver's strength for him not to break down during the service.

For a few weeks afterward he considered selling the business (that had been left to him outright) and moving away. But in the end he knew he was where he belonged. He wished to pass this experience and knowledge on but the child scooting around his property quick as a little roach was probably not the one he was looking for.

Delvin didn't reappear until dinnertime. He smelled of tobacco smoke and his breath reeked of liquor like a loafer. "You are a foolish and wayward child," Mr. O told him. Delvin grinned at him and said he might be but he sure wadn't wasting his time petting dead folks. Mr. Oliver was ready then to whack him one and send him on his way. But something stopped him. Maybe it was a ray of late sunshine catching in the boy's springy hair. Maybe it was an evening bird letting loose a frail sweet cry that touched his heart. Maybe a blip in his brain just then. Maybe only the sturdy-legged boy and the quickened light in his eyes. But he sighed and told Mrs. Parker to get the boy some food. After supper he invited him into his bedroom and they read the newspaper together and then Mr. O gave him a book of stories about explorations in the cold countries and the Arctic. In these stories were plenty of dead men, starved or bear-bitten or shot. Many different ways of disposing of the dead were offered. He thought this would help the boy to revise himself.

He took the boy along when they exhumed the old Harmon woman after the family decided to rebury her remains up north. Coloreds from Red Row, they had gotten rich in Chicago and wanted to dig the old matriarch—the last of them buried in this part of the world—out of the South's bloody ground. A coroner's assistant and a great-grandson down by train and himself and the diggers had driven out there. He and the boy had ridden in the big squared-off Cadillac carved-panel hearse. When they dug down through the yellow, black, gray and red sectioned earth they found the coffin broken through—sometimes after time the weight of the soil itself would collapse the casing—and the body decayed away to the bones. They had brought the remains up in pieces. The grandson had gotten sick off in a tea olive bush. But the boy had been spellbound. He wanted to touch the fragments. A belt buckle, the lapis lazuli necklace she was buried in, were intact. The skull lay in its nest of white marcelled hair. Here and there bits of curled tissue like wispy fried pork skins.

She had spent the last fifty years in the ground. Since shortly after the Civil War when for a moment it seemed black folks might have a living stake in the world's bounty. But that had been only a dream that faded in the hot sunshine of a Dixie June.

As the fragments lay on a white cotton sheet in the tinlined box they would be transported to Chicago in, the boy had reached into the box and taken the skull into his hands. The grandson, a lawyer from Cedar Park, had been too busy upchucking to pay any mind. But Oliver let slip a quivery whistle of alarm. A small outcry, smothered by his habitual discretion. The boy hadn't noticed. He turned the skull in his hands, examining it. Nothing disrespectful, Oliver realized; the boy just wanted to study it.

"Boy," he said, "you'd probably better put that bit of holiness down."

The boy looked at him with a wise and wondering expression. His eyes were lighter colored than usual in one with skin so dark. They were almost hazel.

"Did they stitch her up?" he asked.

"No, son, the lady died of old age."

"But what are these?" he said, indicating the scantlet seams where the skull plates joined.

"That's just where the skull grows together."

"When does it grow?"

"Inside the mother's body, and later when we're little."

"We're just a bunch of pieces, aint we?" He laid the skull gently back in the box. The remnants had a dry smell like unbrushed carpet.

"Why holiness?" he asked, getting to his feet. He skeeted the soil off the knees of his overalls.

"Cause the minister prayed over her," Oliver said. The grandson was wiping his hands on a piece of shaggy green moss.

"What about the ones he didn't pray over?"

"The preacher'd say they are on their own."

"Aye." A tear welled in the boy's eye.

He was remembering something, Oliver thought.

In a way he was. His mother, fled into the wilderness, was always with him, the sadness was, but this sadness had spread out, like a creek flooding the woods, until it soaked everything. He was thinking about all those folks traipsing around in the world, falling over dead or knocked down or sinking into deep waters, who never had anybody to pray for them. These others—they had somebody. Even Mr. Buster Carrie he read about in the paper, knocked down by a heart attack as he purchased a pork roast at Cutler's Butcher shop, or Miss May Wetherburn, whose dress caught fire as she bent over the stove to stir a pot of caramel candy, or Scooter Ellis, visiting from Arizona, the negro paper said, who fell off the mule he was attempting to ride and busted his head open on the iron foot scraper on the steps of the Masons' hall; he expected that each of them had plenty of folks ready and willing to shoot prayers up to heaven or wherever they went.

He watched as the grandson peered at the remains with a look of distaste on his tan, freckled face. "Why aint you sad?" Delvin asked.

The man looked at him with the same urbane distaste. He hated this world down here, restolen from negro folks by Reconstruction, these pitiful luckless helots, still grubbing in the dirt for Ol Massa.

"Time's worn sadness out," he said.

Off across the rolling ground of the negro section of Astoria Cemetery, tucked in between the foundry and the book bindery, beyond the line of blue pines to the west, the sky was filled with a gray pudding of clouds. A vaporous string of red along one seam.

"Time's not going to do that to me," the boy said.

He had just turned seven and had faith in who he was and would become.

"You wait," the man said.

Delvin liked the young man's clothes that were soft gray and had gleaming black buttons. He remembered the gems he had stolen from the shop on Adams street. Where had they gone to? He had carried them in his pocket but somehow they had fallen out, all but the diamond and the cat eye. These two had disappeared as well, lost on the way to the orphanage, or somewhere after he got there. Only a yellow piece left that had somehow by now disappeared too. He felt helpless. Unable to save himself.

He wondered where his sister and brothers were.

As the workers cleaned up and the dismantled body was placed in the hearse and the reclamation party made their way back to the funeral home where the body would be prepared for shipping, by train, to Chicago, and the young man, who knew that the cycle of time is endless, turned his back without sentiment on the green fallen world of east Tennessee, Delvin continued to think of his siblings. The twins had been adopted from the orphanage by a family, so the director had told him, who took them to their farm in Texas. Colored folks owned land out there, she had said, not just little garden plots but whole ranches. They raised beef cattle and grew wheat on the north Texas plains. Delvin wished he could fly out there and see them. Whistler had a little scar on his knee where he had fallen under the bumper of a car he was teetering on trying to hit a horse fly with a rag. Warren liked to sing a little song he called "Homeward" that he said he learned from a woman in a gold dress at the Emporium. Coolmist had picked the song up and she sang it some nights as she washed up out on the back porch. He liked to listen to her splashing water and singing the song in the savory darkness as he lay in bed. Where his sister was he didn't know. She had been standing on the running board of a dusty Ford truck the last time he saw her, wiping her face with a huge red bandana. Had she gone to Texas too? Nothing really seemed to get her down. He was afraid something would. It amazed him how people could get lost in the world.

Soon enough in his early years of dreaming Delvin discovered the second floor, shut off behind a switchback staircase, and climbed up there. The doors along a dim, sullenly carpeted hallway were shut so tightly they seemed at first to be locked, but they weren't. They opened on bed and sitting rooms each fully appointed, everything, including the beds, mummified under big wheat-colored dust cloths. He slapped a bed to see the dust rise in clouds and stood gazing, halfway in a dream, at the motes and powdery fluff slowly resettling. The light coming through the thick, wavy glass windowpanes seemed ancient. It brought to mind his mother's stories. He wished that if he looked closely he might catch sight of her cavorting in a red shiny dress in an antique world, but he knew such thinking was a lie. In one of the bathrooms he stood before a bleached mirror, choking himself with both hands. He pulled his hair, drawing it out above his head. He crossed his eyes and made faces as grotesque as he was able. Once he brought Mrs. Parker's kitchen shears up there and cut his hair short on top, almost down to the skull. Why he did that—when they asked—he couldn't say, but he liked staring into one of the second-floor mirrors at himself. He lay on his back on one bed or another, gazing at the ceiling, trying to slow his heart down to a stop. He wanted to jump into eternity, poke around, see what was there, and jump back quick before the devil caught him. He sprang up and danced wildly. His bare feet slapped the floor. He whirled and capered. "Oh, oh, oh," he cried, "I am nobody's child."

Before long he was eight, then he was nine; in another minute he was twelve.

2

In the evenings Delvin would read to Mr. Oliver. The mortician had come on him in his study lying on the green leather couch scrutinizing a volume of Shakespeare's plays. He barked at him to take his feet off the leather, then asked what he was studying.

"I can't make all of it out," Delvin said, "but I think I get the draw of it."

"Which one you reading, boy?"

"This is one called *Macbeth*. It's about a greedy Scotsman."

"That is a mighty tale," Oliver said, though he was unfamiliar with it. He owned the volume as he owned most of his books: because they gave him a feeling of substance. "Maybe we can study that one out together," he said.

Delvin liked the idea.

They began sessions at night after work was done for the day, or when there was freedom from it. People died at all hours of the day and night. Oliver and his crew had to be prepared to go forth to retrieve the deceased, ready to rise in the wee-est hours to open his house to the dead. The deceased crossed his threshold on stretchers, on doors, on planks and carried in blankets or pulled down from the backs of horses or from the beds of trucks or hauled by hand between weeping, teeth-gnashing grievers, once on the broad iron gate that opened onto the farm of Mr. Wendell Comer, whose only son had been kicked in the head by a mule. Mostly these days they came by ambulance from the hospitals and the morgue. Or he went to fetch them, rising to his midnight errand, a heroic figure, as he saw it, civilization's appointed guide, liaison between the two worlds, navigator and helmsman for the journey to the terrible (and beautiful) mysteries. Oliver had several assistants now, both in the prep room and upstairs in the viewing parlors. He himself was a minister, minister enough, and sometimes performed funeral services in the old dining room that had been converted to a chapel. The boy got into everything, but he hardly learned about anything. Oliver figured the trade—hoped the trade—the seep of it, would infuse him. His dream of finding an heir had settled on the boy—for now.

Both of them enjoyed the reading sessions. They read stories of French kings and stories of explorers and dudes in fancy clothes, but the stories they liked best were the stories in the Shakespeare plays. Propped together on his great bed, Oliver in his wine-red silk dressing gown, Delvin in his green cotton robe and blue pajamas with smiling caucasian faces printed on them, the boy did his best each session to get through a few pages of one of the plays. They made it all the way through *Macbeth* without either of them understanding half of what the boy read; it made them both feel as if they were getting somewhere in life. Delvin was good at saying the words but they were both poor at figuring out what they meant. They got the gist however, or the draw as the boy called it. He had plenty of words Oliver had never heard, probably words that would encourage Mr. Shakespeare himself. "That man had a rowdy life," Delvin said, speaking of the Scottish murderer. "Like a tiger," Oliver concurred. They shuddered and looked off in separate directions, Delvin studying the flame of the squat red candle on the old desk and Oliver looking at the boy's reflection in the window glass. He shuddered again.

"I would like to meet a woman like that Mrs. Mac B," Delvin said.

"Naw you wouldn't, boy."

"How come you hadn't married?" he wanted to know.

"Lots of reasons."

"Name one."

"Not that many care to marry an undertaker."

"Scared, hunh?"

"Mortified mostly."

"What else?"

"I'm busy and don't have that much time to meet them."

"Seems like you'd get first dibs on the widers."

Oliver laughed. "Does, dudn't it?"

"I can help you meet women."

"How is that?"

"I can scout em out for you."

"Don't you be doing that, boy."

"Okay." Delvin snickered. "I won't."

Unless I just have to, he thought, exercising his form of honesty in the situation.

He had already begun to keep an eye peeled for likely marital candidates. He studied the mourners come to view the bodies of their loved ones. The better families preferred to have the remains brought to the house. Some liked to have Mr. Oliver there on the premises with the loved one, others didn't want him anywhere around. For a rich man he had to be awfully humble, Delvin thought. That would not be *his* road to riches. He would—he didn't know what he he would do. Lately he'd been feeling restless. Some boys he met in the alley behind the mortuary told him they were riding freights all over the place.

"For fun?" he had asked.

"No, you little fool," one of them, Portly Sanders, a boy he remembered, or thought he did, from his old Jim's Gully neighborhood, said. "We looking for work."

"I got enough of that right here," Delvin said.

"Bunch of ghouls," Sammy Brakes said.

Delvin had not seen his sweaty face before. "What's that word?" he asked.

"You know," Sammy said, "the ones who dig around in graves."

"We don't dig *in* the grave. We *fill* the grave."

A breeze caught in the tops of the bamboo hedge and passed on. He wanted to hit this Sammy with the greasy, pockmarked face, but he held back. He turned quickly, spinning almost, his arms flying free, and staggered away in mock fright. The other boys laughed.

"Gon miss your train," Delvin said, laughing, and skipped through the wire gate into the backyard where the boys, superstitious and afraid of legal trouble, wouldn't follow him. He waved at them before he went into the house.

Just this week he had been disciplined for fighting with the kitchen boy. The boy had called him a dumb bastard child. Delvin had knocked him into the kindling box. The boy had cut the back of his head on a piece of fat lighter wood. Sunny was his name, but the boy was anything but. Delvin couldn't stand him and would have fought him until he was nothing but another customer for the establishment, but he didn't want to lose his place. Oliver had made him work in the garden spreading horse manure and then working it into the black-eyed pea and tomato rows. From the kitchen window Sunny had eyed him evilly, ducking behind the red cheesecloth curtain whenever Delvin caught him looking. The punishment made him restless, or added to his restlessness, but he didn't want to hit the road, he told himself—if he was *going* to—before he found a bride for Mr. Oliver. He hung around the viewing rooms, wearing the cutdown black suit (once belonging to another favored boy) that Mr. O had provided for him when he rode in the hearse.

He began to ask for the names and addresses and the telephone numbers when they had them of the more likely-looking women. He questioned them, discreetly, so he thought, about their situation. Were they married? What did they think of the mortuary business? Didn't they just love the swank and the soundness of the outfit? Did they know that those velvet curtains over there cost nearly one hundred dollars? That organ in the chapel was over a thousand dollars and Mr. Oliver was planning to buy an even better one soon. He tried to enlist Polly's help, but she was not a willing accomplice. She told him if he didn't cut it out she was going to tell Mr. O.

"He's a lonely man," Delvin said.

"Mr. Oliver is too busy to be lonely," Polly replied.

But Delvin knew his loneliness. They had begun to read Shakespeare's sonnets. The ones that spoke of the absent lover touched them both. In the dim light of the big green-shaded lamp by the bed they had both wiped away tears, Mr. O dabbing with the corner of a blue silk handkerchief, Delvin using the tips of his fingers.

"Here he's saying the only way to live forever is to get yourself a child," Delvin said after reading sonnet no. 12. "If you are going to get a child, you have to first get yourself a wife. Or a woman."

Delvin knew his mother had not married his father. He had been much too young to investigate such business, but once before she ran off as they sat side by side in the God Is Love Beauty Parlor over on Forrest street waiting for Cappie to get her thick crozzled hair straightened, he had asked who his father was and she told him he was a man from the west—an actor, she said. There was a tiny note of pride in her voice. It made Delvin feel as if his daddy was a somebody for sure. Maybe he had acted in Mr. Shakespeare's plays. Maybe in *Othello*, which was their favorite.

A colored general married to a white woman—it seemed a strange dream, so impossible, fantastical, that it had left them breathless. But after that first shock when sitting side by side at the little mahogany table upon which burned an electric lamp softly shaded by a gold paper shade, as they apprehended not simply the facts of the situation but the lack of fear and shame and, better even than that, the kowtowing he received, it seemed a right and proper notion. They saw too how despite the victories he won for them the people of Venice looked down on the general, even as they bowed to him. "Can't get too important not to get your tail set on fire—if you're a black man," Oliver pointed out. Delvin saw it too.

"He works for em," he said. "He's the one they hired to clean up their messes." He said this more to ingratiate himself with Oliver—to get the love going, to nestle deeper into this man's heart—than anything else. "But what about his getting married to that woman?" he said. This excited Delvin.

"Cast that from your mind," Oliver said. A strange look came into his broad face. "It might be a thrill for some," he said. "But not everybody wants to strike that note." He sighed. "Truth is, you never can tell where love is going to hit."

How true, Delvin thought. He was in love with Polly—love had hit him, the soft thin kind that comes in early youth—but he knew it didn't amount to much because Polly, who herself was in love

with one of the yardmen, had told him so. The ache had already
begun to subside. And he was sure he could find a wife for Mr.
Oliver. He had two candidates in mind. Miss Plurafore Conner and
Mrs. Duplaine Misty. Miss Conner had a little candy shop over on
Washington street and Mrs. Duplaine was the widow of Mr. Ste-
phen Misty, former principal of the colored high school over on
Brickson avenue. Both women had seemed suitably impressed by
the deluxe Constitution Funeral Home accommodations they enjoyed at the funerals where he had first spied them. Miss Conner,
a slim woman quick to tremble and shudder, had buried her father
from the Home, and Mrs. Duplaine, a portly, emotional woman,
had spent hours with Mr. O going over the special arrangements she
wanted for her husband's funeral (cornet band, all-white flowers and
four dumpling-sized gilt rings on his fingers). It had been Mr. O's
arm she leaned on—instead of her feckless son's (a nightclub singer
living with a white woman said to be an ether addict—*there's* your
Chattanooga Othello) when she wobbled down the aisle of the Mt.
Moriah Baptist church. Mr. O had put together a perfect service for
her, including a choir of pink-robed singers at the gravesite. As the
last strains of "Cross Over into Campground" had faded into the
pines, Delvin had noticed Mr. Oliver's eyes wet with tears. It was
true that Mr. Oliver was known to weep at funerals—some mocked
it as put-on—but Delvin knew him as a man of great feeling. Mrs. D
saw this too; Delvin noticed her swiveling an eye in Mr. O's direction as he stood tall and plump by one of the brass poles supporting
the green canvas tent over the grave. He had asked tenderly if she
wanted to place anything else in the casket's little memento drawer
and, when she said yes, helped her get the reluctant slide to work
and shielded her as she placed what looked to Delvin like a dried
cat's head in it; he saw how she appreciated this thoughtfulness.
His hand cupped over her hand clutching his arm, he had held
on later as she swayed keening over the casket as it was cranked
down into the layered red and yellow clay. Mr. O had ridden with
her back to the Home and served her brandy and let her cry on his
shoulder and then he'd had Willie Burt drive her home in her own

new Buick and sent Elmer in the big car to fetch Willie Burt, who came in whistling and smelling of liquor.

Mr. Oliver had been similarly attentive to Miss Conner who had needed help with the music for the service and in deciding which suit she wanted her father to wear. She had sat out on the side porch with Mr. Oliver after the funeral and Delvin had heard the creak of the old slat swing far into the night.

When over the next few weeks nothing happened, Delvin decided he had to help the business along. He stole a few sheets of Mr. Oliver's private stationery, along with envelopes and stamps, and wrote notes to the two women. He suggested to Mr. Oliver that he begin home visiting services, especially to the homes of those whose loved ones had been recently interred. "Seems like a funeral home ought to include such services," he said. "It idn't just at the grave that those poor ladies—"

"Which poor ladies?" Mr. Oliver asked. He was at the soapstone sink in the basement outside the embalming room washing his hands with the soap that smelled of lemons.

"Any of em," Delvin said. "I was thinking especially—because they're the latest—of Mrs. . . . ." And he went on to remind Mr. O of the gratefulness shown by the two substantially fixed women whose loved ones he'd just ushered into eternity.

They walked out into the backyard. A new snow had fallen, an inch of glossy powder that emphasized the lines of the old sycamore and the half broken red maple and set tiny gleaming caps on the leaves of the holly bush by the back steps.

"You're trying to push me into something, aren't you?"

"What if I was?"

"It won't do any good, boy."

"Why not?"

"I'm not fit for such folly as that."

"Why aint you?"

"Quit saying aint. I've told you about it."

"I forget. I can't keep every instruction in my mind at all times. My mind is too full of other prospects."

"Other than becoming a gentleman?"

"What good in this world would that do?"

"Kindness—gentleness—will always do."

"You just changing the subject."

"There aint no subject, boy," Mr. O said and laughed his wheezy, pressurized laugh.

They stood a moment looking up at the fuzzy January stars. Orion's lantern, the Sisters' broken stroke aimed at the distant iron mountains.

Delvin went ahead with his note plan, writing in florid ink strokes a message first worked out on a scrap of butcher paper. *I was most grateful to be of service. . . . Would you care to share a cup of tea at the Little Hummingbird cafe over on Jefferson street? If so, please . . . by return . . . yours . . .* Delvin wanted to make sure Mr. O would have to go. Of course he'd be angry but he'd get over that.

Delvin decided to write another set of letters detailing Mr. Oliver's good qualities. *I tell interesting stories, am not stingy with the pocket money, have never been a finicky eater, relish sitting out on the side porch reading good books, am a devotee of worksaving appliances, take no more than a ceremonial sip of wine (no spirits) and act gentlemanly at all times—and I have good table manners and can be counted on in a pinch . . .*

"That is a fine piece of work," Delvin said to himself as he folded the prepared sheets into envelopes he'd lifted from the bunch tucked in one of the cubbyholes in Mr. O's big secretary desk.

Replies to the invites came quickly. Both ladies said they would be delighted to join Mr. Oliver for tea. Delvin was able to determine the exact moment when the funeral director received the first answer. This by way of the loudly exclaimed cry, "What the goddamn hell!"

He also heard Mr. O tell Polly to go fetch him.

He ran out the kitchen door, through the back gate and out into the alley where Willie Burt was washing the old Crane & Breed glass-sided hearse they kept for those few who still preferred the departed to be carried to the cemetery by horse pull. The horses were in a little four-stall barn down the alley. Delvin liked to go out there and sit near their stalls. He didn't particularly like horses but he liked the smell of the hay. He went down there now and pulled himself up on a pile of stacked bales. He pulled the little green volume of *Othello* out of his jacket pocket, leaned back against a bale and began to read. Iago was busy with his underhanded ways. They were nothing to what he, Delvin Walker, former child pretender to the throne of France, was up to. But maybe he shouldn't have done what he did. Lord, I got to slow down. He had already been in one fight that morning. With a high school boy who had caught him the other day whistling at his little plump girlfriend over on Stockton street. Roscoe Blake his name was, a portly fellow with an incipient hump. Roscoe had slapped him in the face. Delvin had fallen back into the manure pile—right behind this barn. He'd got up and hit Roscoe with two chunks of crumbly manure. Roscoe came at him windmilling both fists. Delvin was amazed at how silly he looked. He ducked and poked him tentatively in the belly. Roscoe went down as if he had hit him with a bat. He rolled over three times—like he was going to roll on down the alley, Delvin thought—but then he got up. He shook his fist at Delvin and shouted that he had better leave Preeny alone or worse was coming. "Hadn't seemed too bad so far," Delvin said. Roscoe had walked off stiff-legged like a dog down the alley toward the bicycle he rode everywhere. He was a pretty boy and always had money.

But this episode wasn't troubling him at the moment. I feel burdened by life, Delvin thought. He missed his mother. These days he only thought of her when he said his prayers at night. "Bless Mama," he said as he knelt beside the bed, as he had been taught at the foundling home and required to do. Those two words were all he said. Each night they floated away on a puff of breath to where he didn't know. No one, as far as he knew, had heard news of her. He'd better go over to the Emporium again to check if anybody over there had received word from her, or about her.

Just then, Elmer, resettling the brimless cap he never took off, arrived to say he was wanted back at the house.

"Did you tell em you saw me?"

"I didn't see no harm in it."

"You wouldn't."

Elmer, who had disliked Delvin on sight, laughed.

"You go on," Delvin said.

"Some's got *real* work to do."

"When you run across one you might ask him for a few pointers." Elmer blew air through his fat lips, turned and sloped out of the barn. Delvin waited until he was fully out of sight and sound and then he waited a few minutes longer before he started to the house.

3

One day he took a walk across town to the house where he was born, the canted little shabby place where an old woman whose name he could never keep straight until she spelled it—B-e-a-u-c-h-a-m-p, pronounced Beecham—told him the story of that day, his birth day. (He had already heard it from old Mr. Heberson down at the store.) As the woman spoke he pulled a new penny notebook from his pocket and began to take notes. She said fresh out in the air he'd made sounds like he was talking to himself in an unknown language. Said the day was hot and still, all the leaves in the big poplar tree hanging straight down. Said the big old black rooster over at Hemley's crowed and wouldn't stop. Said, "You could smell the birth from out de alley." She looked hard at him. "You not going to put that in the paper is you?"

"No mam, I just want to keep up with my story."

The house—shanty, owned by Mr. Odel Dupee, an oldtime Red Row colored landlord, with rusty broken windowsills hanging like a drunkard's lip and leaning shiplap walls—was temporarily empty due to the flight of its most recent occupants after a homebrewed liquor bust two days before. Delvin thought of moving back in himself, but he enjoyed living at the funeral home. He thought it would probably be too hard on his feelings if he did. On the porch floor were little cone-shaped piles of sawdust from where the boring bugs had been at the wood. The shabbiness of the place bothered him, humiliated him a little; he didn't want to have to try to fix up the house. The smell he remembered of it (and occasionally ran into out in the world) made him recall the wood as oiled-down, smooth and dark, but in life that wasn't so. The floors, walls—every part—were scabby and dry and smelled of faded and stalled living. He shied from the place.

He walked the neighborhood, stopping at various spots to ask questions about his mother. She had never been apprehended, never heard from again after her flight. Many thought she was dead. At the Emporium she was remembered by a few—forgotten by most—as a quick-spirited woman without guile but fast to anger—if he really wanted to know, real hotheaded. A fat woman in yellow stockings remembered that she liked to tear cloth into strips and try to weave something out of it but was unable to come up with anything much. She had tried to read books, too, but she couldn't do it well enough to make it fun. Tried to play the ukulele, but couldn't master that either.

"She was good at talking to men," the woman said, pursing her large mouth and making a puffing sound, "good at telling funny stories."

The room they sat in that afternoon had yellow-and-purple-striped wallpaper.

"You looking for a tryout?" she asked Delvin and he wasn't sure what she meant and said, no, he didn't think so.

A man in a checked yellow suit came in through a door to the right and he had a pistol butt poking out of his coat pocket. The pistol gave Delvin an exhilarated feeling and he had to press himself not to jump up and run. The man grinned at him. Bunny Boy Williams—everybody knew he lived there. He had two large steel teeth in front. He rubbed the teeth with the side of his left forefinger and grinned again at Delvin and propped himself against the striped wall.

Sweating, Delvin asked the fat woman if his mother had left anything there.

"I don't know about that," the woman said. She was primping a curly bronze wig on a stand as she talked. "You don't have to be worried about that gentleman," she said indicating Williams. "He's all show like a green fly."

"Would somebody else know about Mama's things?"

"You don't have to be afraid to look at him neither," the fat woman said and laughed.

Delvin could feel his face burning. The woman patted his arm.

"Go ask Miss Ellereen," she said. "She'll know."

Miss Ellereen, the proprietress, gave him an ivory letter opener with a broken tip that, so she said, had belonged to his mother. Chinese characters were stamped on the yellowed blade and the handle was shaded in swirls and stripes and looked as if it had once been painted gold; it was a faded blood color. Miss Ellereen said his mother was light on her feet in a way men noticed. "She had a bounce to her," she said. "A quick mouth too."

"You think she's still alive?"

The woman cocked her head to the side and stared at him. A smell of anise and soapy sweat gusted from her. She wore an oversized man's green silk robe.

"I expect she's off in some other swell town, carrying on like she knows how to do."

"She said my daddy's from out west."

"Yes, child, they all are, all them daddies."

His love-pimping for Mr. Oliver had led to his being banished to the yard where he lived for a week in a tent made from an old quilt strung between two trees, and he wondered if word of the humiliation had gotten this far over into Red Row. The thought made him sweat some more. He said something about this and Miss Ellereen laughed outloud.

"You too nervous to know what to talk about, aint you?"

"I *know*, I'm just too nervous to say it."

"Well sometimes that's a good thing."

She waved her fan in a way that made him know his time was up.

He found himself back at the sporting house two days later sitting on the back porch writing in his notebook as Kattie, one of the cook's helpers, peeled baked sweet potatoes and mashed them in a pot for a soufflé. The Emporium was a world of smells. Compounded and contentious loamy perfumes hung in the air like remnants of a gas attack mixed with the rooty odors of female sweat and excretion and drippage and exfoliations and discharge—the blood and the brew, as Portia, a lanky pale-skinned woman from Florida called it—added to the multiple odors from the kitchen of pork-flavored vegetables and chops and hams and frying bacon as well as beef roasts and skillet-fried catfish from the depths of the Tennessee river and the sugary smells of yams and cakes and the sharp odor of turnips and mustard greens and rutabagas and the earthy aroma of grits and hominy and the stinks of lye and the perfumy savors of soaps to drown the lye out.

None of these stinks and perfumes completely masked the early morning stench of sour and near to rot sexualization, the grease and juice of high-velocity cell work, sexwork. The odor trailed behind the women like a beaten puppy as they came down the unpainted back stairs into the kitchen and rear parlor where on two cotton-batting-extruding couches pulled from the main parlor they threw themselves down in various stages of exhaustion or satiety for a last break or breakfast before going off to bed. These were the smells that were the most exotic to Delvin. Each woman had a slightly different odor. Each was in its own way interesting. Loquaty, orangey, musty, green grape sour, smell of rotten tomatoes and smells of the back-house and the sour smells of loneliness and shame, bitter, sugary, burnt, plummy, cidery smells of pulverized bone and of blood mixed with mucosal parts, sweetly piercing, crossmixed with house per-fumes and the faint scents of mold, crapulous, orotund, sleek, conjur smells of van-van and angel's turnip, smells of screech liquor—he aimed his nose at them, face uplifted, sniffing like a hunter as the women passed. Some smells even of the grave, hints, brief passing traces familiar in the funeral home.

Sitting against the porch post with his stretched-out feet as close to Kattie's hip as he thought he could get away with—thrillingly close as she sat on the top step—he jotted this material into his fold-ing notebook. The rich musty smell of the sweet potatoes excited him. Kattie offered him a piece and he pulled it in two and offered half back to her.

"I don't care to eat what I'm cooking," she said.

The red skins lay clumped at her feet. He picked one up, flopped it over his fingers and back and licked it. "I could eat these things all day," he said.

"You'd bloat up like a pig."

"A happy one though."

He always felt as if he didn't get quite enough of whatever it was he wanted. He mentioned this to Kattie. "Why you reckon that is?"

"For you? I couldn't say."

"But I mean don't a lot of people think that? For instance, yall had a duck supper the other night. You saved me out a leg that was very tasty. I wanted some more, but there wadn't any. And then several of the ladies"—he always called them ladies—"said they wished they could have more too."

"Maybe that was just a problem of the number against the duck."

"But look at this whole place. All these gentlemen keep coming back."

"That's just appetite; they get filled up every time."

"I don't know. There are a lot of instances of what I'm talking about. I for one never get enough summer. Or enough of gardenias or lilacs or pe-ony flowers. I like the smell of horses so much sometimes I wish I lived in the stable."

"Sometimes you smell like you do."

"Ah." He shifted his approach. "And *Othello*."

"What's that?"

"That's a play. Mr. William Shakespeare wrote it."

"That's a funny name."

"He's the best of them all."

"Them all who?"

"Playwriters."

"Sometimes we put on skits right here."

"I know. I watched that one about the Queen of Sheba night before last."

"Was that you hiding behind the curtain?"

"Somebody close to it."

"Was that like Mr. Shakebutt?"

He barked a quick laugh and she blushed, ashamed that she would say such a thing but delighted too.

"No. His plays are put on on big stages. In New York and Chicago, New Orleans. Paris even."

"He's from France?"

"No. He's a Englishman. Was."

"Then how do they understand him in Paris?"

"I expect they have to listen pretty hard."

"Well, what about O-thella?"

"I wish there was more of it."

"Does it quit before the end?"

"No, it gets there just right."

"What's it about?"

"It's about this colored general."

"There's no such thing."

"There was back then."

"When?"

"I don't know—centuries ago. Five hundred years maybe."

"That's a lot."

"Sure is. Back in Venice."

"Where's that?"

"Over in Italy I think."

"Does O-thella speak italian?"

"No. He speaks english."

"How about the other people?"

"In the play? They speak english too."

She lay a skin flat in her palm, scraped with her fingernail the stringy remnant of orange meat and licked it off her fingertip. Her palms were the faintest brown, hardly any color at all.

She said, "Sounds like a lot of folks who don't understand a word of what each other's saying. I'm familiar with that problem."

Orange flesh between her teeth made her white teeth even prettier. He was about to tell how the Venice big shots mocked Othello and Iago hated him because he was a negro (but more important than that because he was powerful and Iago had nothing but the black emptiness of the powerless to stare into, and that terrified and ruined your mind, he would think) and Desdemona's father and relatives and Iago's friends and the riffraff and common white trash of Venice all hated him too. About how they tricked him into thinking his wife was running around with another man and how this—along with all the other badmouthing—drove Othello so crazy that he wound up strangling Desdemona with his own bare hands. It was pitiful.

He started to say something but he couldn't. It shamed him too much. He wished he hadn't brought it up.

This girl.

He sneaked a glance at her. It wasn't that he wanted to fool or comfort this ginger-colored girl with her bunchy hair pressed down under a green cotton scarf but that she would look up from mashing sweet potatoes and talking to him of speeches and speechifiers and find him dear. (He was this way with every girl, every woman too. He wanted to tell her this, confess it, but he thought this would be a bad idea and so he kept his mouth shut.) Under a mixed cloudy afternoon sky he yearned.

Just then came a shout from the helpboy John Day over to the side of the Emporium—which was actually several smallish houses linked together by closed-in catwalks around the central three-story house—yelling at somebody in big trouble. He stood up as Kattie said, "What's that?" and he put his hand on her arm to steady her if she needed steadying—and himself, because the shout scared him too—and then he could see John Day down on his knees looking under the big house that in most places—the undercarriage—was covered over with a wooden trellis planted in yellow jasmine but not where John Day was looking and poking up into it with a section of broom handle. He ran out and found John Day poking hard, jabbing at something, and squatting behind him was Bunny Boy holding up the skirts of his shiny yellow suit coat and peering sideways over his shoulder as John Day gave a vicious poke to whatever it was stuck up under the house.

"Come out of there, you crazy fool," cried John Day.

"Go get him," Bunny Boy said.

Delvin jumped down from the porch and ran over to the scene. "What is it?" he said. He trembled with excitement.

"Can you see him?" Bunny Boy said to John Day who was swishing the broom handle back and forth under the house, raising red dust. "Come over here, Joe," he yelled at one of the other factotums, a heavyset man pulling sheets off a long washline over near the board back fence. "And you," he said to Delvin, "get down there and help this boy pull that nonscrip out of there."

"It's a somebody?" Delvin said.

"It's a nobody, who's going to wind up even less," Bunny sneered, ducking his head to peer into the gloom. "Stick yo hand up there," he said to John Day. "Come here, Joe."

Joe came up bringing a shovel. "You want me to dig 'im out, Mr. Bunny?"

"In a minute," Bunny Boy said. "Hey," he said to John Day, "move over let Joe stick his arm up in there. Joe, get down there and grab that rascal."

"What is it?" Joe said. "A possum? I don't want to stick my hand up after no possum."

Bunny Boy smirked. "Some 'ud say that. Not me. It's a lost 'un though."

Joe, a blocky, fidgety man with a small square face, got down on his hands and knees in the powdery red dirt and, shoving John Day aside, crammed himself into the opening and skinnied up under the house. "Grab my feet," he said to nobody in particular, or to everybody.

Bunny Boy indicated to Delvin that this should be his role.

But even with Delvin and John Day holding the man's thick, knobby ankles, Joe was unable to get far up under the house.

"You do it," Bunny Boy said to Delvin. "Joe, get out of there."

It took the three of them to pull Joe out. He came forth covered in red dust, a mummery of himself. Delvin laughed, but the laugh was squelched—Bunny made a flicking motion with his right hand, indicating that is was Delvin's turn at the enterprise.

"What was it?" he said to Joe. "A person?"

"Hard to say," Joe said. "It had human form, but that might not be the telling thing."

Delvin's stomach turned over. He wanted to run away but he was afraid to have these people see how scared he was. A couple of children stood on the picnic table Miss Ellereen kept in the back-yard. One of the children—a boy a few years younger than him—was standing on one leg. It was a clearing day. The sky looked painted on.

He lowered himself into the dust, wanting to hold his nose for the stink he feared was in it and for the germs he'd read about swirling in such places but he didn't and as he slithered into the opening he smelled not a stink but an odor of cleanness and a clayey sweetness that made him want to come back at another time and lie there a while. It was cool and quiet. At first he couldn't make out anyone, but then as his eyes adjusted he saw a form scrunched up against the brick chimney that was a central feature of that part of the Em-porium. This is the music room, Delvin thought; he hadn't realized it. He pictured the ladies sitting up there listening to Punky Wills play the piano. He could hear someone faintly striking the keys, an idler or some lady dreaming of another life far from such houses. He thought of knocking on the floor to scare whoever it was, but he didn't. The form, the dark figure—small, the figure of a boy like him—lay drawn up against the chimney. Delvin could see his shape but he couldn't make out his face.

"You got to come out," he said. "You understand that, don't you? So you probably better just come on. After me they're gon send somebody a whole lot meaner." Little puffs of dust like thin smoke in the half light twirled up where he placed his hands. "Come on now," he said, his voice quiet in the soft dust.

The man or boy let out a low moan.

"You hurt?" Delvin said. The figure didn't answer. "You're scared, aint you? I would be too. But you got to come on. They'll go get the police directly."

Delvin looked back toward the opening. Bunny Boy and Joe peered at him from either side of the torn-away trellis. Bunny Boy waved him on. "Go," he mouthed. There were doodlebug holes in the dust, little cone-shaped depressions. A strand of spiderweb like a wide white ribbon hung from a floor joist. Delvin shuddered. He turned back to the cowering form.

"If you don't come on," he said, "I'm going to have to gather you." He crawled up closer. The figure didn't move.

"Come on now."

The figure kicked at him hard, the sole of his bare foot flashing in the caliginous murk, a kick that would have hurt if it caught him.

"Damn."

He could smell the figure's odor, sour and sharp with the stink of fresh shit.

"Ah well," Delvin said. "I'm sorry."

He knew how he would be in a predicament like this. If it was just him, he'd leave this sniffler, let him work his way out when things died down. But it wasn't just him. Next they'd send Joe up after him with the shovel.

Delvin feinted a grab and when the figure kicked, he caught his fully extended foot. When the figure tried to pull his foot back Delvin caught the other one and pulled hard. The figure—the person— started to kick his first foot loose, and that let Delvin catch both feet in his arms. He crabbed fast backwards, pulling the writhing figure with him.

"Snatch me," he cried to Joe and Bunny Boy.

Somebody's hands grabbed his ankles and jerked him in one sharp motion halfway out of the hole. The figured writhed, pulled partially free and snaked a ways back in, but Joe hauled them both out in a cloud of pale red dust.

Before anybody could stop him John Day reached over and whacked the figure with the broom handle. Delvin was angry too and he socked the figure in the thigh with the flat of his hand. The figure cried out in a boy's cracked voice. He writhed on the crumbly dirt.

"Stand back," Bunny Boy cried, and before anybody could move he flung a bucket of dishwater on the figure and on Delvin who was still holding one of his legs.

The water revealed the albino Winston Morgred. Delvin hadn't seen him since the day he left the africano foundlings home. His orange hair was so thick the water beaded on it and on his pale freckled skin, his flattened nose and pursy lips.

He could pass—easy, Delvin thought, if he cut off that face.

Morgred kicked and Delvin struck him again on the thigh. Morgred moaned and began to cry.

Delvin got up off the ground and fetched Morgred a kick that struck his bare ankle.

The boy glared at him but he said nothing.

Delvin was ashamed even as he made the kick or at least right afterwards, but he knew he hadn't been able to stop himself. In disgust, at Morgred, dirty and peculiar and smelling of shit, scrabbling in the muck, and at himself for even being in that backyard, he turned away from the gathering and went down to the wash shed and cleaned himself with water from the big tub.

From the window propped open with a hickory pole he watched them beat the boy with rough straw brooms and with sticks. Bunny Boy and the others and a few of the women were in on it. One woman swung what looked like a white china figurine at him, but she didn't hit him. Another poked him with a riding crop. Morgred rolled on the ground, crying for them to leave him alone. People called him the Ghost; Delvin remembered that.

"I aint done done it," the boy cried.

Done what? Delvin wondered and then he guessed it was the peeping that he was probably up to, but how could you tell? It could have been anything, maybe even just an outcast looking for a place where he could be left in peace. He had struck him hard in the thigh and meant to and now he was sorry.

Miss Ellereen came out on the back porch and stood watching the boy get his thrashing.

"Don't you kill him," she said.

"You could pinch his head off and it wouldn't kill him," Bunny Boy said, but maybe they thought they were about to because the hitters stopped. Bunny Boy's face gleamed with sweat. The women wrapped their housedresses around them and flounced off, one of them, Aphelia, with a broom twirling on her shoulder.

Avoiding the scene, Delvin crossed the yard back to the porch looking for Kattie, the cook's helper, but she was gone into the kitchen.

"Don't you have something else to do?" Miss Ellereen said, giving him a sharp look.

"Yessum, I guess."

"Then you best haul along and do it."

For a second he felt it would cost him his life not to peek into the kitchen after Kattie, but he would have to knock Miss Ellereen down to do it so he stepped back and headed around the side of the house, in his chest a scuff of frustration and another feeling like a weakness, some low-water place where nothing was. He stopped to look back and saw the boy Morgred crawling on his hands and knees. Blood dripped from his heavy, listless mouth. The water tossed on him made the pale red dust on his torn khaki shirt redder, its color for the moment deeper even than the blood. His drenched clothes were torn nearly from his body, and as he watched, Morgred's pink penis swung loose from his mucky torn trousers and hung free. One of the girls on the steps whistled and Bunny Boy and Joe laughed. Morgred reached and fumbled with himself and tucked the member into his clothes but it wouldn't stay and he had to hold himself with one hand as he crawled. As he crawled, lurching on his knees, the penis began to extend itself in an erection. He had begun to cry. The tears dropped unimpeded into the dirt.

Delvin wanted to run back and put a stop—to what? To the painful feeling, some painful feeling. Make Winston pull himself together. Something in him felt like beating the poor fissle til he quit crawling. Felt like hauling him to safety.

The men walked away from the half-wrecked boy. The women hooted at him from the steps, shaking their flimsy morning skirts.

The boy gathered himself and got to his feet.

Joe stepped up and gave him a kick in the ass, sending him stumbling into a trot that carried him right at Delvin who stepped back to let him pass. As he did he smelled again the odor of shit, now augmented with the wet, sour-smelling dirt.

The boy fumbled at the low side gate of unpainted wood palings that separated the back from the front yard. Delvin came up behind him and snagged the latch for him and swung the gate open. The boy looked wildly at him, his pale eyes blinking in the light that had always seemed too much for them.

"I just wanted to get down in the dim spot," he said.

Delvin didn't answer. He didn't know what to say.

"You didn't have to pull me out of there."

"Yes I did."

With the side of one finger Morgred scratched his eyebrows hard and then he screwed his eyes tight shut and opened them. His eyelashes were orange like his hair.

"You got a dime?"

Delvin started to say no but then he said, "I got one."

"Let me have it. I got to get me somethin to eat."

"Way you look nobody'd sell you anything if you had five dollars."

"Let me have the dime."

"I tell you," Delvin said suddenly, and it was as if he had fallen through a shaky patch of leaf shade, "you follow on behind me to the house."

"To the undertaker? I'm scared to go there."

"You're safer there than anywhere else I can think of."

The boy dropped his eyes then looked quickly up as if trying to catch Delvin in some piddling joke at his expense. Delvin could see he was done in, that he had no other place to go.

"Just lope on along behind," he said.

He started out across the street and ran along the dirt path that served as a sidewalk in Red Row and turned right onto Sweet August street running fast. In his mind he didn't know if he was leading the boy or trying to lose him; maybe both. Children played in a puddle under the big gum tree that stretched heavy, grooved branches over the dirt street and humped it up out in the middle with its roots.

Delvin gave the children a sharp eye as he passed but still he could hear them hooting at Morgred as he came along. The path went up a plank step to the section of wooden sidewalk in front of New Big Bethel Baptist church. The wooden portion ran along the rest of the block and dipped down again two steps into the street.

Delvin ran steadily and he only looked twice to see if the boy was still with him; he was, both times, straggling but coming on in a half-lame trotting style, holding his pant remnants up with one hand and his pale squinting eyes looking squarely at him.

They came up the alley from wind-flecked Brocade street. Delvin checked off the flimsy leaves of chinese elms hanging over the board alley fence of the Askew house and then the great blanket of cherokee roses sagging from the crumbling brick fence of the Lewis house, running. Then came backyards opening directly on the alley, exposing gray- and yellow-streaked red packed dirt yards stacked with boxes or old horse collars or fragments of no longer identifiable machinery, pump parts or busted forge buckets or pieces of streetcar undercarriage or canvas-covered piles of plaster or old weathervanes—roosters or codfish or racehorses—and, in each yard, lines of washing; raised among these like guardhouses were the neighbors' wash sheds and kitchens emitting mixed and penetrating smells of lye and raw ashes and boiled pork-fortified greens and cornmeal and brushwood fires. He checked these off and he checked off old Mr. Berke petting his blind german police dog and Mrs. Sanderson accompanying her tiny triplet daughters sitting side by side tied into a little blue wagon and Billy Batts who wore his engineer's cap at all times and sang sorrow songs as he dug holes in his yard searching for confederate gold and Mrs. Opel and Mrs. Crawford, the former dancing twins, not dancing this afternoon, and a couple of the Pursleys who all looked exactly alike and Mrs. Vereen carrying on a big tray several of the fruit pies she baked and sold at the market over on Leopardi street on Wednesdays and Saturdays, and he checked off Mr. Campson who was home sick from the grocery store he owned at the edge of the chinese quarter, and Biddy Comber, the retired boxer, once a sparring partner for Jack Johnson and father of James who loved only the piano, Biddy standing in the center of his yard staring up into a pecan tree as if from there the Second Coming might commence. Hello and hello and hello. Hidy, yall, he said, checking each one off.

He already felt trailed—hunted really—by the boy loping behind him. He wished he hadn't said anything to him. The Ghost. He gave him an angry look. Elta Napier, a girl his age, stood out in her yard stringing ragged shirts on the washline. She wore a white shift that dragged up her thighs as she reached to pin a fluttering gray shirt. Delvin wanted to leave his self-appointed duty and go speak to Elta. Her thick hair was tied around with a pale blue cloth. His heart took a leap; it was a day, he thought, for heart leaping. He wanted to rush across the yard and push Elta to the ground. He wanted to fly to her and kneel on the packed and swept dirt at her feet. He slowed down, stopped and gave her a wave; Elta waved back without looking at him.

The boy came and stood close enough behind so Delvin could smell him.

"I thought you was going to show me a place."

"We're on our way to it now," he said without looking at him. "I thought I told you to hang back."

"I got to lie down."

"Well come on then."

He led him to the shed and piled a bed of straw for him in one of the unused stalls. As Delvin worked, the boy watched without offering to help, an impatient, grieving look on his face. The two horses shifted uneasily. The big gray nickered at him and Delvin stroked his nose. "Yall be friendly," he said to the pair.

"You can camp here," he told the boy. "I'll go up to the house and get you something to eat."

Willie and the yardboy Elmer were nowhere about and Delvin wondered where they'd gotten off to. No one was in the kitchen either. Delvin went into the pantry and made up a basket of food from the array of delectables they had received from the two funerals Oliver had presided over earlier in the week. The pantry was always

stocked with a bounty—layer cakes and big yellow hams and roasts
in gelatin and eggy puddings and covered casseroles and blueberry
and huckleberry pies and tureens of soup covered with cheesecloth.
Delvin made a couple of ham and roast beef sandwiches on thick
slices of white bread he cut from a long loaf. He filled a bowl with
Brunswick stew made by Mrs. Constable Brown to serve at the funeral of her husband Harry J, the bullying boss of a negro road crew
working out on the Capital highway.

Where was everybody? He went out to the dining room and
stood listening. In the big enameled tin plates propped along the
chair rail Delvin could make out his distorted reflection. No sound
in the house except for the hollow ticking of the big clock in the hall
and the finches Mr. Oliver kept in the big cage in his office. The
birds peeped and rustled and the familiar sound seemed the sound
of the house itself. Then he picked up the low sound of voices coming
from the workrooms downstairs. He went back through the pantry
into the kitchen and down the back stairs where he met Mrs. Parker
coming up. She was wiping tears with her apron.

"Lord," she said, "they done hung another one."

Delvin felt a hard exacting chill.

"Help me up these stairs," Mrs. Parker said.

He took her arm and helped her up and got her a cup of coffee
from the big tin pot at the back of the stove and sat her in the rocking
chair she kept by the breakfast table and then even though she asked
him not to leave her and then told him not to go down those stairs he
went. He had forgotten all about the Ghost.

4

Willie Burt and Elmer and Polly and Mr. Oliver's assistant Culver and a large dark-skinned man he didn't know were in the cool field-stone hallway outside the embalming room. The room was faced along its full length on one side with frosted white glass, and the darkwood door in the center was in the top half panel covered by the same glass. The word RESTRUCTURE that had been there when Mr. Oliver arrived was painted in black on the pebbly glass.

Mrs. Brass, who worked with Polly, was sobbing loudly, as was the big dark-complected man who held a red bandana to his face. The others were quiet. Their faces looked like masks. Polly, tears on her cheeks, came up to him and took him in her arms. He felt her body in the long length of it against his and felt the remarkableness of it—she had never hugged him before—but this was so in the midst of the choppy, ice-laced fire in his gut.

As Polly held him the door opened and Mr. Oliver stuck his head out. "There you are, boy. I need you." He came out. He was wearing a cordovan leather apron that covered his body and under the apron a white shirt with the sleeves rolled up and his black funeral pants. He stepped to the crying man and put his hand on his shoulder.

"Carl," he said, "dear Carl."

The man lifted his eyes from the bandana. His eyes were so wet and red they looked bloody.

Delvin let Polly go and followed Mr. Oliver into the embalming room.

A twisted, naked, half-charred corpse lay on the marble table. Delvin cut his eyes away but not quickly enough, and he wanted to run out of the room. Mr. Oliver closed the door and came up behind him. He put his arm around Delvin's shoulders.

"Come help me with this poor boy," he said.

The man's name, boy's name, written in green ink on a square white card and propped against an empty water glass on the counter that ran along one side of the room, was Casey David Harold.

"Seventeen," Oliver said. "Caught sneaking, they said, from a white woman's bedroom—they said—with a gold acorn bracelet and a ruby necklace and some of the woman's clothes stuffed in a valise."

He touched the crusted forehead with the first two fingers of his right hand, lightly but without hesitation, as if this was some imprimatur he was placing there, resolution of flesh on flesh, from wretched life to life everlasting.

"They put him in the jail over in Custis," he said, "and shortly after midnight last night some men came and got him out of that jail. They put him in chains and hauled him in the back of a truck out to the river where they tormented him with fire and water before they cut his hands off with an ax and then raised him up to hang him in a hickory tree beside the dirt road they came in on. Then they set him on fire. The fire—as you can see—burned him on one side only."

His voice was hollow, oratorical.

The boy's burned side was drawn up in a strange lopsided way and ashy now and showed streaks of gray and red flesh under the black rubbled crust. The other, free of rigor mortis by now, was loose and askew, the handless arm with its projecting inch of bone thrown out like a sharpened white pointer aimed at the floor. The body looked like halves of evilly treated people joined together, two people without relation to each other except in the mystery of there being no limit to what human beings could come up with to do to each other. This angel who didn't know he was an angel, burned and strangled by furious ruffians who didn't know they were angels too.

Sweat stood on Oliver's brow. The helper, Culver, washed equipment in the big metal sink on the other side of the room, banging metal against the sides. The boy's face was blistered and distorted but not terribly burned. Everyone could be thankful for that.

On the counter, beside a red celluloid pinwheel and a line of photographs of male negro movie stars and an ivory frame containing a photo of an elephant the white folks had hung right after the Great War for misbehaving, in open cherrywood boxes the glass bottles of numbers 17 through 52 brown dyes, of conditioners, humectants, anti-edemics, lotions and perfumes waited. On a rolling wooden trolly the big galvanized tank of formaldehyde; gray rubber tubing and silver hand pumps on a tray underneath. One gallon of juice per fifty pounds of corpse. Delvin knew this already. He'd seen corpses, by now he'd helped out.

But he shivered and turned from this one, crowding against the big galvanized tin sink. The clear water running steadily from the tap soothed him. Culver's presence soothed him. The equipment, gauges and hinges of bright metal, scoops and forceps in their clattering, soothed him. These matters are ordinary and superficial, he thought. No, they're not. (They are too weighty to be stood up under. No shelter can keep off the load.) Yes, they are. When he turned back to the lighted body he saw he had not fixed his mind and turned again to the sink. The clean gray mottled galvanized bottom, the smoothly whirling clear flushing water. Culver's wet arms gleaming as he lifted them in the light pouring from the downturned trays on the ceiling.

Delvin stood quietly. He thought about the woods where he liked to stand at the end of the Little Hollow Road trail and ponder on the thousand secrets hidden among the trees. Secrets not like propositions and facts you could come to know but true secrets, mysteries and puzzles you could never discover the answer to or reason for. You could only stand there, like a mourner before a grave, and wonder. He thought of his mother, who was alive, he was sure, moving through that forest of secrets, finding her way. He could feel her, sense her, tracking across the landscape. He bore down steadily—in the few seconds of time that seemed to stretch before him like a day or a year—and once again he could almost find her, almost see her, trailing her blue shawl behind her like a flag. But once again she eluded him. He gasped. He was back in the room. He ran water over his hands, cleaned them with soap.

Wearing green rubber gloves he helped as they washed what remained of the boy and gathered up the pieces that had fallen or been torn off and that came loose as they as gently as possible washed the body. Culver tied off and bandaged the wrists. With a sure hand and tiny stitches Mr. Oliver sewed up the mouth that had been ripped open by blows. He attempted to inject the embalming fluid through the big neck vein and then through others in the thighs and under the arms, but none would hold the slick greenish fluid that drained out onto the white marble table and ran along the gutters into buckets. "It's all right," Oliver said when Elmer began to cry.

They had wrapped the torso and legs loosely in yellow oilcloth when a hard banging began on the door. Then the glass pane broke and Mrs. Arctura Harold, the boy's mother, rushed screaming into the room. Her left wrist streamed blood where she'd cut it breaking the door using the small brass cuspidor that had stood beside it.

Oliver sprang nimbly for so large a man to meet her. He caught her arms and drew them together, crossing them, and pulled her to him and held her against his chest as she screamed. Her scream was like the scream of a creature from the ancient dark of the deepest woods, a creature everybody has forgotten about except when on times like these some ruined individual screams and they suddenly remember.

At the scream, surging and smashing and excavating with a frenzied dedication for the soul already fled the premises, all the strength went out of Delvin's body. He leaned against the sink, catching himself on the lip of it. The woman wouldn't stop screaming. Why should she? he thought, amazed at her lung power. He wanted to scream too, but he was already sobbing and the whole front of his body was numb.

And then, from outside the room, from the hallway that had been filling with people from who knows where, came more screams, loud mixed voices, human voices, crying out, yelling and shouting and screeching until Delvin thought the air itself would shatter and fall down and they would be standing screaming with forsaken eyes in the face of heaven or whatever monstrosity or nothingness was behind the world.

The screams went on and then abruptly they seemed to collapse on themselves and they trailed away. The mother of the boy croupmoaned in Oliver's arms. He began gently to speak to her, but as he did she broke away and lunged at the table. Outside the room a low groaning and keening had begun and as she moved, the crowd, that only a few of could see into the room, swayed and trembled like a sea, moaning and making little chattering and clicking sounds, little human expressions, nicks and chips at the unholiness, at the failed light, whispers and clucks, tiny hisses like spray blown off the tops of waves, all entirely human, pure and unbreakable in perfection, the only perfection left to any of them just now.

Mrs. Harold had thrown her body across her son's body and she was kissing his sewn-up lips.

Still bent over, she took a shuffling step back, placing her hands not on her son's body but on the marble table. She raised up. "Oh, Lord, do not," she cried in a wild voice. "Do not, Lord, do not. Do not ransom this child."

She began again to scream, to shriek in a high, unworldly voice, but before she got well begun her voice sheared off and she dropped to the floor. In the hallway, like a sea, voices massively groaning. Oliver had tried to catch her, but she hit the floor on her side. Both Mrs. Harold and Oliver were smeared with blood that was seeping from the cut on her wrist.

Oliver called for them to get the doctor and he and Culver lifted Mrs. Harold onto the auxiliary table, an old steel-topped folding table used when he had to travel out to the country to work. With alcohol and a tourniquet and hard pressure that made Mrs. Harold cry out again, Oliver was able to stop the bleeding. He had Culver and Elmer carry Mrs. Harold out the double back doors and up to the back screen porch where they could lay her on the big daybed kept there along with folding cots for sleeping on hot summer nights.

Out in the hall he comforted Mr. Harold, who had not come into the embalming room.

"She just got a nick on her wrist," he said. "The doctor will be here in a speck."

Then he went himself and phoned from the telephone hanging on the wall of the embalming room. He came back and said, "The doctor is leaving now." Dr. Mullens lived in the next block and was the only africano doctor in the city at that time.

Oliver spoke gentling words to those standing in the hallway and came back inside and shut the door behind him. Culver had hung one of the big aprons over the missing glass.

"Thank you, Culver," Oliver said and leaned against the wall. "Thank all of you." He closed his eyes and pressed the unbloodied knob of his wrist against his forehead. He looked over at Delvin and smiled a sad, weary smile that brought out his dimples. "Take a long breath, son," he said.

Delvin breathed deeply in. His chest was a dusty empty room filling with a burning wind. His face was wet, and he realized he was crying. He wiped his eyes on one of the gray clean towels stacked on the counter. The shouts, the screams and yells, had been like huge scouring pads, rubbing the feeling off his skin. He was numb—in the places he wasn't still burning. He felt a pressure in his head like a trunk filled with something creaturely that was pushing to get loose. He sat down in a chair by the sink and pressed his face against his knees. The blood rushed and dammed and he sat up quickly. He was about to faint. He grabbed the edge of the sink, pulled himself up and vomited. Culver came over to him and said he ought to go outside. But he said no. He wanted to stay here as long as he could. He thought he could make it through. "I'm doing all right."

"Anymore all right as that and we'll have to take care of *you*," Culver said. Nothing ever seemed to bother Culver.

With the paints, some of which he had mixed himself from raw earth he collected in the ravines and from under rhododendrons growing below the ridge and had drawn from roots collected in the deep woods and dug up from clay pits and boiled out of leaves and bark, Oliver painted the broken boy's face, and with other paints, commercial cosmetics mostly, he added color to his cheeks. He picked the boy's hair loose and oiled it and brushed it back from his bony forehead and then for the second time in his life as a mortician he bent down and kissed the product of his ministrations, this ruined child, on the forehead. He had not looked directly at Delvin, who had stayed in the room for most of the work before he remembered Morgred waiting in the horse shed and became distressed and nervous because he didn't know what to do and told Culver, a small tidy man worn to exhaustion by now, that he had to pee and went out and carried the food he had packed in a small hamper out to the shed and gave it to the Ghost, who knew nothing of what had happened except he said for the hollering somewhere off there, and was peevish and unfriendly and, so he said, starving.

"Me too," Delvin said, but Morgred didn't want to share his food with him.

"I can't afford to," he said.

Delvin laughed. "You can't?"

"I'm mixed up," the boy said.

"Bout what?"

"I know this is you all's food and so I ought to give you what you want of it, but then I am starving to death and don't know where my next bit of panbread for example is coming from. So I wants to keep it. But if I do you might just take it from me and kick me out of this stable."

"I might." He laughed. "You go ahead. I'll get something inside."

"Naw. Take one of these sandwiches."

"Okay. I'll take half of one. Give me the ham."

"I want the ham."

"Okay. Give me half the roast beef."

"There it tis," the Ghost said, handing a pinched piece. His voice had a little of a cicadas' unraveling buzz in it—no bounce, no pick up, only a background of scrub fields, wet basement steps. The look in his eyes was dull as corn meal. He shied and slanted. It was as if he had spent too much time on the Blue Ridge's bare rocky tops where only stunted blueberries and coarse tufts grew. The juice and kick of the city was dried out of him. Delvin was too twitchy to ask him much. The left side of the Ghost's face was puffed out and red, and with two scuffed fingers he rocked a tooth like a tiny post set in too large a hole. He breathed shallowly, with a little hiccup like a rut at the end of each breath. He was a blinker.

Delvin turned away from the boy and looked off into the corner where hay was stacked in bales. He rubbed his hand against the un-sanded stall wood and felt a tiny sharp splinter slide into the flesh under his thumb. Barely go in. A dot of blood. He sucked the blood and tasted it in his mouth and then in his throat and thought of the boy they couldn't get the preservative to stay in, saw it running out and pooling on the table, the clear green glistening liquid that was beautiful and made you want to run your fingers through it, which he had done, sliding his hand—this hand here—discreetly along the slab until he touched the tensile edge of the juice and felt it cool on his fingers and he looked up and Mr. Oliver was looking at him with an expression on his face of such sadness as he'd not seen before.

He got up and went outside into the mid dark of night. People who at first had stayed away for fear of the police and the angry white folks had begun to collect in the alley. Small groups clustered across from the back gate and around the garage that let onto the alley and onto the curved drive at the side of the house. Men and women from the neighborhood and others he didn't know, relatives probably of the deceased. They had brought the body in the back of a box-nosed Ford truck that kept breaking down, they said. The men had worked on the motor with the body wrapped in a quilt in the back as cars passed on the unpaved road at the junction into US 83, and they had felt the weight of the curiosity, of the snoopiness and greed in people's glances, seen in their faces the hatred and disgust and fear (and seen the desire to feel something strongly enough to wrest them free of their own misery); and how hard it was *to know they*

were thieving our own hopes, someone said, from the dead body of
this son or brother or nephew, feeding like buzzards on the dear remains. And some of those white folks spit from the windows of their
automobiles, and others, *you could see,* one said, were gloating and
making ugly remarks among themselves—*sho nuff,* someone said—
and others turned away in shame, but even these looked again—
they wants to see the blood of the black man, another said and others
agreed: *yessuh, yessuh*—staring, and you could see *how hard it was
for them not to stop they cars,* one said, and *get out and beat this poor
child some more—oh, Lord*—and desecrate his body further—He's
whole before Jesus someone said—Yes, I guess he is, but *we are left
here with the mortmain and the grief,* the voice said.

All the time, so Delvin noticed, a cool breeze was softly
blowing—*Lookout breeze,* they called it in Red Row—flowing down
from the big mountain carrying with it the scent of sweet laurel and
woodbine blossoming in the cuts and protected places. Mostly these
people were silent. But then one or two asked him about the Harolds,
mother and father. He'd not seen the father, he said, but the mother
was grieving deeply.

He stepped away, walked to the end of the alley and looked out
at the big field across the road. The wisteria looped and trailing
from telephone and electric wires running along poles out on the
old circus ground had bloomed for a second time this year, but the
flowers were gone now, and the leaves were turning gold early, before
fall had near come. Each year the wisteria, that was to him like some
tropical effusion, bloomed early in May, surprising him, and each
year Mr. Oliver, laughing, asked, "Where is your head, boy?" and
he wanted to say, "Where it ought to be," but he just laughed too
because Oliver wasn't mad, it was just his way of drawing him close,
and both of them liked that.

But now, standing under the sweet gum listening to the heavy
leaves make their swishing sound like big skirts rustling, he didn't
know what to think. There didn't seem to be any happiness in any
direction. Before him, the big rusty and ragged field and the meat

packing plant and the dusty fertilizer plant, the auto shops and the
foundry and the smelting plant, and then the public road running
through the mountains and Tennessee into Kentucky and Ohio and
Indiana and Canada—all of it—was a wilderness and unsettled; it
was all a land of monsters. He shuddered. The wind was cold. It
tasted of unvisited streams and rock. He wondered again how it had
been for his mother making her way in the dark over the mountains.
Had she forgotten him? He couldn't sense her out there in the wilderness, but he believed she was there. But where was *he*? And *what*
was he, standing at the end of a leafy alley in Chattanooga, Tennessee? His hands were still attached, his face uncut, his side unburnt.
But for how long? How easy it was to step off into ruin. He wanted
to slip into the crowd and stay there in its midst, jostling and petting
and sliding body to body, smelling and tasting and touching. And he
wanted to haul off by himself, crawl up under a bush and roll into a
ball like a possum, sink down into a musty hole like a gopher, hide
deep in the rocks like a bear.

When Mr. Oliver had discovered what he'd done with the ren-
dezvous women, tricking them and him into getting together, he was
at first so mad he had ordered Delvin out of the house. Get out and
be gone, he'd said to him in as stony a voice as he'd heard coming
from him. Delvin had walked out not knowing whether he meant
just for now or for all time. The yard that night was fragrant with
mock banana flowers and peonies. The twins heaved their lanky
selves toward the west trailing Cassiopeia and Taurus. Delvin had
stood at the end of this alley feeling his life like snow falling on him
or the stars falling in cold white bits off the heavenly firmament and
the night had seemed too much for him but still great and wonderful.
As scared and hurt as he was, he had laughed outloud. Now the stars
were something else entirely. Bleak and wind-polished, half sopped
up by wads of cloud blowing from the west. There was nothing in
the stars. He stood on the shore of a dark and terrible sea.

But that wasn't true. Where he stood was not a shore.

The breeze picked fitfully at the mimosas bent over the fence
behind him, nicked the roses on the Ballard's fence, scuffed its

knuckles on the loose grass behind Capell's. Somebody in the Lewises' yard was banging on a piece of metal. Not hitting it hard, just lightly, marking time. It made a hollow sound. He turned and it was a turning back into a world corrupt and ruined, a dirty place with a stink on it. But it was still the world, white quartz pebbles mixed into the grass track down the center of the alley, the sound of Big Archie the bay horse whinnying, somebody singing *Do, Lord* in a soft way.

He walked down the alley, speaking to people as he passed, telling them he was sorry, doing what Mr. Oliver did, a facsimile of it. Folks knew him as Mr. Oliver's ward. He was a good boy they thought, but what did they know. In his heart he was an unruly force, battering mountains, a wild lover ravaging the world's naked body.

On the way back to the shed he decided he would get Morgred to join him in a flight to another place. To Texas maybe.

But when he got to the shed the Ghost was gone.

"Got hisself run off," Mortimer Fuchs, who was petting the gray's face, told him, "cause he was about to steal one of these horses."

"I needed him for something," Delvin said. Yes, he was going to leave Chattanooga.

"If I knowed you wanted him, I'd ah helt him for you," Mortimer said.

"That's okay. I'll find him." He pulled out his notebook, intending to write Oliver a message—*Headed West.* "Would you do me a favor?" As he said this he felt a pressure in him. He couldn't leave now, not with all this hanging over Mr. Oliver, over Polly and Mrs. Parker and all of them. He would have to stay. But right now he needed to be somewhere else.

He scribbled a note, folded it and handed it to Mortimer.

"Would you take this to Mr. Oliver for me?"

Mortimer, a naturally troubled-looking person, looked scared.

"If you can't find him, give it to Polly. You know who that is?"

"Sholy I do."

"She'll give it to Mr. Oliver. I'm Delvin."

"I know who you are too," Mortimer said, offended that Delvin might think he didn't.

"Thanks."

"Taint no trouble."

He walked the streets of Red Row looking for the Ghost. On the backside of the quarter the streets played out into the woods, climbing uphill into the mountains. On the opposite they funneled into Washington street, which paralleled the gully and crossed it back and forth in half a dozen places, bridged and unbridged. Other streets shanked and flopped over each other and wound like a snake. If you tended west most likely you'd eventually reach Morgan street and the block the funeral home was on. East they met the white section of town across a dusty unpaved street of mixed domesticities, white and black staring face-to-face through the red dust, and beyond this standoff the railroad tracks beyond which the real white world began.

Delvin worked his way along, asking for the Ghost. Adam street was the Row's main street. It ran perpendicular to the gully and white Chat-town and on the other end petered out like an exhausted shout in a track that ran past houses jacked on stilts and up into the leafy mountain woods. On the town side were the stores and other commercial and professional establishments. There was the Peanut Shop (also selling pecans, walnuts, hickory nuts and filberts), Bailey's Flower Shop, the newspaper office (*Mountain Star Weekly*), the office of the Ministry of Lost Souls (Protestant), barbecue, chicken and fish shacks (the fish shack attached to Dillard Fish Market), Bynum's Hardware, Arthur's Hats and Shoes, Smithwick's Clothing, the Grand and Benevolent Order of Right-Way Men's Hall, Kurrel's Insurance, Elmer's Garage, painted blue with a flat red roof with Elmer Bainbridge's name painted in white on the asphalted gravel covering it (24 HOUR WRECKING AND TOWING, a swinging metal sign out front said), and other outfits and materializations appearing from time to time in one or another frame building or in the upper floors of the only multistory structure on the Row, the Brakeman building, conjure shops and false prophets of one kind or another, too, hovering over the hearts of the community for a week, or a few, and then disappearing, whisked away in the dark of a night similar to the one in which they arrived.

But the Ghost was in none of these places. They hadn't seen him at Pell's or at the pool hall or in the Occasions Restaurant or at the Pig Grill or at Shorty's. He wasn't upstairs at Fitt's Grocery where the men played poker five nights a week. He wasn't at the regular Baptist church or the Holiness or the AME or the primitive Baptist either, and not out back of the Free Will Baptist where a few families were eating the latest mess of fresh souse meat somebody'd cornered over at the stockyards. And he wasn't at the Emporium.

He told himself the reason he was looking for the boy was because he wanted to bring him back to the house, but that wasn't it. He didn't want to go back to the house. *That* was why he was looking for him.

Everywhere he went people knew already about the killing. At Porley's, young men without attachments drank and loudly raved, but every other place was muted, abashed. Extra white police sat in cars at the bridges and rode in cars through the quarter. They hung from the sides of the cars; like monkeys, Delvin thought, or maybe the start of a police migration. Near the old Morrison livery stable and mule barn, now a garage, he picked up a rock, but even though he carried it for a dozen blocks he didn't throw it. He didn't know where he dropped it. The people weren't out on their porches mostly, but he could see them sitting by kerosene light or electric behind curtains in their front rooms; their shadows were still and waiting. The quarter seemed to swell with brooding, with a sadness that had not yet broken forth in mourning. Flaked mother-of-pearl clouds flew along under a sky sprinkled with coldly glittering stars.

In the Emporium most of the white customers had stayed away. But Frank Dumaine and his buddy were there, as were Mr. Considine and Billy Melton who was kin to the family that owned the First Pioneer Bank downtown. There were a few older white men who had come. These the woman pointed out to Delvin; they couldn't keep from it. Many of the white men arrived not knowing about the killing, but in one way or another they quickly found out. In the parlor, except for Billy Melton, nobody was dancing. In the dining room Dumaine and his friend ate chicken stew. Delvin realized he was hungry and went back in the kitchen looking for Kattie. She was upstairs, the cook told him.

"Working?" he asked.

"She's trying it out," said the cook, a large woman whose dark-complected face was deep red under the black.

Delvin felt a pain in his breast. The cook caught the look on his face.

"This not the place to be rummaging around for a sweetheart, honey. Unless you a rich man. But then you gon be rich someday, aint you?"

"How's that?"

"Aint you that old mortician's boy?"

"I work over at the funeral home."

"Yeah, that's you. You the one everybody says he's gon leave that place to."

Delvin felt a warmth in his chest. "It'll be a long time," he said, "before Mr. Oliver leave's the Constitution to anybody. By time he's ready I'll be long gone from this town."

"I hear you on that one. Lord, hit don't near stop," she said, flicking at a musing fly standing on a meringue curl atop a lemon pie. "I don't think it ever will."

"It'll wear us out eventually," Delvin said. "And we'll throw off that yoke."

"Be careful how you talk, boy."

"I'm not talking, I'm just saying."

"These white folks aint never gon take they foot off of us."

"We'll knock it off ourselves."

"I think only the Lord can do that, honey. Though I have to say he's mighty slow-minded about getting to it."

"Idn't that the truth," Delvin said and they both looked away and laughed.

He walked out in the backyard and peered up at the second-story windows. They were lit softly with red or green or blue lights, some with a rich yellow that laid dim oblongs of light on the grass. Maybe the red one was hers. He stepped into the red rectangle that was more black than red and stood in it. He tried to put aside Kattie's new business, but he couldn't help but picture it. It wasn't just the booting itself that got to him, it was the mechanics of it, the body angles and the wrenches and the wringing and the slop-overs and the beads of sweat and the stickiness in your mouth—he saw too much in his mind. Some other—some white man's greasy face—naw, it was worse for it to be a colored man's—panting his liquor breath into hers. He didn't mind the *business*, not generally; it was his mother's . . . and where was *she*?

He looked up at the sky. Clouds at night. He loved clouds at night. And electric lights in daytime; he loved those too. And him lying on his bed with the shades pulled reading a book. Mr. O had put in another butterscotch leather chair in his bedroom and at night they sat on two sides of the little marble-topped table reading their books. Shakespeare and Milton (*Paradise Lost* and *Paradise Regained*) for Mr. O, Shakespeare and Conrad for him, or the explorer books he had begun to prefer, Arctic adventures, dog teams, adventurers stranded on shelves of blue ice.

Just then a flower—a dark carnation, possibly red—sailed by his ear. He looked up to see Kattie standing in an upstairs window. She hissed at him.

"Whoo, you boy, go get me a glass of punch."

Hearing this, his body turned to stone and as quickly turned back to flesh. But a changed, suffering, jellied flesh, wobbling on jelly feet. He couldn't speak. When he could his voice squeaked in his mouth.

"Go on, boy," Kattie said.

He stumbled across the yard into the kitchen and dipped a glass from the crock sitting under a piece of cheesecloth on the counter. The punch was dark red and smelled of wine. He touched the surface in the glass with his tongue. It tasted sharp and sweet, a little of cherries. He carried the glass up the back stairs and into the hall that was lit with widely spaced electric bulbs with square red paper shades covering them. A large negro woman in a maroon silk dress so dark it was almost black snoozed in a brocade chair against the wall. Kattie didn't even tell him the room number; no, he forgot to ask; he'd just run off like a child. But he wasn't a child. He had been with a woman—Miz Pauly, a widow he visited, and Eula Banks, a girl others had too, who gave easily because she liked it. None of these pay-as-you-go gals either. But never Kattie.

He knocked on the door he thought was hers, but the laughing voice that answered was somebody else's. The next down he found her. Even the words *Come in* were spoken with an imperiousness he hadn't heard before. But he understood where it came from. The first time Mr. O had let him drive the horses—down the alley and across the road onto the circus grounds—he had felt like a king. This was the same thing. But that didn't stop it from hurting. One hurt piled on another tonight; piled on all the others, he thought, as something twisted inside him, something acidic and sour. He entered the room with a sneer on his face.

She lay alone amid the fouled bedclothes, wrapped in an old silk robe that belonged to Miss Ellereen. He recalled it from years ago. Yellow silk with pictures of seagulls and sailboats stamped on it. "My mother wore a robe like—" he started to say, but she stopped him with a finger to her lips. "Shh," she said. A yellow robe Miss Ellereen had given to Cappie and then taken back when she saw how she looked in it, back when Miss Ellereen was still one of the girls. That was the story about his mother Coolmist had told him as they lay in a foundling bed on a hot summer night that smelled of the creosote the city oiled the dirt streets with. He remembered the smell of the creosote and the story and his Coolmist crying tears of frustration. A yellow robe with sailing boats on it. No one else was in the room with her, not a man, not Miss Ellereen, not the Ghost, not his mother.

He placed the glass on the little parson's table by the bed; hesitated.

"You can go," Kattie said.

She was wearing lip rouge and her cheeks were powdered the color of cornmeal.

"No," she said, "stay."

"What you want?"

"Stay a minute."

She pulled her legs up under her robe, indicating for him to sit on the bed. He let himself gingerly down on the lumpy mattress. She canted her face and looked at him with a bovine expression that dissolved and was replaced by pique. But not before he caught in her eyes the strangling disappointment and lonesomeness. Something in him that he hadn't even paid attention to, something hard and ready to strike, whirled slowly.

"You never have anything to do, do you," she said, "but hang around doing nothing."

"I got plenty to do. You didn't hear about what happened to that boy?"

She pulled the robe tighter around her. "It's got all these women scared to death. Not just them."

"And what about you?"

"I been shivering all day."

"Me too," he said.

She looked at the punch.

"I didn't really want that. I just wanted you to come up here."

"For what?"

"You don't have cause to be angry."

"That robe you're wearing used to belong to my mother."

"I know your mama worked here."

"There's nothing wrong with it."

"What about me?"

"You working here? I'd rather you hadn't started."

"I'm middling about it. I don't like it much, but I don't mind it much either. I been doing it a while now," she said, her voice wandering off, "and I don't mind it much." She fingered her lapels. "You want me to take this robe off?"

"No. Not right now."

"Miz Ellereen give me this robe."

"She took it back from my mama."

The sense of shame he had suffered under since the boy's battered body was brought in deepened. The unruly thing in him—
hard as slate—began to slide under. He reached for it but he couldn't
pull it back up. He lay back on the bed. She raised herself and bent
over him, looking into his face.

"I don't even know you," she said.

A crease ran down the center of her bottom lip. What caused
that? he wondered. He turned on his side. Suddenly he felt like a
man waking with fever in a room where nothing matched. He scrambled off the bed and stood up.

"I got to go."

"You don't really have to."

He stared at her. "I'm glad you got that robe."

"How come?"

"So somebody—so you're walking around on the earth in it. I
like it that it's still lasting."

"I don't know how long I'm going to last."

"You seen the Ghost?"

"That boy they pulled out from under the house? He wouldn't
come around here again."

"Maybe he would."

A silence then. Somebody down the hall was laughing in a high
unhappy voice. The walls of the room were covered in flocked
pink wallpaper. Small places in the paper bulged out like there was
something behind it. Anything could be there. The hardness had
slumped, drained. Who was he? What was it he was about to do?

He said, "I'd go crazy having to be in this room all night."

"Why don't you get out of it then."

It was like a light flashed across the back of his eyes. So quick he
wasn't sure if he'd seen it or not. He got up, reached down and pulled
hard at the yellow bedspread. He pulled it off and her with it. She hit
the floor and rolled over and scrambled away from him.

"You get the hell out of here," she cried. "Lola!"

He cast a look of scorn at her. Not at her, at what was in the world behind her and all around them. If he had a match he could burn the place down—the row, the whole city. He didn't have a match. He turned and ran out and away.

On the way home a man he knew slightly from the neighborhood, a worker on road crews, called to him from the side yard of Boniface Tillman's house. Boniface was a gangster man, a runner of liquor and drugs through the mountain traces.

"Come over here, boy," the man said. He stood foursquare, half in half out of the tree shadow, waiting for him. "I want you to drop over get a jug from the chinaman's," he said when Delvin approached.

Behind the house men moved around a large fire burning in an open space among large oak trees, doing something Delvin at first couldn't make out. Then he saw they were thrashing somebody on the ground with what looked like willow switches.

"I'd be glad to do it," Delvin said, "but they're looking for me at home."

The man grabbed him by the wrist, quick as a snake, and tried to put two dollars in his hand. "You go get that jug," he said.

"I would, but I can't."

"Damn rascal, you take this case cash and go."

Behind the house the shadows flung their arms up into the heavy leaves and brought them swiftly down. Delvin broke away and ran down the street. Across the street, light from an open grocery shone on a big Bull Durham sign painted on a billboard. A boy stood in the doorway eating with a spoon something out of a tin can. Was that the Ghost down on the ground by the fire? Getting beat on? He told himself it couldn't have been and ran on, but he was afraid it was, and afraid—knowing it—for the kind of boy he was for running away.

But it wasn't the Ghost because when he returned home he found him back in the shed, stretched out in the empty stall asleep on his pile of hay. Delvin woke him up. "Where you been?" he wanted to know.

"I had to go see my auntie," the boy said.

"If you're going to see your auntie, why couldn't you stay with her?"

"She's at the jailhouse. But I knew she'd be worried about me, so I had to go ease her mind."

In those days the women prisoners were kept around back on the third floor of the old brick jail. From a grassy hill above the parking lot friends and relatives could shout to them standing in the cross-barred windows. Morgred's auntie, a crazy woman, saved peas from dinner and tossed them at folks. Morgred showed him a pea he had caught.

"Hard as a damn rock," he said. "Lord, it's a terrible thing to be locked up in that jailhouse."

Delvin went in through the big double basement doors and found Oliver finishing up. The dead boy lay peacefully under a mostly repaired face. The smashed-in parts had been picked out with an awl and the dents filled in with putty but they'd left the makeup off so you could see where the work was done. The pick holes and the brown putty. The boy now had hands, or at least he wore white cotton gloves that looked as if they were filled with palms and fingers. "Cotton ticking," Oliver said, the gloves tied with white hemp twine to the wrists hidden under the white shirt cuffs and the black broadcloth coat taken from among the pile in a big cabinet out in the corridor.

As Oliver bent over the galvanized sink washing his big soft powerful hands, he said, "I thought you'd flown the coop, boy."

"Flew but not far. Sometimes all this is a hard thing to bear up under."

The hallway was cleared of everyone except for Culver and Willie. Culver sat in one of the old wheatcloth armchairs against the wall. The big cordovan aprons, hung on hooks by the door, looked as always to Delvin like the skins of cadavers that somehow hadn't made the grade for burial. "Leftovers," Culver called them.

Now Culver looked up at him, ashen-faced, his eyes blood-veined, hopeless. But as Delvin passed, his hand shot out and with his knuckles he rapped Delvin on the thigh.

"You're a good boy," Culver said, turning his head without shifting his body, which leaned over his knees. And George, the handyman, leaned against the wall, smoking his corncob pipe. "Rumpled us down to the ground," he said in an uninflected voice.

"Come on, you men," Oliver said and shepherded them all up to the kitchen where Mrs. Parker had prepared a night breakfast of cheese eggs, ham, hominy and biscuits.

They sat at the honey-wood table eating and then at the end they cut open the white steaming cathead biscuits and poured wide rivers of cane syrup from the big round tin spilling over the plates and sopped the syrup up with the biscuit flesh and chomped it down as the sun, in yellow and peach streaks it slowly gathered into itself, came up. The new day laid its foundations on the windowsills and pushed gradually into the room, lit by the big electric bulb hanging from the ceiling under a green shade and by a coal lamp on the counter, and Delvin, his eyes so packed with sand he could hardly keep them open, was sorry to see these two lights extinguished. He wanted them to keep burning into the day in memorial to the day passed and its events.

But the sunlight that couldn't be stopped shone on the red breadbox and on the bottle-green icebox and on the blue, marble-painted crock containing cucumber pickles and on the polished black enameled woodstove and on the pale blue safe with the pink floribunda roses painted on the two doors, and he watched all these take their true colors back to themselves and the faces of the men and Mrs. Parker take on the colors and shapes that they carried through daytime that were different from their faces at night under even the brightest light, somehow more supple and creased and softer really than at night, even if they looked more battered and old. He could smell the scents of mock banana flowers and gardenia and pine rosin from the yard, and smell the grass and the dew itself, and it was as if the sun brought these in too. And all of them, including Oliver leaning against the counter sipping a cup of black coffee, felt something hidden inside themselves brought back out into the open, something made up of sorrow and vigor and reverence all bound together. They felt restored, resolved. And this feeling, too, like the tide of light, passing even as they felt it.

5

The funeral was held a day and a half later at the tall narrow Jericho
Holiness church fourteen miles outside the city near the old negro
community of Middle Horse among the remnants of a neglected
pecan orchard surrounded by mixed cotton fields and woods. But
before this, lines of silent mourners trudged through the funeral
home to pause before the white-painted pinewood box plumped with
quilted blue satin complete with a blue satin pillow for the boy's head.
They'd been coming through since first light. CASEY DAVID HAROLD
was etched into a round brass plate on the coffin lid. His mother sat
in one of the plush red quilted armchairs in the little family room
off to the side of the viewing room, moaning and gripping herself
in her arms. Her husband, a heavyset, feckless man taken by drink,
skittered around the room laughing in a strenuous false manner and
shaking hands with everyone who came in. Behind his gay mask his
eyes burned with a fever of grievous perplexity. An air of mortifica-
tion and sorrow filled the room. A compressed vulcanizing barely
contained energy swelled. And in some spots hope guttering.

"We'd have held the viewing out at our home in the country," Mr.
Harold told folks, "but it was just too small."

The funeral expenses were being paid by Mr. W. B. Bickens, who
had also offered his house for the viewing, but he was relieved when
Mrs. Harold said no, she wanted the people of Chattanooga to get a
look at what those white men had done to her child. (No white folks
showed up at the funeral home.) Oliver had worked hard to bring the
boy back to the look of health. Mrs. Harold had broken into the room
a second time and ordered him to stop fixing her son's face. At first
Oliver had thought he misunderstood her, or he told himself he did.
She said, "I don't want you making a fool of my son."

"I wouldn't," he said, "I won't . . . I couldn't," and let his hands drop to his sides.

"I don't want you fancin' him up."

A sadness had filled Oliver's body. The tips of his fingers were shriveled from the ingestants. He wiped his hands on a clean towel he took from a pile on the counter. The towels were usually kept in one of the cabinets, but this case was such a mess he had Culver bring them out. "I will—"

"Stop!" she cried. "Don't say what you will or you won't. Just quit trying to replace my boy with somebody else. Put him back like them white mens left him."

In the end it was a mix. Oliver could not bring himself to wound the boy's half-restored face again. But he didn't go further. The cuts were still apparent, the lip with its vertical gash like a field-dressed wound. He had wept in frustration and despair as he worked. In the end he was left with a weariness he hadn't known he could experience and still walk around in. His legs hurt, and a hard pain had worked its way into his shoulders and roosted there.

The boy looked the victim of ugly drubbing and of haste and unrectified fear and sorriness. There were stitches in his forehead, and one eye was sunk into his head. Wads of putty like the clay we are made of. Everywhere in his face was the strange seriousness of underbone. His artificial hands of cotton in their white gloves looked like doll hands. Shame tinged Oliver, but he wanted to give the family what they wanted. He knew it would all work out in the ground.

In the parlor viewers recoiled trembling. Some fainted, others stared, many wept seamless tears and clutched their hands to their hearts, held each other, others passed by mutely, some stared avidly, feeding, some wanted to touch the body, even caress it, others squeezed their eyes shut. A photographer, a small broad-shouldered man smelling of ferrous sulphate, had come in and taken pictures. He had fumbled with his equipment. He dropped two plates, ruining them. A tiny ball of sweat collected by his ear and trailed slowly

down his jaw. His eyes rapidly blinked. He sighed. His hands shook
and then they steadied and he was able to take the pictures that ran
two days later in the africano *Mountain Star Weekly* and appeared
later in papers up north. Spikes, cascades, flushes of anger and sadness. Many felt new weights added to an old heaviness and it was part
of life for them, understay and manacle, what you grew up with as a
counterpoint to tenderness, murder on the other side of the door. *My
soul has been tipped into a deep well,* somebody said.

Solomon Baker took off his glasses and rubbed them with a blue
silk handkerchief.

"How much, Lord?" somebody said.

"How much longer, Lord?" somebody else said.

The people trooped by through the day, through the evening and
deep into the petty hours of night. Into the buckled and slumped
hours of false dawn. The yeasty realness of life was in their breasts,
and even as they grieved many experienced themselves as held
deeply in the weave of being and even smacked hard by grief were
grateful. Others were simply glad it was not them. Oliver lay on the
hardest of the two couches in his office, trying to rest. Delvin came
in and without turning on the light lay down on the floor beside him.
A night bird asked a question, waited, and asked the same question
again, a question never answered on this earth, unless the earth
itself was the answer. Oliver let his hand fall from the couch and
seek the boy's face that he touched so gently Delvin could barely feel
it and then he groped for his hand. Delvin caught the older man's
fingers and he felt as if he was catching him as he sank into the sea;
he gripped down hard and the older man spoke out and Delvin said
he was sorry and then in a soft seep he was crying.

After a while Oliver said, "This is only the second time I have
had to do this. Usually they take the poor fellow out to some hollow
or country pasture and bury him without calling on my ministrations." He blew his breath out and breathed it back deeply in. Delvin
could smell the cigar on his breath. Oliver said, "When she came in
the laboratory the last time—to tell me not to fix her boy—I thought

I would explode. With frustration and regret. I was afraid I might strike that woman. Oh, I knew I wouldn't, wouldn't ever, but I felt so consternated." He turned heavily—Delvin could smell his musky cologne, and the horsehair in the couch—and his wide face seemed to rest disembodied on the edge of the couch, like a face in one of the books he had read as a child, disembodied and filled with curiosity. He said, "For a second I thought I would strike that woman and walk out of the room and keep walking until I came to some other world to live in." He looked in the dimness at Delvin with eyes that contained a shadowed mournfulness. "But there is no other world." A crinkling, whispering sound then where Oliver's silk robe rubbed against the couch. "I could walk for a thousand thousand years," he said, "and not find any world but this one. Lord." He patted the edge of the couch. "A mortician's not supposed to feel like that."

"What about Africa?" Delvin said.

"What's that?"

"When you're walking."

"Walking—hunh." He was quiet a moment. Then: "Africa. That old bushy place? Those folks over there have forgot all about us. We wouldn't fit in. Despite what old Marcus Garvey in his big hat and with the whole UNIM behind him says."

"What about some empty place? Some place nobody stays in and nobody wants?"

"Only place like that is a place nobody can live in. Shoot, I'd go live on an iceberg in the Arctic ocean if I thought it could be done. But even there the white man would come and run us off. Wouldn't want us mixing with the polar bears."

"I don't want to mix with them anyway," Delvin said for the laugh in it, but he was thinking, *Always the hard way's the only way.*

Oliver let loose a long rattling sigh and then silence fell again. The night bird inserted its ascending cry, only the final note a true question.

"I've known rivers," Delvin said.

"What's that?"

"I've known rivers as ancient as the world and older
than the flow of human blood in human veins.
My soul has grown deep like the rivers."
"That's beautiful, boy. Did you make that up?"
Delvin didn't say anything.
"It doesn't matter. It's strong and faithful, faithful to the truth."
Oliver raised himself. "You ought to say that at the funeral tomorrow. Or I mean today. This afternoon."
"Oh, no," Delvin said.
"I wish you would. I know it would be a piece that would be a great help to everybody."

Though he wanted to claim the words as his own, and might have if he wasn't spooked by Oliver's proposal that he say the lines of Langston Hughes's poem at the funeral, he admitted they were the great Harlem poet's and not his. Oliver looked him in the eyes and smiled, knowing what the boy had almost done and not offended at all by that sort of humanness.

"You're an uncommon young man," he said, words that Delvin would recall often—sometimes derisively—in years to come.

"I might be," he said, "but I don't want to get up before those people and say anything at all."

"I can't make you, boy, but I would be happy to support you in saying them."

They were both exhausted, and shortly after that, after the whippoorwill's duty was passed on to a widow bird offering its own cranky cry, they fell asleep and would have slept right through the funeral if Polly, who had cried half the night, hadn't kept calling from the door until they waked. Delvin, despite the occasion, experienced a jolt of happiness when he saw her standing in her fresh navy-blue dress in the doorway. He spoke to Mr. Oliver, who lay on his back on the long couch, thinking—so he said in a moment—about the net sack of oranges a white woman had given him one Christmas when her driver stopped her carriage in the middle of Valhalla street in Montgomery and called him to the door. Later three africano boys had taken the oranges from him.

They got up and moved quietly in the faint clattery silence of early morning.

The leaves of sweet gum trees made moving shadows on the walls of the church. Across the yard was the old church, a tiny square wooden building, hardly bigger than a cotton house, with a cocked steeple the size of an apple crate riding the roof. The old structure had become so infirm that it had been locked for years and would have been torn down except for the sentimental and historic value it had for the community. It had been recently whitewashed, thanks to Cordell Meeks, a parishioner whose cotton fields bordered the property, and this had made the congregation proud. The new church was an elaborated version of the old one, planed boards, a shingle roof and a tin steeple perched on the roof line like a squared and pointed hat. There were hitching posts for the mules and horses in front of the old church. A cleared space for cars in front of the new. Mostly folks came in wagons. Many sat now in their wagons, two hours before the service, patiently waiting. On the other side of the red dirt road sheriff's deputies sat in two big black cars.

They pulled up and backed around to the door of the new church and several men stepped down from the wagons, blistered men, men of sorrows and men held in contempt, men in washed overalls and starched white shirts, men who didn't know how to read or had never held in their hands any other book but the Bible, if that, men who took the long view that the Lord was waiting for them in heaven, these men, who Delvin was thinking of and had been thinking of now since last night when he watched the last of them come through the parlor of the Home and stop and stare down at the unrefabricated dead boy, the illuminated and beaten but not destroyed boy, standing in a moment of capacious silence that in itself stood for four hundred years of isolation among men—he had thought of these men who had hardly ever known an unbullied moment in their lives but who went on anyway, wondering what they believed in those nights in the country when the last lamp had been put out and they lay beside their narrow wives in the dark that was of a blackness impenetrable by human eyes as skeeters and fleas and flatbugs went about their cunning business, wondered if they thought of anything at all—these men helped unload the burden and carry it into the church.

Those who hadn't gotten a chance to view the body in town got one now. There was rustling and whispering and fresh bursts of tears, and voices cried out, making hollow despairing sounds against rafters and roof. After a while an old man in shirtsleeves held off his wrists with black silk garters began to play a large nickel-plated accordion. "There Is a Balm in Gilead" was the first selection, and then Delvin didn't pay attention because he was harried by nervousness concerning the poem he was supposed to recite. Mr. Oliver was busy with the family. Many cousins and uncles and aunties and brothers and sisters in the Sunday clothes they had worn just three days before at services in this building. A small black stove in the center of the floor was draped in blue cloth and a basket filled with daisies and meadow rue and daylilies set on top. The windows along the sides had been raised and Delvin could smell the dry, rusty scent of new cotton in the fields. A pale green damselfly, elegant and hesitating as it came, drifted in and floated over the assembling congregation. With the paddle fans taken from a box by the door, women fanned themselves vigorously. The fans had advertisements for the Constitution Funeral Home on one side and a color picture of a beautiful sloping tree-shaded field bordering a quiet river on the other.

The place grew warm, and the people, already exhausted, coming off little sleep and the work of their home lives, leaned back on the music for support of a weariness that never really left them.

Delvin, standing next to the open window through which a lazy green fly buzzed slowly back and forth, looked out. Beyond the little ragged graveyard, now rife with fresh flowers amid the undersized gravestones and ceramic urns and worked wire markers, was a big hickory-handled plow with ponderous coulter leaned against a pine tree. He wondered why it was there and wondered what it would be like to plow a field. Beyond the plow the great expanse of cotton hung heavy with hard green bolls.

Now the minister, a deeply black portly man in a black suit with vest and a soft gray tie, ascended the three plank steps to the altar and took a seat in one of the big cypresswood chairs behind and to the side of the pulpit. He was followed by a thin young man in a brown suit who sat down in a similar chair on the other side. The choir had come quietly as ghosts through a door at the side of the church and was now sitting in two short rows farther back on a low platform behind the ministers. They began softly to sing. The accordion that had been playing steadily, the rangy musician pumping, never stopping once to wipe the sweat running down both sides of his face, stopped. The choir sang about how it was going to cross over into campground. Out the big open windows the leaves of the sweet gum soughed and sighed and squared themselves and shook in the breeze that barely reached the floor of the church. Crickets sawed their legs. The bob-white cry of quail. Without Delvin realizing it the service had begun.

The minister gripped the pulpit, thanking everybody for coming and giving the title of a hymn, "Uncumbered Grace." In a light sweet voice he began himself to sing a line that was picked up by the choir. The congregation sang the line back to them and so the hymn followed: a line sung by the minister and choir and repeated by the congregation. Then another hymn, this time "The Ship of Zion," sung by everybody together.

As the last phrase died out the minister stepped to the side of the pulpit and kneeled. In his hands was a large white handkerchief stained rusty brown in places. The preacher raised the handkerchief in both hands and began to pray.

"This bit of cloth, Lord, was found in the pocket of the young man before us today. It is a handkerchief given to him by his auntie for his birthday this last May. Casey carried it with him everywhere and used it to wipe the sweat of life from his face. But night before last he didn't get the chance to use it. Life had already been stolen from him before he could."

The preacher, who had been twisting the handkerchief in his two hands, raised it again. Many in the crowd had lifted their eyes and were looking at the handkerchief. A rusty tail fluttering in the warm breeze. A woman gasped. Another groaned.

"Blood from this boy's body stains this hankie, Lord. Casey didn't have time and the occasion was not propitious for him to draw this square of cloth. Those who kindly cut him down found it in his one unburned pocket. Now this memento belongs to his mother. She will not wash the blood from it."

He held the handkerchief in front of his face, and Delvin thought for a second that he was going to wash his own face in it. But he didn't.

"Heavenly Father," he said, his hands trembling slightly, making the handkerchief flutter, "you have sanctified this blood by your own sacrifice. You too lost a son. A son who washes us all in his own blood. You too grieved. As we here are grieving. This blood, as the blood of any child does, mingles with the blood of the Savior. We here are all sinners, Lord. Fools and strayers, wayward, bumbling folk. This young man whose body lies here before us is cleansed now of all that. He lives with you in heaven. Have mercy on us here, us strugglers and sinners, those left behind in this cold world. Forgive us our sins that we can't keep from committing. Wash us, Lord, in the blood. Wash us in the blood of the lamb. Heal us, Lord. Hear us. We cry out to you in our grief."

He lifted his head as cries of *Amen* and cries of *Thank you*, cries of *Jesus is Lord* filled the sanctuary. The minister got to his feet with the ponderousness of a large man and staggering slightly took his stand, entered the pilothouse of his pulpit. He grasped the front rail as a captain would grasp the wheel of his gale-tossed ship. His raised face seemed lashed by a windy force. He looked out over the congregation, in his deepset eyes a sad fondness.

"There is much I could say about this Casey today. When he was a boy of twelve I baptized him in the tank out behind the church. I

watched him play at the edge of the fields and I watched that play
turn gradually into the work of a man. He used to have a little one-
shot rifle that he carried with him into the woods and he was a
mighty hunter with it. I could tell you stories all day long, as many of
you could tell stories to me." He turned slightly so that he was half
facing the young man sitting in the other cypresswood chair. "But I
want to let this young gentleman up here beside me get up now and
talk to you. He is the uncle of this boy, arrived last night from Nash-
ville. Reverend Arthur Wayne is his name. He is a preacher himself
and has asked to speak to you this afternoon."

He turned fully, offering his hand to the slender man, who rose
and took it. The minister pulled him fluidly and gently to him.
Grasping the man's elbow with one hand, his other behind the man's
back, he guided him to the pulpit and shuffled backwards to his seat.
Delvin at first thought the man was blind. The way he sniffed the air
and raised his eyes to the place where the wall joined the ceiling. But
then he looked straight out into the congregation, and Delvin could
tell he saw just fine. He had a large, hawkish face. He stared into the
crowd, letting his eyes rest on this one or that. A silence grew heavier
as it lasted and filled the sanctuary. People began to grow restless,
and Delvin could sense the nervousness rising.

Reverend Arthur Wayne smacked his lips once, loudly. He threw
back his head and laughed. The laugh made a high keening sound,
the laugh of a madman. Many found the laugh painful to hear, many
were disturbed by a mad-sounding laugh coming from a preacher
and told themselves what they heard wasn't so. Some experienced a
stab of anger. Others were openly frightened. The man smacked his
lips and laughed again, Rev Wayne. He swayed in the pulpit, rocking
from one arm to the other and back. The older minister—his name
was Oriel Munch—made a half move toward him but thought better
and sank back into his chair. The young man caught the sides of the
heavy rostrum. His dark-complected face shone with sweat. Some of
the women wanted to go to him. He stared again into the depths of
the congregation, and now many shrank from his eyes. They were
afraid he would pick them out. Rev Wayne opened his mouth, show-

ing a fine row of upper teeth missing the dog tooth on the right side.

He bowed his head, perhaps in brief silent prayer, raised his face, and in a gentle, even voice said, "Devilment." He smiled again, this time without opening his mouth. "Yeah," he said, "devilment. That's what brought you here."

Beyond the open window, beyond the graveyard, a breeze tugged at the tops of the cotton. Delvin felt a prickliness, as if the breeze carried with it a tiny sting like nettles or a sticker bush. Something out there seemed to touch something inside him. A precision, unlifelike and false, that carried harm. A glint of sunlight on metal. He stepped carefully back—into safety, into the other world beside what was in fields and roads and common rivers.

"Devilment," the preacher was saying. His voice was soothing and even this word, a shocker, soothed. "We can't help but stare at it," he said. "We are drawn to it. I want each of you to make sure you take a good look at the devilment lying here before you today. Not the devilment in this boy. There was never any devilment in *him*. Not any more than you could find in any prancy young fellow. No more than any of us had when we were his age. The devilment is the devilment that was worked upon his helpless body. His mama didn't want the good Mr. Cornelius Oliver here to fix him up. Mr. Oliver is a magician with his chemicals and his cosmetics. He could clean up the devil himself, I guess." (Oliver looked blandly back at him.) "But this boy's mama didn't want Mr. Oliver to fix this boy so he looked like a fresh youth resting after his happy run through the world." He drummed his fingers on the edge of the rostrum. "Why you think she didn't want him to rectify and embellish this boy? I'll tell you. Because she wanted you to see what the devil had wrought. Here before you, in this holy place, before God and his mighty works, the mightiest work of His Holy Hand lies before you torn to pieces. Men did this to a boy."

He shook his head. His long stiff dry crozzled hair swayed slightly. He raised his left hand and with drawn-together fingers wiped his face. The back of his hand was lacerated with white scars. Someone gasped. A moan went through the congregation. He again looked out. He looked straight out. "Are we children of God?" he asked.

Somebody answered yes, an old man with close-cropped gray hair, Hardy Purcell.

"Yes," the young preacher said, "yes we are. We *are all* children of God. And it was children of God who did this in the dark of night to another child of God. They performed an act of devilment on their brother." He pressed his forehead with the heel of his left hand, pressed hard as if pushing back against a pain there. "Now what would make a man—make men—do this?"

"The devil!" somebody cried, a large woman, Maggie Cagel, fanning herself rapidly with her paddle fan. The swish of fans could be heard throughout the room, like the sound of bee wings.

"Yes," the young preacher said. "The devil. But what is the devil?"

"Tell us," another said.

"The devil . . . and all of you know him . . . he's inside each of you . . . is . . . *trepidation*. It's dread, it's consternation, it's fright. Trepidation. That's right. Misdoubts . . . and dismay . . . and recreancy. The bugaboo, the bogie, the hobgoblin. You all know that fellow, don't you?"

"Oh, yes."

"You all been scared. Some of you—with good reason—maybe *most* of you, are scared all the time, scared out of your wits."

"O Lord."

"But those men the other night. Those men carrying torches and kerosene and guns and knives and axes and a rope. *Those* men were afraid. They were scared to death. The devil had entered them and scoured out all the holiness. Or most all of it. He had scoured it out and refilled the hole with trepidation. What was it they were scared of? Were they scared of governments . . . or guns . . . or God?"

"No sir."

"They weren't scared of *them*, you are exactly right. They were scared of this child . . . whose broken body lies before us now. This boy who just a few days ago was walking along the road out here picking blue-eyed grass and singing a song to himself. They were scared that this little boy was going to take something from them that they couldn't do without. What was that something?"

He leaned forward, a look of pain in his face. Nobody had answered.

"I'll tell you. There're many names for it. One of them . . . is strength. Another . . . is honor. Another is courage. Another's goodness. Kindness. Mercy. Steadfastness."

The room was quiet but for the faint buzzing and shuffling and clicking sounds of the living world. Rev Wayne looked around, fixed on this or another one. Then his eyes seemed to fix on them all.

"Those men were afraid that this boy, this sweet and generous child, was going to steal these properties from them. But these men were misinformed. This child wasn't going to steal anything. They had it backwards. This child could only add to them. The good of one adds to the good of the many. But these men could not see this. Their scarediness had taken them over. They had become for this time . . . maybe for all time . . . the captives of this trepidation. Guarantors of the devil."

He cupped his forehead briefly in the palm of his right hand, then held the hand before him and looked into the palm and let the hand drift to the pulpit.

"We have come here to pray for and bless and bury this child. And that we will do. We do it prayerfully with hearts weighed down by grief. But this child does not need our prayers. This child shares none of our grief. He is in heaven right now. He has been in heaven since the moment the blow that separated him from this world was struck. He is snug in the arms of the Lord. A blameless, emancipated child. It is these others who need our prayers. Those so consumed by their trepidations and frets that they were led to do evil deeds. Some of you want to flee this horror—hide yourselves. Others want to turn and seek vengeance against those who committed it. Others want *justice.* Others want simply to forget. But there is no hiding, there is no vengeance, there is no justice, there is no forgetting. There is only the Lord. That hatred we feel rising up like a streaming flame. That trepidity that makes us want to run into the woods and hide under the bushes. That misery. That grief like a block of stone laid upon our hearts. The sweat on our bodies, the aches, the faltering, the falling. There is only the Lord for that."

He looked around. In his eyes a look of despair.

"So fall," he said. "Fall to your knees."

As he said this he fell, like a man shot. His knees hit the planed boards with a cracking sound. He winced and almost keeled over but was able to right himself. His face was drawn, famished, gaunt even. Others had followed him to their knees in a symphony of groans and creaks. The preacher raised his scarred hands and held them before his face as if he was holding in a blessing or curse or the split words of a raveling faith. Slowly he lowered his hands until he could look out over the closed fingers. Then his eyes closed.

In a choking voice he said, "Fall on your knees, yes. Offer what you have to the Lord, yes. Offer the misery and the scarediness and the hate and the rage, yes. Lord!" he cried, his voice reedy and broken. "We here are scared to death. We are miserable. We are filled with hatred. Take these putrid products and like the water you changed into wine, like the loaves and the fishes you enhanced to feed a multitude, change, enhance them, until they are transfigured in the fire and love of your being into a faith that will sustain us. Help us, Lord! We cannot help ourselves." He leaned so far forward it seemed he might pitch off the platform onto the ground.

With a struggle he righted himself. His body slumped. He forced air through nearly closed lips. Drew a rattling breath.

"Ay, Jesus," he whispered. Silence. People looked from under lowered brows. The silence extended like a dark and steady wing over the congregation. Delvin could hear the wind rustling in the trees. At last the young preacher spoke. *"Be kind,"* he croaked, *"Be kind."*

He staggered to his feet. He slumped before them, held up by what they could not tell. His exhausted face looked as if he was no longer behind it, as if he had been taken by an imbecility, a loose dumbness.

Cries began to pass through the assembled.

The minister Rev Munch rose and grasped the younger man's arms from behind. He drew Rev Wayne to him and slid his arm around him and they stood together, eyes closed. Both prayed out-loud and no one in the congregation was sure of what either said. Their prayers mingled and coiled about each other in the sun-filled air aswim with motes and drifting bugs. As the prayers ended the choir started in on another song. *Good news,* they sang, *chariot comin—good news.*

Soon they were all out in the cemetery grouped around the big green canvas awning above the yellow hole in the ground. The air smelled of the dusty cotton plants. A warm breeze as if idly looking for some-thing lifted the leaves of the gum trees and set them back. All around them at other graves bouquets of phlox and jacob's ladder and yarrow and wild carrot and even the yellow blossoms of the humble dusty miller plant gave the scumbly ground a festive and mournful air.

A tall gaunt man stepped forward and began to sing the jubilee song "Before I'd Be A Slave." "O freedom . . . ," he began.

From the corner of his eye Delvin saw a bright shawl of fire shoot incredibly high over the roof from in back of the church. Before the fire became a thought, he heard the thunderous explosion and was pushed against Mr. Oliver's broad belly.

People screamed.

A siren somewhere off in the woods behind the church began to wail.

Another explosion, black and lithely red, hit the retired church across the yard, seeming to lift and set it momentarily back on the ground before it split apart and collapsed into burning boards and shingles.

The people, until this moment weighed down and nearly immo-bile, were suddenly roused. They cried out. Many ran crying and screaming into the fields and toward the road that was empty now of the police cars that had trailed them to this site.

A green glass bottle flew through the air, landed beside the side wall of the main church and exploded in fire.

Delvin, shaky but still upright, crouched under the open awning. The coffin perched on narrow boards above the grave. The older preacher, Rev Munch, lay in collapse across a couple of wooden folding chairs. Some people back in the crowd thought he'd been shot and this was how that story started. The younger preacher, partially recovered from his struggle, knelt beside the coffin. At the explosions he had winced and leaned away as if blown by their wind and looked up with an anguishing face and gone back to his praying. The singer held tightly to one of the brass tent poles.

The siren that had provided a back noise to the occurrence keened higher and faster, rushing until its noise became a wheezing sound like a giant trying to scream through a madness.

More fireballs, sputtering like sparklers, rained down.

Delvin and Oliver and Willie Burt helped the clerics and the singer and those knocked to the ground by the suddenness and noise to get up and get away from the grave.

Some people were crawling on their hands and knees. Others ran full out. Others, dazed or in shock, stood doing nothing.

A man with a smoking back ran by. A woman stumbled along fanning herself with a punctured derby. Little girls screamed.

There was nothing to do but leave the coffin where it was.

Fire caught in both church buildings, rose thickly from the remains of the old church and licked around the corners of the new structure

Delvin's group joined the crowd fleeing. The dozen automobiles and trucks had created a traffic jam. Those in wagons attempted to get their mules and horses into action, but these animals were generally so frightened they couldn't be controlled. Several broke loose and at least three rigs were hauled off across the cotton field bouncing and knocking through the thick knee-high bushes. Others rigs were trapped, tangled, forced back on themselves, animals driven to their knees under whipped reins, shying, kicking, knocking people to the ground, dragging them. Two horses, riderless, made it to the road and were pulled up by quick-acting mourners who grabbed their flaring reins. A little boy was grazed in the forehead by a mule kick and knocked out, but was otherwise unhurt. Many were thrown off their feet and Sunday clothes were ruined and bruises and scrapes were applied everywhere. Some lost their shoes. The hearse was deeply dented on the passenger side by the kick of a mule.

Many people ran away down the eastward slanting road. Others headed through the fields back toward the settlement.

Oliver had gotten in the hearse and had been trying to start it when the mule kicked the door. "Get in," he cried, not realizing what it was.

Just then Delvin tried the passenger door, but he couldn't open it. Oliver turned his head and looked at him. The boy was far away, speaking without sound. Then he was close and Oliver could hear him shouting. *Reach this way!* The boy grinned crazily at him. Oliver grinned back.

Delvin tried the back door and this one worked. He climbed in and then crawled through the interior window space into the front seat. He hugged Oliver and in the hug Oliver could feel his life—that had been leaving him, leaving without his even knowing it—reviving in his body; it was as if the boy's life poured into him. They grasped each other and held on for dear life and then as if a cue was taken by both they let go and looked each other in the eye. Both knew inexpressibly a great thing.

Oliver began to feel his life moving again at its natural speed. He started to cry—small, singular tears, each carrying a little bouquet of humility and gratitude. Delvin kept patting him as, mouth open, he stared out the window.

They sat side by side watching the clash and bang in the world around them. A young man trailing a long blue scarf ran by. A hugely fat woman in a large funnel hat stumped past waving one white glove. A man swung a wooden crutch at a woman who was shouting at him. A small boy climbed onto the hood of the hearse and stood waving a checkerboard bandana as if signaling and then jumped off and disappeared into the crowd, no one, as far as Delvin could tell, having responded to the signal. A skinny man clapped his hands, threw back his head and hollered. Everybody hollered. Curls of smoke licked at the web-footed sweet gum leaves. Somebody was singing, some woman, at the top of her lungs. What firepower, Delvin thought, and it was about the woman not the fire he thought this. But the fire—able to take care of itself—was a circus of color all around. It raged and kicked with great blossoming fusillades like a flotilla of gunships firing cannons. Splashes and rents and gouts of flame. All handy combustibles in terrible trouble. A singing, whizzing noise. Up above everything, Delvin could see patches of blue sky, un-shakeable, mute. Something in him pulsed and seemed to surge toward the sky. He felt a hugeness inside him as if he had broken open. An agitation came with this, a sense of things lopped off and falling, the old fearfulness careening through. He shuddered and drew his chest in. Then, as if a wave had passed through and gone on, a quiet filled him. He felt a rocking motion, a calm and a rec-titude in himself, a shyness. Sunshine picked among the flames, distilling light. A sense of ease came on him, and it seemed natural and right that this was so. He would recall this feeling later in his life, but not for a while. He leaned back, or seemed to, as a swirl of smoke, black and tinged green, rolled past the grit-speckled wind-shield. He was back suddenly in the car.

The rear door opened and Willie Burt pushed the two preachers inside. They brought with them a powerful mingled smell of cologne and gasoline smoke. Rev Munch, sweat-soaked in his clothes, a spray of grit like tiny black stars across his forehead, had his arm around Rev Wayne. The skinny young reverend wrenched himself loose, scrambled to the far side and pressed against the door with his eyes closed. His clothes twisted around his thin body, he seemed to be talking to himself. "Lord," Rev Munch said, "what a struggle."

Willie had run around the hearse, shoved Mr. O aside, gotten in under the wheel, and started the motor. Oliver told him to wait. They had to anyway because they were still blocked in.

Delvin got out of the car. Both churches burned elaborately.

There was a well but no bucket, no stream, and no barrel of water standing by. Men ran to look at the blaze. No one seemed badly hurt. Several knelt praying before the fire. Lobbing prayers up into it, bombing away. The siren had ceased. Somebody, a short man in bright yellow suspenders, said shots had been fired back in the piney woods, but Delvin hadn't heard them. He began to help move the stalled and tangled vehicles.

It took nearly an hour for everyone to be moved. The churches, large and small, had burned avidly, the big church burning more wildly than the little one, but gradually the fires subsided. A group of boys in sooty white shirts picked a broken-down Model T truck up and moved it out of the way of a farm wagon. They waved at Delvin to come help but he didn't.

Oliver had gotten out and stood with both hands pressing his sides as if he was pumping himself up. A flight of distant birds, maybe a hundred out over the cotton field, veered suddenly as if they had just noticed the trouble and headed off north. Dust clouds hung over the road in both directions.

"We have unfinished business," Mr. Oliver said to Delvin when he came around to him.

They all got out, moving in a new, weightier gravity. They helped the younger preacher out. He seemed overridden by his own deepset ailment. By now most people were gone. But a few remained. Among these was the family of the dead boy. They stood off to the side under some old, shaggy cedars near the cotton fields. The mother sat on a canvas camp chair somebody had provided. One of her living sons fanned her. They had carried the coffin with them under the trees. A few relatives stood around it, protecting it.

Before long the worst of the burning was over. The roof of the big church had swayed and collapsed with a huge growling noise, smothering much of the fire, and the fire in the other, the small one, seemed about to extinguish on its own. It smoldered and smoked and burned in patches. Now and then something popped in the fire, sending up a screen of sparks that quickly subsided. They could hear a baby crying.

The police cars had vanished. There were no signs of siren-turning or bomb-throwing white men anywhere.

Oliver directed Delvin and George to re-erect the collapsed funeral tent. The graveyard looked like the disestablished drift scene of a great passing wave. Flowers scattered everywhere. Chairs knocked over. A silver mouth harp lying by itself on the lip of the grave. Pages from some book or songsheet lay like leavings of another occasion entirely. The big green funeral tent was unburned but they had to skeet the red soil off it with a broom somebody produced. Several of the few people left were crying or wiping away tears that had mingled with smoke and dust; their hands were dirty. No one had come out of the woods to kill them. That was where the siren noise and the firebombs had come from. Those left stood by the coffin and among the cedars waiting while the church finished burning.

After a while the people felt safe enough to continue. Black broken beams fire-whittled to sticks poked out of the wreckage. The front of the church was streaked with soot but intact, as if the fire itself was prepared to leave it as a warning or memorial. The side walls had collapsed and burned in a series of combustions, some as small as campfires. A few sooty boards had fallen into the scorched grass, burning separately, like dropped torches. The sun off beyond the rise past the cotton fields was taking on the heft and fullness of day's end, lolling in a vast orange net. To the southwest sundogs ran along through silky clots of cloud. The tops of some of the cotton plants were dusted with soot.

The bereaved family had brought a hamper of food and they passed items around from it. Nearly everyone got a piece—partial piece—of fried chicken and a wedge of cornbread.

When the people were finished eating, Rev Wayne gathered them at the gravesite and they completed the service. The only sound from the woods was the soft sough of breeze in the pines. The older preacher spoke as funeral ministers do of the misery on the earth, of the inevitability of grief. And of joy that comes just the same. Delvin wanted him to stop this time at the grief part. At funerals he often thought of his mother. He experienced a strange, exfoliating, shuddery feeling at the thought that she was still alive somewhere.

The singer—the skinny tall man (Delvin had seen him hoist himself into a moving wagon)—had fled, but at the end of the service those left behind sang his jubilee for him. In smoke-cracked, mournful, wheezy voices they sang, quietly, softly, as if in a secret language they wanted not only strangers but the trees and the air itself not to overhear. Delvin was not asked to recite the Hughes poem he had memorized, and this disappointed and relieved him.

The dead boy's brothers pulled the planks from under the coffin and Elmer and several others lowered the box on ropes into the dry yellow earth.

"Let this soul cross over into campground," the old preacher said.

Sometimes at funerals in these carefully discharged final moments there seemed to be a promised land after all. But for most of those standing on the sun-warmed, fire-heated pebbly ground, Delvin among them, not today. A sudden swell of grief overtook Delvin and he burst into tears. Tears like a sudden wind that shakes and releases a tree.

Before the first water was hardly out of him the wind had passed. Oliver pressed his hand. Delvin pressed back, glad to have somebody close who knew who he was, knew his name. He thought of the Ghost and wondered where he might be. A flock of crows raced westward as if they were trying to catch the dying sun. Close up he could smell the rich scent of the cedar trees. And he could smell the turned earth of the grave, a scent that always made him think of farming, of himself as part of a life of sowing seeds in a field, a promise or memory that was not even his, come back to him.

Those nearby, the poorly outfitted mournful members of the killed boy's family, to speak of them, were crammed up with grief. It was nearly impossible to move in any part of their bodies. As if the organs themselves had solidified and the muscles and streaks of ligament and tissue hardened and, too, even the heretofore streaming blood congealed. They felt leathery and stiff and mired. When they did move, and they did, under the peeling sky with its bulging veils of smoke, it was as if a peculiar narcotized influence had taken them over, as if the hand raised to push back the air, the shoulder lifted in shuddering refusal, the lips licked to soothe the dry cracked skin, the twitch, the wave, the brush, were kineticized by some airy unregulated pointless dissipate energy. The world was a mist of shadows and smothering floods. They were drowning without dying. The mother was an empty corn shuck tossed into the corner of a rained-in house. No one would ever come back to look for such as her. She wanted to cry out, to scream, to yell for help—for anyone, anyone who might remember her, to find her—she had to go get her child— but her voice was too weak to carry. She was stricken with remorse. The father, for the only time in his life as a man, in a flicked on and off vision, saw himself as a small boy, a boy dumbly chasing a rusty windblown handkerchief into the dark under some trees. His face looked as if it had been bitten mercilessly by insects.

After a while the Rev Munch shambled off and stood by himself before the remains of his church, crying helpless tears. No one appeared to be seriously hurt, not physically.

6

Carrying his old single-shot .410 shotgun Onely swung the creaky screen door open, grinning as usual like he was the sly one when he wasn't at all, and they walked up Constable street to where it became a path rising into laurel scrub. They climbed through Virginia pines and young oaks to the ridge and crossed over into the cove where Hoppy Butler had been shot in his underwear by sheriff's deputies, a spot marked by a hickory slab upon which were burned with a hot nail the words Son O Man, and climbed transversely along the far ridge and crossed the summit of Bald Face mountain and descended laterally, following a deer trail through a grassy meadow filled with blossoming Joe Pye weed, the pink shaggy flowers nodding in a cool breeze, and entered a flat area of hardwoods.

The trees in this place, mostly white oaks and tulip poplars and chestnuts, were the largest he had ever seen. Onely said they were the oldest leafy trees east of the Mississippi river, a fact passed on by his grandfather and confirmed, he said, in *Collier's Encyclopedia*. They had brought chicken and gravy sandwiches and a chunk of hoop cheese wrapped in wax paper and an apple that Onely cut up into chunks with his single-blade Barlow knife. The flesh was mushy and hardly worth eating. They were hunting turkeys. Delvin thought he heard a gobbler as they entered these woods, but he was not sure. The trees, some of them, were ten feet through the base and soared up a hundred feet or more. The tulip poplars had bark that had whitened almost like the peeled places on a sycamore. The leaf tops were sparse in a way that made Delvin think of old wispy-haired men, white men. The oaks were more fulsome, fully decorated with leaves so dark green they were almost black, and the chestnuts had what he thought of as an aristocratic look. There was hardly any undergrowth. Only a carpet of fallen leaves on the rocky floor. It was a hushed place and even the wind was stately and mindful, striding in sockfeet high up through the insubstantial leaves.

When they finished eating, the boys made little beds for themselves among the big tree roots and took a nap.

When he waked, Onely was still sleeping, so Delvin walked off alone under the trees. Every step opened a fresh avenue, no need for paths. He had heard of these old trees before Onely told him. The wind in the tops made a rushing sound, steady and grave. Delvin pressed his palm against the creased bark of a tulip polar. On the ground were scattered a few orange and green tulip flowers. They had the same sweet smell he was familiar with, no codger odor, tree variety. He craned his neck looking upward until he almost fell over. As he watched, an orange and green flower twirled slowly down and came to rest at his feet. Gift from the sky, he thought. Lately he had been thinking about getting up high. Not tree high, not mountain high, but far up into the sky. He wasn't thinking about flying in a plane either though that would be thrilling, he was thinking about something else. It was like a dream. He couldn't quite put into words what he meant. But he wanted to be far up, riding right at the border between earth and space. Hang waist deep in the blue air and look up at the stars in the cold black sky.

From off beyond the trees came a faint striking, slapping sound. Maybe it was a bear nosing about. The woods had always been strange to him, he was uneasy in them, nervous. He shied behind a tree and stepped a few paces along a quartering line, taking care on the hard surface of black dirt and leaves, on the chunk granite and schist, not to fall. The sound didn't come again. In several places there appeared to be regular paths. He followed one. Up ahead he could see sunlight and he hoped it was a meadow. Meadows, pastures, planted fields, these were fine; he preferred places of human habitation, some sign that people were busy with life or had been or might be again soon.

The path curved west under the trees. It made him nervous to follow but he thought he ought to, ought to brave it. A breeze made a whisking sound high up. The path sloped gently downhill. He could hear what sounded like voices. Also a clattering of metal. He ducked off the path and made his way across the leafy ground, drawing closer to the light. He could see an irregular ridgeline way across there, mottled dark and light green patches. Then he could clearly hear voices, white boys shouting. The voices made a high, looping sound, a sound as if they were imitating the sound of owls or wolves. He drew closer, crouched behind a bank of serviceberry bushes and looked out.

Two groups of boys on opposite sides of a narrow grassy field were running toward each other. They carried leather straps and lengths of rope and sticks and some even had long poles the bark had been stripped off of. They ran at each other swinging these—they were weapons. Boys about his age, fifteen, going at it.

Delvin dropped flat to the ground. His heart began to beat hard. The ground had no give at all, a rock floor. He raised himself and peered through the gray, starchy-smelling leaves of the closest bush.

Out in the field the boys ran hard, yelling. With a crunching, pranging sound they struck each other with the flexing weapons, clashing, unchecked and swinging. Those who didn't fall or drop down or skeet off to the edges limping and hollering ran on to the other side of the grassy field. Only a few had hit the ground and most of these got quickly up. One or two rested on a knee. A boy licked blood off his wrist. Another lay on the ground wailing in a high, unlucky voice. One of the fallen got up, limped over to a fallen boy nearby and dragged him to his feet. The fallen boy had a long bleeding scrape on one arm. He grasped the arm above the elbow, like he was shy with it, and tried to lean his head against the other boy's shoulder but the boy wouldn't let him. All the boys were wearing hats, turn-brims, chocked out as if they were stuffed with something.

The boys gathered in separate groups on opposite sides of the pasture. They shouted at each other, insults and curses, none of which carried any heat. One boy waved his hat and strutted with his hand on his hip. Two sashayed arm in arm brandishing their sticks. Taunts, boasts. This was some kind of game.

From among the bushes Delvin watched them regroup and with

a shout again run at each other. Shrieking, hollering, they swung straps and sections of yellow rope and peeled sticks and met with a clattery jumble of weapons and bodies. Blood spurted from the ear of one boy. Another cried out with a sound like a child. Two stood off to the side hitting at each other with the long white poles.

Delvin raised higher to see more clearly. Stalks of pokeweed and wild carrot standing up in the field like markers swayed in a quick little breeze. The boys shoved at each other, stumbling, falling and getting up, crouching, darting in with a swing of rope that looped and whistled in the bright air.

Gradually the two groups began to break apart, passing agitatedly from gathering to separation, the boys moving off with twitchy arms and trembling legs across the bent-down grass, leaving behind the three or four more damaged boys to drag along after.

Delvin didn't see the white boy coming along the edge of the field, a small boy moving dispiritedly just inside the cover of the trees, fleeing the struggle. The boy came up on him. Suddenly they were looking into each other's eyes. Neither said anything. The boy, who was skinny and wore a red bandana around his ropey neck, stared at him. He had eyes as blue as the blue-eyed grass. He stared at Delvin as if he was looking at something he had never seen before. In that moment Delvin saw all the way into him, all the way down the long hallway of his spirit right to the bottom where the boy lay curled up in terror. The boy knew he saw him and he saw Delvin too, saw fright mixed with wonder. In that way they were not brothers, even under the skin. There was variation, an offslant both experienced, a dizziness of estrangement.

Both ducked to the side, the boy thrashing through the berry bushes flailing his arms, swimming through greenery. He was not trying to call attention, he was trying to get away; Delvin saw this. He had ducked too, and as he saw the boy swinging his arms he began to run.

Some other boy, a boy with narrow muscular shoulders and a crusted star-shaped cut on his cheekbone, a boy done with fighting but afraid to say so, saw Delvin as he raised up and started to run.

He cried out. "Yonder's a black 'un spying!"

Others too had had enough. They too were ready to retire.

"Get him!" they cried.

The boys were quick in this way, instantly and solidly opposed to an africano person watching them in their secret white boys' Sunday afternoon battle that they'd come up with to break loose from the boredom and dreariness of their lives. But this here was better.

Whooping, cawing like crows, they took after Delvin.

Delvin was fast, and he remembered the way he'd come. It was easy to run among the trees. He sprinted up the track, cut between two big chestnut trees that said *shoo shoo* in low windy voices as he passed, dashed straight up the hill and cut over to where he'd left Onely. The white boys came on behind him running, not in a bunch but spread out through the woods. Virgin forest, Onely had said this was. Delvin was wearing sneakers so old the white canvas had turned green. He could feel the rocks and the hard ground through the gutta percha soles.

He reached the spot where they'd napped, but Onely wasn't there. Maybe he'd mistook the place, but no, he recognized the tulip poplar, a black streak on it about head high.

"Onely," he called in a low voice, "Whoo, Onely."

"Keep on coming this way," said Onely's voice from on up the track. He stuck his head around a large oak. "Come on," he said.

Delvin ran toward him. Behind him he could hear the boys coming. As he passed him he saw from the corner of his eye Onely get to his feet. He had the .410 up and pointed. Delvin ran on by him. Then a shot. The gun going off with a loud crumping sound that seemed to slam against the trees.

A cry came from the chasing boys.

"He hit him!" somebody yelled.

Delvin had continued on up the track thinking Onely would follow. Now he did, sprinting right past Delvin. Delvin heard what had happened—heard the shot and the cry—but he didn't want to know it.

He ran as hard as he could and they continued running up the

ridge and along it through the long grass and a stand of yellow birch
trees and down into a mixed wood of maples and poplars that made
a sound as if it was raining in the leaves (it wasn't) and on through a
canebrake in a hollow where they hid for a minute but couldn't stay
because the fright was on them in a punishing way. They crashed
through the limber cane shoots and ran past a huge cherry tree and
ran on without fatigue across the shoulder of the ridge and down and
across another sun-splashed swale where blackberries were making
among their own white flowers. Two young africano girls were picking the ripe berries and dropping them into buckets.

Onely yelled at the girls to run away but they stood looking at
them. Delvin grabbed one girl's wrist and began to pull her along.
He stopped when the other didn't come and said to them both that
crazy white boys were coming and they had to run. The other came
along slowly, swinging her bucket. When Delvin started to run again
they ran too. He was thinking wildly, coming up closer in his mind
to jumping off into some hideout or cave he couldn't find and he
wanted to start shrieking and yelling (all the while mutttering "damn
damn damn") and then in the next moment saw ahead of him the
cuts and swerves he would be racing along in just a second and he
couldn't get it straight exactly what was happening or even who it
was happening to, saw the jostle in a chokecherry branch and the
sideslip of some tiny creature exiting the premises, and didn't know
anything, he thought, but just run and run.

Onely had disappeared up ahead but Delvin ran with the girls.
One of them was crying but the other ran with a solemn face, not
saying a word. They made it to the top of the ridge and when Delvin
started down toward the north the solemn girl whose wrist he still
held tugged him the opposite way.

"We got to . . . ," he said, but he didn't know what, and when the
girl pulled him again hard, in her face still wordless a look of severe
intelligence and knowing, he went with her.

He couldn't tell where Onely was. With the girls, the one whose
hand he was still holding now leading—twelve-year-old girls, thirteen maybe—he crossed the long bottom where jack-in-the-pulpits

bloomed in mucky soil and climbed through a complex understory of rhododendron bushes and laurel beneath tall loblolly pines to a ridge covered in holly bushes that the girl knew a path through and down into a gully that they followed, jumping from rock to rock, until they were suddenly back in Red Row at the head of Jersey street.

He stopped, winded, run through with an exhilaration that made him want to run some more, keep on running, maybe cross out of the mountains to the flatlands that spilled toward the Mississippi river and then rose again to the Texas plains where maybe his mother was if she wasn't all the way to California and Hollywood or some other flimsy place—stopped and bent over his knees and drew in big breaths that he suddenly wanted the girls to see, notice the heroic boy who'd just outwitted the white people once again, a fine fellow. But when he raised up he was dizzy, and swayed, almost fell. The girls, particularly the one solemn-faced pretty girl, didn't even seem to be ruffled. Even as he was telling them not to say anything about what had happened, the one he was still holding (for dear life) broke free and together the girls ran away from him down the street, their bare feet kicking up puffs of dust as they ran.

At the corner the girl he'd run with stopped and looked back at him. Her face was solemn yet. For a moment she studied him before wheeling about and disappearing beyond the porch of a man's house whose wife had been buried the week before, he remembered, by accommodation of the Constitution Funeral Home.

Then the truth of what kind of trouble he was in poked its snout up like a ground rat.

He wouldn't be safe anywhere and he knew it. If that white boy was killed—even if he wasn't—they wouldn't stop looking until they found him. He would have to head right back into the woods. He felt sick to his stomach. Just like his mother he was going to have run off into the mountains.

But before he did that he wanted to go home. He loped across the Row, running like a boy who had somewhere to get to but didn't want anybody to know it.

• • •

Many people saw him that evening, a well-formed boy with a bush of thick hair cut in a high part and the handsome face of a blackness that even africano people remarked on, a good boy, they said, son of a murderer who had escaped retribution, a lucky boy despite that, who, so they figured, would some day come into one of the three or four largest fortunes in the quarter—former dewbaby, as they called him, black as grandmama's skillet and kindly.

He was sure they would be looking for him at home so he ducked around behind the big yellow frame AME church on Jefferson where under a pollarded magnolia three little girls were playing fly the hoop. One of them skipped and fell in the dust. She looked up at him as if he was the cause. In the office he found Miss Marvie Appleton who let him use the phone to call the house.

Miss Parker said no one had been around looking for him. He asked her to put Willie Burt on and after a few minutes his raspy voice said he too hadn't seen anybody looking. But then maybe, Delvin thought, it was too early. Had Willie seen the Ghost? Sho, he was out in the shed eating apples he stole from Mr. Oliver's supply. Well, would Willie tell Winston to come meet him over behind Miss Louise Marchant's house where he was working on something for her?

"What?"

"What what?"

"What is it you be working on?" Willie wanted to know.

"I'm helping her to write a letter."

"Okay," Willie said, "I'll tell him."

"I need him to come fast."

Which the Ghost did, hotfooting across the Row to the back door of Miss Louise's lime-green house. Miss Louise was the unmarried sister of Rev Poulice Marchant who for forty years was the minister of the Sweetwater Holiness church and now ten years after he died continued on in fine form and local respect (Miss Louise did) in her small two-story house that was the only one on her block that was painted. As Winston started up the brick back steps Delvin called to him from some redtop bushes by a runoff ditch at the bottom of the yard. The Ghost gave him a misshapen grin and loped over.

"Hey, my boon," he said.

Delvin told him he needed him to go around to the police station to see what he could find out about a boy being shot.

"Ju shoot him?"

"No. It wadn't me."

"Okay, fine," the Ghost said. He'd been living in the shed semi-permanently for a few weeks now, despite being run off twice or three times by Willie or Elmer, slinking back each time under Delvin's protection.

"I'm going around behind Heberson's and get something to eat. Let's meet right there in two hours' time—around back."

The Ghost said this was fine with him, grinned and took off running across the yard in his hunched, loping style, his head stiff on his shoulders and his arms swinging as if he was about to grab something.

It was full dark out and gloomy without lights along the streets except here and there on the corners and little wicklamps burning in the houses like it was still the nineteenth century. Instead of going straight to the store Delvin made his way to the Emporium, slipping along the alley behind his old birth house and ducking into the bordello's wide yard, easing in under one of the big magnolias in back. He wasn't sure what the Ghost would do and he felt safer near the bordello. The magnolia's branches drooped all the way to the ground. He climbed up among them, feeling his sense of hopefulness, his strength, ebbing as he climbed and pushed into the smooth fork and lay along the high limb panting, nauseous and afraid he would vomit. His life felt emptied out, like earth from a barrow, and he saw himself alone, a trembling haint on the edge of the world. His mother must have felt like this. He let out a small cry, a squeak of pain and fright. He wanted to throw himself into the air and fly

away but there was no way to do that. His felt his spirit leap out
from him like a skittish bird, some creature without knowledge of
the world or a way to go. He was suddenly dizzy. "Little Time," he
said, "Little Time," addressing the tick of his life as if it was a small
goblin he might appeal to. But there was nothing. He was terrified
of every house in the quarter—in Chattanooga—in the world—but
at the same time he wanted to rush into them and beg to be hidden.
He thought of the Ghost crammed up under the Emporium. Lord,
he would jam himself even deeper if he thought he could stay. He
shivered, pressing his face against the tree body. His fingers moved
across little whorls and striations like ancient messages age-carved
into the bark, indecipherable. "Help me," he said, "Dear God, Little
Time, help me." His heart hammered like a crazy man trying to get
out—or in, he thought, trying to burrow deeper into his own body.

At the three-quarters chiming of the second hour by the courthouse clock he shinnied down and made his way across the Row to
Heberson's. The Ghost was crouched behind a line of garbage cans
out back. His eyes gleamed like a cat's.

"Yeah, they's been some kind of shooting up that old mountain
way. They was talking about it round the jailhouse."

Delvin felt his insides clutch. A slashing pain driving down his
body. He felt suddenly as if he needed to evacuate his bowels. "They
say what they have on that?" he said in a crumped, rustly voice.

"Not to me, no, but they was talking about somebody's got shot
up on the mountain and they's had to carry him out. Haul him out
or something—somebody, some mosying wanderer or something
or maybe it was a bunch of em up there. Or something else, I can't
remember. It's mixed up. Shell Pickens—they got *him* on a drunk
charge—was shouting in the back."

"Was it a boy?"

"When? Yeah, I get you. Could have been. You done shot a boy?"

"No."

"Was it a white boy?"

Delvin ignored the question. "Did they say who did it?"

"They aint come down real hard on that yet. Leastways not in my hearing. Maybe they holding back on it. Maybe they don't know. That'd be some luck."

Delvin turned away. He was afraid he was about to start crying. He felt as if a huge part of him was breaking off, shelving away—as if he was big as a town or a continent, something huge about him that he had never noticed now shifting, rumbling and sliding down, contravening solidity and the future. "You got to excuse me," he said, ran and pushed through the door of Heberson's outhouse, shucked, squatted and let loose his bowels. Even as he did so something urged him to flee instantly. He had to grip one of the worn two-by-four supports to hold himself in place. He felt sick, as if his insides had melted in a corrosive heat. He strained over himself, the pungent stink rising as he did so. "Lord God, suppose me," he said. "Suppose me into your way right now. O Help me help me help me." He was falling through himself and for a second thought he would pass out. But he came back. He tore off a sheet of the old *Collier's Encyclopedia* hanging backless on a hook and cleaned himself, fixed his clothes and came out again into the vaguely light-muddled dark behind the store where the Ghost, pale and swaying, piecing out a mountain tune, waited.

"You done fo it now, aint you?" the Ghost said.

The stars faint above the city like pale drops flicked off heaven's fingers. Never to be the same again. Tick time, he thought, Little Time.

"Was there anything going on at home?"

"I aint been over there, but when I left out Mr. Oliver was preparing a body—Miss Freedly from over on Godown street, that old woman who used to boil up those pots of molasses in her backyard? You didn't shoot *her*, did you?"

"No. She died?"

"Yeah. Waked up dead in her bed this morning, Elmer said. Mr. Oliver is probably just finishing with her now. Funeral's tomorrow."

"Would you tell them I have some business over in town and probably won't be in tonight?"

"Will they believe me?"

"Tell em I'm going shining for rabbits with some boys."

"Can I go?"

"It's just something I want you to tell them."

"Okay."

They were sitting now on a couple of bottomless rush chairs that Mr. Heberson had set beside a storage shed for possible repairing. Mr. Heberson ran a sideline in repaired used furniture. The backyard was piled with couches and broken tables and smashed-up chairs. From the grocery's double back doors came the sound of Heberson's crystal radio playing white church music. Delvin listened for a minute; a few passages were soothing, then a run of growly, stiff exhorting was not. He wanted to phonecall Mr. Oliver, but he better forgo that. A wan emptiness revealed itself under his heart. He longed to go lie down on the big red and gold rug in Mr. O's bedroom and read his book on sea voyages—longed to be there right now turning the big stiff pages, listening to Mr. O humming under his breath. But he didn't want to have to tell him what happened. The Ghost's information had plunged him into a terror so brusque and enveloping he could hardly think. As if a whole scotched world has just shook into place and he stood in the middle of it. A scotched world in a scotched world, he thought and almost laughed. Poor white boy. He hoped he wasn't dead. Off in the lonely leaf strew of the mountain. Loneliness flooding along inside him as he thought this.

He told the Ghost to run on to the house and then he waited a while before going into the grocery and buying a bag of crackers and some store cheese. Then he crossed the Row to Onely's house. It was a shanty made of boards tacked onto poles and a roof of slats covered in disintegrating tarpaper. He sneaked up through the smelly yard, a skinny pale dog snuffling and bowing-up with delight at his side, and looked through a crack. There was no sign of Onely. As he walked away down the alley Onely called to him from a mass of elderberry bushes. He stepped out to meet Delvin. The alley smelled like dead animals. Gray puffed clouds were out all over the sky, sliding along, hauled like barges by a great current before a pinched moon. Onely had a hat, an old soft snapbrim with a hole in the crown, pulled over his eyes. He didn't push it back to talk to Delvin.

"I was afraid you'd run off to turn me in," he said. His large teeth gleamed as he spoke.

"I wouldn't do that. I didn't even think of it. Besides, we're two colored boys. They'd be more happy to fry two than one."

"I hadn't seen anything unusual around here," Onely said.

Delvin told him about the Ghost's visit to the police station.

"That humbugger. He probably turned us in."

"He wouldn't. He's a free-hearted soul."

"You think they want to keep it quiet til they catch us?"

"They couldn't do that. This is the kind of thing word gets around on. You sure you shot that boy?"

"You heard him cry out yourself."

"I heard somebody."

"That was probably the somebody that said *They shot 'im*. Dang. Even if we'd missed him by a mile, they know we's black uns and they'll come at us just the same. You shouldn't a spooked em."

Delvin thought that too but he didn't say anything.

He wanted to tell Onely how scared he was but he thought better of it. If they got out of this Onely might hold it against him, or, before that, he might think Delvin couldn't be trusted and no telling what would happen then.

"I'm shook," he said, unable after all to help himself.

"You not the only one."

In the dark stinking alley piled along one side with barrels containing not yet expendable refuse, they stood in the deeper dark cast by the shadow of a tin-sided shed. Delvin leaned against the tin that was cool and made a low crackling sound as it slightly gave. He pulled himself back upright.

"I was thinking of running off into the hills."

He hadn't wanted to tell Onely that either, but maybe he would want to come with him. In the dimness Delvin could see in Onely's eyes knowledge of his life. You can tell what people know, he thought. That was the difference between eyes of the living and eyes of the dead. Dead didn't know anything. Once he had realized that, he was no longer nervous around corpses. He studied Onely's round face.

"What are you going to do?"

"I'm gon catch a train. I was on my way to the yards when I saw you coming around the corner."

"I'll go with you," Delvin said, and the two of them started out. But when they reached the train yard just beyond the south side of the quarter he changed his mind. Not at first but during the time they waited for the train to form up.

"In twenty minutes on the roads we'll be in Georgia or Alabama and they won't come looking for us down there," Onley said.

"I wouldn't count on it."

He'd be trapped on a train. He wanted to be on his feet, running.

"I don't think this is for me," he said.

But he waited with Onley in the empty boxcar they'd crawled into.

"As soon as this thing starts I'm gone," Delvin said. But when the car jolted and stopped he only looked up without moving and when it jarred into motion he got up and went to the door but he didn't jump out. "I'll ride a little ways with you," he said coming back to where Onley sat with his chin tipped up and his eyes closed.

He stayed on until the train passed the junction at Buttonwood, first settlement inside the Alabama line, where he intended to jump down, but he stayed on instead, through Buttonwood and then through Shelby and then Holderness and Barwick. It wasn't until the train rattled through Slimton, just past the two straggly, crooked blocks of the town, as the freight began to pick up speed past the long curve leaving the Culver Ginning Company behind, that he jumped down, rolled into a dry ditch, got up and walked away down the road, heading, to his vague surprise, not back to Chattanooga, but west.

"Since then," he said, talking to himself as he walked along a hard dirt road, "old Delvin's been on the loose end of loose." He thought of turning up in Chicago, half dead, penniless, and making a life for himself as a musician. He had heard Louis Armstrong play on the radio and had once seen Duke Ellington walking down Adams street on his way to conduct his orchestra at the Harmony ballroom. He carried a light cane that he swished like a little limber sword as he walked. Or maybe he would live on the rough streets until winter came to Chicago and then catch a train to Miami.

He was still breathless after a mile walking on the side of the road. Nothing ahead but farm fields and woods. No telling how many miles of them. Why not go back and catch another train? Why not go home and hide under the house? Watch the legs of the police as they rounded everybody up. Oh Lord. If he was going back he would have to walk through that little town. These farmers would eat him alive. Oh Lord. He stopped and stood in the middle of the road. A consternation came on him so powerfully he thought his head would burst. What the mercy do I do? He scuffed the light, speckled dirt. It smelled of the country, of country life. Tall sumac bushes nodded darkly and gave in a little breeze. He thought he might walk on a bit farther, see what he could see. He started out.

As he continued south he would step off the road and crouch in the ditch when he saw car lights coming. The ditch was dry and sandy at the bottom. There weren't many vehicles, maybe six between when he was set down and when the first gray shadings of dawn began to appear over grassy hills to the east. He stopped to rest. He lay down in the ditch grass. He shut his eyes but he could see the white boys running after him. Then he could see the solemn-faced girl. She was a plucky girl; he hoped their paths would cross again. The grass itched through his shirt. How would he ever get home? He began softly to cry, holding the tears in, ashamed of them, as if there was someone around who might see and rate him. After a while he slept, but just barely, always near the surface where it seemed white boys carrying big sticks were about to catch him. At the earliest shadings of dawn he was up and walking.

For nine months he wandered, catching trains out of little shapeless burgs, riding all night peering up from splintery beds

of flatcars at the drifting stars, wondering who he was and where
he would wind up, taking his meals at back steps and in alleys
behind little restaurants, gnawing on hard store cheese and
crusty bread, wondering where he was going and when he would
get there, crossing rivers and blackwater sloughs where buzzard
delegations perched in tall cypress trees and passing fields ornately
laid down, riding and working and pulling his socks off only when
he came to a likely stream he could wash in, laying low on the lowdown, a railroad angelina shy of bulls and yeggs, careful with his
few cents, taking his time to question others who might look likely,
flailing in dreams, and wondering if he would ever again light on
somewhere to stay. But time passed, the world edged into fall, and he
grew homesick. Outside Barwick, Alabama—the closest he'd been
to Chattanooga since he stepped down from his original freight—he
caught a ride with a farmer who took him home on a work plan, and
all the way Delvin was making up a story, not his, he knew that already, but the man's, story of a skinny fellow with a wrinkled brow
and slim shoulders and a partially withered arm, some farmer with
a mystery in his life that he couldn't express and needed old Delvin
to get him going and help him tell his tale. Everybody had a mystery
and on the roads you heard versions of mystery like fairy tales and
legends continuously revised. Stories of great fights and punishment
and loss enduring like an eternal flame. Stories of marriages gone
sour and children lost in a fire and stumbles that threw a man down
into pits and left him crawling in dark hallways under the gaze of
strange faces peering ghostly through windows, and floods come
like destitution itself, and somebody had his left hand cut off with
a pirate cutlass and another had his back broke by a cotton wagon
and somebody else discovered his sweetheart in a junction between
towns where nobody would tell you the truth about anything and he
said to his sweetheart I will go get us something to eat but when he
came back she was dead in the road with her throat cut. The stories
stacked in your head like painted plates and you could take them
down and read the life of the country in them and he liked to do this
even though each one made him lonely. Here was another.

For the next five weeks he stayed on the farm working for the Bealls, that was their name, a husband and wife, africano folks who owned their own farm. He cleaned out the chicken yard and house and hoed the garden and picked vegetables. In the kitchen he worked peeling tomatoes for canning and putting up pickles. He sat at the kitchen table eating green tomato pickles that were so sweet they made his back teeth ache, reading aloud to Mrs. Beall from a book of fairy tales. He read her the story of Sleeping Beauty and the story of the Lost Prince. In both these, one the tale of a single woman drugged and stashed by a thug in the woods and the other of a young man who could not read the signs that were as plain as day, Mrs. B found her life.

I too have been asleep all my life, she said. I too could never read the signs.

She was a stout woman with a plain open face. She voiced these statements in a way that made Delvin feel she knew the stories well and had spoken these sentiments before. Yet she made them with fervor, as if realizing truths about herself for the first time. Her long broad bottom lip trembled. I wonder where my prince is, she said, as if she had just misplaced him, and where is my crippled but kindly dwarf to lead me from the dark wood. Another story about a prince defeating three wily witches did not interest her.

I just don't believe no prince is going to outwit such remarkable women, she said, baring her stained childish teeth.

This remark too seemed prepared. Maybe, Delvin thought, he was not the first traveler to sit at this table. It was covered with oilcloth printed in tiny red flowers on a blue background. Small red mallow flowers filled a cloudy glass vase set in the center. She picked new flowers every day from the garden, always red mallows, but only the small ones. Others, rose pink and red-streaked and as wide and fat as a dinner plate, she left alone. The kitchen smelled heavily of peeled and blanched and pureed tomatoes, as of a tomato wine.

The first sleep there, morning into afternoon, just before he waked, he had had a dream of his mother kneeling beside a mountain stream dipping water in a yellow gourd. She looked young and

healthy and vigilant and she was carrying a large bunch of white
flowers stuffed into a sack on her back. All in the dream seemed right.
But she did not look at him and he did not call or go to her. In the
dream he asked himself why not, but it did not seem an important
question. He waked in the late afternoon with the dream still alive in
his mind, a little sad, and refreshed and alert and hungry again. The
room was filled with a fine-grained aged-yellow light coming in a
narrow window at the foot of the bed. He smelled some lemony herb
he didn't know the name of, some kind of mint, he thought.

He lay on his back feeling surrounded by big events. These events
were at a distance, like lights on the horizon. Last year they had buried
out of the funeral home a man who'd committed suicide by setting
himself on fire. He'd been burned worse than that boy. The man—
Stacy Beltram—had bought half a gallon of gasoline that he pumped
himself into a little tin jug and out in the alley behind his house under
a big blossoming mimosa he poured it over himself and set a match
to it. The fire had burned him up and the mimosa too. "That was
typical of him," the man's old father had said about his ruining all the
fuzzy pink blossoms. At the graveside service Delvin overheard a tall
man in an army uniform, a man some said was once Mr. Beltram's
best friend, say, "He set fire to himself trying to buy a little time off in
Hell." The other people who heard him laughed with their hands over
their mouths. The burned man had been a cardsharp and a japer, a
grifter who was once put in jail for selling worthless insurance policies
to old ladies. What had been coming for that man finally caught him,
Delvin had said to Mr. Oliver as they washed up at the soapstone sink
in the basement hall. What caught him, catches everybody, Mr. O had
reminded him. Chickens wing home to every roost.

He stood at the window looking out at the poultry yard. Evening coming on out of yellow swirls and loose red patches in the
west. The chickens were starting to make for the roost in the chicken
house. They clucked and quarreled as they trooped toward the short
board inclines, and a few of them continued scratching in the dirt as
if the dark wont anything to worry about. But in a minute even the
brave ones would pick up and climb aboard. Chickens couldn't see

at night, so he'd read, that was why the fox could catch them so easy. Among other reasons, he'd thought.

On the day they finished canning the tomatoes it was still early afternoon and Delvin walked out to the pasture beyond the garden. Off to the left a distant truck boiled along a dusty road, probably Mr. Beall, on one of his errands. Mr. Beall often left after breakfast and was gone for a good part of the day. He would return bringing a small shrub or turnip or some seeds folded in a small newspaper packet or once a slender carved wood figurine he said had been brought from Africa. He did a little work around the place, but that usually involved encouraging the chickens and once or twice taking one of the roosters out of the small cages and exchanging its place with the rooster in the big pen. Delvin followed him into the pen the first time, but when Mr. Beall put the fresh rooster down he immediately attacked Delvin, coming at him in a ruckus of feathers and kicks. Mr. Beall had laughed when Delvin ran. I wish I could have got a picture, he said, when he caught the other rooster and shooed the angry cock away from the boy. Delvin figured he could have stomped the rooster if it came to that, but he wasn't sure. If that devilish bird had gotten him on the ground no telling what would have happened. From the safety of the farmyard he eyed the new rooster, a red and green and black cock with a large red wattle that swayed as it walked. The rooster lifted itself on its legs and let loose a sharp crow. Delvin decided not to let himself be drawn into a battle with the cock. When Mr. Beall invited him into the enclosure again he passed. I'm too young to let myself be killed by a chicken, he said. Mr. Beall had laughed a friendly, farmer-knows-best laugh.

Past the yard, past the garden, Delvin stood in the pasture sniffing the wind. A stand of yellow phlox caught at a bit of breeze, shuddered and let it go, the tall shaggy flower heads fluttering. A meadowlark flew his way, checked and veered sharply off, exposing his yellow breast feathers. The blue sky was strewn with small round clouds, like puffs of cannon fire. The path was wide and grassy, but in the middle of it a narrow strip ran that was sandy, without growth. There were faint footprints in this strip. He experienced a consternated shiver. He began to follow the path, and as he walked the fear or nervousness at first grew, but then gradually it began to subside or if not quite subside, to be replaced by another kind of trepidation, not just a fear of police agents or detectives trailing him, but of some other presence. The path dipped toward a branch, left the pasture and entered a gray wood. Long spindly trunks of mottled gray trees he didn't know the names of held up small collections of pale green leaves. Below them crooked skinny bushes with hard glossy leaves squatted. A sharp fluttering came from behind one set of bushes—a bird spooked by something, maybe him, maybe something else. Badgers came to mind. He had been reading in the *Britannica* lately about badgers, about their implacable fierceness. In the drawings, despite their fur, they looked flattened, like some turtles or other reptiles. They had hard black curved claws. He stopped. The wind soughed in the tall thin trees, making a sighing sound. In a minute, he thought, it's gonna start moaning. The path came to a plank, railed bridge over twenty feet of a tea-colored creek. He made himself stop in the middle of the bridge, carefully lean on the rail and look at the water that had no discernible current. Green and yellow dragonflies darted and hung over the surface, hesitating, tipping, angling, sliding down almost to the water and hovering there as if discovering and examining tremendously interesting material on what to Delvin looked like a glozed, chocolate-colored sheet. The stream had a pleasant peaty smell. The bank on the far side was sandy, speckled with brown and black bits, but the stream itself was opaque; dark water that might contain anything. But no police down there, he thought. He'd never gone fishing, except once when Mr. Oliver and George had taken him to a little pond behind a client's house out in the country. Nothing but a little black turtle had bit their hooks. He'd like to try it again.

Looking up the trail that continued through the leafy trees filtering into piney woods, he debated whether to keep going. These moments of hesitation were familiar to him. Seems like that's where I really live, he sometimes thought, not in the *doing* of one thing or another. He didn't really want to go on, but he felt he ought to, ought to be brave enough or interested enough. Or was that a way of really wanting to do something—thinking he should—and hiding it from himself. He'd like to go into the little room where he slept and lie on the bed and read something, maybe the book of fairy stories or a newspaper. In their parlor the Bealls had *My Bondage and Freedom* by Mr. Douglas and *Souls of Black Folk* by Dr. Du Bois, but he had already read those books. He wanted to read another masterpiece, like *Ivanhoe* maybe, that he had read last summer lying on an old couch up in the attic at Mr. Oliver's. He liked stories of struggle and questing in distant locales. Reading was natural, Miz Parker the cook said, to moody boys, and you are a moody boy. Maybe too moody, he thought, to be out alone in some thorny wood.

Then, without as far as he could tell having decided anything, he continued across the bridge and up the path that was strewn with waxy needles and rose gently into the pine woods. Just a few steps in it shaded off to the right, passed a large hedgelike growth of ligustrum that ran fifty feet in a high green wall and left off abruptly at the edge of a clearing in which there was a small white frame cottage. On the front porch of the cottage in a rocking chair much too big for him sat a tiny white man. The back of his chair soared high above his rusty white head. On one of the posts was hung a gray Confederate battle cap. The old man was looking straight at him. Delvin would have ducked and shot off from there, but the man called to him in a sweet little white man's voice.

You, boy, welcome, he said.

His voice came so quick it caught Delvin before he could swing around. He must have been listening to him come along the trail. Those are some ears, Delvin thought, on an old man.

Did you bring me my candy? the man said.

No suh, Delvin answered.

Well, come on up here anyway and sit awhile.

Delvin came slowly up a sandy walk that was bordered by bricks set on edge and end to end and painted white. A low tea olive hedge was planted around the base of the front porch. The old man smiled as he came up the steps; he had been smiling since Delvin came in

the yard. He half rose from his rocker and stuck out his hand. Delvin
didn't at first know what to do.

Well, the old man said, let's shake on it.

Delvin bowed his head, took the old man's hand that under skin
so soft it felt like it would pull to pieces was as hard as wood. The
man pumped his fingers and let go.

It's good to get the human touch as often as you can, he said sinking back into his rocker. He sat among plump red cushions looped to
the back of his chair. He wore a blue-striped white collarless shirt and
a pair of nutbrown heavy cotton trousers. On the crest of the cap were
two crossed swords. Delvin knew these caps from the parades in Chattanooga. The old Confederates marched together or were wheeled in
their big wooden chairs in the group that grew smaller every year.

I see you're studying my headpiece, the old man said, though
Delvin had only glanced at it. He didn't say anything. That's from
the independence war, the old man said.

I've seen em before.

They getting scarce, aint they?

I was just thinking that.

Where you from?

Atlanta.

Hm. Your accent sounds a touch farther north. Got some mountain in it.

Atlanta's where I'm from now.

Well, Atlanta. Now there was a fight. Did I introduce myself?
Probably not, I usually forget. I'm so happy to get a little company I
jump right in. You'll be lucky to get a word in yourself, young man.

I'm pretty much the quiet type.

Well, that's too bad. By time I get wound down I like to hear from
the other party. I'm Mr. Jobeen Mitchell. He cocked his head to the
side. His old flesh slipped on his face as he moved. His nose, long
and drawn down to a point at the tip, was waxy and gleamed in the
soft light under the sighing pine trees. You been to any extravagant
spots lately?

No sir, not lately.

Fletchy up there—you come from the house?

Yassuh, I guess—

Fletchy comes down here to read to me from her fairy books, but I don't particularly care for them wispy tales. You like em?

I like about anything that's written down.

Well now that's a good way to be. Or maybe it aint. It's a question I ask myself. Is it a man's duty to let the ramblings go on unchecked, or is it his duty to at some point put a stop to em? That was the question old Ape Lincoln answered with a war against us. The old man knocked against his chin with two fingers, stretched out his jaw. What if he hadn't won that one?

The Civil War?

That's what I'm speaking of. War of Secession.

I'd probably still be a slave, Delvin said, thinking, as if I wadn't one yet. His voice sounded funny to him, clipped, squeezed; maybe that was how they talked in Atlanta.

A slave? the old man said, throwing his head back. Oh, I doubt that. I spect the shame of that arrangement would have gotten under the skin of even these hardskin folks down here. But then, you probably feel like you even now are a slave.

Sometimes I do, Delvin said. Maybe he *was* under a spell, and this codger was some kind of old man witch.

He was still standing. At this point the old man indicated the companion rocker, also a tall chair. I'm sorry, he said, I was so glad to see you I forgot my manners. With nobody around my mouth gets backed up.

Thank you, Delvin said, and sat down.

I was a corporal in the Sixth Alabama Volunteers, the old man said, looking at him with eyes the blue of which had soaked into the white, a fighting regiment that mustered in after First Manassas and mustered out after Appomattox. I lived personally through eleven major battles and a sack full of skirmishes, all before I was twenty-one years old. The war put itself into my mind in such a way that nothing after it has been able to take its place. He looked away. His profile was jagged, bitten looking. Near bout nothing, he said.

Some of these old confederates, so Delvin knew, believed the war was still going on. This man seemed to be one of them. Twenty-one in '64—that'd make him eighty-six right now.

The old man pushed back in the rocker and as it rocked back seemed about to go out of sight in the violet gloom of dusk, and then as he caught himself on the return seemed about to pitch into Delvin's lap. Whoa, the old man said. You come from the house up yonder, didn't you?

Yessir.

Howse Fletchy doing?

Mrs. Beall?

None other.

She appears to be fine. We been putting up tomatoes.

Well, I hope she brings me a jar of them. He looked in a wistful way toward the trail Delvin had come down. I used to live up in that house.

It has a gentle seat, Delvin said, quoting Ivanhoe.

Howse that?

It's a good-looking place.

Me and my daddy and his daddy were all born in that house. Fletchy was born up there too—not directly in the house, but in a little house down from it. Her folks used to work for my people. Howse she doing by the way?

She's doing fine. We been reading in her book of fairy stories.

I gave her that book when she was a spring child. A beautiful young girl she was. She had the jumpinest legs. Just springing about everywhere. You ought to have seen her leap a fence. He stared hard at Delvin. You one of J. D.'s kin?

Nawsir, I'm just down visiting.

From Atlanta?

Yessuh.

J. D. comes from over around Anniston. He come over this way following his daddy who was a preacher in one them nigra denomi-nations. You go to church, boy?

Well, I do and I don't.

You being smart?

Nosir. I work at a funeral home and we are in church quite often. But I myself am not a member of any given organization.

You educated, aint you, boy?

It thrilled Delvin to have the man think that, even if he was spiting him. He said, The man I work for lets me read some of his books.

Careful they don't smoke up your head. The old man barked out a laugh that sounded like he was cracking pecans. I guess they couldn't smoke your feet, could they?

Nosuh.

I myself got so interested in life that I never had time for reading. I spose I could have during the winters—like when we was holed up from fighting Useless Grant—but even then I found so much to do in the world I din't even think of it. And look at me now, he said, running his stiff hard mottled hands down his thighs. Under the age-softened cloth they looked like two-by-fours. He looked again toward the trail. Delvin had the sense that he spent his time looking up that way. The edge of the ligustrum cut off sight; from the porch he could only see the sandy white path itself wandering on past the house into the deeper evergreen woods. The old man had the air of somebody waiting for something. D'I tell you I used to live up at that house?

Yessuh, you did. It's a fine house.

I gave that house to Fletchy when she married J. D. I gave her this whole farm and much else besides.

Delvin didn't say anything. The old man appeared to be in the grip of great emotion and Delvin figured anything he said might offend him. Mr. Oliver was very good in these sorts of situations. He brought a peacefulness with him that soothed others. But Delvin was a little jumpy. Yet he too cared about the bereaved folk, and this rickety old white man appeared to be one of the bereaved.

Is there anything I can do for you? he asked.

The old man looked at him with his blue-flooded eyes. Naw, son. Not unless you can make time run backwards. He smiled, revealing a snaggly mouth of isolated yellow teeth. And even then, how could you make it stop at just the right intersection?

They sat quietly for a while. His mind wandered to the cot in the Bealls's back room that wore little shoe polish tins on its feet, filled with water and a touch of coal oil, just like the beds in their little house with his mama. Keep the bedbugs and the roaches and the ants out of bed with you. When he waked in the morning he smelled smells, little trickly odors, that made him want to cry for the memories they brought with them: creosote, rue, soda biscuits: cottagey smells from the long ago.

The sky still held on to its fading blue, blue almost gone to gray now, but the world around the two of them was turning on to black.

They surprised us naked in the woods, the old man said.

Sir?

Old George Thomas's boys. We was bathing in a creek off from Chickamauga—it was before the big fighting began—and they came upon us washing ourselves. Must of been at least a dozen of us stark naked when they rushed from the woods. They was trying to capture us. I got away but it was without clothes or any weapon. I walked thirty miles through the night and all the next day before I got back to this farm and I was a naked man the whole way. Once or twice I could have maybe got some clothes off of this or that farmstead home but I didn't, I don't know why. Maybe it was the dogs, maybe I was ashamed, maybe I just didn't care. A fit of some kind. I arrived here in the dawn of September twentieth, 1863, last day of that battle that was the last fight we ever won, and I walked up the back steps of that house up yonder naked as a jaybird and there I found . . .

His voice trailed off.

Yessir?

The old man looked at him out of eyes that continued to hold the limitless attachment irremediable and without effort on his part. He made little squeezy sounds in his throat and then he was silent.

After a while he said, You better go on, boy.

Delvin got up, thanked the old man for his time. The white man waved a rickety arm loosely as if it was waving by designs of its own but he said nothing. Delvin started back up the path. On his way he noticed a wide white sand wagon track behind the house running up through the darkening woods. This was probably where Mr. Beall came to when he went off in his truck, or maybe it was. These were some unusual living arrangements, Delvin thought, but, by way of the funeral home, he had become privy to unusual arrangements. So often who was whose, or had been, lived on as secrets in the hearts of the living. Women revealed as grandmothers, not mothers, aunts who were mothers, sisters who were mothers, mothers who were nobody at all. Same for fathers on their side. Husbands who had been forgotten or simply never mentioned. Children who had been run off and left and who now claimed the first seat on the mourners' row and wouldn't be displaced without a fight. He had seen both men and women—and children—leap into the grave hole, trying to continue the struggle with the dead, right on into eternal life. He had seen furious left-behinds hammer with their fists on the coffin and at least once break through the lid and beat the unresisting face. Some had to be dragged kicking and screaming out of the grave, some came wailing, some came limp as the freshly dead. Fistfights broke out at times among the bereaved. Once a pistol had been pulled and with a single shot one of the mourners, a smirking brother, had been sent to join the dead child on his journey. He'd seen a husband arrested at the funeral of his wife. You never knew what might happen as the dirt shoveling moment approached.

Death brings out the real person, Mr. O always said. You can't hold these commotions against anybody. Some of these folks, he said, some of them have waited a lifetime to let the cat out of the bag. We are helping them to do for themselves what nothing else in their lives could. You see estranged children at last drop their hatred and become loving. Others go right exactly the opposite way. Sometimes you can see how happy a spouse is to be finally free. And you can see the ones who know they will never be free. If I wanted to go into business—or get married, he'd say with a look of false horror on his face—I could make up my mind who not to do it with or who would be the best choice just from how people show themselves during the time of bereavement. But it's our job to provide a backdrop—a stage for these dramas. Without preference. Their lapses or breakouts are safe with us. Think of it, he would say, puffing on one of the tightly rolled Cuban cigars he had begun to smoke after supper, some of these folks have never in their lives been able to trust anybody with the secret of who they are, not the loved one or the preacher—not even themselves. But they can trust us. We don't bring it out—death does that—but we make it so they can feel at home with their fit. Some of the displays, Delvin thought, were so public that those folks would have to trust the hundred or so other folks who watched them squeal and roll on the ground begging Mama or Daddy or sweet Sue not to go, and not just Mr. O and his boys. At least once Delvin had seen a man who had just shouted out in glee at the sight of his dead wife fresh from the embalming room threaten Mr. O with a future pistol shot if he did not keep his mouth shut about his delight. Mr. O, trembling a little and thinly smiling, had promised that no word would escape.

The afternoon had slipped quietly away. The evening star was out in the east, trembling as if it had been struck with a hammer. He stopped at the section of the garden where they'd planted strawberries. The fruit time had passed, but all the berries hadn't been picked; some had withered on the bushes. On the north side of the garden were a few apple trees. The little striped apples soon would be ready for picking. He felt a strange emptiness. It had come so quickly it was as if he had stepped unnoticed from one body into another. The old white man had spent his life in love with the woman he called Fletchy. That was the story he had not quite told. But now he lived in a little house in a pine wood. And the woman, a colored woman, lived with her husband, a colored man, in the ample farmhouse up the hill. But Delvin did not especially care to think on these things. The world was an odd place. He only wanted to stand in the sandy path, smelling fennel and the light dry smell of the broom grass and feeling what was happening to him. The emptiness; as if everything he depended on was gone. As if it never was. He felt as if he could see a hundred miles. As if the rough pasture that ended in a buff dirt road, and the distant cotton field, and the line of pine trees beyond were not there, or if they were they were really miles and miles away. As if in ordinary calculations the ordinary miles or so between him and the horizon were filled with hundreds of miles of dirt and trees and bushes and wild hay. No, it wasn't emptiness he was feeling, that was the wrong word. It was lack. As if who he was had vanished. As if he was simply a floating heedfulness, not hovering or lying in wait but simply present in a space and time that was so full of variety and mixes and complications that the ordinary measures of space wouldn't fit it. The trees were a mile away and they were a hundred miles away. He lived in an endlessness in which everything was also confined. A sense of quiet unchangeableness was all around him. Nothing was required. As he rested in this state gradually it passed, fading slowly like a long twilight. When he stirred again the ordinary world had regained its normal proportions. No residue of special arrangements or tricks remained. Without his noticing lightning bugs had risen from the grass. They swayed and flickered, holding their yellow-green lights aloft. He wished he had a jar to catch them in. His mother once in the backyard had caught a handful and tried to keep them in a big handkerchief she tied around her head, but the tiny lights faded and it was only dead bugs she shook from the cloth. She had given a half sob and laughed in a peculiar way that he could feel in his belly. Coolmist had stroked her arm and he wanted to say something, but he didn't; sometimes even around his mother he was shy.

For supper that night they had hominy and thin slices of salt ham cut from a large ham hanging in the pantry and tomatoes stewed with okra and for dessert hot soda biscuits slathered with salted butter with cane syrup poured over them. Mr. Beall had come in from his afternoon trip. He looked at Delvin in an odd way, not unfriendly, almost sad. Delvin asked about the old white man down in the vale, but neither of them would go very far into it. He was their tenant, Mr. B said, a man who had once worked this land but was now retired. Delvin studied Mrs. Beall's face as best he could without being rude, but she showed no special feelings about the matter. She didn't ask after the man.

After supper Mr. Beall and Delvin went out on the side screen porch and sat in the dark looking out at the night. The tin foil Mr.

Beall rolled from his cigar made a crinkling sound. His big sulfur match flared light and stink and the end of the cigar flamed and Delvin could see the ball of smoke and then there was only the red glowing tip in the dark. From the woods an owl called, looping its brief two-speed call out like a lariat. A whippoorwill offered its question and continued for several minutes before falling silent, answered or tired, no way to tell. Another night bird, peewit or thrush, let loose a short burst of sharp small cries that seemed to run along the tops of the field grasses, as if the little bird, in a panic, was hurrying toward a still distant roost. In the apple trees by the garden they could hear blackbirds jostling for their final places before sleep. After a while Mrs. Beall came out bringing cups of sassafras tea. He'd never drank this kind of root tea before. It had a sharp cedary smell and tasted faintly of wood. With the honey she also brought it was all right. They must do this often, Delvin thought (though it was the first time they had done it since he came). Sit out here among the birds and woods creatures listening to this racket. Country people. Like they were tiptoeing around in this big greeny world. Folks who lived out here had special secret places they retreated to—so he imagined— canebrakes and branches, caves under the fox grapes where in shady green citadels they could sit undisturbed and think about the world that couldn't find them just now. *All* this rural world was like that for him. Not just some hideout in an alder thicket or ramshackle cotton house, but all of it, the whole parcel of woods and rivers and planted fields and all the houses and other buildings and sites too. Nobody in the world knew he was here. He could stop and loiter among the sedge and thistles like he'd done this afternoon and let himself think about things. It didn't even matter what he thought; the thinking was the point. After fear of the police it was loneliness, he remembered now, that had driven him on. Thoughts of Mr. Oliver and George and Polly and the Ghost and a girl he saw over at the Emporium one night standing in a window winding her brassy hair in her hands. Thoughts of his brothers and sister and his mother. The tenderness he felt sending him off looking for more of it.

Mr. Beall looked up from the tea he'd been steadily slurping for the last five minutes and asked if he would accompany him to town tomorrow. Delvin, brought sharply back, said yes sure.

The next morning he waked as Mrs. Beall was bringing the fire up in the kitchen. She didn't always make the fire, or when she did, she'd bank it for restarting in the morning. Just the two of them out here, she said—we don't need it. But this morning she built it up and made a large breakfast for them. While he and Mr. Beall were eating she packed a lunch in a small shellacked wicker basket. They had given him clothes to replace the dirty ones he showed up in. He carefully folded these and set them on the soft green coverlet on his bed and changed back into the washed originals. No one said anything to him, but he knew what was up. When in town Mr. Beall stopped the truck, handed him the little basket and told him it was time for him to go on his way he was not surprised. The old man pressed two one-dollar bills into his palm. Delvin hesitated a moment as if there was something he wanted to say, as if you could in a slender second or two like this somehow recount the goodness you'd found, the walks in the garden and the light shining unhampered over the fields and especially the human company, its softened edges and wandering, sympathetic talk, but there was no way to do this; he thanked him for his hospitality and started across the courthouse square. Four big water oaks squatted at the corners around the big rough granite building. He felt a sharp aloneness. He didn't know where to go. The town was small but he had to walk half an hour before he discovered a small colored neighborhood. It was really only two short streets past the cotton gin and a couple of warehouses. Cotton lint hung in the trees. It looked like dirty snow had fallen. Women, their lower lips pouched with snuff, gazed at him from their front porches. He went in a store and bought a grape soda. The woman who sold it to him studied him carefully. She seemed as if she would let him go without speaking, but as he turned away, she drummed her big fingers on the counter and asked, Who you visiting?

I been out here to see the Bealls, he said.

Oh, you're that boy.

Yes mam.

You off again.

Well, I would be, but I don't quite know the way.

Looks like you don't know how either.

No mam, I don't.

Where is it you headed?

Chattanooga.

I thought you was from Atlanta.

Well, I am, but I got folks to visit up in Tennessee.

She studied him with a sharp black eye. Her face was grayish as if she was not well, a thin woman wearing a khaki dress almost completely covered by a worn gray apron. Without turning her head she called out, Hankie!

A voice outside the back door called back, Mam?

Come in here.

A skinny man in faded overalls came in carrying a bucket.

Go over yonder and ask Mr. Sterling if he's going up to Chattanooga this morning.

Yessum.

She said all this without taking her eye off Delvin. You had your breakfast? she said.

Yes I have.

Well you can go wait out behind the store til Hankie gets back. Take your drink.

Delvin exited by the back screen door into a yard that was filled with stacked-up wooden crates of all sizes. On one side a bushy camphor tree with elegant dark leaves. On the other perched above a shallow ravine a small board cabin. He walked to the ravine and looked down into it. Trash of all kinds filled it. A pig tied to a stake ate melon rinds. On the other side two skinny brown dogs glanced up and went back to their meal. Delvin couldn't see what they were eating. Odd that they didn't bother the pig. On the far side of the ravine was a wide path bordered by a half-broken-down board fence. Beyond the fence were houses in dirt yards, a few fruit and chinaberry trees. A girl in a pale blue dress walked along the path. She carried a large basket of laundry.

Hope your day's going well, Delvin said across the divide.

The girl didn't answer. He watched her continue along the path and turn down a street out of sight.

He finished the drink and put the bottle in the little basket, sat down on a crate and began to make up a story. He hadn't done much writing work, but he figured his trip would give him many things to write about. He thought about the ex-confederate soldier living in the cottage. He might tell a story about him. This old white man who loved a black woman who had betrayed him with another. And so the man, who was much older than the young black woman, had given her and her husband the farm he owned just to make her stay close to him. He made them sign papers so they wouldn't move away or throw him off the place. He had even paid them to stay, a salary drawn off his accounts that he had set up from the sale of property he owned here in town. That was why the couple didn't do too much work. They were on salary. Maybe that was the story. Delvin wished he had a notebook with him. He had left in such a hurry that he hadn't thought about it. Remembering, his fear came back. Maybe he should stay out of C-town longer. He had been away a few months shy of a year. The police were probably looking for him still—or ready to start again if they caught a lead. They would always be looking for him. A sadness crept in on him. It was like an old unfriendly cat. Just then the girl came back around the corner. She still carried the now empty basket.

That your job? he called, delivering laundry for the neighborhood?

It was a foolish thing to say, he knew, but the girl's prettiness confused him.

The girl didn't look at him. Least I got one, she said.

He thought he caught a glimmer of a smile and didn't feel so alone. His old fantasy of being the intrepid man alone—one of his fantasies—had fallen quickly apart. The morning had a dewy, comfortable feeling to it. Salvia and mexican sage bloomed along the sides of the ravine. He walked along the way the girl had gone— she'd disappeared into one of the yards up ahead, but he didn't see

a way to cross unless he wanted to wade the rusty little stream at
the bottom, and he didn't. He liked wearing clean clothes, liked the
feeling of fullness from breakfast. Liked waiting.

He returned to the yard behind the store. The sky was touched
up here and there by a few high clouds like smears of white. The day
would be hot. He took a seat on a crate under the camphor tree. There
were camphor trees in the negro section of the municipal cemetery in
Chattanooga. He wondered who was on the funeral list. Mr. O studied the paper and listened to stories from the neighborhoods of Red
Row and kept a list, sometimes on a sheet of linen stationery in his
bedroom, sometimes simply in his head, of the ones who would most
likely be needing his services soon. He never spoke up ahead of time,
but he was ready when the day came. Often before he was called. Mrs.
Turnipseed was on the last list he'd seen, a middle-aged widow dying
of bowel cancer. Her whole house smelled of shit, somebody said.
One of the boys he smoked cigarettes with in the alley. And Rufus
Wainwright who had taken to his bed with rheumatism. He lay in a
room wallpapered with newspapers, listening to band music on the
radio, reading the headlines out loud. And they said little Eustace
Rogers, eleven, who had fallen off the roof onto the sharp palings of
an old wooden fence his father was keeping around, hoping to set it
up in his yard, wouldn't recover. There were others, the sick and the
aged mostly, occupants of the waiting room, Mr. O called them, and
Delvin had pictured them sitting in the colored-only room outside
the heavenly office, their straw suitcases and carpetbags closed with
string at their feet, old people and young, children too, some weeping, others stoical, others not understanding why they were there and
maybe only slowly figuring it out. What was the weather like outside
the window? There had to be a window. He pictured himself in that
room. He would be looking out the window at whatever was growing
in the yard. Probably mallow bushes and mock banana, a few straggly
corn plants, a rosebush dripping pink blooms, tomato vines lying on
the ground. He was coming to love the smell of the fields.

A little boy threw open the screen door and rushed out into the
yard.

Don't hit me with that switch, he cried to the woman who chased behind him. She was carrying a long, limber elm switch.

The little boy circled the yard, coming in close to Delvin under the tree. He shot him a glance of humiliation and regret and ran on by. The woman—his mother, Delvin assumed—stood just outside the doorway waiting for him. The little boy stopped on the edge of the ravine and looked at her.

You gon come here, Stacy? the woman said.

I aint coming to take no whipping, the boy said.

Well, if you don't then you don't get to come home at all.

The woman stared at the boy a moment longer and then wheeled and vanished back into the store. The little boy, six or seven, squatted and began to cry. Delvin watched him. After a while the boy dried his eyes with the bottoms of his hands, straightened up and came over to Delvin.

What you doing? he asked.

Waiting.

For what?

The bus.

Aint no bus come back here.

It's a different kind of bus.

You think my mama's gon whip me? the boy said with an almost saucy air.

Sure does look like it.

Well, she won't. I'll just wait out here til she gets lonely for me then I'll mosey on home.

How long will that be?

Oh, bout five minutes. He scratched his arms. Delvin could see the faint raised red circles of ringworm on his tan arms.

Shouldn't scratch that, he said.

I don't see how you can keep from it.

That what your mama's after you for?

That's it. He began to cry again. That doctor, he sniffed after a minute, wants to shave my head bald and paint it with grease that stings like fire.

That bad?

Sure is. I seen it done.

But those worms'll eat you alive.

He scratched mournfully at the rings. It's a problem that's got me in a vise grip, he said.

Just then the boy's mother pushed the screen door halfway open. Here's a strawberry drink, honey, she said, her voice light and tender. Come on now.

You gon beat me, the little boy said.

Come on sugarbite, his mother said, and the boy walked to her and took the drink and she put her hand on his shoulder and steered him into the store.

After a few minutes Delvin followed the boy inside. The pair were gone, but some men were sitting at a corkboard table set on a crate in a cleared space off to the side in back. The woman behind the counter looked at him as if she didn't know him. Then in a blink she did. She wiped her forehead with the back of her hand.

That's Sterling, she said to him, indicating with her elbow one of the men sitting at the table. They weren't playing a game, they weren't really sitting around the table, they were just near it. The man she indicated, a middle-aged stocky man with bushy hair mashed down under a forage cap, gave him a one-finger salute and said, We're waiting on my sister's boy. He grinned a grin of uselessness and amiable futility. Another of the men, an older fellow wearing a greasy black vest over a clean white collarless shirt, offered him a chair. Delvin slid in and joined the little confab. He was used to sitting with adults, listening to their talk. He had sat up in the viewing parlor or in the Home parlor on call for the bereaved who spoke in all kinds of ways, very often about things that had nothing to do with the dead. People, no matter what happened, kept their eye on the living side of things. The third man, a slim geezer with a fist-sized red rose pinned to the lapel of a yellow bathrobe he kept pulling tighter around himself, looked as if he might be joining the funeral list pretty soon. I'm Albert, he said, offering slim shiny fingers for Delvin to shake. Yes, he said, turning back to the group, my grandfather won that election fair and true. Eighteen seventy-four, he said, turning his narrow face to Delvin, Slidell—fair and true.

What for? Delvin asked.

Why, the US Congress, the man Albert said.

He went on to tell how his grandfather had served two terms before he was thrown out of office after the soldiers left in '78.

They put it to him straight over the barrel of a Spencer rifle that it was not in his best interests to run for Congress, or any other office, again, he said.

Sho they did, the older man said. Happened all over this country down here. After the US government left.

He was a tall man, Albert said, six and a half feet. He had a natural bearing to him. A smart man, too. He proposed we open the southern part of the state with canals to help with trade—dig em straight to the Gulf—but nobody would vote for the measure. He never got over losing his office. He wound up living out on Mr. Roscoe Tillman's farm.

Up here, Mr. Sterling said.

Sure. Out in one of the cabins down by the river. Just sitting out there on the front porch in a old rocking chair, like he was dreaming with his eyes open.

Did you know him? Sterling asked.

I did when I was a boy. He wore his Congress suit of black cloth, white shirt and a little black string tie. He was a handsome man.

I remember him well, the older man said. He came up here eventually to live with his sister, aint that right?

Yessuh.

They sighed and made soft sounds like swallowed humming and Delvin listened as the stories went around. The old man told a story about a magician who kept losing things. You know that magic's just a trick, he said, but this fellow—lived over just outside Birmingham in a little crossroads settlement I believe it was, called Cherrytown, and he had a magic act at the Gifford show.

What you mean he started losing things? Albert said.

These objects that he made disappear, for his show act, he got so he couldn't bring em back. First, so they said, it was a blue rubber ball. You know how they wave a cloth or some such thing and it'll disappear? Well he waved his cloth over this blue ball and it disappeared, but when he went to wave it again it wouldn't come back.

Where was it? Albert asked.

That was the thing. He didn't know. He looked everywhere for that ball but it didn't show up. He wondered about it, so they said, but he didn't think too much of it. Maybe it had rolled off under the couch or something. Then a Mason jar filled with honeybees disappeared and was lost forever. Same way as the rubber ball. He waved the cloth over the jar and presto it was gone, but then it wouldn't come back. That jar filled with bees—he'd punched holes in the lid so they could breathe and so the customers could hear the bees buzzing—was gone for good.

Haw, Sterling said. It had to be somewhere.

Well, where was it? Nobody saw it again. He tried the trick again, with a new silver dollar and . . . wham! . . . it vanished and was never heard from again. He couldn't find it in any of the pockets it usually wound up in. He tried the trick on a little hairless dog and the dog vanished. Gone for good, though his little girl, whose dog it was, said she sometimes could hear the dog's squeaky little bark, ghostly like, as she lay in her bed at night. Well, he didn't know what to do. He didn't know whether he had discovered a blessing or a curse. He tried it on a bushel of fresh peaches and lost all the cobblers his wife was planning to make for the lawn supper over at the church. He tried it on a pile of trash in the backyard and found a lazy man's way to work.

It was gone too, Delvin said.

Like it had never been there. He decided that this was a power that he had to be careful with. It was too important to use as a trick. He wouldn't use it at all. But then a thought began to come on him. He started to wonder if it would work on a person. He'd never got along with his wife. She was a fine woman, but she had a sharp tongue, as the wives of magicians are said to have. She was on him night and day. Even with the new power he was still not bringing any income into the family circle. His wife began to nag him to use the power in his act. He would become the best known magician around, and maybe the richest. He pointed out that not being able to bring back what you made disappear cut into the value of the trick. That didn't matter to his wife. She went right on picking at him. Plenty of folks, she said, want to get rid of things. Think about all that trash, those busted wagons and such and old barrels you see piled up in people's yards. You want me to be a garbage collector? I want you to collect a few dollars, she said. Well, finally he decided that he would use the trick one more time. He'd use it to get rid of his wife.

Albert guffawed.

Yes, thass right, the old man said, bending toward his listeners. He licked his narrow black lips. As his wife sat sleeping in her porch rocker one Sunday afternoon he took out his cloth, so they said, and with his daughter and his daughter's new fyce pup watching, he waved it over his wife. The old man paused. Could you get me another lemon drink there, Sally? he asked the proprietress. And sat back in his chair.

Damnation, Sterling said, what happened? Did she disappear?

Naw.

It didn't work?

Oh, it worked.

But she didn't vanish?

Naw. *He* did.

Albert guffawed as Sterling sputtered. He half-raised a fist in mock attack. You rascal.

It's a true story, said the old man, smiling behind white store teeth.

There were other stories. A man in khaki clothes, juggling boxes of 20 Mule Team Borax, joined them and told a story of his uncle who walked from California to Alabama, traveling through the desert for hundreds of miles carrying water in two army canteens. He said his uncle, Uncle Dorrit, told him that one night the stars filled the sky so thick they looked like they were poured out of a bucket. They formed themselves as he lay watching them. Took shapes, like clouds on a summer day. They made shapes of houses and horses and absent relatives and the shape of a huge angel right at the top of the sky. The day after this happened his uncle came on a donkey walking loose in the scrub and he rode this donkey through New Mexico and across Texas through the byways and little hamlets and across Louisiana, through Mississippi into Alabama and all the way to his home on the Jemeson farm out from Dothan.

I thought you said he walked, Delvin said.

I did, but I misremembered. He only walked part of the way.

The man in the bathrobe, Albert, told a story of a two-headed child who strangled one of the heads so he could have the whole body to himself.

The others laughed, but Morris said the story was true. The man told the family that the other head—his brother—had died during the night. They had to cut the dead head off and they buried it in an apple crate. But the man felt so much remorse for the murder that he fled his home and disappeared. It was said that he traveled around the country by himself, taking a job here and there—bean picker in California, deliveryman in Kansas for a dairy—but never staying any place long. In some places he pretended to be his brother, even though no one in the place knew either of them. He called himself by his brother's name and wore the kind of clothes his brother preferred. At night in his room—he stayed usually in a rooming house—people could hear what sounded like two people talking. Sometimes they'd argue and sometimes one begged forgiveness from the other, a forgiveness the other would never give, and sometimes they would sing a duet. How that could be no one knew, but two voices is what some people said they heard, singing old songs like "Wonder Where Is Good Old Daniel" and "'Buked and Scorned." Almost always the old jubilees, folks said. He was a good worker, people said. He had a habit of leaning his head over to one side, like he was resting it on something, and when he did this a wistful, tearful look would come into his face. He never stayed in any job long, never stayed long in any place. One day you'd see him on the road walking toward the next town. Or maybe you wouldn't see him at all. The housekeeper would come into his room and find the bed made and the towel and washcloth neatly folded and dust tracks on the floor where he tried to sweep the room clean. Usually there was a note and the note always said the same thing. *My brother and I thank you for our stay.* It was said he left the rural life and moved to the city where he took jobs in restaurants, working in sculleries washing dishes and such. Some people in the cities had heard of the two-headed man, some had even heard that one of the heads had died, but nobody suspected this man of being that person. It was said that in the beginning he lived in rooming houses, even in a small apartment a few blocks from the river, but then, so it was said, he began to appear in flops and missions where often his few belongings were stolen and his wistful look was taken for a sign of weakness and he was sometimes beaten up. He moved to the streets, where he lived in alleys and parks. On summer nights sometimes you could see him sitting by the river. Some said he had a little dog, a spotted mongrel, that followed him everywhere. Others said he had no dog. Eventually no one saw him again. Once or twice some reporter, having got wind of an old story that was said to involve such a man, something overheard in a newsman's bar, would look for him, but he was not found. It was said that one summer night—when Castor and Pollux were in their ascendancy—he slipped into the river and was carried away.

By this time a couple of others had joined the group around the makeshift table and they too offered their stories. One spoke of a pack of wolves living in an abandoned house on one of the great cotton plantations to the west. Another told of money, confederate gold, buried in malachite chests along the Porterville Road, some said, at the bottom of a pond in a cypress grove. Another said he knew that grove, but he had heard of no money buried out there.

Wadn't no gold left among those folks after the yankees got through with them, Albert said and everybody laughed.

Around them the great fields of cotton stretched away in every direction, the last fields in the last big cotton county before the mountains. The split bolls leaked white fiber and on a clear night the earth seemed covered with small showy stars. As the stories went around a feeling grew in Delvin that his life's journey had begun. He had not thought of journeys in particular, not his or anyone's, outside a book, but the strong feeling came that he was beginning on a journey of journeys. Not just this little jaunt down the road from C-town, but on from here (even if he was already on the way back to his birthplace) farther and farther. He wanted to ask Mr. Sterling when they would be leaving. He was afraid to, what with his circumstances; he got up, went over to the corner and sat down beside some stacked boxes of canned beans. In a few minutes he had drifted into a light sleep. He dreamed of a boy tussling with another boy who was as tall as a giant, and of leaping off a viney bridge into a great green river, and of dancing in front of a pretty girl, and of washing long yellow rolls of cloth in a barbecue restaurant kitchen, and of a dog that understood everything he said. He could still hear the voices of the men droning on. They were trying to top each other's stories. He wasn't sure whether he was awake or asleep. He started to say something and then Mr. Sterling was shaking him by the shoulder. He jumped to his feet. In only a few quick minutes he was out front in bright sunshine tossing his bindle into Sterling's dusty Chevrolet pickup and the two of them were headed out of town.

He rode turned away from the man—older, with ragged gray hair under a gray felt hat and above a dark-complected face—because he had an erection. It came up shortly after they got in the car. Sterling had glanced at him and Delvin thought he saw his minor predicament. The town flowed away from them and they were in the country. Tall red spires of sumac flowers by the road, cattails in the ditches spilling their stuffing. In front of a squashed-looking white house, lumberous oaks with dark green leaves. The trees made the house look small and lonely. What was it he had been dreaming about? He remembered: fights and friendly dogs, and something else, something muted, stepping from a stillness that didn't want to stay still. His plans seemed silly now as he traveled through the farmed countryside. What of the old man in the cottage? Would he just sit on his porch waiting for the woman until he died? Was there a contest, fight of wills and desire and hopes going on without cease on that farm? Did the Bealls lie awake at night struggling with loss and consequences, decisions made that changed everything? The path down into the piney woods was well traveled. By whom? It hurt that he would never know.

Delvin's familiar erection passed. He didn't know where these traveling erections came from, what they were about. He wasn't charged up by sex right now. They hung around then drifted off like some corner rogue who'd thought of something else. A streak of high white cloud narrowed in the west. The fields were planted with cotton mostly, some with barley, some with hay grass. Mr. Sterling talked of his family—a wife and two boys who were mostly grown. The boys worked in town at the Easy Buy Tire store, fixing flats and putting new tires on trucks and tractors. In houses they passed—isolated farmhouses, tenant shanties, farmworker cabins in a row under sycamore trees—tragedies, commonplace occurrences, religious makeovers, births, nonsensical familiar arguments, were taking place. A wife threw boiling water at her hateful son and missed him. An old man lay in bed choking on a radish. A little boy with a pale white scar on his heel stood on the seat of a hay rake, tottering, about to fall into a harrow's teeth. A man spoke on the party line to his brother, wondering what they should get Mother for her birthday. A tea caddy? his brother asked. A young woman who had lost her husband's gold-plated watch cried in her bedroom, sorry she had ever married and left her home. An aging ne'er-do-well, father of eight, paused on the back steps to look back at a field of flowering purple vetch, thinking that the beauty of the world was endless.

Time passed and the closer to Chattanooga they got the more scared Delvin became. He had tried to forget his predicament but he couldn't and now it flopped out onto him like a bitter truth. The closer he got the surer he was that he couldn't go back. The police were waiting. Delvin knew what the penalty was for shooting a white boy. His mother had fled a killing herself, taking to the woods after she had brained that old haberdasher in the hallway behind his shop. No forgiveness for her in this world. And none for him. He felt a rush of feeling for his mother, and tears rose in the corners of his eyes. He trembled and he put his hands on the dashboard to steady himself. His hands looked wrinkled and old and this frightened him more. As they passed through a small railroad hamlet he asked Mr. Sterling to stop the truck. You all right, boy? the man asked. I think I changed my mind—I forgot something back yonder. Well too late to go back for it. I got to, Delvin said. The old man pulled over in front of a small hardware store on the main street. Behind the store the train tracks ran north and south. Thank you, sir, Delvin said, and he gave the man his one case dollar left. The man didn't want to take it but then he took it anyway. Delvin got down and stood in the dust watching the truck go on up the road. A crow, passing from here to there, croaked as it flew. He headed around back to the tracks to wait for a train.

So his real travels began. He rode the trains that passed through dinky towns and entered big cities through the back doors and he rested on the top of boxcars smelling of rotted grain and rode the gunnels when he had to and swung onto the metal porches of gondolas and spoke with men who had wandered so far that they had almost outdistanced their own bodies and become ghosts, and he learned to dodge the bulls and the rough riders, and he picked up what he could working here and there, baling hay and hoeing bush beans and winding tobacco leaves onto sticks, and everywhere he went the stories collected and the unpainted domiciles of black citizens stood before him like memories of olden times and he entered new worlds life by life and gathered there his tares and offered what he could and the days passed clanking or whispering along the chain of his life. At night sometimes a loneliness like a lost letter found him in his bed in a cottonhouse or on a forest floor or inside the patternless wooden walls of a boxcar and it tried to explain to him that he would never find a home but he refused to listen and turned his back and gazed out at the moonlight standing in wet grass like an angelina too shy to come inside. Time sang its cracked songs in rail yards and along the edges of the fields and passed on, leaving half memories and slights and a false heartiness and belly laughs and cold suppers on somebody's sagging back steps: the poor-mouthings of a crass deceiver he took little count of and rarely worried about.

The dots of blackness on each calendar date, marking another day when the police did not come pulling at him, rousting him from a hobo jungle or barn or back steps, added time, freedom from what he knew was awaiting him. He carried this knowledge of the pursuit like a stranger, dark man, darker than he was, accompanying him into whatever town he passed through, whatever road he walked along, slipping with him at night into open fields or woods or along leafy riverbanks. It was in this flight, in these days, that he touched his mother again. Beside a stream in Louisiana choked with rusty foam he found himself dreaming of her so profoundly that he thought he lay with his head in her lap listening to her sing "Old Johnny Jones," one of the songs she had sung to him under the little peach tree in their backyard in Chattanooga. He too was a runner, he had wanted to say, he too knew pursuit, but she faded before he could get the words out. In dawns of swirling fog he called silently to her, but she never answered. The days came up, wintry or steaming with heat, and in them he felt the press of the law. But always he felt the reassurance of his mother, escapee and wanderer, out ahead of him somewhere on the roads or crossing a river on a hand-pulled ferry, sitting by a campfire or dancing on a stage before admiring crowds, and gradually in these dreams, these fantasies or reveries or boy's make-believe, she bent toward success, toward kindness and elaboration, rosy with life, resting as a free woman in a happiness that was the happiness of dreams, and in these dreams he too was free.

BOOK TWO

1

He was walking one fall day along an unpaved side street in the dark quarter in Yellow Cross, Mississippi, when he passed a black-painted truck the size and shape of a small moving van. The truck was parked in front of an African Holiness church. On the side in dusty gold letters were the words *Negro Museum of the Americas.* In back was a door and a fold-down set of steps. A slim middle-aged africano man in a long tan canvas duster shiny at the elbows and a soft black felt hat sat on the step eating cantaloupe chunks out of a white bowl. Delvin asked him what this was, this museum. The man cocked his head, continued chewing until he could swallow good and then turned and squinted up at the high back of the vehicle.

"You mean this here?" he said, smiling, showing flat white teeth. "This is the only traveling museum of the american negro in existence."

Delvin felt a jolt of pleasure. "A real museum," he said.

"Exactly right. Photos mostly, but in fact a record of the negro's trials and sufferings and joys on this side of the Atlantic ocean."

"Could I take a look?"

"Why certainly. Only cost you a nickel."

Delvin allowed as he had an extra nickel at that time and would be pleased to spend it on such an operation.

The man put the bowl down on the steps, took out a large yellow handkerchief and with gestures ceremonial wiped his mouth and hands.

"You produce the cash and I'll open her up for you."

The man had an accent like a northern white man, and his facial features—narrow nose, thin lips, soft green eyes—were those of a white man, but he was as black nearly as he was—sealblack, they called it.

The man—Professor Carmel, he called himself—produced a flat
brass key, opened the back door and ushered Delvin into the van,
stepping ahead of him to raise the canvas shades on one side. Along
the back and other side walls were photographs, hundreds of them.
On a table running down the long closed side were stacks of objects,
jumbled together, among them skulls and batons and whisks and
feathery headdresses and flutes and what looked like a gilded cham-
ber pot. The photographs dominated the exhibit.

Delvin walked around the room that was as large nearly as the
house he was born in, looking at the pictures. The man lit a kerosene
lamp that made no impression on the daylight streaming under the
rolled-up canvas shades and hung it from a brass hook in the ceiling.
Delvin studied the photographs. Flat black-and-white representa-
tions, the stillness of each, the caughtness, gestures trapped, looks
riveted to the paper, people turning and never getting there, the place-
ments, the issuance of cries uncried, the smiles or grim looks, the
sadness in a boy's eyes, the girl looking at her mother who was fixing
her hair with what looked like a gold bobbin—these only gradually
touched him. Records of a moment pressed on either side by what
came before and what was coming after. They all—all the africanos—
knew what had been, had a pretty good idea of what was on its way.
The proprietor, bent down under the table, fiddled with something,
made a quick frantic motion and suddenly the scratchy voice of Bessie
Smith flew up like a big yellow bird filling the van. Hurt and desolation, the crime of being black, the uselessness of fighting back, fear
like a grime covering every surface, the tremors and quakes, a softness in the heart you couldn't obliterate. He saw the hoes lifted in
cotton fields like the specialized instrumentation of an anonymous
and preposterous camarilla, men poised like dancers in barn rafters
lifting long sticks upon which were strung the limp assegaial tobacco
leaves, children standing waist deep in dew-drenched fields of cotton
tobacco corn beans and peanuts bushy as gallberry shrub, or men
posed in ditches over a dark infrangible corpus with pickaxes raised
like the ceremonious antlery of some white man's loony pestiferation.
He had seen much on the roads, much that wasn't found here, or

not on this day. Old men battered until their faces looked like a coal seam turned inside out. Boys used for the smoothness of their bodies. Women squatted by the tracks, heads and shoulders powdered in coal dust, waiting like mail sacks containing no good news for the next hard hook to snatch them up. Some of this was here. The music pressed him on, pressed the pictures as if they were leaves of a tree gathered again in reverse progeneration into the big armory of leafage.

He couldn't take in half of these photos, not a tenth. Many were stuck like markers in big books. He liked the books themselves, the large folios, cloth and leather bound, stuffed with progeny. He ran his hands over their covers as the keeper showed them to him. The music scratched itself out. Suddenly he had to get away.

He rose up qualmous and shaking, abruptly overfretted in his mind. No not that exactly—scared he had for a second lost his sense of where he was, like the time he'd dreamed a moment longer than he needed to and almost pitched headfirst off the ladder of a Baton Rouge–bound freight car.

He set the book down (he had been by now sitting on the lowest of the van's two back steps, out in the air) and staggered across the dust-charged street into a field grown up in plantains and pokeweed. He thrashed through these greeny drifts and pulled up in a little cleared space where somebody had once made a campfire. Some wanderer. "That is what I am," Delvin said. Said and slumped to his knees and over, passed out, like somebody graved into by the heat.

He came to with the professor man dripping cold water in his face.

"Come on boy, you're not all right but you will live."

"Don't be so sure," Delvin said.

The man rocked back on his heels and laughed. He raised the white china bowl that now contained water. "Here." He held the bowl to Delvin's mouth and let him drink. The water tasted pleasantly of cantaloupe.

He told Professor Carmel that he had for many years worked—was raised actually—in a funeral home, and when the prof asked which

one and he told him he said with a broad smile that showed off his
fine large teeth that he knew old Oliver well.

"A bit spendthrift with his emotions, but honorable and a fine
consistency of service," he said.

It made Delvin less lonely to hear this. He had been lonely for
several days, maybe longer. Riding freights was generally a social
activity of a kind, but due to a sweep by railroad detectives along
the Southern line, he'd had to lay low in a canebrake by himself for
three days before catching a local freight out of Metusa, a rattling
train empty of cargo but for some loads of furniture and no other rail
companions.

"You know something about the departed," Prof Carmel said in
a friendly way.

"I know something about how to prepare a body."

"Fancy up the meat," Carmel said.

"Most folks consider it showing respect for what's coming.
Don't want to meet the Lord in your work clothes—"

"Worms and beetles are what's coming," the prof said.

Delvin believed pretty much the same thing, cosmologically
speaking, but he didn't generally like anybody else pressing on him
in some righteous way that he had to believe this too. It didn't matter
what side of the theological fence people were on, they got hard-
shelled about it quick enough. But the professor had given his cor-
rection or opinion in a genial way.

"Yall photograph up there?" he said.

"You mean the deceased? No, we don't. Some do it by their own
arrangements, but we don't encourage it."

"Why not?"

"We don't discourage it either, but I think Mr. Oliver would
rather people mourn by way of living memory. He's not pushy about
it though. He just doesn't promote the service."

"People are interesting no matter what shape they're in, don't you
think?"

"Yes I do."

"Look at these," he said and pulled a long drawer out from a flat cabinet under the table.

Attached to big sheets of thick black paper were photographs of negro men hanging from the limbs of trees by their necks. Here we add to the number, he thought. Here we add to it. He wanted to turn away again. A nausea gripped him. Good lord, good lord. That boy out in the country, hanged and chopped and burned half away. It had been too much. It was still too much. This was too much.

As he bent to look at the bodies, some broken-necked, some burned so their arms were tapered stumps, some denatured, some with whip marks showing on their blood-greased naked backs, some gutted, one wearing high top shoes with the laces still tied in immaculate bows, another looking like the man who used to sell parched peanuts on the courthouse square—every one somebody, looking like somebody—he experienced a collapsing sensation as if he had soiled his pants, but he hadn't. His private self shrank from the surface of his body, yielding inward like walls falling in on once safe rooms. He didn't like it that Carmel had held these for last. Crippled, scarred, half-skinned, mutilated—still it was the faces that held him. Lonesome negro faces surrounded by the upturned faces of white men. No, not lonely, he had it wrong. He hadn't been looking close enough; he had hardly been looking at all. But he saw it now: the faces of those no longer there. But not even that. No. He saw it: only the white men were there. All alone in the world they made. They were the ones who lived again in a universe made up of only their kind. Not again, but for once, finally. He shuddered. Many of the white faces were blank. No, not blank—he couldn't get it right at first either—: addled, sated, entranced. But not that, no, not even that. They had the look of the rapturously crazed. Something tucked way down behind their souls had leapfrogged to the front. Yes. But not so quickly—and this is what he saw—that he couldn't make out the shocked and hopeless expression still visible behind the stuporous glee. And this, the pictures whispered, to his face or behind his back as he turned away, is your fate. He shuddered as a chill flashed across his body and he staggered, catching himself against the table. He coughed into his fist.

"You see how human beings really are," said the professor.

"White men," Delvin said. He just said that. It was like saying "The devil." No need to mention him.

The professor went to pull another sheet out, but Delvin stayed him with a touch of his hand on the tray. He turned back to the pictures on the walls. The van smelled of onions and sweat and of another, chemical, odor which the professor said was ferrous sulphate, from developing the photos. He stared again at the faces of the living. A little boy trailed a cotton sack behind him like a long fat grub. In his face a guilelessness, a comfortableness, you could call it a happiness. Shirtless, in overalls, and wearing a huge sombrero style hat, he looked back at Delvin with a gentleness that nearly brought tears to his eyes. Crying not for the dead—he'd learned this in the funeral business—but for the lifebound living. This wasn't the only face that held him. There were others, skips and jumps of faces, expressions, dull and crisp and bloated or filled with a fierceness that stirred him and scared him and made him feel a churning in his guts and even deeper. An old woman with a wide fleshy gleaming face and flared nostrils looked out with an eagerness to please and so much . . . it was sorrow . . . that he laughed outloud, himself shocked. In many faces fright mingled with a desire to please. Others were as nearly blank as the faces of the lyncherous white men, though not so often erased. A man caught for murder (so a hand-lettered tag said) looked at him with cold eyes in a grimly smiling face; his lower lip looked as if it had been bitten in two and sewn roughly back together. Stunned faces, terrified faces, smashed and reconstituted faces, organized faces and the faces of the holy and the hustling, the light-complected face of a man in a high white collar and thin tie who looked as if nothing in the world could touch him. Faces that wanted to shame him and faces that made him want to slap them. A little girl with a high wide forehead and small intense eyes he wanted to kiss. Two old men sitting on the front steps of a grocery store laughing fit to bust.

And behind him the white faces of men looking up from the

lynching field at the body of a black man or gazing at the camera as if they didn't know what a camera was.

But then here were others, pinned to the opposite wall, spilling out of other big flat books, flows and gatherings—of silliness, of running and jumping, of yelling and delight. A woman laughed open-mouthed, a man beat time with sticks on a porch floor as two other men out in the dust before a spurt of campfire danced an ebullient jig. A congregation lustily sang. A man petted a horse's face, the look in both of their eyes, horse and man, compelled and kindly. A boy called across a river to other boys rising like dolphins from the glassy water. Children rode a mule, old men played dominoes, gripping their laughter like it was a great fish they were landing by hand. A band marched, brass raised, down a sunny street. A little boy on a top step contemplated his stretched-out feet. An old woman whelmed with glee. A girl in a checkered headrag wiped sweat off her forehead, grinning over a big bowl of ice cream. A man in a dark suit bent over a tablet. Cascade of fellowship, of tickling or guffaws or brimmed-up festiveness. Children on top of a wagonload of cotton high as a house. Chuckling babies, women shouting in joy.

He turned away with tears in his eyes.

"Yessir," Carmel said as he tapped the flats with the heel of his hand to straighten them, "you can see the true life of the race in these pictures."

It took a minute for Delvin to draw himself together. A coolness came into his mind, and it was only then that he realized how tired he was.

The museum keeper had turned away, giving him time, rustling among his photos, gathering, careful to keep his fingers from the impacted centers of the paper.

"Ah, lord," Delvin said.

"Yes, sholy. Like a mashed-up sweet potato."

Delvin smiled. He indicated a photograph of men and women standing in front of a white-painted church with a half-finished steeple.

"That's over in east Tennessee," Carmel said. "That church has since been burned to the ground."

It was the church where the funeral for the slain boy was held. "I've been there," he said. "I *was* there."

He told Carmel about the fire (set by unknown white men) and a little about his life as an undertaker's assistant, parts of a past he rarely talked about for his aging but still lively fear of Chat-town police.

"That's quite an education," Carmel said. He looked at the boy who was disheveled and needed a haircut, but who had the gleam of intelligence in his fine brown eyes. "You just touring around the country?"

"You might say that."

"They kick you out of the funeral business?"

"No, 'twern't that."

"You don't have to go into it. We all from time to time stick our foot into the dung heap."

"I'm looking to further my education," Delvin said. Said it and meant it—had said it before—even though he was tired out by all the instruction he'd received in the van. But he liked the smell of the place, liked the old man puttering about.

"Racewise you got a full education gathered right here in one location, my boy."

Delvin on the spot decided to postpone his rod-riding travels. He spent the night in a hobo camp outside town and returned the next day and the next. On the third the professor invited him to hang around and gave him little chores to do. On the fifth day he proposed that Delvin join him on the road.

He saw that Delvin carried a little blue notebook and a couple of cedarwood pencil nubs and told him to take notes if he wanted to.

"In fact," he said, "I recommend it."

He spoke to him of the great power and destiny of the African peoples. The Wandering Negro, he called them.

"That's us," he said. "We are loose in the world, free to wander the earth poking our noses into whatever interests us. Many will complain and grieve about our plight, and it's true it looks, especially in certain areas, as if the white man has the upper hand, yes.

But this is only appearances. In the kingdom of the spirit, we are so far ahead of these lily-livered folk that it is really our job to take care of *them*. Look at us. Stolen from our homes and sold into slavery, mistreated, raped and lynched, and still we find a way to love the work of the Lord, if you want to call it that, or the natural creations of the universe if you don't. That church you are familiar with. It's not just a house of worship—rebuilt, by the way—it's a depot, a trolley stop, a way station and refreshment stand for those traveling this world of pain and struggle. In religion after religion you find at the heart of God a mystery. That same mystery is in everything, every rose—it's in every dog or pig, every human being. In that mystery is the power of life. Not only the existence of life, but the purpose as well. The mystery is at the heart of life itself. A perplexity, a boggler. Everywhere you turn you find it. Who are we? Who is that lovely young woman over there? What did you mean by saying that? Who are you? A life of questions. Well, we don't need so many questions really. Our job, son, through living, through love, through helping one another along in this wilderness, is to snug up with it. Simply that."

He stared at Delvin with an expectant expression in his cool green eyes as if he had just explained everything.

Delvin looked him straight back. "With the *mystery*?" he said.

"Damn, you're right," Carmel cried, chuckling. "That *must* be what I mean." He laughed, a croaky, slappy laugh. "Yes, son, with the mystery. We are the ones supposed to get up close and hug it till it squeaks."

"You mean, colored folk?"

"I do indeed. We are the only ones got the heart for the job."

He went on to explain that this wandering life—plus, he said, the willingness to bear burdens without complaint—was—"were," he said—exactly the recipe for getting down to the heart of said mystery.

This last was spoken at a dinner they ate at Fanny's Hot Shop over on Washington street in the quarter. Carmel informed Delvin that he was on the run from forces that were dedicated to the elimination of the negro race in general and him in particular.

"The materials I carry in my little traveling museum are a threat to the well-being of certain elements that will not be deterred until they have put out of existence the truths these materials contain. And I have to admit, it is true that in some quarters what I carry has the eliminatary aspects of a bomb. Built to blow the foolish, sanctimonious notions of these folks right out of the water. In a generous, in a kindly, way," he added, his eyes twinkling.

As it turned out, Carmel had received this caravan of truths from a white man, his former employer, Dr. Haskell Sullivan, the famous ethnologist from the University of Chicago. Dr. Sullivan, with whom Professor Carmel had worked for many years as driver and helper of all kinds, and finally as partner, "in the ethnological enterprise you see before you" (they were back with the van, parked now in a field next to a little brushy river), had passed the outfit on to Carmel when he was taken with spasms and became too ill to continue.

"What kind of spasms?" Delvin asked.

"Hard to say. Gut mainly. He'd also lost a bit in the head department. I had to put him in a home over in Jackson. I left him on the front steps of the Berrins Home for the Aged with a note pinned to his coat."

This was six days into their association. Delvin sat in sweet-smelling roadside grass on a rice mat provided by Carmel. By then Carmel had told him to call him Professor. They were drinking sugar cane juice from white china mugs.

"It was five years ago this September," the professor said, "that I said goodbye to that fine white man on the steps of the charity home. When I am in the area I stop by and check on him. He is still alive, but only in body. His mind has become part of the great mystery."

This mystery the professor spoke of hung like a misty picture in Delvin's mind. His life was filled with mystery. Everywhere he looked he was baffled and diverted.

In days to come the professor gave Delvin books to read: novels, poetry, polemics, race stories, histories, uplift books and books de-

signed to probe the ways of men on the earth. Many of these books
were written by black authors, and not just the big-timers like Du Bois
and Washington and Sojourner Truth. There were slim softbacks
printed on flimsy paper written by men sweating away, so Carmel
said, in Manhattan and Brooklyn tenements, and books written by
africano men living over in Europe, and men in Chicago, and even
Memphis. Why, in Memphis, he said, there was a small publish-
ing house that specialized in literature written by negro men—and
women—for the negro race only. He owned some of these books.
They tended to be long arguments concerning the superiority of the
negro race, most of them, as well as a few that counseled brotherhood and love. In one Carmel showed him, the author Seneca Wilson—a nom de plume, Carmel said—wrote of the vacancy in white
men's faces and the "digested fullness" in black faces ("This goes
right along with what I've pointed out to you in the photographs,"
Carmel said, smiling). The faces were empty, Wilson said, because
white people, by way of their long defense of their "rightness," their
right to consider themselves the top dogs in life, had lost touch with
faithfulness. This showed in the wrenched-up greed in their faces
("When the disease of corruption has reached the bone, there's
nothing left but greed and self-importance," he said), whereas the
negro man, who lived in a disheveled and turmoil-filled state, one
he was constantly having to call for help with and constantly getting knocked around by, had thereby come on a much deeper understanding of the great mysteries of being. As you could plainly see in
the face of every negro person you met.

It wore Delvin out to read all this.

Other books proclaimed the day when the negro man would rise
up and by force of simple righteousness take his rightful place at
the head of the table. It scared Delvin to read these and gave him a
guilty thrill. He had not thought particularly of these matters. The
world belonged to the white man. Delvin and his kind were merely
scumbling through it. They were stranded in a country whose language was not theirs and whose customs were foreign to them. They
did their best under these circumstances. Nothing he knew of had

corrupted the spirit of negro folk, not in any significant way. Even the lynchings. Sojourner Truth said it was most important to show love and concern for those around us, colored or white. This was the only way to show our love of God, she said. Love meant freedom from oppression. Somehow it soothed him to read this. But many of the negro writers appeared to be girding up for a fight.

He spoke of this to Carmel who listened with his small cropped head down. They were parked behind the Bethlehem Baptist church in the african quarter in New Hope, Mississippi.

"If it's their country, then where is our country?" Carmel asked.

"I thought you saw our greatness as being people not tied to any place."

"It *is* our greatness," Carmel said, stretching his short legs out in front of him. He sat on the van's back step; Delvin sat on the tufty grass in front of him. The summer-dry leaves of a sycamore above their heads creaked in a faint breeze.

"And though we are become a wandering people," Carmel said, "we nevertheless come from somewhere."

"Yeah—Africa."

The professor held up his hand. The butterscotch palm was crossed by a wild hatch of lines.

"Wait. I know a couple of those books say we arrived here in big ships swung down from the heavens—from outer space somewhere parked on the backside of Jupiter—but truth is we come from the great empires of Africa."

"I just said—"

"Wait. We are the descendants of mighty rulers." He went on to explain how the stepped-on negro folk of the US of A were the natural children of great chiefs who had ruled vast African empires. "Just imagine how much fortitude and imagination it took to rule a continent as fierce and wild as Africa. That's not one of those puny so-called civilized countries of Europe. No sir."

He went on to explain how this fact was not so much the important consideration as the fact that Africa was the cradle of life, home of the original Garden of Eden and other great gardens and general stomping places, the most ancient of lands on the earth and thereby the place not only black people but all people must one day return to. "Except this time when the white people show up," he said, "they will find the colored folks in charge. They will have to ask us about how the proceedings are supposed to go."

"And what will we tell them?" Delvin said.

"Why, we will tell them to pick up a hoe and get to chopping that cotton." He laughed. "Go forth," he said, waving his hand, "that's what we will tell them—and get yourselves a little first-class suffering."

Delvin couldn't help but laugh, it all sounded so comical. But he also couldn't help being excited by what he heard and what he read in the slim floppy books. He'd agreed by then to come along more or less permanently with Carmel and work as his helper. After a week on the road he was driving the van and doing the cleaning work on the exhibits. The prof had not only photographs but a small collection of artifacts that included woven baskets, quilts, pipes, drums, fired bowls, woodcarvings, a few painted pictures (of well-dressed, healthy negro folk giving speeches, preaching or gathered together by a river talking among themselves), two Union army uniforms, a few bushee sticks for warding off evil at night and goofer bags and other conjur potions in little blue bottles and a collection of ty-ty seed and claystone necklaces.

"I intend to rustle up more of these curios," he said, "when I get more room."

"Are you looking for a home for all this?"

"I am and I am not," the professor said. "I want to transfer this knowledge into as many minds as possible and in these dreary days it is best to bring the knowledge to the people instead of the other way around. But one day . . . one day," he said, smiling his wide, thin-lipped smile. He began to laugh as if everything he was saying and everything he was doing was a pleasant joke he was playing on the world.

They drove from town to town, parked in the africano sections and opened for business. A nickel per, able to accommodate ten people at a time, the money added up. They ate at colored restaurants or stood in line behind white restaurants at the window for colored folks or supped in people's homes when invited (which happened not as often as the prof would have liked) and slept on the floor of the van or out beside it under a canvas awning. They were usually not bothered by the police and the local white population because the professor generally stopped off at the station first thing to offer a contribution to the police general welfare fund. He was well known and genially mocked in most towns and usually left alone. Since he stayed in the africano areas only he did not interfere with the dreams and illusions of white folks and trouble if it came was usually unco-ordinated and of the variety that included fruit or hand-sized vege-tables thrown at the big black van. Once a bucket of limewash was thrown from a passing vehicle, but the bucket missed and splashed across the front steps of the Pisgah AME church in New Constance, a town that over both east and west entrances had white-painted fili-greed rose-climbing arches welcoming all good christian folk.

Delvin met stern-mouthed gents and audibly sighing women and little boys carrying big bandanas in their back pockets and fisher-men who propped their cane poles on the side of the van and left their shoes outside and harmonica players and anonymous connivers and scoundrels and a tubercular essayist visiting from Boston, who mocked them both, and a retired sideshow Wildman of Borneo and various cute girls and several wanted men and loquacious clerks and bosomy, chuckling women; and he met some of his own kind—as he saw them—boomers and breezers of the great continental rail-roads, hoboes and angelinas like him (formerly) who flapped dust from their shirttails, laughing and telling stories about wild rides on the gunnels. He met buckheads and jeffs and caledonias pretend-ing to be upright women and drunks and wine drinkers and some on dope ingested by way of syrups and elixirs, and he met bright-skinned dancing women and conjurers—all of whom, travelers and squinchers both, so the professor said, were on their way to Bee-luther-hatchee.

And he met the grief-stricken and the celebratory, the quilters and choristers. He met people at weddings and football games and pasture track meets and at barbecues under voluminous oaks by blackwater rivers where the smell of slow-roasting pork filled the woods with its sweetness. He met peddlers and dodgemen offering burial and life insurance for pennies a week and truck drivers and higglers; and he met preachers, jolly ones and severe ones and ones who told funny jokes at dinner and ones whose speech was so filled with extraordinary locutions that he wondered if it was a special language taught only to preachers and understood only by them; he met schoolteachers and doctors and barbers and lodgekeepers and tinners and ragpickers and butter and egg men and grifters and ex-bindlestiffs turned shouters, and a sightless wanderer who liked to fondle the porphyry necklaces. In Tarbitha, Alabama, he watched a silky-haired copperbright woman throw back a glass of red wine punch and thought his heart would stop. He met africano policemen wearing cracked Sam Browne belts and met house painters and a writer of tall tales that he said were better than the Uncle Remus stories that newspaperman Harris had stolen from the colored folks over there in Georgia. He met undertakers and talked shop with them and by way of the undertaker railroad you might call it sent messages to Oliver, telling him he was on a mighty adventure.

2

In the passing nights, the old days—of youth already encrusted with memory and the peculiar visitations of dream time—in these short summer nights and fall nights when the dust was lifted from the dry fields and sailed in clouds before the moon, turning the moon to rose— more secured now—again he brought back Oliver, Polly and the Ghost, and brought back the streets of the Row where he was a prince of boys, a wanderer among familiar byways, poking into the unusual facts and alliances of a neighborhood built on the lives of patrimonial and historical mimicries. He caught himself coughing quietly, from no dis- ease other than the heart's tendernesses, and pressed his hand on the floor of the van to steady himself as he shook with dream tears over the days gone from tarrying in the kitchen talking to Mrs. Parker about her adventures as a freight hauler's wife in Florida, or the times, at the end of short winter days, when he sprawled in the voluminous armchair in Oliver's bedroom reading of the high kings of Scotland and Venice. From a silence that seemed to flow endlessly both backward and forward he reached toward the shade that was his mother—shade of lingering breath. On cold days his own breath seemed at times to be hers too. The extensions of himself, the remainders, and especially the folded notes he sometimes handed to visitors asking them to pass the notes on if they were ever to come on an aubergine-faced, beau- tiful, springy-haired woman talking about the lives of kings—these scraps haunted him, their messages of hope and descriptions of some adventitious moment, of pulling on an oversized red sock or eating supper with gypsies or of waiting at a railroad crossing on a clay road in the late afternoon watching a breeze pick up and sort through its scatterings of yellow leaves. As far as the scribbled notes went, he had no idea if they found her, but he told himself—sometimes—that they did. *This was his homemade religion, as the roads and the little towns smelling of wet ashes and pork grease, their painted arches welcoming everybody—so they said—and their overfed trees and storefronts where he and the professor caught themselves reflected with the same articulation and clarity as any other passersby, were his religion, and the cookfires they built and the august and pilfering nights and the collection itself, the big portmanteau they hauled around like medieval peddlers rolling their creaking schooners of trade goods, all these, and on some days not only these but everything he saw, touched, smelled and chanced on like motherless foundlings beside the road, were his religion. He tried to remember them all in the prayers of his noticing and his footsteps, especially his mother Cappie, offering a nodding and insufficient worship. Meanwhile in sleep he wrestled so mightily that the professor told him he would put him outside under the truck if he didn't quiet down. It took a long time to ease up in the dreams. But the professor never did put him out. It was a secret ministration he thought and he thanked him for it. The old man's clucky, crusty ways did not interfere with his kindness. Raised around childless grownups, Delvin was used to the standard selfishness of the lonely and habitbound. He had been studying people all his life so far. "Some kind of lookout," the professor said when he told him. "You could say that," Delvin said. Out the truck window the wind stroked channels and currents through a field of yellowing barley as they talked.*

At a funeral they caught on a pass-through in Coldwater, Louisiana—trying a little utility work to drum up business—as he eavesdropped on a gassy and trouble-infused woman describing her husband's medical symptoms (bilious fever, bone shave, a gathering in his feet and a little apologetic cough that was driving her crazy), past her terrapinate chewing brown jaw, across the room and out the window and on the other side of a little yard, standing in front of a piney wood the understory of which was filled with blossoming blackberry bushes, he spied a woman, no, a girl, who was the most compelling person, femalewise, he'd ever seen. She was slim and nearly blueblack like him and had bushy hair that looked uncombed and untreated—never treated—and in her wide face was a look of barely suppressed outrage and a sorrow and under this an astonishment that as he looked seemed the most familiar and unusual and irresistible expression in the world. As he watched she bent her head back and caught the sun in her face. She opened her mouth and he watched the sun catch in her white teeth.

Crimped, exhilarated, trying not to draw attention to himself, he scooted out and dashed around the side of the house to introduce himself. But when he got to where she'd been there was no sign of her. Usually shy, usually a slider along the edges, he asked five different people if they'd seen her and would have asked more, but the fifth, a salesman for the Universal Encyclopedia Company, with a leer that would have been a wink except that he had a lazy eyelid, told him she was in town visiting a local friend from college. The salesman didn't know her name but the local woman was Annie Bawnmoss and she lived two streets over, back from Till's grocery between the house with a lopsided porch and the Free Will Baptist church.

Delvin hustled over there and arrived just as the two young women were climbing the front steps of a small brick home.

"Hello," he called from the street and the local woman, Miss Bawnmoss he figured, turned and looked at him.

"Do I know you?" she said.

The other, the one who looked so familiar and unusual at the same time, turned too and looked at him as if she was interested in who he might be.

"I'm Delvin Walker of the American Museum of Negro History," he said breathlessly, trying to get a smile to set right on his face.

"You look like I'm supposed to know who that is," the first girl said.

"No way really that you would, unless you are interested in negro history."

"Negro history," the other woman said, not a question but musefully.

Delvin wanted desperately to ask her name. "Yes," he said.

"Hello, I'm Delvin Walker—with Professor Carmel. I help put on this traveling museum show we got about negro history."

"Traveling," she said, still not a question.

"Oh yes. We got a big old truck type van with the whole museum inside it."

"I'd like to see that," she said.

"You could come right now."

The woman continued to look at him in her museful, slightly dislocated way. Delvin immediately retrenched.

"We'll be parked over at the Melody AME church, over on—where is that?—on . . . ," and he looked at the local college woman, who had a narrow face and hard, intelligent eyes.

"Come on, Celia," she said, "these wandering wooly heads come through here all the time."

"That extension off Foster street," Delvin said. "I could come escort you if you like. When you like."

"That's all right," the woman called Celia said. "I can find my way over there I reckon."

She smiled. It was a friendly smile that Delvin took to heart.

"Well," he said, almost choking, "I'll look out for you."

The two young women went into the house.

The next morning he swept out the museum and dusted the photos and opened the flat books to what he thought of as the most interesting examples of africano life. His favorite photo was one looking up a dirt road at a grocery store that looked like a little wooden ship drifting in a forest. You could see two small boys sitting on the grocery steps and up ahead a wagon pulled by a mule. It had a grace and loneliness and a passing air about it of quiet welcoming that created a sweet place in his heart. He had already arranged the display cases to include the photographs of the people whose faces he found most interesting. He shook the thin mattresses and the checkered blankets out, rolled them up and shoved them into their space above the cab. The professor commented on his quickness this clear late spring morning, but Delvin didn't explain. It was a beautiful day. A sky with blue depths and puffed-up complicated clouds. The dew brought the smell of the roses in the church's side garden and the junebugs were just tuning up in what Delvin thought of as a harmonious fashion. He stood by the back steps listening to them climb their ladders into the higher reaches of sound and stop as if they had been caught at something. Wonder what it is? he thought.

By dinnertime they had made a dollar and fifty-five cents off a first-grade class from the little deckleboard school behind the waterworks. The teacher had to snap her fingers at him as if he was a schoolboy to get his attention on the presentation articles. The professor called him on his distractedness, but in a friendly way. Delvin had mentioned that a young woman might be coming over. They ate noon dinner at a slabwood table by the church garden. Bees tumbled among poppy flowers and floated over the big puffy hydrangeas.

"It's a miracle I guess that these Methodists allowed themselves even to plant a garden like this," the prof said, indicating the colorful array of blossoms. "They are so hard on themselves about appreciating any beauty but that of their lord and savior. It is the most foolish response to the truth that I am aware of in these parts."

"What do you mean by that?" Delvin, only half listening, inquired.

"Anybody who tarries long enough in the quiet of the day will shortly see that the most profound world is intangible. Invisible," he said, laughing his wheezy one-horse laugh. "Like in that photograph you like so much."

"Which one?"

"The one of that shady road and that wagon climbing the hill."

"Invisible?"

"You know what I am talking about. We love being under big trees, in their shade, because they return us, partway at least, to the mysterious world."

"How come we knuckle down so hard in this one? Everybody I know is trying to make a killing right here."

"Looks that way, dudn't it?"

"In the funeral business you see the ones who gathered the most headed out in the slickest style."

"Still we wonder where they head out to."

"I wonder about it all the time."

"All you got to do is slow yourself down a little. Put aside this grasping."

"You mean like right now?"

"Well, right now you have the hidden world appearing in its most concentrated form. Or about to. Or you hope it will."

"You mean . . ."

"Exactly. She is the most familiar representation of this other world—or at least what we feel about such as her is."

"I feel so jumpy I am about to crash out of my skin."

"Pretty likely." He looked off toward a large blossoming crape myrtle. "How you doing with those books I gave you?"

"Right well. I been reading *The Blue Horn*, that book by I. B. Connell. He says that desolation and dread are our oldest feelings. That this whole world of cities and government is just our attempt to build walls against them. God, too. He says these are the comedies of foolishness. We got to discard them. Walk away from them like they were a dead dog in the road and make a new life in another place, live in another way."

The professor looked up at the sky that was so clear by now it was almost white, summer white.

"What kind of life?"

"He doesn't clearly say. He just recommends that we vacate the premises."

"Yes."

Delvin looked off toward the van. "I guess we pretty naturally are living that way right now."

"Our ambling way of life, you mean?"

"Yessir. Traveling from town to town."

"It's a splendid life, I agree, but it doesn't appear to be for everybody."

"It pretty much suits me."

"You are one in a thousand, my boy."

It was difficult under the circumstances to keep up his end of the conversation but he felt it was his duty to, and besides, at least on most occasions, their talks excited him. But today his spirit lay sunk in longing and the afternoon was a parched plain spread around him and the food he ate unidentifiable. He kept getting up to go check the street in both directions; the professor had to call him back to the table.

Just before sunset, stepping out from under the blue shadow cast by a big box elder down the street, Celia appeared. She came with her friend. Delvin, his throat so thick he first had to step around the side of the van and hack and take deep breaths, showed them around the premises. Miss Bawnmoss held back, allowing that she was not at all impressed, but Celia—she said to call her that—wept a quiet seep of tears before a stack of pictures of suffering and degradation, of hangings and burnings. Delvin did not interfere. He had learned from Mr. Oliver that there was a proper distance to allow grievers to express themselves without them feeling that they too were being urged into the pit. She leaned with her hand propping her body against the long table. Before her men with blood gleaming on their backs knelt under the whip hand. She swayed slightly. Her face gleamed with tears. She cried without making a sound. He wanted to touch her. Just before his hand rose she turned blindly from the helpless bodies, first toward the front of the van and then, catching herself, turned back and stumbled by him and out into the fading light. He followed her to the door and then down the steps.

She crossed the sidewalk and stood in the grass beyond it. The sky looked like a piece of pale gray silk stretched tight. The trees had darkened almost to black. Between them a few sips of color, of peach and cherry, shone through.

Miss Bawnmoss came down the steps and stood beside him, wringing her hands in a white handkerchief.

"It's her father," she said.

"In the pictures?"

"No. But her father got killed by white men. Over in Mississippi."

"They hanged him?"

"No, it wasn't that."

She didn't go to the woman, who had stopped weeping and was standing now in the churchyard looking off into the distance.

What have I done? he thought.

"They drowned him," Miss Bawnmoss said.

"Aie, Lord."

She went to her friend. The two woman embraced. Celia's right hand fluttered down to her side and hung there like something forgotten. She separated herself from her friend and came over to Delvin who stood now in the shadow behind the truck.

"Thank you for showing me your exhibit," she said. "I guess I was just surprised by some of it."

"I'm sorry about your daddy," Delvin said.

"Yes, thank you," she said, looking at him with a softness that Delvin could feel in his body. He wanted to take her in his arms, and would have and walked her away into the mustering dark and kissed her if she let him and would do this even though he knew it was the wrong time and place, but he was a few days or hours from knowing her well enough yet and that stopped him.

"Oh me," she said, "I guess I'll be seeing you."

"Can I walk along with you?"

She looked lightly at him, a look like a flutter of lace in a summer window, and said, "I suppose."

Delvin walked with the two women back to Miss Bawnmoss's house. There was at first a little light talk from Miss Bawnmoss, but this died quickly and they walked in silence. Down the dirt street three boys played with a ball made of cloth scraps, tossing it high in the air and jostling each other to see who would catch it. On the front steps of a crooked house a little girl combed a small black dog with a hairbrush. A woman in overalls sat on a rough wood porch husking green corn. Smell of pine smoke. Dusk easing along.

A man leading a mule on a piece of cotton plowline passed. He tipped his white straw hat to the women. They both laughed with a gaiety that surprised Delvin. The next moment the two women began to run. Celia looked back at Delvin and waved, her expression a mix of mischief and melancholy. "Come by tomorrow," she called.

He stood in the street watching them run. "Never saw anything like it," he whispered, took a breath and whispered the words again, saying them because he had suddenly always wanted to in just this situation.

That night he walked through the half-lit gloom of the quarter to the edge of town. The quarter was separated from lush empty fields by a wide ditch grown up in gallberry scrub. On the other side and about a half mile down, close to the railroad tracks, was a hobo camp. Above him a scattering of stars were as hard and white as quartz chips. He was filled to the brim with thoughts of the young woman Celia. He went down into the little depression where the camp was and sat down by the fire. A few of the hoboes had visited the museum, including two white men who said they had been teachers and were now on the road. Last year the stock market had tumbled like a man falling down a flight of stairs and this year brought new travelers to the roads, but in the South the hobo life and bad times were long established. Dixie hadn't come back from the Civil War, it had just kept going on the busted-up same. The white folks weren't about to change and they didn't let the negro folks change either, or tried to keep them from it. An antique asked if he wanted food but he thanked him and said no. The antique was a rough-looking colored man with a dent in his chin. Delvin accepted a cup of coffee, drunk from a partially crumpled tin cup the man offered him. They sat side by side on a downed chestnut branch with the leaves still on it. These trees were dying off, too, poisoned by blight. They talked about the state of the world and agreed that it was, as ever, going to hell.

After a while Delvin got up and walked around the camp. He thought he recognized a few of the men, but he wasn't sure. These days he often saw folks he thought he had seem somewhere before.

He walked down the eroded slope into the ditch and sat by the milky waters of the little creek and thought about Celia. Her cheeks had a slant to them that made his heart break like an egg. Her eyes were fully black, and shiny like something brand-new, and she had looked out of them as if she'd never had a chance to use them before. She had to live with her father being killed by white men. But it didn't seem she'd been turned to hate. You couldn't always tell. Had she glimpsed her father's picture in the museum? They had pictures of drowned men; maybe he was one of them, maybe the ashy-mouthed man, naked but for a torn white shirt, hauled up by three men from the dark waters of a country pond, was him. Or the man snagged on a grappling hook and lifted like a big fish out of the Tamal Canal onto a wooden bridge. Or the half-burned man lying in the reeds west of New Orleans. It seemed like life could suddenly snatch you up and kill you, *this* life could. But the professor said every step we take leads us to our destiny. We never make one false step, he said. Delvin stretched his foot out and flattened it against the hard sand. Next step, he said and brought the foot back. Does that one count? A man squatting in a little clearing on the other side of the creek waved but he wasn't waving at him. A breeze stumbled around in the gall-berry bushes, ruffling the flimsy tops. Back at the camp somebody hooted and another voice broke into a clumsy out-of-tune song and stopped. Celia had slim hands, long fingers that slid along like she was about to poke them into something. Her shoulders were square. He wanted to go on a long walk with her, tell her about his travels, hear what she had to say about her life.

He got up, stepped across the creek, climbed the low bank and headed back to the van.

Over the next few days he spent time with her. Due to his putting together a small concession with the negro primary and elementary schools that brought their classes over to look at the exhibits, the professor wanted anyway to stay over.

"It's a sure two maybe three dollars a day," he said.

He planned to head northward, summer coming, the wild mag-nolia trees already blossoming in the woods.

Celia seemed to like walking with Delvin. They drove to the

country in her car (she was the first africano woman he had met
who owned her own car, a small Chevrolet coupe). They had to be
mindful of where they went; they didn't want to upset the white folks
by alarming them with a couple of out-of-town africanos in an automobile. You got along if you smiled and said yessir and put on a
humble front. But even so, the white folks were sometimes spooked
by the appearance of a strange africano person. Her cousin Samuel
had been beat up in Shelby, where she was from, because he let his
irritation at the dumbness of a white store clerk show through.

They had put a couple of cane fishing poles in the rumbleseat,
and when they wanted to walk some they would carry the poles with
them. Fishing negroes were a familiar and reassuring sight in this
part of the world. Delvin had never fished in his life, except for the
comical trip he took to a pond with Mr. Oliver, where they both fell
in, but he enjoyed walking along with Celia carrying a pole.

It would be pleasing to catch their dinner, maybe sometime they
would do that. But neither had brought bait and they didn't know
how to find any. Worms, Delvin had read, or grasshoppers, were
good, but where might they be? It was early in the summer for grasshoppers anyway. Celia was no help and they chided each other in a
familiar way that made them tense and happy and they tossed their
unbaited lines into this or that murky body of water nonetheless.
They had remembered hooks and the bobbers made of bits of cork.
They liked best, as today, simply to walk along the side of a stream
with the poles on their shoulders, and Celia didn't seem to mind the
water dripping off the wound fishing line onto her blouse; he liked
that. They spoke of the lives they lived—the traveling in his case,
school in hers—and of the towns they were from and each told the
other little almost secret details that thrilled them to say and to hear
and their skin tingled and their eyes shone and each more than once
felt a sudden joyful weepiness come on that each stalled and then
rushed past, scattering details and sudden declamatory claims about
life and themselves.

Celia's stepfather was a doctor—as her father had been—trained
in Chicago. ("My favorite town," Delvin crowed, though he allowed

under questioning that he'd never been there—"but I have read much about it," he said.) Her family lived in the little town of Shelby in Louisiana just south of the Mississippi line, and also in Chicago. She found the South strange and scary ("Like living in a perilous fairy tale," she said), but the people, "the africano people down here," she said, were warmhearted, even if they were nosy and gossipy and often chuckleheaded folk; they gave you the feeling they had found a way to some happiness about themselves that she missed up north.

"Everything there split up?" Delvin wanted to know. "Between the white folks and the colored?"

"You could say yes," she said, but it wasn't quite so open. The races could sit together in the picture show or even eat together in some restaurants, but there was a feeling that was always there that you might at any minute be called for trespassing. People didn't pay attention to colored folk like they did to white; you were overlooked, left out. They didn't mind if you got a little successful, but they didn't want you getting too close to them.

"Down here we're all jumbled up together," Delvin said. He didn't know why he said that, but it seemed so as he said it.

"Long as you return to the Land of Darkness," Celia said and laughed. That was what everybody called the quarter, in most every town.

They had stopped under a big oak that had a peltlike green moss growing on its limbs.

"What are you going to do with yourself?" he said. She was at least two years older than him and he could see she looked on him as a boy or tried to. Long streaks of pale cloud ran east to west. Near one a little double-winged airplane chugged along. Only last year, he thought, he had begun to notice airplanes flying; before last year you never saw them, except maybe at fairs and exhibitions.

"I guess I'll be a doctor too," she said, switching the end of her pole against some dusty tickseed plants.

"Can you do that?"

"I don't know for sure. There are places in the east maybe, but I don't know."

"You don't sound too red-hot about it."

"I know. I've always thought I would be a doctor like my father . . ." She bit her lip. "I used always to say *Father*, but now I say *my* father . . . I just realized that a couple of months ago."

"It's natural, idn't it? My mama ran off when I was little, and I always say my . . ."

Her silence stopped him. She stood looking down at the little brush-tangled creek.

"What does your mother do?" he asked.

"She teaches in the negro women's college in Shelby, english literature."

"I knew it. I knew she had a job too. I'd like to meet her."

Celia's nose was long and straight, her lips had a thin sculptured rim. She opened her mouth but didn't speak.

"You were talking about being a doctor."

"No, I'm not . . ."

"It's all right. I want to know."

"I think about going to medical school, but when I do—think about it—it seems as if I'm just marching . . . you know, as if I am following orders."

"Does your stepfather want you to be a doctor?"

"No, I don't think . . . well, he never speaks of it. I guess he would like . . . I don't know . . . it's some feeling I get that I ought to be doing something important, when I don't know if I really want to do anything at all."

She looked at him in a slightly embarrassed way and he could see in her shining black eyes that she thought she'd said too much.

"Nothing's clear to me," he said and laughed.

"Well, you're young." Saying this her mouth turned down in something like chagrin and she touched his wrist, lightly, a touch he would later recall, little pats not of electrical fire but of restoration.

"It's not that," he said. "I mean I know what I want to do, but . . ."

"What's that?"

"What do I want to do?"

"Yes."

"I want to write books."

She didn't laugh but her face became serious and she turned her head away. A flock of blackbirds streamed westward. They were walking again, passing in and out of shade. The grass where the sun touched it was the color of brass. The earth under the trees gave off a musty smell, smell of mushrooms and the drifting underworld.

"A couple years ago I started keeping a notebook," he said.

"Do you write stories?"

"Mostly I take notes, write down facts, the names of things. I make a lot of lists."

"Of what?"

"The names of railroad companies. Flowers. Different kinds of rocks. People's names, their accents, hometowns, words they use a lot." It sounded silly as he said it.

She glanced at him out of the corner of her eye—something wild in there—turned abruptly and said she had to go back. Had she changed—what was it? He wanted to stop her, to kiss her, but he couldn't believe she'd let him.

"Wait—"

"No. I can't."

He reached out his hand—as if it was the last, the only thing he could do—and touched the sleeve of her cotton shirt, but she was already turning away, already walking.

They returned along the path to the car they had parked under the short wooden bridge. Instead of getting in she walked to the creek and stood gazing at it. The water was black and shiny like the skin of fox grapes. He followed and stood beside her. He wanted to take her hand, but she was holding it in a way—clasping her left wrist with her right hand—that made it difficult. Across the creek three buzzards resting in a tall cypress got clumsily up and rowed off. Delvin watched them go, thinking that they were so black and large and ponderous that you wanted them to have some big meaning. He said this to Celia.

"Like something tragic," she said.

"Like a sign of death or something."

"Well, they are that."

"Since they eat dead animals. But you'd think that creatures so striking ought to have an independent meaning."

"You don't think they do?"

"No. In the funeral business you hear a lot about remarkable meanings. People talk about premonitions of dying and about what the deceased had to say before he or she passed or how the death means something special was or did or is about to happen."

"And you don't believe any of that."

"I believe dying strikes people really hard, most of them, and sometimes it shakes them loose from what they were holding on to."

"You're pretty smart."

"Well, in some areas I've seen a lot."

"Dying scares me. I don't like to think about it."

"I guess it would scare you."

She gave him a searching look. "They told you all about my father."

"Yes. What little a stranger could tell."

"I shouldn't talk about him as if he was still alive, but I always do. I'm one of those who got shook loose by somebody dying."

"Me too," he said. "Dying—or missing."

"What do you mean?"

He told her about his mother's flight.

"Did you look for her in the photographs?"

He brightened at her thinking that. "Yes. She wasn't there. But I wondered last night—again—if I might have overlooked her."

"I don't want to think you might have a picture of my father."

"We don't."

"How do you know?"

"We don't have anybody who fit the description."

She clasped herself in her arms and turned away from him. A truck rumbled over the wooden bridge, making running slapping sounds as the tires went over the boards. Around the creosoted wooden pilings the current displayed little brown froth collars. At any minute, he thought, the water could pull the bridge away. A thin shiver went through him; he wanted to run. But he made himself stay still. His head had begun to hurt.

"Are you all right?" she asked.

"I'm okay."

"You look discomposed."

"Sometimes I feel like everything is about to collapse. As if the next second it'll all be knocked down and swept away."

"I feel that way too sometimes."

"Or sometimes I feel like it's already happened. As if I'm standing in havocs and confusions."

"Yes."

"I used to sit at night out on the back steps of this orphan's home I lived in and it would seem like if I got up I wouldn't be able to prevent myself from stepping off into the dark that would swallow me up. Nothing I could do to hold myself from it. I'd sit there shivering, afraid to move at all. I could hardly call myself. Somebody'd have to come get me."

He'd not talked like this to anybody before. And it was as if he'd not thought this way or felt this way or had these things happen before he said them. As if his life was not something that occurred out in the world, but instead was a collection of stories that came to him out of his heart and mind. He thought of telling this to Celia, but he knew he wouldn't say it correctly.

"Sometimes," he said, "I touch some living thing, like a bush or a bit of slick grass, or a . . . cricket . . . and I feel like I'm going to disappear."

This was no better, and he flushed as he said the words. She was silent. He could not put properly what he felt. With a feeling that he must or die he wanted to tell her how it felt to be pulled into the state he was trying to describe, but he couldn't. Maybe every part of this had only to do with her being here.

Below the low gray bank they stood on was a narrow stretch of white sand. He had seen this before, white sand under cutback dark soil. It too had given him a peculiar feeling. He was full of peculiar feelings. He didn't want to let her know what a curioussome person he was, but then he did.

She put her hand again on his bare wrist. The touch felt so powerfully delightful that he thought he could run up the steps of it right into her heart. But it was only a friendly touch, a pat. She smiled at him and her smile was congenial, nothing more. Way back in the woods a bird, some unidentifiable, ridiculous creature, let loose a single cry, round and sweet as a scuppernong grape. He jumped down to the sandy bar and stood there peering upstream under the bridge. Big clots of brush tucked under the eaves. He had a great desire to jump into a boat and float away down the stream, but the stream was too shallow, the dark water turned thin and copper colored as it washed the sand edge, and he had no boat. A turtle with a saucer-shaped black and yellow shell perched on a slanted log. It wobbled and fell into the water; he didn't know they were so ungainly.

She walked away, but still he stood there. He picked up a piece of pine bark and sailed it at the water. It flipped and parried off, catching on the surface as he stood thinking. Everybody he met had a different dream. Every dream was strong and secret and clung-to and hoped for with all the dreamer's might. One wanted a little patch of good soil, another folding money on the section, another a hazel-eyed baby with a burblous laugh, another rescue rolling in from a far country. Each thought he could find his soul's satisfaction in a single scrap of creation . . . and build his life on it. But the air or water or bit of ground that separated you from the dream . . . how could you cross it?

He climbed the bank and walked back to the car where she sat waiting. He had hoped she would look up, look away from where she had stored herself these last moments, look at him with delight, but she only looked half pleased at seeing him, half annoyed at having to wait. He got in the car and leaned toward her to kiss her anyway, but halfway there he stopped and smiled at her. It was a forced smile that felt cracked and stiff on his face.

"You know," he said, "I think you and I fit together better than any two . . ." And then stopped. He slumped back into his seat as she started the car. She didn't need a crank, the machine fired right up.

"I like you," she said, understanding everything, he thought, seeing right into him, "but I am older than you. I feel kind of sisterly toward you."

Oh no, he wanted to say and raised his hand as if to stop her: Don't talk that way. "You and I would be perfect together," he said.

"None are perfect," she said, "and we both have other plans, other lives we want."

He turned away, for the moment defeated. The car chugged, creaking and shaking up the bank and stopped; the bank was too steep. She gave him a scared look. He told her to drive it back down and turn around. After she did this he took the wheel and backed it up the slope, something he had seen a driver do before. Her face was flushed a hidden, rising red, strongest in the point of her cheeks, and a bead of sweat slid down under her ear. At the top, after he'd wheeled around and stopped, as he leaned back in the seat under big mossy oaks, a smoothness, a calm in his body, she darted in and kissed him on the cheek. They changed places and then sat a minute on the grassy shoulder. The dirt road was a soft orange dusty color. She looked as if she wanted to kiss him again but she only put the car in gear and they started out.

"That was too scary," she said.

"Wadn't much to it."

"I'm so thankful you knew what to do."

"Me too," he said and smiled.

"You're a curious boy."

"Not in a bad way."

"No, no, I don't mean that. It's just . . . you're out here in the world wandering around on your own."

"I got the professor. I got a job."

"I don't mean to insult you."

"It's all right."

They were silent. The pine woods streamed by. A distant hawk, drifting in its singleness, tipped and slid off to the west.

"Thank you for telling me everything you have," she said. "I love listening to you."

"You said you didn't really want to become a doctor. What is it that you want to be?"

"I'd like to do something like you're doing," she said, reaching over and touching his hand. "I'd like to ride around showing people things."

"Why don't you come along with us?"

She smiled at him and then she tossed her head in an artificial way. "I probably will become a doctor if they'll let me. A nurse if that's all they'll allow. And then I'll travel around helping sick people."

He could offer her a lot of things better than that, he thought.

"What people really want," he said, "is to hook up with somebody they feel comfortable with and then get on with living."

"I don't really think much about that," she said.

"But you don't have to. We got it in our nature already. You don't have to cozen it up."

"But I have other things to do first." She smiled again, fondly; distantly. "And so do you."

"No," he said emphatically, hurriedly. "The somebody you hook up with goes right along with all this other business we got to do. They're a natural fit. One helps the other."

"Still, I don't think I quite would be . . ." She stopped talking. They were passing a small cane syrup mill. The press turned by a single gray mule attached to the end of a long pole. A white man wearing overalls and no shirt fed stalks of purple cane into the mill.

"You want some syrup?" Delvin asked.

"Oh, I'd love some . . . but I don't know."

"Sho. Pull on in."

She parked on the road shoulder just beyond the cooking shed and they got out and the man watched them walk back to him as he continued to stuff stalks into the press. He was a thin white man, his skin clammy pale where it showed under the overalls.

"Could we buy a jug of your syrup, mister?" Delvin asked.

The man went on feeding the long purple stalks into the press. Delvin could see his left nipple, like a dark brown button, slip in and out of view as he worked.

"Excuse me, suh."

The man just looked at them and went on feeding in the stalks. The mule, head down, had nothing on his mind but muleness.

"Do you sell cane syrup, mister?"

The man stopped feeding, stepped to the press, unsnagged the full bucket of dark juice from under the slot and walked with it past them to the cooking shed. He poured the juice into the kettle, stoked the fire with a billet of whiteoak wood and then stood looking across the fields that were planted in cotton. He did not appear any longer to be aware of their presence.

They got back in the car. They drove a couple of miles down the road before Delvin said, "Sometimes a white man will act like a human being, sometimes he won't."

"He didn't like to see negro folk riding around in their own fine car." She laughed and then they both laughed. It seemed so funny and ridiculously humiliating to be treated like that, so crazy to them both, that they couldn't help but laugh. He reached over, fumbled with her face, managed to turn it toward him and kissed her partially on the lips.

She smiled again, the fond now slightly askew distant smile, and said, "That's sweet."

He drew instantly back and looked straight ahead at the road that seemed to be running through exotic green country. He didn't feel any more like laughing.

Soon they were back in town, bumping along the main street of the quarter. The day was hot. Two lines of sweat ran down her face as she laughed at his story about a peg-legged man who, in Fitzgerald, Georgia, had challenged him to a foot race and beat him.

"He wanted to wrestle," he said, "but I told him I didn't think I could take being mortified twice."

They parked behind the van, through the open door of which the prof could be seen sitting in his collapsible canvas chair drinking from a tall glass. Without getting up he waved at them. They didn't get out of the car.

"You think you want to have children anytime soon?" Delvin asked.

Instead of mocking or laughing she looked searchingly at him and said, "I'm troubled about all that."

"How so?"

She made a discarding motion with the gathered fingers of one hand and said, "I sometimes feel this yearning for children—it's like, I don't know, a searchlight of happiness has found me out in some swamp of myself and I think a child is that light, but then I feel very calm and cool about the whole thing and believe I have so much to do in this life that I am not interested in children or not interested right now or in this situation or in that person and I just let it sink away from me. Like when you're thinking about eating a peach and don't for some reason and you just forget it."

"What is that?"

"Oh, I'm not making sense, am I?"

She was speaking rapidly and almost frantically, as if she had herself caught on to something and wanted to elude it.

"The professor says it's good to marry early and have children early and all that—get started," he said, "on what life's really about."

"I don't think you can avoid that—or avoid the opportunity."

"Shoot. You ought to ride the trains. Wasted lives. Ruined folk. And then you come to town and you see most people—those that got a chance—white or colored—can't get away from that study quick enough."

He too was talking fast. He didn't want her to go away, that was why. Probably she wouldn't come back. Maybe if he tried everything she would go for one something. But he was going too fast.

"Can I buy you a lemonade?" he said.

She would sit up nights trying to feel at ease enough on the earth to go to sleep. Some nights she thought the fighting in her would never stop. It was always the same: whether or not she was a good girl, a girl God could love. Girl a man could love. She didn't believe she was that girl. In the half light of her college room, with her roommate's little tuk . . . tuk . . . tuk snores gently percolating in the next bed, she would wrestle with herself and always lose. She would rediscover herself as a bad person who could never get free of her badness. Always she would begin silently to apologize: *I'm sorry I'm sorry I'm sorry.* But not even this let her sleep. Only the vague exhaustion that came over her, thoughts like musty gray shadows settling around her, tucking the space like moss. This boy pushing her was scary.

A breeze felt around in the trees. Down the street a couple of little girls playing hullygully.

"No, I can't do that," she said.

"No lemonade? Everybody needs lemonade. Except for my foster uncle Herman who got his stomach tore out during the war—everybody but him."

"I have to be at Annie's for supper."

"It's still early."

She gave him a look that stopped him.

"All right," he said, dashed. Then, brightly, "Can I ride with you over to your house? I'd like to air out a little and I can start from there."

"Oh yes," she said, abruptly lighthearted. She put the car in gear and they drove slowly through the narrow, tree-lined streets.

"Why don't you talk more about little things?" she said. "All these big topics wear a person out."

"You mean like love and marriage?"

"And the rest. Look at this." She held her right hand out, showing on her middle finger a ring with a cut violet stone.

"An amethyst," he said.

"Aren't you smart."

She was patronizing him and they both knew it, but they both knew it was because she was a little hurt. He didn't rebuke her.

"My father gave this ring to me. Or it was passed down to me after he died."

He wished he had a ring to give her. "Let me look at it."

He took her hand in his and with the fingers held together it was as compact and slim as a mockingbird; opened (his fingers brushing her skin as if there was a magic he could unsettle and start with a gentleness), the palm was a pale, yellowish tan, beautiful. He tried to hold it but she spread her fingers. Then she closed them and let him hold her hand and they both knew she was doing this, doing what she'd come to in this way, her hand relaxing in his so it felt softer, yet at the same time more full of life. Gently she pulled away from him.

"I can't drive," she said in a small voice.

They said nothing for the last block.

She pulled into the dirt driveway and parked beside the sturdy brick house with the big shocks of daylilies blooming against it. He wanted to sit in the car and talk, keep her with him somehow. Her flattened, coarse, springy hair caught the fading light as she got out. It was impossible that in a minute she'd be gone.

"I thought . . . ," he said, but she was already around the side of the car, opening the door for him.

He reached to touch her hand on the windowsill but it was gone too quickly and she had already turned to climb the two white painted steps to the little porch. She stopped, pivoted on one foot, looked down at him still sitting in the car and thanked him for going riding with her.

"Come with us in the van," he blurted and he saw in her eyes that the offer touched her, that she yielded to it and let it enter her and he thought he could see it in the moment of early twilight swing through her, circulating, but she only smiled, a smile diminishing in clarity and strength as she slipped further away. As she reached the door he thought she almost turned back but she didn't. She gave him a small, sliding wave, a soft almost slicing motion of hand, as she went in. The screen door and then the white paneled main door closed and it was as if she had flown from the world and left him there.

He let out a small cry. He wanted to rush after her, overturning rooms until he found her and made her let him touch her fingers again, made her let him kiss her and have her.

But he only sat there, still inside the car—like a dummy, he thought later, walking home—dressed up in thriftshop clothes, with cotton ticking in his hair.

The next morning the sun came up through thin peach-colored clouds and seemed to Delvin to be filled with the promise of love, but he had to stay where he was because a group of fifth-graders was coming to tour and the professor had an early appointment with the negro dentist who visited that area on Thursdays (he needed a filigree on his bottom teeth, which were worn down to stubs and hurt) and so he did not get over to the charmed house before nearly noontime. He could smell greens cooking as he walked around to the back door.

Celia was not there. She had left at first light to get to Birmingham before it got too hot.

"Well, it surely is hot," he said, a look on his face that made the woman who cooked for the family think she'd hardly seen a person look so catercornered to hisself. She wanted to laugh at him, but as the laugh rose in her it changed to pity.

"She left a letter for you," she said, this woman about whom he was wondering if she could tell him what he was supposed to do now—*what now?*

"A letter?"

"It's right here on the speckle table," she said as if he was inside the house, but she hadn't let him in, and she turned, went away and got it and brought it to him.

He accepted the letter like a starving man told the banquet was not for him but he could have this chunk of cold cornbread here. Those riches! But still, here was food.

Like a dog, he thought as he went down the steps with the letter clasped against his chest, I scurry off to eat my little mess of leftovers in secret.

But he was not bitter, not yet, or ever would be really. Even later, out in the rain-drenched cotton fields of the state prison system as he trudged barefoot along the rows chopping nutgrass with a hoe, he would not cast blame on her.

He kept the unopened letter in his breast pocket safe like a tiny coiled lifeline until after dinner, that he ate alone behind the van under the little detachable awning at the small round folding table they used for meals and sometimes card games on cool nights when the mosquitoes weren't too vicious. When an older woman carrying a blue cloth parasol with a wide chuffed rim approached, asking to look at the exhibits, he got up, let her in and showed her around. When he stepped out to finish his ham sandwich, she stole half a dozen photos, a fact he only became aware of after the professor got back and discovered it.

The professor was in a foul mood over his teeth. The fretwork hurt and had cost him more than it should have and on top of that among the purloined snaps were two of his favorites. He swore and ordered Delvin out of the van and off the property.

"You firing me?" He was stricken and angry himself.

"Just go on," the prof said, sitting down in the chair Delvin had vacated. "Leave me be." The old man felt like closing the museum and driving off someplace by himself to grieve his wounded teeth and the loss of the photos (grieve the founderings of time, the raw blast that had wakened him that morning with thoughts of his own demise, grieve the single-minded woman he'd left back in Biloxi years ago, a woman with shiny hair and a quickness of spirit that sat him up straight in his chair). For the moment he felt as if he could not go on. The boy—damn the boy.

Delvin walked fast away from the van. He had been about to read the letter when the professor appeared. He walked until he was out of town and then crossed the gully and entered the hobo camp. It was mostly deserted this time of day, but a few men were lying under a large persimmon tree smoking and talking. He didn't want any company, he only wanted to feel less peeled. He was so nervous his hands shook. He walked through the camp and into a field of broomsedge, made a little clearing for himself and sat down in the grass. A ways farther on a little willow stood up from the field, its branches cut partially back and heavy with leaves. He got up and went over there and sat down in the shade of the tree. A killdeer fluttered up and made her little flopping display trying to draw trouble away from her chicks, but he didn't pay any attention.

The letter was brief. *I thought so much about our talk and was glad, but I know it is best if I go back to where I belong now. Maybe you would like to write me sometime.* She gave her address, not the school's address but, so he assumed, her parents' house, or was it her dormitory, in Shelby. She signed it simply Celia. He spread the single pink page out and ran his fingers lightly over it. He sniffed the spicy, brassy scent, her scent. His heart pounded. He jumped to his feet and started to run—stopped and sank back into the dry grass. The long-fingered willow leaves rustled and shifted and settled.

I thought so much about our talk . . . , he read again, stopped and restarted, forcing himself to read again, *I thought . . .* First she wrote *I*, the side of her hand pressing against the paper. She was thinking of him at that moment. *I thought*—had she paused then and struggled to decide what to say next? What did the letter mean? Did it mean for him to forget about loving her? Maybe not.

He lay back in the grass with the letter pressed to his face and for a few minutes inhaled its smell into his body. Part of her was on the inside of him now, filtering through the pipes and tracks, easing in among the muscle and bone, settling into little culverts and housings, finding shelter, seeping into his being. We leave these little trademarks and gizmos and reliquaries behind us. Little stacks of dust in a corner. That others snuff up and take away. Now I am one of them.

He turned over on his stomach and, propped on his elbows, read the letter again. She had sneaked away, that was a fact. But maybe because she felt too much to speak to him. Yes, she felt something strong. But maybe not. Maybe she was used to boys approaching her, used to giving them rides in her car. We didn't even go to a beautiful spot, or beautiful enough. And what was an africano girl doing owning her own car? This was Bee-luther-hatchee, not Chicago. Not even Shelby, where they had a college. It was Ginny Gall. Bad things happening over on this side of the universe.

He jumped up, fierce in feeling now, ready to go save her. It was not a boy's notion, or only a boy's. The grass surged heavily under a freshening breeze. He shuddered—like a mule, he thought, old Stubbornness, twitching off flies—and a hooting, wailing thing slid off from him, peeling away into depths inside. It trailed a whole lifetime of griefs behind it like knots pulled tight in greased rope, headed toward a howling. He staggered and had to catch himself to keep from falling. What is this? His body, the inside of it, seemed to have slid down, dropped, concentrated itself in a heap, a muddle. He didn't want any of this now. Not now, not any time. But here it was. Something sharp as a hawk cried *Run!—run for your life!* But before he could act it threw ropes around him. He was being squeezed to death. In a blur he saw his hand out waving, or falling, in front of him. He could feel his forehead burning. *I'm a crazy person.* She was headed at high speed away from him but she was not diminishing in size. Wadn't that funny. He paced a circle in the grass, catching switches of it, crumbling the feathery tops. Gradually the influence subsided. Somebody over at the camp hooted. Another let loose a high cackling, hateful laugh. Delvin got up and looked over that way past a broken-down fence and a few thin chokecherry trees. Nothing unusual. Down at the far end of the gully, where it passed under a low railroad trestle, he saw some men waiting. They were figuring to hop the westbound that would still be moving slowly after picking up freight in Eula. He thought of joining them. He loved riding on top of a car in good weather, watching the country pass. But he could catch a train any day.

Ah, jeez—he felt like lying down and not getting up. He wanted to run after her without stopping until he found her. Just to get a look at her. What was it—five days since he met her? Before Tuesday he hadn't in his whole life had one single thought about her, didn't expect her, wasn't looking, and now he'd do anything just to touch her hand again. A breeze charged the thin hair on his arm. He closed his eyes. He was an inch away from her. Then she was gone like a bird flown. He ran his fingers along his arm but they were only his fingers. His eyes stung.

The train, pulled by a scuffed green locomotive, rumbled out of a woody area just east and came smoothly on around the big curve

before the straight run to the trestle. He watched as the men got to
their feet and stood brushing off their patched pants, resettling bindles and soogans, jostling or joking or just standing alone looking.
They were like passengers at the special open-air station—like fleas,
he thought bitterly, returning to the dog. Sometimes the bulls got
after you, but lately, so he'd heard, there'd been no real trouble of that
kind. It was news you couldn't count on. The train rolled clacking
over the trestle and the men began to find their way onto the gondolas and into open boxcars, climbing ladders or pulling themselves
through the doors. Many of the gunnels were already taken. In cities
you could board a standing train, but there was sometimes more
risk. No hobo names on the weigh bills. He wanted to run along and
join the boys.

He took a few steps in that direction, folding the letter as he
walked and sliding it into his breast pocket. He was about to start
running, but he stopped himself. A bitterness that had risen into his
throat subsided. The men were scattered across the cars. Some he
knew. A baraby wearing a patched crushhat, Parly from Denver, gave
a slow looping wave and made a finger sign of good times. Delvin
gave a small cocked wave back. He could still make the train, but he
didn't try.

He wasn't sure why he stopped himself and maybe he was making
a mistake. It was right, when something said go, for you to go. He believed this, or thought he did. He wasn't sure. Something about the
letter, about what had happened in the last two days—he'd come on
another sense of things. Small but particular, not a dominion, but an
understanding. He couldn't tell what it was but he knew he wasn't
going to make a sprint for the train. He waved again, a larger wave
this time, and made a sign of good luck to the nomads settling into
the open doors of the cars. In the west the sky was blue and streaked
with long fish-tailed clouds.

As he walked back into town he felt a twice-settled weight in him, the
dashed freshness of missing the train and the heavier bundle of this

new loss. But it wasn't a loss, the second one, this woman or girl who had driven away in the gray sweet-smelling morning in her own car. She wanted him to write her. He wanted to get back to his museum job and regular place in the world and now he did that.

The professor was glad to see him. He put him to wiping with a dry rag the glassine folders they stored the extra photos in. Delvin was happy to do this. He finished and then went out back to the little table and wrote a letter that he walked down to the post office and mailed. In it he told her how happy he was to meet her. He told her he would carry her with him everywhere and neither of them could help it one way or the other, that they were in each other's life now and don't worry he welcomed her into his.

He wanted them to put the letter on its way immediately and thought of carrying it himself part of the way. Her home was in the extreme western part of the state, other side from the way the professor said they were headed. They were on their way through the eastern towns and north then to Tennessee and on the professor said to Roanoke where he had people he liked to spend a couple of weeks with in the hottest part of the summer. Delvin was planning to get off in Chattanooga.

Back at the van he sat in the shade under the little orange awning writing another letter. Later a few boys came by, paid their nickels and he took them through the exhibits. They liked the pictures of baseball players. He didn't show them the murder photographs and it was because he didn't want them to feel bad. He didn't want to be part of anybody feeling bad just now. One of the boys said the little painted reed baskets looked like Indian ware. Well, Delvin said, there was cross-marrying among Indian and colored folk, that was a fact. Another boy said he had Indian blood. The others began to joke at him and they made their way out of the van laughing. Delvin stayed inside. He needed to study the photos a while. This was something he did regularly. After supper he sat at the little fold-up table inside the van and studied photographs by the light of the coal oil lamp. The professor was off trying to get a donation from one of the churches. This was one of many such nights.

The next day they were on the road, headed for Cary. Then on to Dumont and then to Cromville. They drove past the long finger lake, Rommy Run. Inland gulls, white and gray, their sickle wings catching the late afternoon light, wheeled over the dark green waters of a little cove. They made it to Depburg by dark.

3

From time to time, but regularly, after the museum closed, after he wrote his letter to Celia and posted it, he studied the photographs. Looking at them—for signs, clues, entryways into mysteries, facts, solutions—he wondered if his own face were not a collection of hidden messages, like one of the notes posted on signboards at crossroads stores and post offices, readable by all, telling stories, revealing secrets, offering humorous bits or pitiful revelations; in the triangular piece of mirror they hung on the back door each morning for washing he began to study his face to discover what was there, what hidden messages or revelations were posted for the searchers of the world and the passersby . . . and not just the traditional indicators such as a weak chin (his was short but square) or ferrety eyes (his were large and hazel), but others, the special sign in the slightly curled and hard-edged upper lip that he was a man who dreamed of silver flying fishes and an empty caleche on a tropic shore . . . and a crease at the corner of his mouth that revealed the love of a duplicitous but comely woman who would leave him for a mule trader, say, who was losing his business to the tractor companies . . . or a level gouge above his short chin that revealed his susceptibility to the taste of quince and vinegar pie . . . a tiny curving indentation, a hook, at the edge of his left eyebrow that foretold hard days in the cotton and sweet pepper fields above the Acheron river (unknown to him as yet), as well as the throbbing soreness in his chest on evenings smelling of rust and sour pecans . . . and the tiny indentation below his left nostril, put there by a wasp sting when he was three months old (he'd been told by Coolmist), that signified the suffering of humankind . . .

The future, like a purple martin swooping in the last light of day, was almost near enough, clear enough, to see, to fix . . . but then it was gone.

His face collapsed back into a pudding of dark lumpy skin. It had no character, he thought.

He went back to studying the faces of the mostly anonymous photographed negroes. These faces were fascinating to him. He had asked the prof why they didn't take more pictures themselves, and the professor had said creation was not his line and besides he was baffled by some of the complex workings of that craft. Delvin himself was not particularly interested in taking pictures but it bothered him that they didn't add more of their own manufacture to the lot. But they didn't have money for a new camera and the one they had was busted when the professor threw it at a rabid coon.

Despite all this Delvin had begun to study the faces of those who came to view the exhibits.

He began to jot down descriptions of the clientele. He looked for signifying features, marks, signs. In this one he saw by the slant of a nose the confusion and the name-calling that was coming. In another down-shaded mouth he thought he perceived the impotent attempts to shift blame. In a drooping earlobe he saw bitterness against children. He liked the bumpy spots in faces. The knots and swellings. He himself had two small knots on his forehead and another just back of his chin on the left side. What they were caused by he didn't know, but they worried him; he hoped they weren't infant goiters. The hen's egg on the forehead of a workman in Bayless fascinated him. He described it as a hen's egg, duck's egg, eagle's egg, as a marble under the skin or a lump of custard. He wanted to run it between his fingers; squeeze the juice out of it, he wrote. The left half of one woman's lip was swollen and droopy. She wanted to hide it with her hand (he wrote), but she'd decided not to. Bravely, she entered the museum with her head high. It was only as she re-entered the brilliant waxy sunlight that she ever so slightly flinched. He wanted to kiss her lip and tell her not to be ashamed and thought of Celia whose lips looked carved, long lips with the narrowest ridges running along their edge and tiny lines stroked vertically into them—lips

he wanted more than anything to kiss. He described her face before
he forgot. He kept the written-down description of Celia's face and
returned to it in the night, adding a little, taking a little away, raising
her cheekbones slightly, tapering her eyebrows and plucking them.
She was fading. Without the description he couldn't picture her.

He turned to describing what was around him. The truck was
once black: *but now it's gray*, he wrote.

It's becoming ghostly. We're the ghosts of present, past and future, slip-
ping through the towns. In the morning sometimes when there's fog
the truck disappears and no one can find it. It's as if all this huge
collection of photographs, of pictured history, was erased, as if it never
existed at all. Something makes me want to cry. Not just for my own
troubles, which are pointed and rolling right on, but for everybody's.
Each photographed face is something true about the world. The happy
ones, the sad ones, the lost ones, the found, each one telling its story.
The truck hauling this great assembly through the towns. The people,
the dazed and the suffering . . .

and then he quit the writing. It was becoming too grandeed. He
had a tendency in this direction that he recognized. *Everybody got*
to do something, the professor said. He got the canvas bucket and
hauled water from a well in the front yard of a slanted negro cabin and
washed the truck. It didn't come back to shiny black; it still was gray.

They were in Cullen, then Astor, then Cumming, then the old coal
town of Radsburg. How did they, two negroes in a shabby van filled
with photographs, escape destruction by the white race? In each
town the strict divide between the races was carefully and forcefully
maintained. *Place* was most important. *Remember your place, boy,*
the instructions lettered invisibly but legibly on every sign and atti-
tude and takeout window and coldwater shanty said.

The professor said, "When your own unholiness gets you burned
down, shot, cannonaded, trampled, your close relatives killed, and

the victors dig up the dead and drunkenly dance with them by bon-firelight, which is just what happened to these white folks, what you want is a world or a section of the world where what was lost can be rebuilt, and, most important, none of those you wronged can make a move on you. You want a world that *stays still*. 'We will live not in a spinning remnant,' they say, 'but in a world in which what stands for who we once were can be reconstructed and preserved without the shadow of death falling across it.' But this is impossible to do. Life, snorting and fretting and sniffing around for something sweet, once loosed, can't be fetched up. Even if it's not loose, it will get loose. That's the thing about life that makes it different from the stones: it moves around."

But alien negroes driving a large truck—it was a kind of truck, built by the Ford Motor Company—bringing a celebration of things negroid, was pushing the limit. How did they get by without being lynched or at least beaten senseless, their van confiscated and their pictures burned with the yard trash?

The professor first thing when he arrived in whatever settled nervous burg they visited (they didn't stop in every one) dropped by the police station and paid a bribe, made a donation, to the chief, yes, as said. And he made sure the chief and the city government understood that they—the alien purveyors—knew how stupid these dark folks were, showing each other photographs of their comic faces. They made it clear to the authorities that the exhibit was a folly, a cunning joke on the negro race, a lampoon and antic burlesque designed to humiliate and poke fun at every one of them. Make sure, Your Honor, these simple folk are in their place. What a hoot. He showed them examples of those feckless, half-wit darkies, grand-daddy or some youngun napping in a porch swing or grinning big or a look on his face, as he stared off at the sun slipping down behind the pines, of foolish wonder. The police grinned and patted their bellies and laughed, mostly. Other times the professor cut it close, sometimes a little too close. But few wanted trouble, with negroes or any other group. (Times some defeated person, some sap that hatred had knocked down so many times until he had to use a grudge to build himself back up, some fool who didn't know better, some ex-tormented-child who wanted revenge, a self-despiser, would swing his feet back under him, rise up and knock the black man down. "But you always apologize," the prof said, "and then you get back up."

"I know about that," Delvin said, remembering his scrape in the dress shop, and other venues.)

What up north they called the Depression circled like a flight of buzzards over every town. People still thought business would pull the country out even though business, since 1863, had not been able to pull the South out of anything and the new Depression was just a doubling up, locally.

"Yall just keep that race nonsense off among yourselves and don't bother nobody," the suzerains said to the professor, "we got real wor-ries now." Anyway, they had, since the war, quickly tied the black race back up in knots and they didn't have to worry about them. Nor any fake professor and his truckload of comic photographs.

Into the negro half-towns and sham-cities Delvin began to go at night. He walked the streets of the Overtowns and Undertowns and the Congos and Mississippi and Louisiana quarters. The Lands of Darkness. Unpaved, they were often hardly streets at all. More like lanes in medieval towns of Europe or villages in Africa—streets filled with the smells of woodsmoke and spices and antique senso-ries made of bits of prehistoric matter and dried long-extinct flow-ers. On the creaky lopsided porches vague lights shone like bits of webbing or mist, casting huge shadows on the bare lopsided front walls of the little frame houses. Under the trees the tiny diastolic glimmers of lightning bugs ticked, becoming whiter the higher they rose. Up among the branches pinches and bits of gleaming too faint to cast shadows stayed on for hours. Up ahead, in the middle of the street, human shapes dipped and swooped in unhasty dances as the barely perceptible music of guitars and hand organs made their soundings in the deeps of night. Cries and hoots and whisperings.

There seemed always to be a bit of fog at the end of the street. Cats moaned in their long nights of suffering. Dogs barked with a sound like consumptive muted coughing. As he walked the streets in the deepest parts of the night he could hear people talking in their beds. Old men confessed to their snoring wives the secret affairs of their youth. Old women spoke of masked riders galloping furiously down the roads on huge dark horses. Children spoke of boogeymen with hands growing out of their knees and bellies. In dreams girls whispered to kindly lovers. Boys answered questions with wit and intelligence.

Who dat dar? a woman's voice called, but not to him. He carried in his heart the drubbed and muzzled love of a disallowing woman through the faintly whispering, crepitant streets. He believed this walking eased him and made him able to go about without so much fear he had to run away. He was scared all the time. *What have I come to?* he whispered in the dark caverns under oaks, and he was old enough—had been born old enough—to ask this question. He believed that whatever he was had to be played out in the world. He couldn't hold off from it. What he was scared him. What he believed he was. Seventeen and strong, not very strong, but strong enough and able and filled with beef, with get-up-and-go, with pep, zip, vim—with *lifting power*, which the professor said was the greatest thing, lifting power—and he had an inexhaustible need to exercise himself on the earth.

In the shadows by a boarded-up livery stable, in a little town so small the africano section was only half of two streets next to the town dump, he waited as one would wait for a carriage called to take him to the far places of the world. The air smelled of pine smoke and rotten apples. Down the street a man in a long white nightshirt stepped out of his door and looked at the sky that was still dark. He waved at something in the sky and Delvin wondered who it was, or what, and thought he knew. *What is coming?* he wondered, but no one and nothing in the world could tell him. The man made a large sweeping gesture, turned back in and slammed the door behind him. The sound was like the last clap of a civilization closing up.

• • •

In Salisbury, Alabama, in the northwestern part of the state up near the Tennessee line, one clear night lit by stars, he walked by a church where choir practice was being held.

The choir was singing one of the old sorrow songs, a jubilee called "The Ship of Zion." He stopped and stood under an open window to listen. Someone in the choir kept making a mistake, a woman. Each time, the director, a man, would stop the singing, crying out in a frustrated voice, "Halt!"

After a few busy-sounding and angry words from the director the choir would take up the song again. Again a mistake was made. With the same word—"Halt!"—the director would again stop the singing. This went on and on. A brief patch of silence, just a moment, followed each time at the quittance. In one of these empty moments, someone, a woman, maybe the erring singer, let loose a small, despairing cry. Her voice was like the voice of a child and maybe it was, but he didn't think so and, studier of many faces, he thought hers was probably the face of some reedy girl, just in from the country probably, some plain-faced young person who just wanted to join a choir to praise the Lord and maybe meet people, maybe meet some boy who might like her, but who was finding out that she couldn't really sing. Or maybe she just couldn't please this stern master.

The choir started up again and once more the director stopped it with the same word; again Delvin heard the thin small wail.

The director spoke harshly again, this time ordering the woman out of the group. There was another silence and then came the sound, very quietly, of weeping. Gradually the weeping faded, as if the woman was leaving the room.

The choir started up again. This time the old jubilee went sweetly by without a hitch. But it seemed to Delvin there was a gap in the song, a little hole or gouged-out place where the young woman's voice had been. He could hear this place. It was an emptiness like the silence inside the narrow circle of a well.

He shivered. He was cold though it was a warm June night. A desolate feeling came over him and he thought he couldn't bear what it meant to be a human being on the earth. This feeling welled up and slowly ebbed as he walked on thinking of it.

Back in the van, lying on the floor on his cotton pallet in front of the door, he could still feel a little of this impression or inclination, and he carried with him for days the recall of a faint sadness. It became something he didn't completely forget. He returned to study and wonder about it, the singular occasion of reprimand and the grief it uncovered and the moment of silence it revealed and how this silence or space with nothing in it seemed so important.

Nothing where everything is, he would think and draw tiny circles in his notebook and make dots.

The professor, who dressed generally in the same clothes every day (so he didn't get distracted, he said, by sartorial concerns), continued to instruct him by way of books and disquisitions on the meaning of existence, and Delvin found this education to be interesting and informative, but he preferred other written words, stories he found mainly in books in the small libraries he encountered. These libraries were mostly in churches. Many of the town libraries were not open to colored, and not many people in the quarter had books, but some churches had collected a few and he read many with inspirational themes. These, together with the books from the professor, formed the basis of his education at this time.

He thought of Celia daily and told her of his reading in the letters he wrote, listing the books he read and telling her his hopes for exotic travel. He sent her his itinerary as he learned it as well as his address in Chattanooga; he would occasionally receive a note from her. She was in her third year at college and found it more difficult than the first two. She was studying literature, but found herself pulled more strongly by her science studies. She was lonely often, but she met regularly with a circle of young women to talk politics and literature and social life (*Quite often we get bogged down in the last*), but still, afterwards, she said, on the walk home through the campus or after she was supposed to be asleep, she would feel a loneliness. *Maybe it's only something trying to tug me into another kind of life*, she wrote, but she didn't know what it was. *I sense the world standing ready for me like a big feast, but I feel scared and unsure of where I want to start. I'd like to find some work that is so demanding that I won't think of anything else. Isn't that crazy?*

I wish you would write some about us, you and me, he thought, and added this to the bottom of the letter he was writing. *I think of all sorts of things we could do together.* He told her about the little zoo they visited down in Treesburg, Louisiana, that had several goats and snakes and raccoons and a panther with the mange and a skinny bear that slept all the time. In Suberville he had climbed an abandoned fire tower and looked out at the country that seemed hapless and dull in its monotony. *I want to see the world*, he wrote, *but only the parts that are surprising.* In a note he read on the worn stone steps of the post office in Mooksville, she said she was the same.

It was in Mooksville that he got in a fight with a couple of white boys. Negro on the run, he should have known better. The boys had mocked him on the street for receiving a letter. The letter was written on green stationary and smelled of Celia's cunning perfume. He had it spread out on one hand as he stood under a big live oak tree.

"Look at that nigra acting like he's getting mail," one of them said. "Hey so and so [some derogatory racial term and why repeat it], who you think'd be writing a dumb whatchamacallit like you etcetera etcetera. Who you know anyway who can write?"

"And what you doing pretending to read?" the other, a towheaded skinny boy with a slight limp, chimed in.

"You hang around I'll teach you to read *and* write," Delvin said. He didn't want to be bothered by these silly boys. Celia was speaking in dark blue ink about a jar of pickled peaches her roommate received from her family. She was also describing her Freud studies, which she found gloomy and a kind of outrageous European voodoo. *It's a lot of wishful thinking*, she said. *But really smart. Even if there is a lot more mystery in the world than this man has any idea of.*

White people always like to put their thumb on everything, Delvin thought. They were scared not to.

The boys were like yellow flies stuttering about. He shooed them with the letter. The nearest, a stout boy about his age with coal-black straight hair cut short and a lopsided evil smile, came up close and slapped him in the face.

Delvin was so startled he lost his footing and fell, or half fell, onto his side. He pushed up, jumped to his feet, and backhanded the boy across the forehead, hurting his hand slightly.

The other, more slender, but with a strange, sterile look in his eye, hit him hard in the face. He again lost his sense of things. But didn't go down. Then the other walloped him and he was instantly numb on the left side of his face and to his surprise revolving slowly, wondering where Celia had got to.

Right after this the police came by and he was thrown into the back of a Ford automobile, driven to the jail and locked up in it. The whole ride to the jail he shivered and wanted to cry out, sure this was his fallen day in which the clamps of white men's justice would take hold in his life. The long rope that stretched from Chattanooga to this village in Alabama had tripped him. What was he thinking, to hit that boy?

But he was wrong about the ubiquity of the law. And it wasn't the last time he hit a white boy.

The professor found him in the whitewashed brick jail the next day—after Delvin had been brought before the judge and given thirty days for fighting and assault. Justice was a quick and handy business for africano folks in that town. As Delvin stood before the judge, who wore not robes but a red-striped collarless shirt and black suspenders, he thought he could smell the citrus perfume on Celia's letter and looked around wildly for her come to help him but she wasn't there. The letter was gone and this hurt him in his heart. Just then the judge was speaking directly at him.

"I'm sorry, Your Honor," Delvin said, "I didn't hear you."

The judge added five days to his sentence for impertinence.

The prof wasn't on the crime scene, but by nature of his relationship to Delvin he was implicated in the offense; the town took custody of the van (it wasn't the first time the museum had been taken in) and planned to hold it until the authorities made sure the professor was not up to any illegal activity on his own.

In these situations usually the africano elders of the town would explain to the white fathers the value they placed on the museum, on enterprises of this sort, if not this particular enterprise, and hoped and pleaded, *Your Honor, that you might let us enjoy this celebration of simple american negro life.* The fathers, sometimes more jocosely than not, would liberate the van, not because they believed in the efficacy of nigra museums but generally because they didn't want to get these black fools in a stir. But this time, in Haplessburg or Muttstown or whatever it was called, they were not so quick to see the good side of the museum's existence.

"You are already stirring up trouble with that vexacious tribunery," they said. "If we release it, you might cause even more trouble."

"We receive so little in the way of education about our people . . . ," the professor began, but one of the fathers, a usually genial druggist named Mames, stared at the pencil he was holding as if it might be a magic wand of some kind and said, "What you talking about—your people? You aint got no *people.* You're a nigra—am I right?"

"Yessir, I am."

"The nigras are not a people. They are just—what's the word I'm looking for, Monk? Not a herd—"

"A flock?" Monk Wilkes, the florid owner of the hardware store, said.

"No, damn it!"

"That's a quarter for swearing in the meeting," the mayor, a disputacious little lawyer and landlord, said.

"Not a flock," Mames said, "no, they're just—well, there is no name for what you are. You're just an ordinary part of the life of folks in this area, like junebugs or dirt daubers or possums. Wait—okay:

Folks is what you are, just folks. The Israelites, *they* are a people. The *Chinese* are a people. *Americans* are a people. *You* are *folks*."

He smiled complacently at the professor who stood before him in what he called his presentation clothes, a pair of faded but very clean black broadcloth pants with a yellow shirt and cream-colored canvas jacket, waiting patiently for a chance to speak. When it came, he said calmly that he believed the exhibit helped colored folks—folks, he said—to appreciate how good their lives were down here in the rural south. Let them know how rich and pleasant it is. (Truth was he believed that, despite all this nonsensical fuss, it *was* a good life—a good life being possible under almost any conditions. This was one of his major philosophical points.)

The mayor screwed up his little empty blue eyes and said, "We will take this matter under advisement and let you know."

The professor attempted to plead further that the museum was his life's work and only means of earning a living and so forth, but these pleadings did not sway the fathers. They waved him out with the disinterested courtesy of retired mule skinners seeing an oldtime customer onto a bus, and the chief of police ushered him from the room.

4

From the moment he was in the hands of the police Delvin experienced tides of nausea that rolled in carrying his expectation of discovery of his Tennessee crime and rolled out with any sort of courage he might have. He stayed by himself as best he could and thought distractedly of escape. He watched the fields of corn that stretched away from the central compound. He walked the fence line and gazed at the play of fat cumulus drifting across the blue sky. Trapped, he thought, I'm trapped. Each day, when any of the officers spoke to him or came near him or appeared around the deckle-braid corner of the barracks or hollered for the prisoners to truck it up and climb into the rickety dust-splattered bus that carried them out to work in the vegetable fields, a tension gripped him by the shoulders, stiffened his face and bent him down and robbed him of readiness to confront what he was sure was coming. The other prisoners noticed his state of mind. A couple tried to calm him, pointing out that his sentence was short and the work at the farm was not any harder than it would be on the outside. "You gets three squares and clean bedding every two weeks," Sully John Baker, a short gray-headed man, told him. Delvin thanked him for the info and continued his distracted wandering around the compound. It would have been easy enough to escape (in the cornfields they were often out of sight of the guards), but he didn't want to take the chance. And he didn't want to get the professor into any further trouble. After a week he began to calm down. He began to believe that if they were going to discover him they would have done it by now. He relaxed enough to be able to sit in the little shed they used as a dining hall and eat a healthy portion of his cornbread and stew beans. It was at this point that twin brothers from the west side of the county, also in for fighting, decided to test Delvin along these lines. Delvin pointed out that he was not a fighter at all but simply a man who had been assaulted by white men (they were in the colored section of the county farm). The brothers did not consider this a sufficient disincentive and waylaid Delvin at the outdoor washing area and knocked him down. He slid half under the sidewalk-like boards before the washstands, cutting and twisting his ankle. This laid him up for five days in the farm hospital where he spent his time reading religious tracts. He considered himself lucky not to have had to suffer more of this material. The Bible had been always too bloodthirsty for his taste, a mix of self-glorification and sideshow magic that led only to feeling bad about yourself.

When the cut on his ankle healed a little and the swelling from the sprain went down Delvin was given light duty checking equipment in the work shed. He checked and handed out hoes and mattocks and the cane poles used to knock pecans out of the farm trees as well as the canvas picking sacks for the apple orchard. The work was not onerous and he had ample time to jot descriptions and compose letters to Celia into his notebook that the professor had brought him. He posted his letters in the wooden box nailed to a post by the camp store. He was nervous about them going out stamped with the return address of the work farm, but he figured Celia would understand his situation, which he explained in his second letter; *I have nothing to be ashamed of*, he wrote. She said as much in her first letter. *It's hard to live without getting stung by a bee once or twice in your life*, she answered. He read this sitting on the screened back porch of the potting shed where he was working, potting geraniums for the farm shop in Mooksville. His hands even after he washed them in the big galvanized sink still smelled of the sludgy potting soil that was made from mule manure and vegetable compost. He held her letter with the tips of his fingers. It smelled of her orangey perfume.

Segregation on the farm was strict. There was no mixing of the races, at work or at meals or in the barracks. The white folks, determined and nervous, felt better when it was like this. Delvin didn't mind. He'd had only a slight and glancing contact with white people; he never missed them, busy as they were organizing themselves and battering the world into shape. He was happy sitting on the bench among the spindly young geraniums. A slight breeze eased through the screen, cooling him. He wished he could swing the flimsy door open and walk out to meet Celia. He thought of the small indentation on the right side of her nose. He thought of this place often. He could remember it when he could not remember (without his crib sheet) the other parts of her. He wanted to sit in a cool place and talk with her about the books they were reading and about the tiny flat pressed-in place on her nose. He had proved slow in the fields, weak really, knocked back by the heavy sunshine, and fell behind early. It made sense to transfer him to the potting shed, and after he was wounded to check-out and -in duty. Much of his time was spent in the shed alone. Here he wrote his letters.

But what could you do, he wrote, *when you find people you cleave to who are up to things you don't go for?*

I guess you get used to what's unnatural to you, she wrote back, *if you can, or try to, but sometimes maybe you can't and I guess that's one of the places grief comes from.*

He could tell she was edging away from him. He mentioned this in a letter, but in the return she didn't address it.

Afternoons in the potting shed he looked out of the half-painted window, thinking of the people he knew, calling their names in a low voice. His mother was first, then his brothers and sister, then Mr. Oliver, then Polly, then the professor and Celia, and on down the line through the boys from the alley and the others he ran with in the woods and climbed with into wild cherry trees in June and the children from the homes and people he had met traveling on the trains and working in the museum, to finally the crew he had met at the farm. He had met a man named Jim here, a limping solitary prisoner, aloof and with eyes that carried an assurance that irritated the white guards and the white prisoners he encountered. Tuesday before, a guard had knocked him down, but he got right up and stood in front of the shabby overweight functionary who had only his outrage and the whole white nation to depend on, looking him straight in the eye.

"You don't sass me, jig," the guard said and hit him in the face again. The lieutenant stopped him from beating Jim further, but he was sent forthwith to the box, a large freestanding tin-roofed closet behind the barracks they used for unreasonable prisoners. A small closed room with a slot in the door for food. Jim stayed there a week and was no different when he came out. He excited Delvin because he seemed able to survive with only—as he saw it—his determination for company. The older man, red-haired like some odd negroes, including the Ghost back home, was not interested in Delvin until he found out he could read and write. He asked Delvin to write a letter for him, which he did, a letter filled with pleading and sadness.

Dear Zee, he dictated as they sat on Jim's narrow cot,

I can not go on no longer in this foolish world without you, not a minute it's likely sometimes, and the dust chokes me and the foul food and the whole wretched disorderly world of provocation and misery. There is no light, no place to rest in this world. I am alone with only the hope of your caress. Come to me. I am alive, trapped behind wire like an animal in a cage built on a sand hill. The sun beats down on us with a force that makes me think the god who designed this world was a madman. I must find shade or some way to believe there will someday be shade. It is not through power or money or arms that this can be achieved. I am left only with love. What a meager portion that seems some days. But it is great and endless, I know it. The love I mean between a man and a woman and through them to the children. This is my only hope in this bitter world.

There was more and Delvin's hand grew tired trying to keep up. Jim would stop, hold his face to the light, sniffing like a hunting dog on a scent, and wait impatiently for him to catch up. "Yes," he said, "the word is *dereliction*, spell it as best you can. It means wreckage." It was strange that he would know so many unusual words and not know how to write. Or read either. Jim said this was because he had been read to in his youth by an actor traveling the vaudeville circuit out west. This actor, a black man, a feeder in a crow act generally but a sometime comedian himself, had found him wandering on a street in Dallas and taken him in.

"I had something like that happen to me," Delvin said.

"Not like this," Jim said. The man had raised him and he had traveled with him as his factotum for several years. The man had held him in the thrall of an iniquitous sexual relationship it had taken years to extricate himself from. He had finally had to beat the man half to death and throw him down the stairs of a boarding house in Kansas City and leave him for dead to get free. "Free," he said smiling sarcastically. "There is no damn freedom for the likes of me in this damn world."

He believed everything in the world was corrupt and diseased.

"Except for family love," Delvin said.

"Yeah, that," Jim said smiling grimly. "There's that, thank God; if you can get to it. This world," he said, looking around as if it was sneaking up on him, "is crooked and defiled. Yet *still*, right down to the smallest speck and scurrying roach, it runs *just fine*. Which leads you to the conclusion that crooked and corrupt is how the world *likes* it."

His glance then from his cot where he sat scrunched up against his knees was haggard and determined, winded.

"What's a man like me to do?" he asked. He looked around as if a crowd was waiting for his answer. He blew his breath out, not a sigh but so he could draw in a strong one behind it. "I conclude it is me who is out of step. I am a foolish man bound for ignominy. But I too it appears have a right to the tree of life. How do I know this?" He twirled his right hand as if he could spiral it through to the truth. "Because I am alive. If I wasn't meant to be here I wouldn't be able to suck breath, I'd be like a fish when you snatch it out of the water. Smothered by air. But I am not, am I? I draw breath and breathe and my heart beats and food sustains me, so I must belong here too. What do you reckon that means?"

He hadn't waited for Delvin to answer any of these questions.

"It must mean that the opposition I bring to the facts of life is necessary too. So it doesn't matter what these dumb white boys have to say about me because I belong here just like they do. And my opposition to them is just as right as theirs is to me."

Delvin said, "I don't think their opposition is right."

"That's because you haven't got the heart yet to look at the world as it is," Jim said. "Maybe that day will come, maybe not. For many it never arrives. Most, really. They see only their side of the struggle."

He blinked into the dimness and made a smacking sound with his full lips. "Well, I am getting tired," he said, and with that he turned on his side and went to sleep.

This is a crazy man, Delvin thought as he sat in the shed, but he was excited by what he'd told him. He missed the professor. He missed riding along dirt roads in the van hauling photographs around the states. *There* was a foolish bit of activity. But he loved sitting out behind the van on summer twilights with citronella oil burning in the little china dish for the mosquitoes, letting the world row darkly along beside them. Time creaked by on those wandering days.

A few nights later Jim was caught trying to escape. They hauled him down off the wire fence, took him into the guard shed and beat him until he couldn't stand and threw him into the box. He might not get out of this simple work farm alive. The farm grew corn and tomatoes and field greens and a little cotton for market and squash and butterbeans for the table. A small community of men working the sandy fields of west Dixie. Every one there except for three or four would go back to homes in the county. Some of the men were related. The white men knew the colored men and vice versa. Delvin was one of the few strangers. Everybody knew his place. Life here was unstirring. Fixed. Moldy, Delvin thought. The white folks hoped they would not have to make another big fight, but they were prepared if one came. Nobody gave up land and power without a fight. Well, what to do? The quiet in the evening here, he thought, is peaceful. It can't help itself. Even in a war they can't be firing the guns *all* the time. There has to be these quiet moments. *In these moments I am refreshed.* He had read these words somewhere. He remembered: Stanley Terrell, the negro philosopher from Harlem, a man known only by negro folks, who wrote that in the clamor and frenzy of the white-run life they were being hustled through, there were still times when we could take our rest, find peace and happiness. *We do not even have to seek them out. There are already here, in moments by the well or behind the barn or walking back from the store carrying a ten-pound can of lard. In the city you can look up: above you is the endless wilderness of sky, a promised land and free to every man, a country unsullied and unclaimable, yours as well as any other's.* He had started looking at the sky more often, studying it, at least for a while. What was that old song Mrs. Parker sang in the kitchen? Yeah: "Before I'd Be A Slave," also called, she said, "Oh Freedom." Oh, freedom. Terrell said freedom was everywhere. In these songs, in the quiet of the day, in the sky when you stop at the washboard and feel the softness of a piece of cloth in your hands, in the eyes of your loved ones. But of course that didn't stop the whip from coming down.

He didn't feel too bad sitting in the shed stuffing flowers into the brown clay pots. He waked each day with a feeling of possibility, a sweet joyous feeling sometimes. The white guard was just outside the door beating a train rail with an iron bar. The prisoners slept side by side on their rough cots and had very little to their names in this place, like sailors out at sea, and in a way this suited Delvin. He had written the professor care of general delivery and got a single answer that he was working in the kitchen of the Gold Flower restaurant on Main street washing dishes and doing a little of the short work. *They are still pondering,* he said, *whether or not to release the museum. Maybe watching to see if it will sprout arms and legs and jump on them. Nothing to do but sit and wait.*

One of the prisoners had a mouth harp that he played the old songs on. Others mocked this music and called out for something more timely. But the player, a small man with close-set lively eyes, refused. So somebody took the harp away from him. Others rose up and tried to get the harp back from the robber, a short man with muscular forearms. He in his turn refused, so they beat him. In the struggle the harp was crushed on the concrete floor, smashed by the heel of a Georgia Logger boot. Now the owner of the instrument cried in his sleep. Delvin wasn't the only one who heard him.

So life went; they had stew beans every night for supper and some kind of pig meat, usually sowbelly, and a corn dish, usually grits, and cornbread. These were among Delvin's natural favorites. Nobody was sentenced here for more than a year, though some had their sentences lengthened for what the white men called misbehavior. Sentences of over a year went to state prison. This is a work farm, they said, not a prison. What did they know?

By time he got out there had been no word from Tennessee and he hadn't heard from the professor for over two weeks. A man Josie got out with him and the two of them walked into town together on the dirt road that ran through the corn and tomato fields and the fields of sweet peppers. Delvin appreciated the company, but he wasn't interested just then in any more lectures about philosophy or racial politics, which this man Josie was known for. Josie said he didn't mind and then launched into a monologue about general restrictions placed on negroes and what this fact represented in the larger scheme of things. The negro's hidden superior strength was what the gist seemed to Delvin.

On a little rise Josie stopped and told Delvin to turn around and look and he did and the two of them gazed back down the long slope at the farm, a shabby, roughhewn settlement among its vegetable fields.

"A place you could rub out with the bottom of your hand," Josie said, "a ridiculous congregation of punishment for forgetful or over-energetic colored men, a crushed, upended heap lying like a dog exposing its spotted belly to the high-class sunshine pouring down upon it."

On a wide leather band he was wearing one of the first wrist-watches Delvin had ever seen and he had a faded straw panama set back on his head and he snorted through his gob of a nose and spit a white fleck that snagged on a pepper leaf. He stretched himself and worked his shoulders—throwing off the shame and degradation, he said. "I can feel it sliding back down this hill," he said, smiling his snaggle-toothed smile.

Delvin had been returned a short gray pencil and his old blue flip-top notebook as well as a copy of the passing novel *Flight* by Walter White of Chicago and printed in that city by the Constant Press. As he read the book—as he did with every book—Delvin had turned back often to study the title and copyright pages, wondering about the world that had produced the volume. He was touched by the county's willingness to return his property. He had thought the authorities would simply throw his belongings away, or at least complicate their retrieval, but it had them ready in a paper sack with his name scribbled in black ink on the side. They even gave him the sack.

He mentioned this to Josie, who began to make crowing noises, flapping his arms with his hands tucked under his armpits as he jumped around him.

"Well, all right," Delvin said. Jim Crow—he got it. "Where you headed now?" he asked.

Josie paused mid-crow and shook his head. "I'll just trot off in one direction or the other as the incitement takes me," he said with a softened inflection.

Delvin thought about offering him a ride in the van but he wasn't sure the professor had gotten the van back or what he might say about the non-owner offering a stranger a ride. He had been in the past a little testy about such behavior on Delvin's part.

He poked around looking but the professor was nowhere to be found. He could hardly believe he had gone off and left him. With Josie he walked across town to the negro barbershop. He waked the single barber in his porcelain chair and asked him—fat, unshaven, with a merry manner—if he'd seen Professor Carmel, the spare-set gentleman in a long canvas coat and so forth.

The barber said he had indeed and that many like himself—meaning in the negro establishment—had been given a message to pass on to Delvin when he showed up.

"What message was that?"

"Let me see," the barber, a Mr. Floris, said and rummaged in a small counter drawer among combs and hair nets and various pieces of old dismantled hand clippers until he found what he was looking for, a folded piece of blue paper with Delvin's name on the outside in the professor's florid script.

I would have squatted naked in the rain in the public square waiting for you son but they threatened me with the whip and the pains of pitch fire if I did not get out of this town and put at least thirty-five miles between myself and it or that is between the museum and their ignorant dishonorable asses. So I have hightailed it. I am headed to Haverness and will wait if allowed for you there. Don't fret or be low spirited any more than you have to. Obstacles are only a means for sharpening the wits. Glory to you, boy.

It was signed with the professor's full name, Professor Clemens John Carmel MS, a name the first part of which Delvin had not heard the professor call himself before.

"Well," he said, "I guess I need you to tell me how to get to Haverness."

"Haverness," the barber said. "I can not only tell you how to get there, but also where you might find yourself a ride with a gentleman going that way."

He got a ride with Arthur Turnbill, who was hauling a load of sweetgrass hay to Mr. J. B. Suber, a white man up in Conniston county. Josie said he'd like to come along. In the truck Josie squirmed, fidgeted, popped his fingers on the gray metal dash and talked all the time until Mr. Turnbill asked him to take a little time off from it. He then commenced to humming. The humming was tuneless and this drove both Delvin and Mr. Turnbill crazy until Mr. Turnbull, a narrow-faced man with large fleshy lips, asked Josie to get in the back with the hay. Josie looked as if he'd been asked to swim with alligators.

"I'm sorry," he said. "I'm just the naturally jumpy type. They say it was because my mother spilt hot grease on me when I was a baby, causing me not to trust in the given supports of this life, but I am working hard to get over—"

"Please," Mr. Turnbull, himself a nervous man, said, jerking his head and his eyes to the left. He had pulled over onto the shoulder and stopped the truck when he performed this pantomime. The sky was gradually filling in the southwest corner with bruised shadow-gray clouds like big balled fists. Delvin could smell the sweet dry scent of the hay. Off in the distance two red cows stood in the shade of a large oak tree. They didn't appear to be concerned by any circumstance in the world of human beings. Delvin experienced a small quiet flood of happiness. What a thing it was to be alive. The sky was the glossy blue of turquoise jewelry. He started a popping little finger tune on the dash. Turnbill eyed him. "Yikes," he softly said and apologized. "You want me to get in the back too?"

"I want both of you to be still before I put you out walking on the road."

Except for a small burst of song from Josie they both remained silent unless spoken to—both still in the cab—for the rest of the way into Haverness.

In Haverness a row of houses on the highway opened into a district of shops and stores around a courthouse square that pushed up on the far side against a long cotton warehouse. They didn't find the professor, but there was a note from him held by the minister of the Walls of Jericho Baptist church that said he was called away to attend the funeral of his cousin up in Rance City but would wait there for a week to see if they were following. They traveled by freight to RC, but there too they missed Professor Carmel. He left word with another minister, Caleb Jenkins of the local AME church, housed in a green-painted low wooden building behind the Rance City peanut mill. In the note, scrawled nearly illegibly on a scrap of greasy paper bag still smelling of fried chicken, he apologized but said against his will he was forced to leave RC due to complications with the local officials concerning a fracas over some allegedly pilfered property.

Delvin was ready to push on, but Josie was by this time exhausted.

"Our time on this earth is by its nature a trial to the endurance of human beings," he said, "but I see no need to make things worse."

He said he thought he might tarry a while in Rance City.

Delvin said he was sorry to see him leave the expedition, but he understood.

Josie then changed his mind half a dozen times before flopping down on the side of remaining in town.

"I can find work here," he said, "maybe picking plums or some such thing." It was long past plum season and the only plums Delvin had heard of in this part of the world anyway were of the sour yellow variety that flourished beside the roadways throughout. They were free for the picking, but few were known to want to pay money for any amount of them.

"I have notions to become a cook," Josie said. "Cooks have time on their hands and are known for their eccentric and sometimes foolish-seeming ways. My off hours will give me time to work on my book."

This book fascinated Delvin. Josie had twice shown it to him as they traveled, but though he (or his scrivener) had covered both sides of many pieces of scrap paper he carried wrapped in oilskin in his county-issued paper bag, Delvin had been unable to make any sense of it. This, Delvin figured, was the case with many a would-be writer. He himself might be among that unfortunate number. This thought dashed him slightly, but he remembered that he was still very young. This, so he figured, weighed in his favor; he had many years of energetic effort ahead of him, and even if his novice attempts made little sense and were hardly more than notes, quotations and lists of people and items he had encountered on his travels, he believed he would someday have the skill to shape these materials into a narrative stunning in its force and clarity, or at least readable.

"Fruit preserves," Josie said when he asked about the interest in plums. "Fruit preserves are the secret passion of many a soul. Loved everywhere. You ever seen anybody turn down a helping of fruit preserves? Of course you haven't. And what better way to start as a chef than with concoctions the main ingredient of which is free for the picking."

Delvin pointed out that they had missed the plum season by two months at least.

"Gives me time to gather my materials and procure use of a kitchen," Josie said with a ferocious and sly and somewhat doggish grin.

They were both dressed in faded overalls, Josie in a strap undershirt and carrying a greasy leather jacket and Delvin in a soft-collared red shirt that along with his underwear he washed every night and hung up to dry. His shoes were getting old and cracked but he hadn't the money to replace them.

They walked around town looking in shop windows. Josie preferred the hardware stores where he could peruse cookware and other kitchen paraphernalia and Delvin enjoyed office supply stores. They both enjoyed the mule barn. In Rance City mules were sold out of a brick barn attached to a hardware and farm supply store. They worked their way over there past the sewing shop, the department store, the pharmacy with the spinning pinwheels in the window, the dime store (where they stopped off and walked the undulate wooden floors looking for pocket knives which they found and couldn't afford but enjoyed studying through the glass case window), the men's shop, dress shop, red brick hotel and restaurant, paint store, granite bank with recessed windows and big brass door, appliance store with the washing machines and new Frigidaires standing out on the sidewalk ready for purchase, a couple of insurance offices, two car dealerships (Ford and Packard), the movie theater showing a double bill of *Constant Motion* and *The Flamingo Kid Goes to Paris*, starring Manfred Boudin the Dancing Cowboy. He thought occasionally of the life of movie stars, tickled that at the moment he was thinking of Gloria Swanson or Ramón Navarro they were at that same moment, possibly, sitting down to supper in their dining nooks or washing their socks in the upstairs bathroom, maybe cutting pictures out of a magazine to paste into a scrapbook. Movie stars, soldiers, famous negro writers and artists excited him. He was prone, if not to hero worship, to affection for successful people. He felt some of this affection for Josie who seemed far ahead of him with his plans and accomplishments. In one part of himself he knew Josie was scatterbrained and bootless, but still he wanted to believe in his writing plans; he was the first person he'd met who was writing a book, and Josie had encouraged him to begin one too. Plenty of room in that profession, he said.

They talked often of books and were in fact talking of the book *Smashed Idols*, written by the negro thinker Davis Stuckey, who lived, so the flyleaf said, on an island in the St. Lawrence Seaway, when they entered the Harding Hardware and Sale Barn on Stomont street across from the city waterworks. A boy Delvin's age was leading three mules down the low wooden ramp from the barn into the street. He tied the mules to an iron post ring and went back inside. The smells of equine matters reminded Delvin of the stable shed back in Chattanooga. He wondered how the Ghost was doing. Probably by now riding the horses around town with a feather in his hat. And felt a shiver when he thought of what still lay in wait for him there, police lurking, his face most probably still on a wanted poster at the post office (though he'd never seen it out in the world), men growing old but still on standby, keeping an eye out for the cold-hearted shooter of white children, hands ready to reach out quick as a cat to catch that boy should he reappear in the oldtime streets. He shuddered. Nights he had lain awake thinking of the trouble to come. They entered the store and poked around for a while among the metal and leather and wood items. A white man looked hard at them and Delvin smiled a friendly smile. "Cooking equipment," he said. "Over yonder," the man said, indicating with his chin some low shelves. "Thank you, sir." He had never cared much for these stores. In Harding's the equipment, tools, the bulbous or spirally or contorted or bent metal and other work minutiae, baffled and oppressed him so that in a short time he began to sweat and feel as if he needed air.

"I'll be over in the barn," he told Josie and started out of the store.

As he exited through the front door he saw a small towheaded man pass—foolishly—behind the tied mules. One of the mules, in a motion quick as a snake, lashed out with his back feet and caught the man in the forehead. The man went down as if he'd been shot. He lay in the dirt street crumpled on his side with his arms stretched out ahead of him like he was running. But he wasn't moving. His eyes were open and his eyeballs were red with blood.

The stable boy who had come back outside and a white man who leapt suddenly past Delvin both pulled at the mules. The man struck the offending one, a blocky gray, on the side of the head with his fist. The mule's knees buckled and he almost went down.

"Goddamn you beast," the man cried. He then turned and struck the colored boy. The boy skittered away, with the man chasing him for a few steps before he turned and came back.

Delvin was shoved roughly aside by men rushing from the store, but he gathered himself and pegged into the street to look. The downed man, wearing overalls and a gray suit coat, had a fresh red quarter moon mark sunk into his forehead. The mark ran up into his stiff yellow hair. There was no blood and except for his red eyes no other sign of wounding.

"God, Clarence," someone said over and over, "God, Clarence." Speaking apparently to the felled man.

Josie, breathing heavily, joined Delvin. With a loud clatter that made people jump, a big wooden barrel containing rakes and shovels by the door was knocked over. The implements spilled onto the sidewalk. A large man stepped on a shovel and stumbled and fell to his knees. "Oh, Jesus," another man said. Two women in light summer dresses had tears in their eyes as they rushed up. "Help him," one of them said, like she was ordering schoolchildren, even though people were already bending to the fallen man. The men had pale or red or red and pale mottled faces. The faces of the africano men watching darkened.

"Get back," a large white man yelled. "Get back, you"—as if everybody was trying to assault the man on the ground.

Somebody spoke from the crowd to the fallen man as if he were only sleeping, telling him to get up. "Get up off the ground, Clarence," the calm clear male voice said. "Get up now."

A man in a dark suit knelt beside him. Another man knelt on the downed man's other side and raised his limp hand and massaged it. Another negro boy led the mules back into the barn. They too had an agitated look, and one kept stepping sideways. The boy hit the stepping mule with the flat of his hand and the mule dropped its head and came along. Delvin couldn't see where the first boy had gone. He hoped he was all right.

Police arrived in a car and then the boxy ambulance hauled up just ahead of a dust cloud that rolled over the assembled. A woman began coughing and couldn't stop; a large man in a checked coat started to pull her down the street but she resisted until he quit and then they stood looking at the ambulance attendants as they bent over the man, who hadn't moved.

One of the attendants, a slim man wearing a white coat over a gray long-sleeved jersey, carefully straightened the man's arms and then, as if he didn't quite know what to do with them, folded them over the man's stomach. The man's eyes were open and he was looking straight up. It was clear that the fallen man was dead. This fact spread through the crowd. People gasped and somebody—it sounded like a man—began to cry.

The limp body was lifted onto a stretcher, placed in the ambulance and carried away.

Delvin and Josie stayed until the area had begun to clear. Far down the street, under a large sycamore tree, two colored boys stood in the street, pulling a piece of rubber between them as they watched the dispersing crowd. A policeman asked Delvin if he had seen the accident.

"Nawsuh," he said, "I didn't. I come out and saw the gentleman on the ground." He'd known he was dead though, he said.

"How is that?" the policeman, a man with white-blond hair and a creak in his voice, asked.

"I use to work in a funeral parlor."

"Around here?"

"Nawsuh. Up in Illinois."

The policeman asked what his name was and what business he had in Rance City, but before Delvin could give him the name he had used on the work farm—Custis Jones—he was called away.

Delvin knew better than to open his mouth with the authorities.

Whatever you said, there was no telling how they would take it. Why had he done it? What was wrong with him? He was a fugitive for goodness' sake.

Josie had edged off and disappeared around the corner. Delvin couldn't pull himself away until long after the dust had settled and the crowd had moved on. The store personnel returned to their tasks. Inside the door the mules stood in dimness at a hitching rail. They were eating out of feedbags. The gray stamped one foot and swished its short black tail. Delvin watched them thinking—he didn't know what he was thinking. *What did it matter what you did?* That was what he was thinking. The hoofprint a death's grin on the man's forehead. Then he too turned back to his life and hurried around the corner and up the rising street toward the courthouse. He didn't slow down (couldn't walk *too* fast, might catch the white men's attention) until he was on the other side of the square where Josie waited.

"Let's head over to the tracks," Josie said.

"You change your mind about coming along?"

"I'm stud'n it."

As they walked through the small colored quarter—shotgun houses painted in flat strong colors (yellow, blue, green) faded to a soft cloudiness—Delvin had the feeling he was being followed. When he turned around to look he couldn't see anybody suspicious. A boy down the street was turning his dog in a circle with a piece of pork rind. A girl tossed a jacks ball against the low brick wall sunk in the grassy face of a small hill before the Antioch Christian church. A man dusted with his yellow handkerchief the hood ornament of a Pontiac automobile parked in front of the Casual Grocery. People on front porches waited for news of the death that would soon provide an evening's chinning material. But no sleuths, no lurkers. Still, as they walked he felt as if somebody was on their trail.

"You're just shook up," Josie said. "Death'll do that to any man."

"I've seen death before," Delvin said, though the sudden sharpness of the mule's kick and the man falling as he did, straight down with his arms thrown out, had shocked him. He really wanted to go off by himself and think about what he'd seen, let the troubled, disconnected feelings run through him. Too quick, he had thought. Too impossibly quick. What did it matter what you did? It made him sick to think that.

They crossed the double tracks and walked along them toward a low place that was bridged by a creosoted wooden trestle. On the other side, where the tracks curved in toward a pecan grove, was the town's small hobo camp. Just before they reached the trestle Delvin said he didn't want to go down there right then. He wanted to stay in town. He returned along the tracks without Josie who said he'd wait for him at the camp.

On his way he met no one he thought might have been following. But when he reached the quarter and began to walk its dusty gray dirt streets he again sensed that somebody was behind him.

He stopped in the shady yard of a little frame church and sat at a picnic table under a big pollarded magnolia and wrote another letter to Celia. Having an interest in a woman gave a man something to do in unsettled times. He told her about the dead man.

His face, he wrote, *had a puffed-up, stubborn look, as if he was refusing what had come for him.* Get up and run, Delvin had wanted to yell to him.

He was a short man, slim, maybe hiding a secret flaw or vice he wanted no one to find out about. Maybe he owed money, maybe he had recently hurt somebody he cared for. Soon he'd be naked in a room he'd never visited, might never have thought of. Washed and cleaned of his last bit of earthly dirt and dust. Mr. Oliver always left just a little place of unwashed skin so the deceased could be recognized, he said, by the dust that awaited him.

This was not true but he wrote it anyway.

He stopped writing. A little boy in blue shorts stared at him from the street. Delvin waved—the boy continued staring at him—and went back to his letter.

I've felt for the last hour or so that somebody's following me. It's an odd feeling, but familiar, and that's odd. When I saw the man fall down—

*when I saw he was dead—I thought What does it matter what you do?
I hate thinking that. It's got to matter. I felt so frustrated. It was like
the words were written in the dirt and I wanted to rub them out. But
they were in my head. I want to rub them out of there but I can't. What
does it matter? Aren't we supposed to . . .*

He stopped. No one out in the street looked suspicious; maybe
his tracker had ducked into a house or store. Or maybe it was a different kind of follower. What kind was that?

I'm on my way back to Chattanooga, he wrote.

*I think of you off at school. It's hard to picture. Big buildings I guess.
I saw a college once—on top of a mountain, but it was a blacksmith's
college. They had fires in caves. Where was that? I studied with Mr.
Oliver at home. We read all of Shakespeare and many of the classics
like Sir Walter Scott and those boys. Fielding and Tobias Smollett,
who wrote a very funny book. Englishmen. Except for Othello they
didn't have any colored folks over there. Daniel Defoe. He wrote a
scary book about the black plague. It had nothing to do with negro folk.*

He was rambling, passing time, making up his life. Out in the
street a small man with a shiny black head stood looking at him.
He was fanning himself with a large yellow straw hat. When he saw
Delvin notice him he started toward him. He walked straight up the
little two-track church driveway, came up to Delvin and stuck out
his hand.

"What's that?" Delvin said. He shook the man's small puffy
hand.

"My name is Ornelio P. Rome," the man said in a high, slightly
hollow voice with a little stuttery wheeze toward the end (pleasant
for all that). His shaved head, the color of the dark shine on a crystal
ball, gleamed.

"Did the professor send you?" Delvin asked, suddenly sure that
was it.

"Sho nuff he did."

Mr. Rome put his hat back on. It dwarfed his face and made him look like a wise child. Delvin just caught himself from laughing. Mr. Rome was wearing a stained and rumpled slightly shiny green linen suit.

Raring back into a squared-off stance, chest thrust forward so his flesh pressed against the buttons of his dirty ruffled sky-blue shirt, with his hands on his hips, the little man in a cracked approximation of the professor's voice said, "Professor Carmel has this to say to you: 'Continue on, my boy. Do not be daunted and do not feel as if you have to catch up to me. Life takes us in the direction we are meant to go. We do not know who we may meet, how long we may travel along side by side, or when we may part. If you and I have come to a parting, then fare thee well, my boy, godspeed and thanks for your company.'"

By time he finished the speech, for that is what it was, he was wheezing more heavily and making little *tick tick tick* noises. Mr. Rome had removed his hat during the last bit. He brandished it before him like an offering. Delvin almost took it, but the gesture was preceding a half bow.

"O. P. Rome, Verbatim Messenger, at your service," he said.

"Verbatim?" Delvin didn't know whether to laugh or clap.

"Word for word. Word by word. You express in your own personal form what you want to say and I will repeat it to your recipient, verbatim—word for word—so there is no mistake as to your intentions."

"How about the, uh, what is it—the feeling?"

"Ah, yes—the tone, the timbre, the gusto, or lack thereof. Yes. There, my boy, is where you find the art. Any parrot can be taught a speech. But only a great actor—no, not even an actor—a great *expresser*, let us say, can put across a verbatim line. An actor—you never can be sure if he means what he's saying. Every line sounds sincere. But with yours truly, it's clear where the meaning begins and where it leaves off and we return to the ordinary business of living. I take it you were moved by your friend's . . . enthusiasm?"

"Why, yes, I was," Delvin said, still wanting to laugh or at least chuckle. "How is the professor?"

"Dauntless, but sad, I would say, moody a little, more weary than

he would like to admit, but valiant still, a great captain of the everlasting road."

"I'd say I've grieved for him, but I've been so busy trying to catch
up with him that I hadn't had time to settle down and really pine.
How much do you charge for a message?"

"Two dollars for that last."

"Could you repeat it?"

"Yessir. You get one free repetition. Then the price is a dime."

"Fine."

The man repeated the message with the same worldly-wise brio.

"It's kind of a farewell," Delvin said.

"I would say it fits into that category."

"Do you have set messages, or does everybody have to make up
his own?"

The man pressed his cheek with the side of his thumb, leaving
a faintly gleaming grease mark. "I do have a selection of messages
appropriate to the occasion."

"Could I send one back?"

"You could try. But I might not be able to find the gentleman you
are looking for. That is sometimes a problem."

"If you can't find him do I get a refund?"

'Yes, but only half. I have to cover my expenses."

"Where did you meet the professor?"

"In Cullawee."

"That in Alabama?"

"Arkansas."

"Whoa. I'm way behind."

"Life has swept him along like a leaf before the wind."

"Is he all right?"

"He's doing fine, but last I saw of him he was in a hurry to be on
the road."

"Where to?"

"I believe he is heading west."

"I'm going to miss him," Delvin said, and as he said this he experienced a pulpy plummeting feeling in his chest and a dampness in

his eyes. He looked down the street where two men in dusty clothes were backing a mule up to a buckboard. The cuffs of the men's pants were ragged and the shoes of one were tied around with hanks of pale cloth. *Mules going contrary all over the city*, he thought, the words like a sentence he wanted to write down.

"So no return," the little man said.

"What's that?"

"On the message?"

"No, I don't believe so."

"Ah, well," Mr. Rome said, looking around without much relish. "Maybe I will find some business in this town."

"All your work long-distance?"

"Only about half. I get just as much local as out-of-town. I've begun to prefer the in-town, actually."

"Why's that?"

The man had taken a seat across from Delvin. He was so small that the tabletop came up to his puffy chest. "It's hard to make a profit of these long journeys."

"You travel by train."

"Boxcar class, yes."

"You been on the western roads?"

"Have I? You name the line, I've ridden it. I've been a passenger on the Espy, the GN, the Katy, the Octopus, the old Cough & Snort, the Damn Rotten Grub, the UP . . . You traveled in the west?"

"No, not me. But I'm about to catch a ride out this afternoon, headed northeast."

Mr. Rome said like as how he would be leaving town himself.

"Thought you were looking for local business."

"These little towns don't often care for my services. They're packed so tight they don't need me. Sometimes though—well, you never can tell."

Delvin got up and they walked together down the dusty street that smelled of hardwood fires and the sweet tang of summer dusk to the camp. Later that afternoon, with Josie, they caught an eastbound L&S freight.

• • •

The sun snagged in the naked branches of a far-off grove of dead trees. Through the trees Delvin could see glints and lusters where some body of water caught the light.

In an empty wood-paneled B&O line boxcar Delvin settled in next to a skinny older negro man carrying a greasy carpetbag. The car smelled of the dried corn it had most recently transported. The man smelled of road wear and animal grease. He introduced himself as Frank Brooks.

Delvin introduced Mr. Rome, who was pressed up against the front wall of the car. The waning daylight shone through the box-car's open door.

Mr. Rome said he might return to his home base up in Roanoke. "I miss the smell of the hemlocks," he said.

The man Frank was traveling from the west—Phoenix, he said, where he had a wife and two children.

At the other end of the car a few white men sat with their bindles. There was race mixing on the trains, but without much friendliness. People sought those they took to be their own, were nervous about other races. Negroes were called dinges, shines, skillets, by the whites, the whites, ofays, slicks, jeffs, by the negroes. Bindlestiffs, beefers, zips—the criminal element—were enough of a concern without adding racial confusions to the mix. Delvin, no longer an angelica or a gonsil, no longer a reg, was now a stamper, maybe a jack, so taken by some or would be soon enough.

Frank, this new fellow, a jack, settling his back carefully against the warped boxcar wall, said last week he'd seen a fight where a jeff— "big pink-faced monstrosity"—had thrown an africano man off a train. The fight had got more than one hurt, on both sides, Frank said. "Like you couldn't trade out of it," he said, raising a grimy cap that reveled a lighter tan forehead, "like you got somebody there—some colored man—who all of a sudden lost his everything, you know, like some magic act done took away his humanness—*Get dis sack off the train*. You look at it, think I got to the wrong world. It's a mistake."

"I steer clear," Mr. Rome said.

"Can't always do that," Frank said picking at his bottom teeth with a split twig he'd fished from the inner pocket of his tattered salt-and-pepper jacket.

"That is true," Mr. Rome said with a sigh.

Josie had not come into the boxcar. He was up top or riding on one of the empty flatcars. He said he preferred the open air. Delvin half wanted to go with him, but then he decided to get in the boxcar and try to sleep. He'd felt tired lately, as if the complications of the world outside prison were too much for him; he figured he had to build up a tolerance. When he mentioned this to Mr. Rome, the little man told him he was just feeling the burden of the colored man.

"These white folks are unrightly the black man's burden," he said. "Their foolishness and ignorance." He sat up straighter and looked around, a tiny person of color alone in the kingdom. Delvin asked—off-handedly—if Mr. Rome could give examples of some of his more interesting messages. He was thinking about a bath, a tub somebody'd told him about, carved out of rock in a far island stream under shaggy trees.

"Sans names," Mr. Rome said. "Nor revealing details. That way it's not really divulging secrets." He straightened up and his face brightened. "I am standing under this here tree holding a hatful of cherries," one began, he said; it was, like many of the others, a plea for a lover's return. "I can't sleep at night without you by my side," another declared, a plea from an older woman—"You'd think she might be young," Mr. Rome said—to her wandering husband of nearly fifty years. Another time a one-legged man stranded in a town by a frozen lake in Minnesota pleaded for his sweetheart to relent. "'Your love could melt this icy world and set me free,'" Mr. R quoted in a hushed and passionate voice.

"What you talking about there?" the man Frank said, friendly, working a bit of string between his fingers like a weave. "You some kinda—"

"Oh, no, my son," Mr. Rome said, and Delvin chimed in that Mr. O. P. Rome was a professional message carrier.

"Yes," Mr. Rome said. "Declarationist, full-throated pleader and issuer of challenges and stomp-footed assertations. No word spoken too softly or too loudly for me not to be able to carry its full weight. Nothing loses a ounce on the journey—to whoever, or whatever—I once carried a message to a speckle-faced mule—is able to pay the fee. For a dime I'll carry a message across the room or up to four blocks away. Higher prices the farther I have to go, but I will not only carry an exact rendition of your missive, I will provide the appropriate— that is to say, your own, or what you wish to have as your own, feelings, complete with intonations, speech quirks or added gustatives, per message, limit three to a customer."

"You aint never heard of Western Union?" Frank said, shuffling himself into a better seat.

"Primitive upstarts," Mr. Rome said. "I follow a profession as old as talking itself."

Frank began to peel a potato with his thumbnail. "Yall want some?" He eyed the little man. "Much money in that old racket?"

"Not enough to buy freedom from the white man, but I get by."

"None of us gon make enough to buy that kind of freedom," Frank said. "Though I's heard they's a town down in Florida populated entirely by negro folk—no whites allowed."

"Says the white man," Mr. Rome said.

"You don't think we are free?" Delvin said. Maybe I am haunting this world, he thought, a fluttered-up spirit on the loose. Down the way a knobby little man said, "I got a misery in my leg's been hounding me for three years—"

"Hell, we don't even look free," Frank said. He leaned forward and studied the tiny Mr. Rome. "You probably make your best money when they's a calamity," he said.

"That I do. Folks get talkative when there's trouble. I once carried a message made up entirely of groans and whizzing sighs. But you can't count on calamity's always being in town when you are."

"Profiteer."

"I wouldn't call anything I do very profitable."

"You ever been in a calamity? A big one?"

"A few," the little man said cheerfully.

"Like which?"

Mr. Rome pressed his thumb against his cheek, a fond gesture. "I was in the Boveen, Missouri, tornado last year. You read about it in the paper. And year before that I was in that big hurricane that wiped out the whole east side of Texas. I almost drowned in that monstrosity. And I was in Houston for the big Whiteside warehouse fire where thirty blocks went up in flames. I carried three dozen messages after that one. Mostly in-town, but one I carried by rail and bus and dusty aching foot all the way to Shield, Saskatchewan—Canada—to a little white house in a walnut grove where an old woman lived with her thirty-five-year-old deaf and dumb son."

"What'd you tell her?"

"Wadn't for her. The message was for the boy."

"What was it?"

"I'm not free to repeat messages where you might be able to tell who they were from or for. I've let slip too much already. My customers rely on my discretion"—diskretchen, he said—"as you can understand. They're only for those paid up to receive em, but I can say it was one of my greatest challenges."

"You just write it out for him?"

"I figured writing the words down was not giving full service on the dollar. And I'd had to charge extra for the stretch and general botheration."

"So what did you do?" the man Frank said, tapping his narrow forehead with the thumb and middle finger of his left hand. He had a sharp vertical crease running down the center of his forehead.

"Well sir," Mr. Rome said—he was collecting a little pile of corn kernels in the brim of his hat that he held before him in his lap—"I of course had to act it out for the boy. I call him a boy even though he was a solid sturdy gentleman with big rough hands he kept flexing like he was working up to break something, but he had a manner that was like that of a child and his mother treated him like one. He may have been mentally slow as well as D and D, but I realize that is no excuse for treating any of God's creatures as less than precious.

Anyhow, I had a cap the man had given me in Houston, a greasy, faded red cap he'd passed to me for just this situation. I'd been studying all the way across the country (I was on the Espy, then the Falls & Canadian) about what it was I ought to do and I'd come up with a good show. I went to whooping and hollering and swooping and rolling on the ground and beating on my chest like a wild man, repeating the message as I went. This boy—this bald-headed near gray-headed man—started to shrieking. It was one of the most peculiar noises I ever heard in my life, that shriek. He began to mimick my actions, jumping and swooping and rolling on the ground and throwing dirt up in the air and making this shrieking noise like some kind of demented soul—just an awful sound—until he had me so worked up that I'm embarrassed to say I busted out into tears. Right there in front of both of them. I just sagged against this big wire rabbit cage they had there by this old walnut tree we was standing under, sobbing like my heart was broke, which it nearly was. Hell, the man I was reporting on was alive and here I was bringing the happy word to his family and I was crying like a baby. And fool thing was, when we all finally got calmed down, the woman told me her boy read lips. Just like he was hearing what you said. Damnness."

"Maybe you aint exactly cut out for the work," Frank said.

Mr. Rome eyed him. He sucked his gray lips in and puffed them out.

"Fact that I have continued on after that particular episode might tell you I am. Oh, I'm a natural for it, that's for sure. It was something else, the weeping." He looked off to the open boxcar door where the day's sliding-away blue sky shone brightly in its last moments on earth. His looking extended in time, seconds ticking along. The clack of the wheels came up through the floor. Somebody down the way, a white man, made through cupped fingers a bird call like a lonely thing. Mr. Rome peering off somewhere. Like he was hearing words. "So freedom can never be taken fully from us," he said finally, "who knows if even death can do it." This man maybe not even noticing the sky but soaring through the wild prairies of his own mind, voiceless.

"Well, what was it?" the man Frank said, pulling gently at his bottom lip.

"What was what, son?"

"What something else was it that made you sob like a baby."

"Oh. Fatigue. Mere fatigue."

To that Delvin wanted to say suddenly no. No. It's all right, he wanted to say, to be sad. You don't have to be ashamed of it. Go on and speak. But he didn't. He too was tired, and not sad enough, felt ghostly, as if his foot, his hand, his whole body, could sift right on through the bottom of this car and disperse.

"What about you, my fine young man," Mr. Rome said, addressing him. "What interesting tale have you to tell?"

Delvin rubbed silky corn dust between his fingers. Down at the other end of the car the white men were playing cards. In the middle space, leaned against the opposite closed door, a man mended with a needle and thread a pair of sky-blue pants. Delvin had never seen trousers that shade of blue, and satiny, shining. He wanted to touch the cloth. "I think I want to get you to carry a message to a friend for me," he said.

"Say and it's done," Rome said.

They settled on a fee, and Mr. Rome promised to carry a message to Celia if Delvin could come up with the two dollars.

"I don't see how you can make any money at all," Frank said. "Mail a letter for two cents."

Mr. Rome agreed. He was an agreeable man.

"Back in Tulsa they could have used you," Frank said.

The little man shuddered. "You talking about that lamentable time, aren't you?"

"I can call myself doing that," Frank said. "I just come through there is why I do, day before yesterday. Tulsa's where I's born and raised. And it brought it back to my mind."

"Were you there during the massacre?" Delvin asked. Everybody'd heard about that. He wanted something to eat, but he had nothing beyond Frank's shared potato. Just then Mr. R pulled a squished ham and mustard sandwich out of his coat pocket, tore it in three pieces and handed two off to his fellow passengers. They sat quietly for a minute or two chewing. Somebody down on the other end was whistling "Barbry Allen," the sound clear and fresh over the clack of the wheels.

"Yeah," Frank said, "exactly." As if they had been conversing all the time—words moving about, arranging, preserving, stacking in his mind. "Riot the white folks called it, but massacree it was."

They all knew the story, even Delvin, who had heard it from the professor. Three hundred negroes killed, eight hundred wounded, all because a white girl had gotten upset when a black boy tripped and grabbed her arm for support.

"Yessir, I know all about it," Frank said. "That boy, Dickie Do Rowland, was one of my cousins. He wadn't nothing but a shoe-shine boy in that office building downtown. The white woman—she was just a seventeen-year-old girl—operated the elevator. When old Dickie Do—he was nineteen but you would have thought he was still just a child—when he took a break from his shoeshine stand to use the restroom upstairs he tripped coming into the elevator and grabbed this girl—her name was Sarah something—"

"Page," the little man said, "it was Sarah Page."

"That's it. And the one who *really* caused it, this white clerk in a close-by clothing store, this dumb jeff, heard her scream—I guess she was just a nervous person, scared of colored people—and rushed to her and saw Dickie leaving the building—*running*, the man said, as who wouldn't if a white woman started screaming—and he come on this girl and said she was all shook up—about being *assaulted,* when it was just a case of a poor chuckleheaded boy grabbing to hold on. That's how it started. The police come and took him the next day, little Dickie Do. He was sitting at home eating his breakfast and talking to this little puppy dog he used to have, little black and white spotted feist that could do tricks—he talked to that dog like it was a human being—and they came up on the porch and hollered for him to come out, Dickie Do, and talk to em. He knew right off what it was. He maybe could have turned tail, but he didn't, even though my auntie said he'd been up worrying hisself, about what she didn't know, for half the night. She had to get up and make him a milkroot punch to get him off to sleep. But they took him down to the courthouse and put him in jail. Somehow the word on the affair got in the paper—"

"The negro paper," the little man said, "won't it?"

"Yes, it was, the *African Tribune*. They'd got the word that the white mens was coming to lynch him. That's when it started. My uncle and a bunch of other mens put on they uniforms—

"This was right after the Great War, wasn't it?" Delvin said.

"Yes, it was," Frank said, "pretty near. And a whole bunch of em put on they army uniforms and got they guns and marched down to the courthouse to protect Dickie Do."

He reached between his spread knees and patted the dusty floor with both hands. "Well, the white boys heard about this and they grabbed *they* guns and *they* marched down to the courthouse. There was a standoff, getting nowhere, and after a while some of the colored boys went home after the sheriff told them he would protect Dickie. Everybody was scared because just the month before these white boys had lynched a little jew man because they didn't like something *he* was doing. They didn't like nothing they wont doing theyselves."

Frank sifted a little corn dust from one hand to the other. "Well, it rocked back and forth with some folkses leaving and more coming and the sheriff and his boys up on the roof and hiding in the office behind tipped-over desks and such at the top of the courthouse stairs and outside the white boys pumping themselves up and the colored boys scared—everybody scared about to pop—and then the city police and the National Guard showed up and they went over to the quarter and began rounding up our boys and taking them over here to the fairgrounds where they had fences to stick em behind. All the while the white boys down at the courthouse kept trying to make our boys leave, but they had already left and come back once and won't leaving again. It was night by now. And then they started shooting at each other and that was it."

He leaned back against the pale wooden bulkhead and then he sunk his head and looked at the floor. He stayed that way for a long minute. The train hooted at a crossing, long singlethroated dying wail. Lights far off at some settlement or other. Then he raised his head and looked at his listeners.

"I was down in a ditch behind the Lazarus department store talking to my friend Hoster about getting on to the courthouse when came a wave of colored men running the other way through the alley and out into the lot where the ditch was. I got down in a big old pipe that stuck out of the ditch and I watched those men, colored men, come leaping over that ditch like they was horses galloping, just leaping. Some of them stopped to fire their rifles back the way they'd come. And then a little later here come the white boys. They was crouching and running. Ducking down and kneeling down to fire *they* rifles. It was dark enough . . . flames shot out of the end of their guns. One white man stopped in the ditch right in front of me and he knelt down and fired. It was a double-barreled shotgun with rust on it. He had white hair and he was pink like a albino and he fired that gun two times. Sweat was pouring off his face. I could see it in the moonlight. After him I scrooched farther back in the pipe."

Frank looked at Delvin. There was sweat on *his* face.

"Things died down," he said, "but they didn't die out. You could hear the gunshots over in Greenwood—"

"The quarter?" Delvin said.

"That's right. You could hear the *whomp whomp* of the shotguns and the *kee-rack!* of the rifles, but they died down some and I was about to think the trouble was over. But it was just getting started. I'd fallen asleep in the pipe, but the whistle of an early morning train waked me up. The day was coming up clear with a few clouds, looked like big white soft pillows stacked up in the west. I crawled out of the pipe. In the ditch were three or four bodies of white men. They were dead, all but one of em, sprawled out in the bottom where they was a little rusty stream and up the side where two of em looked like they'd been trying to crawl out. There was a colored man dead too, but I didn't know him. He was lying on his back with one fist balled up under his chin like he was about to strike a blow. I picked up a pistol I found and climbed out of the ditch. There was a white man lying over next to a sticker bush crying. I didn't know him either and I didn't stop for him."

Delvin started to ask about the lynching party, but Mr. Rome shushed him. It was Frank's time to speak.

"Whoo," Frank said making a low brushing motion with his right hand, "whoo." His eyes moved back and forth between the listeners. "I slipped along the alleys and made my way into Greenwood where they was already shooting going on over on the north side. Fires had been started up all over. They had burned the Holy Mount church and Stanton's grocery and all the windows had been shot out of Shorty's African Cafe. There were dead people lying in the street. A couple of em had been runned over. Houses was burning and a few people was standing over near em. I don't know what they was doing—taking a goodbye look I reckon. Just then there was the sound of a bugle blowing. A tall woman wearing a man's shirt over her dress shouted, 'Oh Lord it's the vengeance,' and started running down the street. Cries started up and out of the houses came whole families of people. There was shouts everywhere. All the peoples was running. There was the sound of shooting and it was coming closer. There was cars overturned in the street and a couple of em had dead white men spilling out of em. We was fighting in a war and the war was taking place right where we lived. I couldn't hardly believe it. I felt so bad I wanted to sit down somewhere by myself and cry, but I couldn't take the time to. Nobody had no time.

"Well, just then I ran up on Ralph Tompkins—I don't know where Hoster had got off to—and we rushed down the street together. Some of the trees done been burnt. And front porches too and there was burn marks running up the house faces. One house was still burning. It smelled like a woods fire. Ralph had a double-barrel shotgun tied together with wire. The butt of the gun had blood on it. Ralph was sucking air through his mouth as he ran. I probably was too. Everybody was headed over to the westside away from downtown. We could hear the shooting coming closer and sometimes it sounded like they was firing off cannons. Then we saw these white men in they cars. The cars was coming slow down the street. White mens was walking beside the cars and they was shooting into the houses. Some of them went *in-to* the houses—the unburnt ones— and these men were pulling people out and they were shootin em. We ducked down behind the steps of Rum's Fish Shop and fired back at em. I think I hit one of em because I saw him snatch at his chest high up like he'd been bit hard. But we didn't stay to make sure. We ran down behind the houses, popping up where we could to fire at the white men. This activity kept up during the morning. I found another pistol lying in the street and took that. After a while I found another stuck up in the fork of a sweet apple tree and I took that too. I had this desperate feeling like I had to get more guns. I had one stuck in my belt and I was carrying two and I wanted three or four more and more bullets. I didn't have enough bullets. Two of the pistols was .38s and one was a little silver .22. Ralph had a canvas bag full of shotgun shells. Buckshot.

"Everywhere we looked there were these gunfights going on. People was up on rooftops firing and they was collected in little gangs behind cars or piled-up furniture, couches and such, that had been dragged out into the streets. There was too many white men. Some of em was wearing army uniforms. We heard later it was the whole National Guard fighting alongside those crazy white men. Over where I was they had us backed up against this old brick fire station where a bunch of men had ducked in behind a fire engine and some wagons they'd turned over in the street. Behind the station everything was on fire. It didn't look like there was any way to get out through there and so we was making the best of it by shooting at the boys that was coming at us. We must've killed a dozen right in the street. There was some whooping and hollering, but that was mostly on the white side. Them crackers thought they was back at Bull Run or someplace still trying to win that old war. We wadn't hollering much. Everybody was sad and scared and some looked like they didn't care who it was won they was just shooting because there wadn't no way around it. We had dust on us from the street, this powdery light gray dust that made us look like ghosts. But we was fighting hard.

"Ralph had found a carbine rifle to go with his shotgun. A couple of little boys was loading guns for people and there was even a girl, this high school girl wearing an old brown army coat and a straw hat, who was running around carrying ammunition and seeing to the ones that'd got hit. A lot of us got hit, but not me. The bullets came whizzing by, real insolent-sounding. A boy stood up on a roof across the street and he was waving a piece of white cloth, surrendering, I guess, but they shot him anyway. He just pitched on his face and slidded down the roof. He knocked up some shingles as he fell and they spilled off the roof with him. He dropped into a big holly bush. Some more of our boys came around the corner and one of them had one of those big repeating rifles, a BAR. No telling how he got it. Somebody said the armory'd been busted into, I guess that was it. He set this big gun up behind a pile of kettles from I don't know where—they was piled up on a couch—and he started shooting. He hit a man in the head, a big man in a bright blue shirt, and it looked like his head just snapped off. The bullets kicked splinters off this big church pew some of them was hiding behind. He looked at me once and he had a grin on his face like it had been stuck there last night and forgot about.

"Then just about a minute after he started firing we saw the airplanes. They was two of em, double-wing planes flying right down the street. Men was shooting rifles out of both of em. One plane was painted bright yellow and it had the word SKY KING on the side. The other was a army plane, you could tell by the target it had painted on it. They wobbled as they came. They wadn't too high up but high enough so it was hard to get a bead on em. A few peoples at that point started running. The planes flew right at us and when they got close up over us, this man in one of them hung out the side and threw a jug of gasoline with a fuse in it that busted right over the left side of the hideout and spilled fire on everybody over there. That set people to hollering and running.

"One of the ones got hit by the gas was the girl. I was watching. This big tongue of flames shot right up over her back and caught her head and hat both on fire. She tried to run, but she tripped and fell, not ten feet from me. I had jumped back and didn't get nothing but the scorch. The girl was burning all over the back of her and her hair and that hat mixed in was burning bright red like a halo. She wadn't saying nothing. Me and Ralph started throwing dirt on her to put the fire out, but it didn't help much, at least at first. Then we got it out. Her army coat had melted right onto her skin. She was smoking and crusty and the back of her head—maybe it was the crust of that hat— was like a black leather helmet. In one place you could see through to the skull bone. She was still restless. She kept trying to draw up her legs but she couldn't quite. She never had said nothin. She opened her eyes real wide and looked at us, but she didn't seem to recognize us, and then she shut her eyes tight.

"The other plane had gone by and then it circled back, the yellow one, the Sky King, and when it got over us this man in a army uniform threw out a stick of dynamite. You could tell it was dynamite because it was burning on a fuse. The stick missed and blew up in the street. The shock was like somebody shoving against you. We all—the last of us standing—hightailed it then. There was nothing else for it. We ran for our lives, what lives we had. Amazing how beat up you could get and still want to live. That girl died while we was looking at her. She was squirming, trying to get up, til all of a sudden she shuddered, let out a little sigh, and stopped dead. That was it. There was tears in her eyes but you could see she wadn't looking at nobody, least none of us.

"I got out of there and on out of town and hid in the big woods on the other side of the brass works. They say that most of the people in Greenwood was rounded up and taken out to camps over toward the old fairgrounds. Put inside wire fences like they was beasts and left there in the hot sun to suffer. The white boys walked around town, they said, just shooting at will."

He stopped talking and sat quietly, patting the corn dust, leaving with each pat a new print of his palm. Delvin saw in the traces that his two middle fingers were the same length and knew this meant something to fortune-tellers but he couldn't recall what.

"Damn, damn," Mr. Rome said softly.

Delvin felt a running smoothness all along his skin, a smoothness that turned to an ache. But he didn't want to do anything about it. Little worm of despair angling up through his body from a place that hardly existed. *I would do . . .* , he thought, but no, he wouldn't. A crease in his heart like a gouge in rock. Hot tallow seeping in. Hotter and hotter. Tears in his eyes. Tears running down his face. His eyes burning. It was old and had wandered through him all his life—this feeling now. Lonely and helpless and desperate. He pushed up, rose through creaking knees and an unlimberness like a bent branch and stumbled a tiny bit, just an edge of body striking the man, the locuter Frank, but not enough to remark on, and lurched a step or two out into the open space of the car and stood there looking at the door that was a completed picture of darkness. In the distance, low down, a star like a bit of fluff, winking out.

"Airplanes," Mr. Rome said, his voice soft and frail. "They dropped firebombs on us. Like we was the enemy."

"This world is full of murder and craziness," Frank said.

Delvin headed down the car. He'd had enough of these stories for now. You heard them everywhere, a low people telling tales against the ones who held them down. He felt something fade and tremble in him as he walked toward the white men. Three of them were sitting in the open doorway. He stood near them looking out. The train rolled past fields that were glossed under the light of a bruised half moon, the only light for miles. Except for one lamp burning far out in a house across the cotton fields. Some sharecropper up late tending to a sick child maybe, worrying about his life. If you flew in a plane over this country, Delvin thought, you would be looking down into a world of blackness. Maybe we are going to rise up. But he knew that wouldn't happen.

Just then, down among the card players, somebody raised a shout. A shout and a sudden cry of outrage. Came sounds of struggle, very brief as if half secret, then a *tunk* and a thin, brittle, cracking sound, followed by a strange meek tiny despairing yelp. Trailed by sounds of whistling, of sighing, of muttering. The humped backs, dark shirts, the white arm raised like somebody signaling, and dust in the air, drifting like a pale yellow smoke. "Jesus, God," somebody back there said in a big, rich, disappointed voice as the group bowed outwards and men stumbled to their feet, scooted on their butts backwards, and, flailing, rose halfway into the dark above them, half caterwheeling, jumping, getting out of the space occupied by trouble. Leaving what was left, what could wait on trouble now, what could take its time.

At the center of the new circle a man, loosened from his stays, ordinary otherwise, lay on his back not moving, and another man—a little, twitchy man—raised up on his knees, was held in a slump by three other men. The captured man struggled feebly.

"Look at what you done," one of the men holding him said.

Delvin wanted to ask what it was though he could see well enough. He needed the confirmation of voices, but these were white men so he said nothing, only leaned closer to the men standing in the doorway.

"Shouldn't a'cheated I guess," one said.

"If that wo what it was," said another, a man with a heavy shock of dark hair.

The cardplayers holding the man—this short and scrawny man now selected, man with a clean, frightened face smooth as a child's (or somebody very old)—dragwalked him to the door, not even hesitating for those standing there to scramble out of the way, and in a smooth motion that looked almost practiced, threw the little man from the train. He didn't cry out. His arms flailed as he disappeared into the rushing-by dark, but he made no sound.

The evictors didn't even look out after the tossed man. They returned to the one lying on the floor, a man who hadn't moved, bent briefly over him—someone going softly *skeeter bite skeeter bite* all the while—picked him up, carried the middle-sized, regular-looking man, who had a small white bald spot on the shiny dark crown of his head, to the now cleared doorway, and threw him out after the other.

Delvin stood at the side of the doorway looking after the ejected men, but he couldn't see them. The right of way was grown up in marsh grass and cattails. The moon was westering. To the north tatters of clean white cloud looked like the exhaust of machines invisible to the human eye. He shuddered, and felt the shudder traveling through his body. The wispy clouds had been rubbed into the night. Without realizing it he'd sailed out into a country where he was all by himself again; nobody to approach and linger with, waiting out a rain, say, or eating blackberries out of a cap.

Something like that, he thought, half laughing at himself as one of the white men nearby said to another, "Pitch em and catch em, ay buddy," and the other laughed a small tight laugh like you would in front of somebody you didn't want to offend, and the other saying, "He just flung out there, didn't he?" and the first—small, stiff-faced— laughing again the same cramped laugh; and Delvin thought, It hurt him too, that man getting killed.

He wanted to get off the train, wanted to walk by himself down a dirt road back toward that sharecropper light over yonder and knock on the door and ask if he could stay for a while. But what would he find there? Some old snaggle-toothed couple with their raggedy children. Cold grits and well water for supper. Wash your feet in a pan out on the back porch before going to bed. Lie down on the floor and listen to the skeeters whine around your head. Malaria bubbling in your veins.

An ache like a buckled-on harness clutched him. He wanted more than anything to reach his hand out to somebody he loved, just for a minute. It was like a sickness, a feverish radiance. He reckoned that was what was taking him back to Chattanooga after nearly three years away. People who love you, somebody said to him on the roads once, they'll cover your nakedness. Guess you'd even risk jail to get that, he thought. But maybe not jail after all this time. He told himself this, charming himself, maybe not jail. But white men had long memories. But he was wily. Go on, go on—it was an endless chain. Not minding himself, not even figuring, he swayed in the doorway. He tilted toward the dark, starting to fall. A hand reached out and grabbed him. It was one of the white men, the little one who had mis-laughed.

"Watch yourself, shinola," the little man said, grinning cooly. Delvin staggered back a step into the car.

"Thank you," he said.

The little man turned away without acknowledging him further. He felt grateful to him, wanted to say something more, but he couldn't; world wasn't like that.

As if in a dream he returned to his small group and, taking just a moment to dust off a place on the cool rattling chestnutwood floor, lay down against the bulkhead. He slipped his notebook from his pocket into his shirt. His chest felt hot and he let his hand rest there. His heart beat into his fingers, same old cadence, nothing extra. I can't sleep, he thought, and drifted off.

He left the train in Huntsville to wait for the Chattanooga-bound Tweetsy freight. He didn't have the money to pay Mr. Rome for carrying a message but the little man said it was all right and got off with him. Josie stayed on the train. He was on the way, he said, to Denver, where there was a meeting of an anarchist group he wanted to join up with. "They talk about each man having full say in his life," he said, "but they are generally as touchy as any others about who's on top." He and Delvin embraced and then Delvin and Mr. Rome walked off together with Frank into the night. The northbound freight wouldn't be leaving until early in the A.M.—so they were told by a tall spindle-legged man striding along sheltering a young woman who toted a small guitar wrapped in a piece of checkered cloth. The man reminded Delvin of the professional mourner J. O. Shank back in Chattanooga.

Among thin dust drifts, broken bottles, bent gray grass, and a sprinkling of wild carrot in full white flower, Delvin sat up on an embankment, thinking of faces. They were maps, stories, timetables, confessions. The big celluloid pages in the museum each contained fifty faces, a hundred faces, every one contending with what must be revealed and what must not be, all but a few that had conquered the freakish truths trying to bust out or who had given up and stood back while they careened into view.

He broke off a stalk of carrot and pressed the flat white bracts to his nose. It smelled sour and slightly bitter. He wanted to get up and walk two miles through wildflowers. Beside him Frank was sleeping. Mr. Rome was catching a westbound freight. He said he would be in Chicago in two days and would find Celia and give her his speech. He had agreed to do it on credit, payable in ten days at the Constitution Funeral Home in Chattanooga, Tennessee.

Not long after this, but well after the fright had come upon him—the police fright, fright of a murderer returned to the scene of his crime, a murderer who on more than one night had waked from a dream in which he pictured a white form lying still with death in the remorseless shade of big trees, and gotten up from pallet or straw bed and paced, shivering with fright and sadness, a fright and sadness that in the years since had been slowly sloughed off like a dry skin until there were times when he believed he could no longer recognize the accomplice to the lead charge shot into the body of another human being, but who knew in his heart that this was not true, that the crime, swinging shadow to light, back and forth, like a lantern in a deserted house, was not forgotten, or left behind like a broken valise, but was carried by him still, banging and weighty against his own body and soul—after this, a Chattanooga man traveling with a small boy told him that he knew of no crime in the last few years in that town in which an africano had shot a white boy. "That's one you won't miss," he said, and laughed, and his son, a small child with a recessed chin and a wry look, laughed too. "You sure you would know?" Delvin asked. In his wandering time he had run into only two others from Chattanooga and one was too drunk to talk and the other had walked away from him without answering. Mostly he had been too scared to ask about it. He had made a vague partial reference to the professor, who had looked at him with a frank, sad eye and turned away without pressing him. It's all right to carry a misery, he had said over his shoulder. This man said, " 'Cept for this one trip to visit the boy's grandmama in Birmingham, I been in Chattanooga right along." A blank screen, cold and vapid, pulled across Delvin's eyes and he almost fell down. "You all right?" the man said. Delvin didn't answer him. "Look like you seen a wild ghost," the man said. "No," Delvin said, "not that." He thanked the man and walked off. Could what the man said be true? A mixed relief and anguish came on him. Wait—he'd have to wait to know for sure. These years, off in the muddy, punishing world. But how could he call them bad years? Mr. Rome had already boarded his freight, bound for Chicago. I got to get to someplace private, Delvin thought. But he couldn't miss his train. He stepped among the sleeping bodies of the tramps, careful not to lose his footing, and in a little cleared space by a gallberry bush he lay down. He pressed his body up under the bush and found the trunk and gripped the crooked wood with both hands. I am out beyond myself, he thought. Tears hot as dots of acid squeezed from his eyes. "Thank you," he said. "Thank you Jesus in heaven and here on the earth. Thank you everything that walks and rides and swims in the sea." He let go of the trunk and rolled over on his back. Through straggly leaves he could see a few fuzzed stars. His life was a trick played on him in a game he knew nothing about. A feeling that there was a great powerfulness in the world came over him. Maybe what the man said wasn't true. But he knew it was. He cried without knowing if it was from sorrow or joy.

And here came the train, a clanking, slow-moving freight bound for Norfolk.

Frank, a man with a wide guileless face and a limp that seemed to come and go, called to him.

Yeah, okay.

He sprang to his feet. The sharp push of his youth stirred him, his body quivered with his strength. He bounded down the embankment, caught the door rider and swung himself up into a yellow East Tennessee & Western boxcar.

5

Spring had flared out, burned brightly and was smothered by summer, its heroic proposals soon cornered and worn down into soft mountain evenings and hot days nobody wanted to be outside in. Soon fall would be cranking up. Already the tulip poplars and the sycamores showing black-speckled leaves, and the tall sumac reddening in the road ditches. He had returned to the Home, but there was another boy in his old place now, living with Mr. Oliver inside the house; Delvin had to take a berth out in the barn. The Ghost was the regular driver now, captain of the big new Cadillac hearse and even the black-paned ambulance they used to pick up the bodies. They had a contract locally to pick up africano corpses at the city morgue and local hospitals. Mr. Oliver spent much of his time lying on a velvet couch out on the newly glassed-in side porch. You could raise the cloudy louvers and let in breeze and on cool days Delvin would find him out there listening to his new prodigy read to him from the tales of King Arthur and his Knights of the Round Table. The boy was only ten, but he was smart as a whip and to Delvin's eyes a hustling little conniver.

Not that Delvin mentioned any of this. The Ghost, who had told him, laughed about it, but he was on Delvin's side in the matter, if there was a side, as long as Delvin didn't try to push in on the driving. Conspiring young 'uns wasn't much to get charged up about. Not compared to what he found out about what had haunted him the last four years. The old trouble—the shooting, the flight, the law—so the Ghost confirmed, had all been a figment on top of a figment. For a while that busted him up good. As he stood out in the street before the Home on his first day back, still dusty from the rails, the Ghost had come up behind him and cried Boo! Delvin had jumped like a

poked dog. The Ghost gave him a big fool's grin. He'd grown tall,
skinny, and had an orange fuzz settled on his face.

"Expected you back sooner'n now," he said.

"How's that?" Delvin said.

"That old business."

"What so?"

"The one bout shooting that white boy?"

"You heard anything?"

"Nothing 'cept there wadn't no white boy shot."

Delvin re-experienced a clutching sickness in his gut. "You sure
about that?"

"Wadn't nothing but a wisp."

"I don't believe you."

And he didn't, wouldn't, until the Ghost walked him aside, led
him into the shade of a a big half-peeled sycamore and there told
him what was so: there'd been no trouble anybody'd been looking
for him about. No Chattanooga white folks had even mentioned negroes shooting. "They's probably too ashamed to," the Ghost said.

Delvin had stretched both hands out and eased himself close
against the tree. The bark smelled of tree life. He pressed his face
against the smooth skin. The Ghost took a step closer but he didn't
touch him. "We'd uv told you but we didn't know where to write."

Delvin felt a loose trailing feeling like the ragged tail on a kite
falling across the sky. He'd heard this, stray asides or a word let slip,
but he realized none of that had he believed. Now what was so swung
on him like a club and got through. It was as if he was hearing it for
the first time. Tears welled in his eyes, a few, small, crisp as berries.
He waited for them to fall but they didn't. They made a smear where
his fingers touched them. He felt a wobbling in his chest, a raveling.
The feeling that had come over him in the train yard—of happiness
and relief and anger and dumbfoundedness and a solemn castigation
that melted as he felt it into a smooth and easygoing slide, of sorrow
mixed with joy—came on him again. Lord, I've survived. That boy
survived. He wanted to go find him—if there ever was a boy, that one
who had shouted—and kiss his face. What luck. And what a sham-

faced, goddamn— Agh. The professor. Celia. Celia. What luck. When he turned around from the tree, he was laughing—shaking and laughing and crying and about to fall over; the Ghost had to hold him up by the shoulders.

They would sit out in the yard on sunny days drinking Miss Foster's Punch and talking about what they'd experienced in the world. The Ghost had taken to wearing big Redtone boots, and he did a stomp around the yard to show Delvin how well they fit. He carried keys on a long yellow chain that he said was gold but wasn't. He was still an angel turnip, though he lied about this and claimed he had the girls at the Emporium eating out of his hand.

"Those caledonias do anything for a man in a big car," he said, and they both laughed. It was like they could make up anything they wanted and have it be true.

Delvin, leaning back in the big canvas folding chair, breathed in the smell of pine seeds and sun-baked grass and felt for a moment that he was in heaven. A few feathered clouds with an unchased, slow-poke, summery look seemed like they'd still be there tomorrow. The lilt of the new boy's sweet voice came from the porch, interrupted now and again by Mr. Oliver's rich barreltone correcting a pronunciation or offering a remark on some aspect of the latest reading. Like Delvin, the boy—and Mr. Oliver—preferred the parts concerning trips and traveling. Delvin missed his old intimacy with Mr. O, but he was not particularly jealous. To have it again he would have to return to being the boy he once was and he was no longer that boy.

What he was now was shaky and fraught; confused, he thought, about half the time, scared—jumpy, he told Winston, the Ghost—full of excuses and plans . . . and desires, he said, speaking the word softly as if afraid just the word would invoke some bustling over-riding particular; itching, he said, thinking as he spoke of his at-tempts to appear blasé, indolent even, while at the same time—as he thought, and spoke—flexing the muscles in his forearms until the Ghost told him to quit showing off what he didn't have. He picked pine seeds out of their little single wings and ate them one at time and listened to the easy spell of the old knights and waited for what was coming.

For a time he wrote Celia every day and for a while he was engrossed in this, this job really, he thought, his work for now, or part of it; he was deeply involved in what he thought of as the proper way of life. He told the Ghost about her, and the Ghost, who fantasized nightly of high-yella women crossing the yard to find him, was rightly appreciative and admiring.

"I spect you want to marry her and open up a business of your own," he said.

"I might," Delvin said. The rosiness of possibility swelled in his heart. He had begun to believe again—sense, suspect, guess—that he was being followed. "Somebody's tailing me," he said to the Ghost, nervously . . . hopefully.

"Somebody sus-pect you of somethin?" the Ghost said. "Somethin else?"

"No, I don't feel that way. And besides I hadn't done anything. Not a thing."

"People follow me a lot too," the Ghost said congenially. "I got lots of admirers these days. That's probably what it is in your case—admirers. These girls, when they get a whiff of your abilities, they come slinking along after yuh."

"I don't know if it's that. Besides, in yo case I heard it was a snort of that old three jacks and a king."

"I don't need no potion." He shook his head. His greased orange hair shone in the low sunlight. "You rob a bank or something? Shoot somebody again?"

Delvin gave him a look. "No. But I did see a man get stabbed."

"They want you for a witness?"

"It wadn't like that."

He told the Ghost about his experience on the freight.

"You think the fall killed him?" the Ghost asked, referring to the living murderer they threw off the train. "Wonder why they didn't just kill him outright."

"People don't want blood on their hands."

"Even murderer blood? Seems like that would be a badge of honor."

"They don't want nothing on their hands."

Somebody'd tossed a handful of corn dust on a little spill of blood. Delvin'd had a bitter taste in the back of his throat. But after a while it passed. The man who grabbed him at the door and saved him, the little jeff; the man's hands had shook. Lying makes violence, the professor always said.

The Ghost scratched his freckled cheek. He began a story of dash and devilment, familiar to Delvin before he heard it. Women, shiny-eyed girls, who loved him. "Got one over at the Emporium who wears a gold bracelet I give her." Out this way he was ready to take on more responsibility, just as soon as Mr. O thought he was ready for it. Actually not when, but right now, if Delvin knew what he meant. He had a sly look under thick orange eyebrows. Something in his face heretofore hidden had worked its way to the surface. Delvin had seen it before with boys their age. Boys who had once been sweet and shy now become rough customers who pushed others around. Mostly it was the cowed ones, the frightened boys who weren't quick or strong, who stayed gentle, the over-friendly boys who agreed with everything you said. He preferred the older boys—the men really— he'd met on the trains, riders toughened by experience. They scared him but they gave him somebody to follow. And he too pushed and poked and shouted out his readiness to take on the world. He thought of Celia, who had looked at him as a boy who couldn't be trusted yet. Who didn't have the power to—to what? He never could be sure. Protect her, he guessed. I can do that, he thought, but then he wasn't sure, considered himself too rangy-minded, too loose in his ways. He was what she thought he was—a drifter, picking up jobs where he could, a day worker anywhere, in any town—the world's day worker, he thought—picking peaches, sweeping out the back, raking a yard, filling baskets with sycamore and oak tree leaves. But still he wanted to write things down, in books maybe. He didn't just have this in mind. He wadn't no drifter there. He got down hard on

the stories he was jotting down these days, applications of effort and
detail, some loose-jointed boy walking by a string of wild grapevine
trailing up a fence, talking to a brindle cow on the other side about
loneliness, taking the cow's part, taking it back so he could say how
he lived over in the town. Story about a man living in a grass house
in a ditch, about a little girl singing to herself as the house next door
burned down. He didn't show these stories to anybody, but some
time he would.

He turned on his belly and looked up at the porch where the
new boy, Casey, named after the dead burned boy—"My real name
is Henry," he told Delvin, "but Daddy"—speaking of Mr. O—"likes
Casey"—read outloud from antique adventures. He had a thin,
pleasant voice. Delvin *was* a little jealous of him, but he tried not
to let it show. The worry over vengeful pursuit by white boys had
faded away, leaving an irresolute calm. Mr. Oliver was afraid his
return might stir things up—vague things, stirred in a vague way—
but Delvin saw this was as much because he wanted to be settled in
with the new boy, some new boy, as anything else. He wouldn't be
able to stay here long, and this saddened him. He only half wanted
to move on, though he figured it was time for him to. He sat in the
kitchen with Mr. Oliver and Polly—who herself was married now,
living with her husband, Curtis Rodell, a plumber's helper, in a little
cottage behind the big house—discussing what he planned to do.
Polly wanted him to stay, but Mr. Oliver encouraged him to put his
plans into action. He recommended college, but they both knew he
was not really a candidate for that. Delvin had told him he wanted to
write books and Mr. Oliver had been happy for him. That was just
the sort of profession that appealed to him. Get right into it, he said.
Don't delay a minute. Start up and build you a head of steam. Mr.
Oliver offered to stake him, to give him an allowance for a year or
two while he got going. Delvin was reluctant to agree to this because
he wasn't sure how he wanted to go about things. I have more traveling to do, he said. I want to gather more information. Novels? Mr.
O had asked, and Delvin had said he wasn't even sure about that. He
thought he might like to write about real things.

"Thus your travels, eh?" Mr. O said.

"I feel like I'm winding string onto a ball."

He told them a little of what he had seen. It was, he thought, a rich but narrow vein, and not very deep.

"Deep's in the heart, son," Mr. O said. "But you already know that." He reached across the red-striped oilcloth and patted Delvin on the arm and ran his thumb over the bone. His eyes were lively. Casey sat on a stool at the counter putting together a jigsaw puzzle: the Parthenon—in New York City, he told Delvin when he asked.

Sylvia, the new assistant, had told Delvin that these days Mr. Oliver was using a preparation he got from the doctor to get to sleep and he had other drugstore remedies to perk himself up, but Delvin saw no real sign of the preparations affecting him. There was the same risive look as always (riding like a pretty boat on his sea of sadness), maybe a tad more hectic. The boy Casey had his own room—Delvin's old room—but he slept mostly in a little box bed in the corner of Mr. Oliver's bedroom. Oliver kept the boy like somebody'd keep a fluffy little dog. The boy was generally sullen and fretful, but he had a pretty, clear yellow face and shiny hazel eyes that seemed to weigh everything they saw, not always favorably. As they were talking the boy got up without a word, grabbed a cracker from a plate of Graham crackers and honey Mrs. Parker was putting together and scooted out the back door.

"Just like you used to," Mr. Oliver said, looking nervously out the kitchen window.

Delvin laughed. "Don't strain yourself there, Pop."

Mr. Oliver laughed. "I get so attached to you boys."

"And who wouldn't," Delvin said, grinning ferociously.

The old man laughed again, his laugh slightly wheezy, a little hollowed out by time. The world was receding from him, leaving a space that nothing had quite filled in. Life in the end thievery's fool. It made Delvin sad, gave him a trembling in his heart that he thought about on the pallet, smelling the thin sweetness of the hay in his nostrils, and he wanted to write these things down, or no, thought he should, maybe take some notes, but it was hard to do, hard while the facts stared him in the face, panting and wheezing. He would have to wait. Some things he could jot down: the patchiness in Mr. O's face, the smell in the kitchen of roast meat and baking, the wooden counters worn with stains, the petunias in little boxes in the window, Polly reaching back to rub herself low in the back, her hands when she bent them looking like bunched-up brown chicken skin, the faraway look in Mr. O's eyes, the way his mouth worked sometimes without anything in it. *Sadness creeps*, he wrote. But then they laughed too, told stories, lingered on the porch in the twilight listening on the radio to *The Acousticon Hour* or *King Biscuit Time*, featuring Sonny Boy Williams, nobody wanting to go back in the house, even in the sadness something sweet and alive, life itself rounding out like the moon. They turned the radio off and listened to the horses whinnying in their stalls, to somebody down the street calling for May Ella with something sweet in his voice.

Delvin walked the streets. He felt like a sailor home from a long voyage. He still had the feeling that he was being followed. Don't be crazy, he said to himself, but he couldn't completely shake it. At the picture show the couples seemed huddled together in fright. Pedestrians looked lost. Just past the lights of a store he stopped to look back for his trailer, his devotee. There was no one. He was touched by how shabby the buildings were—the Empire office building with its entablatures and foamy cornices, the Western States building with its red brick front and tiny windows that caught the west-tending, falsely glamorous sunlight. The courthouse looked like something left over from the worst of Roman times, a building no one thought enough of even to tear down. Goldman's offered anoraks and Maine jackets and low-priced formal wear. Dark stains on the mock Greek front of the Mountaineer Bank. The Peacock Hotel with its jowly stone face and its gazebos set like little guardhouses on the corners at the top of its six stories seemed to brood. He noted familiar trees. Cracked buckeyes and thick-waisted poplars and hickories that looked bitter and worn by life. He had always loved

city bushes and patches of urban grass and flowers in window boxes
and as he walked he recalled these, mostly gone now except for a big
patch of red-throated nandina bushes over on Story street planted
by the wife of the owner of Holston Hardware to decorate a blank
gray brick wall, and pittisporum at Mott's, Mrs. Combine's mock
banana bushes. He looked in on still-vacant lots spotted with pokeweed and goat sorrel and stopped to gather seeds from bolted morning glories in a fence on Governor Piddle street, where the Munger
house, a large building with peeling french doors and concrete vases
stuffed with ragged azaleas, had been torn down to put up a center
for state culture. He noted broken walls and bellied chicken wire
fences, alleys where old men propped themselves against stacked
crates, splashing their water on the unwashed bricks. People were
living out in the open now, in tents and board shacks and residing
in crannies behind buildings and tucked into holes in embankments
and under the bridge down on Custer where the street dipped low
and made a pond on the rainiest days and down by the river where
the muddy water foamed against the pilings of the Converse Bridge.
Along a yellow wall with the words CHESTER APPLIANCES written
in black letters on it, white men lined up. What were they waiting
for? Tractor wheels propped in a row against a wall behind Puckett
Machine Shop. Broken metal parts and black, oily ground and a big
tub used to cool off the hotwork. He breathed in the rich, heavy,
fluid stink of burning metal and thought he too was becoming a man
like the other men walking the streets, peering into alleys and vacant
lots. In the yard of Manger Auto Repair skeletal cars rested, waiting for armorers to refit them. He preferred—no, not preferred, felt
a wobbly, living nostalgia for—the old wagons, returning to the city
in force now, horses and mules pulling milk carts and Murphy and
Studebaker wagons and buckboards piled with farm produce and,
layered under gunny sacks and crushed ice, seafood hauled up by
night train from the Gulf. At the ice plant big cloudy blocks coughed
out of the chute and were grabbed by shirtless men with tongs and
swung onto the back of Carson wagons and stacked in trucks that
had ISSOM ICE COMPANY written in gold on their green sides. Here

too men hung around, sucking ice slivers, waiting for something to happen. Pointless lines of men, men in bunches and listless groups, solitary men picking shreds of tobacco from their teeth, idlers, worriers, cashed-out men, strong men grown weak and sluggish, skeezing into bars and restaurant doorways. He marked the tremor of a bottom lip, the troubled brow, the picked-at sore on the face of a man reading a newspaper folded to a dozen lines of type; noted the africano lady who looked familiar—but he wasn't quite able to place—with a cast in her left eye that gave her a cockeyed aspect that didn't interfere with the small eager smile she directed toward the Embers Supper Club on Mareton Avenue; traced the harried looks, the looks of displacement and earnest willingness to do anything that might engender money or kindness or love or simply a few moments without being shamed or hit; caught the brokenhearted, the outright weepers, with or without handkerchiefs; scoped the cornered, the effusively lying, the desperate making wild claims. He marked the practiced liars, the hard-pressed guilty, the twitching and fluttery humiliated, the dazed, the obnoxious attempting to pass themselves off as simply loud, the ones with stone faces that hid nothing really, checked the self-mocking and envious. He studied the faces swollen by beatings or tears or genetic malformations, birthmarks and such; angled the ones battered into cripples, or the natural cripples, the deaf and dumb, the palsied, the blind, including the blind seller of peanuts, Willie Perkins, still sitting in his little cupped tractor seat by his stand over on Montgomery street; and Ethel Beck, great beauty of the east side, blinded at age eight by an overdose of wood alcohol supplied by her father, still tapping along—more rapping than tapping—with her bamboo cane painted white. He observed the pinched places in people's cheeks, their noses pointed up sniffing for a change in the weather; considered women barely able to hold back screams, women raging at the mouths of alleys, old ladies pressing their backs against brick walls, mothers crying, laughing, scolding children, harlots with melted ice cream dripping from a paper cup onto stone steps, women without stockings, women with—and men: men resting, waiting, men telling uneasy stories, men shouting into barrels, picking up pennies from the street, men hitting horses, men shaving in alleys, spitting into their hands . . . men waiting for what wasn't coming . . . or what was . . .

He rested his back against a scarred tulip poplar in Constitution Park, watching an old white man peel an apple with a gold penknife for a little girl in a yellow crepe dress. He watched an unidentified africano man with one leg pull himself into the bed of a wagon, work himself onto the seat, untie the reins from the brake, and clop a brown mule down the cobblestone street, the man smiling sarcastically to himself, the mule never picking up its gait as the wagon rounded the corner and disappeared—into time itself, it seemed to Delvin—leaving behind a patch of undisturbed sunlight on the fish-colored cobbles of Tremaine street.

He bought a paper cup of sweet iced tea at the window marked "Colored" at the back of Hunter's Restaurant, these windows and doors and slots and chutes the only places, he thought, where the word *colored* was ever capitalized, smiling to himself as he thought this, tipping his head to the negro woman who handed the cup to him, wanting to touch her hand with his, just for the humanness, the solid pressure of life between them, let her know he was as alive as she was, ready for what came next . . .

He sat drinking the tea on a low wall overlooking the alley in back of a vacant lot between Cooper's Mercantile and the newspaper offices. Rain had left a tracery of red clay veins running among broom and dog fennel in the lot. Out in the alley a yellow mongrel shook a dirty white glove in its jaws. A crow pecked at a ragged bouquet of chrysanthemums and at the entrance to the alley two women scolded three tiny children who gazed up at them with the rapt faces of believers. A breeze picked at the tops of a patch of fennel, touching the pale green filigree with a mindless tenderness, and brought his lost, or never quite found, love, Celia, to mind. Or maybe, he thought, she just came on her own. Or never left. She'd sent letters to the funeral home, letters he dived into as soon as he got the hugs

and handshakes out of the way. He'd tied them up with a string and
carried them with him everywhere in the inside pocket of the brown
linen coat he wore. He took them out to re-sort them, commonplace with him these days. He opened the first and read it again.
Somehow it seemed to have changed. It was not so interested in him
as he thought. It was kindly, but distant. He read another and then
another. The letters were like messages to a straggler. To the one
who couldn't keep up. How strange the world was—how so easily
you could get yourself into a fix. He had a tendency to hang back
in corners, wore the brim of his hat pulled down and stood in the
shade of great oaks—still not sure the law wasn't waiting for him. He
had begun to dream again about his mother. In the dreams he met
her on woodland paths and in mountain fields, the two of them hurrying past each other on unnamed errands. He was already gone by
and into the woods or the next field when he realized that had been
Cappie just lifting her hand to acknowledge him. When he ran back
to find her, she was gone. He felt the mystery of things all around
him. He wasn't even sad, he was only awestruck. He remembered
how the professor had said that in olden times you could be changed
into a bird, a tree, a crawling troll . . . you could become a star or a
set of stars, and the stars could speak, and the rocks and the wind
could tell you who you were and what was about to happen, the gods
or God himself talk to you directly, and an invisible force could be
applied—but none of that kind of speech occurs anymore, only an
occasional pale, barely coherent whisper remains in the world, the
flicker of a conscience, or the sick tug of love that claims to be real.
And this had saddened him and he had spoken to rocks and trees
himself but nothing talked back. But the professor was wrong about
love. It was more than just a whispering thing. It was strong and it
held you up. A happiness had overtaken him—his mother was somewhere out there—he knew it. He would wake with tears in his eyes,
only a few, and an easefulness in his heart.

He placed the packet of letters beside him on the wall. A small
stack, creased and worn already. He leaned down and kissed them
and then he got up and walked away.

• • •

"I believe I will be shoving off in the morning," he told Mr. Oliver.

In the old man's face was a mix of sadness and relief. The relief outweighed the sadness. It hurt Delvin to see it.

Mr. Oliver put his heavy, knobby hand on his. He was wearing a new ring, a chunky gold ring with a crest on it. Delvin started to ask about it, but just then Mrs. Parker brought dessert into the dining room and Mr. Oliver cried out that Delvin was leaving them again and they both began to weep. Casey sat pulled up tight to the table, looking at Delvin as if he wasn't sure who he was and wasn't sure he wanted to know. He too was wearing a crusty gold ring. I don't know what's going to happen to me, Delvin thought. I don't even know who I am.

He repeated these two sentences to the Ghost later as they sat at the card table the Ghost had set up in the old tack room. He now used the room for a combo bedroom, office, dining room and kitchen.

"Probably all the usual," the Ghost said. Just the day before he'd got rid of his beard and shaved his hair close; it looked like a bit of orange mist had settled on the top of his pale head.

"You as saucy as ever, aint you?"

"Worse." The albino half rose from his chair. "Let me show you this." He pulled a new Placer clasp knife from his pocket and laid it on the table. It looked like a sleek silver fish. When Delvin went to pick it up the Ghost skidded it out of reach, pushed it off the table into his other hand and held it up trophy style.

"You gon show it to me?" Delvin said.

"Your hands dry?"

"Let me see it."

The Ghost gave him the knife.

"It's right righteous," Delvin said, though he had no interest in knives and didn't open it. Still it had a lovely heft and felt compact and complete. He turned it in his hand. He would like to give Celia something that had this detailed perfection. He handed the knife back. In his pocket he carried an old tape-wrapped Barlow. "I mean," he said, "I don't know what I'm going to be doing next. In the next minute."

"Me, I know my way on down the road. That's the way I like it too."

"I don't know which of us is the lucky one."

"Maybe neither," the Ghost said, "not in this world."

Delvin wondered if the Ghost wasn't more intelligent than he'd thought.

"You want to go traveling with me?"

"Not for a thousand dollars."

Delvin was troubled that he didn't want to go alone. He wondered where the man Frank was by now. Maybe he should go over to the Emporium, get somebody over there to go with him. But he didn't care to see any of that world again just now. He went back into the house and out onto the porch where by light of a kerosene lamp and sitting beside Mr. Oliver in one of the big pontific arm chairs he read a book the professor had given him, *Who Is the Negro Man*, by Dr. Quinton Merckson of the University of Pennsylvania. Merckson argued that the negro man was the bearer of the world's troubles. This was because he had the strength to carry the weight. Delvin had read this sort of thing before, heard it before. He had a tendency to believe what he read, just because what he read was down in print. Later he would sort through it and find out what fit. For tonight he was the able negro man, hauler of the world's burdens. A soul thing, the doctor said in so many words. The negro man had a deeper and more refined, a nobler soul. He'd heard this from preachers at funeral services. For the trampled-on it always came down to something like that.

He put the book down on a little wicker table and looked over at Mr. Oliver, who was listening to the *Adelaide* concerto, his favorite Mozart, on the wind-up Victrola, turned down low.

"You think the negro man is designed to carry the world's burden?" Delvin said.

"If we are I spect we need to bulk up," Mr. Oliver said, looking down his ample front. He flipped open a wing of his black vest, revealing the red silk underlining. Casey lay on the floor putting another jigsaw puzzle together. Assembled, so Delvin recalled, the puzzle would become a picture of lions resting under a tree in Africa. The tree had a squashed gray top that always seemed to Delvin a mistake until he saw a photo of such a tree in the professor's museum. Acacia. They grew in Africa where everybody in this house was from. *Everybody* came from Africa, the professor had told him. White man caught the first train out, he said.

Tomorrow he would be back on the rails. Mr. Oliver had asked where he was off to this time. Delvin had told him about Celia. "Good, good," Mr. Oliver had said, grinning broadly, "it'll probably help take your mind off rounding up ladies for yours truly," and they both had laughed. Delvin had talked a little about how painful the situation was. "What matters to us always makes us a little nervous and spooky when we draw up to it," the funeral director said. "Look at me. I still live above my shop, like some old grocer off in the big city. I keep thinking I am about to move on to something that will be better, but when I think I am getting there . . . I get shaky."

Delvin hadn't known exactly what he was talking about, or maybe he did. In his eyes the real mournfulness under the professional one. Off to the side most folks had a little sparkle, most folks he knew. Some little graced and heroic frolic. But not Mr. O. He had never criticized Delvin for getting into trouble with the white boys (or the no-trouble). But he knew without being told that he had been the heir apparent and was no longer. This hurt him and at the same time he felt relieved to be free. He had never wanted to run a funeral home. Now there was little Casey. Twelve years old—not ten as he'd thought—and quiet-minded, an able boy who liked to do what he was told, seemed to get satisfaction out of it. The boy already smelled faintly of formaldehyde (always the smell around here, even in the kitchen where Mrs. Parker kept some in a mix for cleaning— except on Mr. Oliver, who was obsessive about cleanliness and well-perfumed—except on him, who had bathed readily out in the stable, washing at the pump).

He smiled, nodding in the old way, got up and asked if there was anything he could get his benefactor.

"The sight of you is enough," Oliver said. The old man—he was not so old, but there was a look in his eyes now, something abashed and wavering. He raised his hand and his hand, wide and furrowed down the back, trembled. They both saw this and Delvin wanted to take the hand and kiss it, press it hard to his heart, but he didn't, he pretended he didn't see the tremor, didn't see the vexed look in Oliver's eyes, only squeezed the hand, softly, like a promise, instead of with the jocosely competitive pressure they had used since he was a little boy. He didn't want to hurt him and he didn't want to let go. From somewhere off in the dark an owl called. The call was followed by the hesitant, falling cry of a widow bird, answering, or commenting, it wasn't clear.

6

In the late dark of early morning Delvin slipped out the back door. He walked through the quiet streets to the rail yards. The west-bound freight was finishing its assembly. A long string of red and yellow boxcars, flatcars and a hook of four black gondolas, all with their big bellies empty, clanked as they were coupled to the big red freight engine. Southern Railroad, Piedmont portion: Bitter Biscuit Line, the breezers called it. Delvin watched from the long grassy hill-side above Wainwright Avenue. Two men, one short, the other tall, in striped overalls, carried small suitcases to the dull red caboose and climbed the three steps to the back porch. He wished he was riding in the caboose. From the cupola the brakemen were supposed to watch for jumpers, but they didn't always do anything if they spotted them. Yard bulls were always a problem, but they too were off somewhere else this morning. A few dozen stampers sat around in the greasy yellow grass waiting for time to board. It was a wonder hawkers didn't work the crowd. In a way they did. There was Little Simp, a middle-aged hoop chiseler from Georgia, offering tiny hand-made dolls for sale. He made them out of gunnysacks stuffed with cotton and colored-in their faces with paints he made himself. There were women in the crowd too, bo-ettes, burlap sisters, zooks, shanty queens, blisters and hay bags they were called by the hobo crowd, janes looking for lost husbands or lovers, mop marys and buzzers. A little boy sold strips of sugar cane. Other men sold whatever anyone wanted to buy, personwise. Most of the shifters it looked like this trip were young, white and colored, boys mostly, looking for work—he overheard a young white boy talking about a big box factory opening in Memphis—and the rest members of the increasing crowd of the out-of-work, troubled or desperate or worn out or knocked to their

knees, or slaphappy tourists, workers or lazers or bindlestiffs and
beefers, dousers and cons, boys eager to make a start, posseshes joy-
riding into their cranky destinies. He had written about these travelers in his notebook. Truth was, you could find just about anybody
on the road these days.

The morning came up sunny, with only a few shredded clouds
in the south. They weren't high enough in the mountains to miss
the humidity. It lay like a film of grease on everybody's skin. In his
notebook he had written *sun plowing the night under . . . day touching itself everywhere. . . .* Were they his words, or had he copied
them from somewhere? Tapping at the page, he couldn't remember
now. He looked around for familiars. Maybe one would show. He
recognized a boy from over on the west side, Calvin Binger, and he
waved to him. Calvin gave him a slow sweep of wave back, which
was his style. They both kept their seat. A man standing in the grass
scratching his thigh through new blue jeans looked familiar, but not
from here. He looked like a yegg he'd run across, or no, somebody,
maybe it was the line foreman Trobilly had pointed out to him in
Baton Rouge. They had been eating coon meat sandwiches, a first
for Delvin, over near the closed-down rendering plant in the Larusse
district near where Molly Picone got killed that time in November
when the weather turned foul and her hincty boyfriend turned foul
with it. That had been a rough time for everybody. They had tried to
pull her out of the rot-choked slough she'd been thrown into—coax
her out—but she was more scared of her boyfriend than she was of
drowning and wouldn't come. She was wearing a long yellow dress
like a wool nightgown and the dress spread out all around her and
as she went under she was singing the Bessie Smith song "One More
Good Time with You." They had stood on the bank crying like
babies. That was where that man he was looking at now, hunched up
under a peaked gray cap, had been pointed out to him—not the first
such a one—as somebody to stay away from. They were the ones you
wanted to avoid on these trips. Wolves and high jackets and crazy
men, desocialized tramps of evil intent and slimy ways, the rail fight-
ers, croakers who traveled the circuit looking for somebody to whale

away on, beat to death and then stomp on the corpse. Few were like that, but there were always those good sense and kindness had never reached. It wasn't always easy to tell, not at first anyway, not until you got a feel for it.

Delvin took out his volume of Du Bois essays and began to read. Du Bois was writing about the threads that bound a people together. Delvin stopped. He was thinking about skin color. The photographs in the professor's museum. Black-and-white photos sure, the mix like out here, but not like out here because here the colors didn't mix, or if they did you were still only the one color, no matter how you fractionalized it; if there was any negro in you, you were negro only. Just a drop would do. Like we were tainted, he thought. But him, Delvin the Dark, he loved the rich deep colors best. His own face was among the blackest. But even among africano folks the light-skinned got the biggest portion. They were treated with more respect. As a tiny child he had sometimes been laughed at, called a dewbaby.

He shivered, and a thin string of anger pulled tight in him. Then the soft drop into gloom. These passed. He liked being dark-skinned. Some of the faces in the photos—he could see all the way back to the African beginnings. It stirred his body strangely to find himself peering through time at faces that carried in them a million years of life and history. As he looked he could feel the wind slipping up a river, turning little dust devils on the dry bank. He could smell the rank stink of a sun-rotted pelt. The people in these faces—what had they been doing out there?

Then he was thinking of Celia. Oh, he shouldn't have left the letters. Maybe he had misread them; he was capable of it. Mr. Rome had not shown up as promised in Chattanooga. He had looked out for him every day, but the reciter had not appeared. Maybe he hadn't reached Chicago, where he was to deliver his message to Celia. In the train yard he had asked about him, but no one coming in had seen him. He didn't know what had happened. He'd written Celia about him coming, but in her return she said the little man had not appeared. He'd asked her to write him in Memphis, general delivery. That was where he was going too, before—maybe—he headed out west. But what was there now in Memphis? His insides clutched. He was a fool. He thought of her dark african face. Even close to her he was looking into time. He wanted to run his fingers over her face, like a blind man, a man who saw the world as black. Maybe he could go find those letters again. Maybe they were still there.

The jacks began to get to their feet. The train was under way. Like grasshoppers the wind shakes from the grain, the hoboes and drifters, the shufflers and stiffs and ex–plow jockeys, ramblers, tramps, and scenery bums moved down through the slick grass to the cinderbeds and crossed the six sets of tracks to the train clanking into motion. They climbed aboard, scurrying to the top or the bottom, into open doors and onto gondolas and flatcars, swung up into the shelter of the two empty boxcars. Delvin hesitated. He felt he was leaving half his heart. Then he ran for the train and climbed up onto a gondola. The last of the travelers boarded. Behind them the breeze shifted and slipped delicately over the trampled grass.

Clanking, screeching, squealing, shuddering, the big train made its way through the yard and out onto the road that passed through the rough western sections of the city, past the warehouses where Delvin once liked to walk inside of with his friend Archie Consadine along the rows of high-stacked cotton bales. Big barrels of water had grease scum on the surfaces of the water to keep the mosquitoes from breeding in them. And past the cotton mills, three of them in a row, painted green originally but now gray with lint. Lint swagged from electrical wires and outlined roof shingles and collected in the eaves of the little shotgun cabins workers lived in and blew along the unpaved streets and every day wisped into the lungs of the workers. And past the rendering plant with its vats of copper-colored solution and its piled white bones waiting to be ground into fertilizer. And past the big pine grove off Dunkins street where little Rozie Coverdale was murdered by two white boys who were caught with Rozie's mother's pearl necklace in the pocket of one of them, a necklace never returned, so the story went, to the family. The white boy and his family claimed the necklace was theirs—they were only retrieving it—and the Coverdales could not prove to the satisfaction of the jury that they were lying. Rozie's mother died without knowing what had really happened, but, so they said, she didn't really want to know what had gone on in those woods that were still used for trysts and mushroom-picking expeditions.

And past the Ombley pasture where Delvin had once played football with boys who attended Fisk University and after the game gave him his first taste of bonded whiskey, a taste he had spit out onto the rocky ground behind the Buck & Buck barbecue restaurant over on Caprice street. And past cramped unpainted houses where the lives of crackers were lived out in pale concordance, and past them and across the spur to Lucasville, where negro folks in similar shotgun cabins with their tiny front porches sporting a rocking chair and maybe a swing and tomatoes growing in No. 10 cans and string nets tacked on one side for trellising confederate jasmine or morning glories, both still blossoming in early autumn, lived their similar money-fretted lives. And past the primitive Baptist church—white cube with ice-cream-cone steeple—manifested by hardshell believers who refused to accept the injunction to send missionaries around the world spreading the gospel, playing it close to the vest with the Good Book. And past the livestock sale barn, an airy structure built of native pine and tin roofing, now derelict after a sustained outbreak of pinkeye and slop foot, along with the shift in agricultural focus away from the rocky farms of the mountain and sandhill country south and westward. And past Angelo's, a combination grocery, Italian restaurant and speakeasy where patrons (white only) interested in red-sauced dinners (with Chianti wine) sat around card tables set among the shelves packed with Idea Starch, Calgon, 20 Mule Team Borax, Ajax, sacks of Water Maid rice, stacks of hard lye soap and shoe polish tins, exchanging vernacular quips with Angelo Depesto, immigrant soul from Pesaro on the Adriatic sea, Coloreds served out of a window in back.

And past Wilbur Homewood's deserted pastures, sold two years ago to the Fox and Hound Hunt Club and left to their natural ways of steeplebush, clover, dusty miller, ironweed, meadow rue, Joe Pye weed and bunchgrass by members who on Saturdays in spring and fall chased foxes on jumpers and farm nags across the rocky ground, a practice they would abandon a few years from then after the last diehard admitted that the granite shelves and schist outcrops of the southern Appalachians were inhospitable to this kind of sport.

Past dumps of generalized refuse and small boys walking along dreaming of adventure and freedom from father's strap.

Past young girls standing at roller washing machines or pushing corncobs on washer boards or lifting soaked overalls out of No. 2 washtubs.

Past wives walking barefoot out of cornfields just streaked with fall's first yellow and old men propping barn doors open and farmers slapping at flies and orchard workers studying rolled-over Beauchamp pamphlets they hoped would teach them to use the english language for their social and economic betterment.

Past the Mt. Moriah cemetery where colored folk were buried under wire and worked-iron tombstones and stone tombstones that had been dug out of some mountainside and under tombstones made of clay pots and some made of wood. Among the graves a group of little colored boys moved about challenging the dead and the spirits of the dead and challenging the whole of life to come and the whole of life never coming again. One of them as the train began to pick up speed threw up a hand and waved, and Delvin, looking up from his notebook, waved back.

And onward, loose finally from the bindery and compaction of cities into the nondescript woodlands and raw weather-gouged fields and clay-streaked grassy pastures of that part of the country.

All these forms and folks and structures Delvin noticed, and some he wrote down in his notebook, the latest version, that was worn by now with sweat and wrung by his hands and bent back, its pages covered in his close and tight handwriting, filled with little stories of birds killed by freeze and sunshine stealing all the color from the grain fields and some woman busting some man outside a bar with her fists and all manner of names and lists of railroad companies and flowers and hymns from the Concord hymnbook used in Methodist churches and kinds of shoes and dances and equipment and road terminology and plow parts and military ranks and characters in Shakespeare and Sir Walter Scott and perfumes and state capitols and freshwater fishes; and much pertaining to Celia including long sweaty passages keeping her informed of his troubling incapacities and failures of heart and his sense of lostness in the world and of the dawns when he woke terrified and shaking, passages never copied into his letters; and the names of friends and brief sections concerning their doings; and sections pertaining to his childhood, of the shanty floor smelling of coconut oil and of the songs his mother sung and of Coolmist leaning down to give him a kiss and of Spokes his little ragheaded doll and of Ri-Rusty his fluffy old dog and of banana pie and of skeeting in rainwater puddles in the street and of the lure of alleys and dead ends and of his mother fleeing into the wilderness wearing an organdy silk dress and of his brothers and sister singing along with Old Shaky Sims and his Talking Guitar and of the foundling home (*lostling home*, he wrote) where he learned to love potatoes and flute music and keened for freedom; and of the funeral parlor where when he was seven George held him up over the prep table to stare at the sunken, dented body and filmed-over eyes of Mr. Harvell Burns, former principal of Tucker Elementary school, allowing him to confront for the first time the obstinate bulkage of the dead, and Mr. Oliver waltzing to Mozart; and back-alley life that smelled at this time of year of crabapples crushed underfoot and dead bees and fired clay and spillings of crankcase oil; and of the terrible battles that took place among boys on this ground; and of the smell of summer mornings in the kitchen garden among squash flowers and staked bean rows and of all the distilled and perfumey odors of high summer; of the time Luther Burdle caught Smuckie Sparks in the ear with the old wooden golf club he'd found in the trash out at the Congress Country Club, cutting Smuckie's ear in half and spraying blood onto Hollie Jo Davis's white confirmation dress; and on and such and through the dribbles and castings and shucks of his life up to this moment as he sat under the overhang of a Tweety gondola headed west carrying a half load of sand (he'd thought the car was empty).

He turned the pages of the small gray book, reading the story of his life. In no other place, he thought, did this story exist, not even in his own head. Only here, and in the other four notebooks left at Oliver's. This is what keeps me from disappearing. In these few years riding trains he had watched and recorded the drifting men rucky times had cast onto the rails. This train was filled with shufflers, jobless characters following the latest rumor of work. After a while the dirt and soot wore in. Seemed like it did. Sleeptalkers, sleepwalkers, divers and chokers, barabys and Airedales. *A trainload of boys*, he wrote, *looking for work*. It's a race. Tramps, not the same as hoboes. And the ones who rode for years without ever saying a word. *Sixty-two cars on this train*, he wrote.

Thirty or forty riders. Say thirty-seven. Mostly white boys headed for (maybe) jobs in Memphis. Nine or ten colored boys. Many dressed in rags, or close to it. One has a yellow bandana tied around his head. A few boys carrying canvas sacks. A couple have suitcases. Soogans. Most of the colored boys aren't carrying anything, maybe two or three have a few items tied up in handkerchiefs.

To the south clouds were filling up the hollow places in the pale sky, but they didn't look like rain clouds, just frothy empties and leftovers from summer. The train was passing through grain fields; wheat, he thought. He stood and reached up to steady himself on the edge of the gondola catwalk. A white boy he didn't at first see, boy with a high freckled forehead, just making his way along the narrow strip below the gondola rim, stepped on his hand.

"Hey," Delvin said. "Watch those fingers, they're precious to me." He was feeling good, glad to be out in the wide world.

"If you want to keep em, chig, then get your ass off the train."

The boy kicked at him, missed.

"You need to watch yo mouth as well as yo feet," Delvin said.

He had been stuffing the notebook into his back pocket when the white boy stepped on him. He almost lost his grip—didn't—but it was not worrisome, little aggravations happened on trains.

"I'll watch you fly like a sack of shit off this train," the boy said. He had fish-colored eyes and long pale eyelashes pretty as a girl's.

A couple of africano boys on the other side of the gondola watched the exchange. Everyone proceeded on his way.

After a while Delvin made a course up the train to one of the two open boxcars and climbed in through the trap. Africano boys were in there talking. They saw Delvin and one waved him over. A burly boy with close-cropped hair said, "You the one that ofay kicked?"

"He didn't exactly kick me," Delvin said. "It was more of a step. Just missed being a stomp."

"That white boy wants to fight about it," another traveler said, a small, slender boy with not very recently conked hair, slicked back. He wore a long green shirt like some medieval woodsman. "*All* them white boys wants to fight. They gon come at us."

"They sure like to mix it up," another said, a blocky boy with a wide, friendly, scared face. "No questions about why or what for."

"No why or what for in this world," another said in a weary voice. He was tall and had narrow round shoulders.

"Long as they got the numbers," another said.

They were all suddenly nervous.

A few pocket knives (if it came to that), a couple of round whittled sticks, a leather sap (the cracked leather showing the lead plumb underneath), and a bag of ball bearings in a canvas sack, these the weapons.

Down at the other end of the car a couple of unhappy, plain-looking white girls, one of them fat. The fat one interrupted chinning with her skinny buddy to hurl a couple insults at the negro end. A few white boys down there too, but they were just looking.

"Those men?" somebody asked, a dark-skinned boy unmemorable but for a small white scar cutting his left eyebrow in two. He was looking at the little group down the far end.

"They's other ones coming," said another boy—they were mostly, but for a couple, just leaving boy life for manhood, fresh travelers, hoboes, Chattanooga and upline angelicas trekked out of the hollows, headed west looking for work. They'd heard the mills in

Memphis were hiring. The mills or the box factory or the riverside warehouses or the meat-processing plant, somebody, someplace. One, a skinny boy with pale gold freckles on a tan face, was so scared already his hands shook; he kept slapping them against his jeans. He was on his way to meet his sister in Tulsa, he said. She needed him to escort her down to Dallas for their brother's wedding.

"I got to get on," he said, and Delvin could tell he wanted to slip away. But he didn't; he was afraid to, Delvin could see this too. Out the door he could see a river, lengths of shining water running between sycamore trees turning yellow.

"Can't help from it," he said slowly, referring to the fight; letting the words out carefully, as if they were precious, like special stones held back in a pouch or wrapped in cloth and stowed in a bindle. A whole speech. Like something from Shakespeare. His body buzzed with excitement. He was not particularly angry. But he wanted to experience—here, now—the exercise of his power, wanted to move harshly against something solid and strong. These white boys. They were hardly real to him. They came and went, and it was always the same with them, they knew only one way, had only one side.

"Knock these dicty jeffs on they diasticusses," the tall boy said, and the others laughed.

The car smelled of cedar shavings. It was beginning to fill up. Two, three, more white boys swung in off the roof and others crawled through the trap at the far end. Tattered boys in denim and patched khaki, farm boys, city boys with shop grease under their fingernails. They too had weapons. Sticks and short lengths of cane pole, what looked like a corner off a metal bed.

The girls started yelling, calling the africano boys names. Nothing they hadn't heard before.

The air in the car was cool, but Delvin felt a heat on him. He trembled and the heat seemed suddenly to fly out of him and he was cold. I must be coming down with something, he thought, and then thought, yeah, scaredy-catness. The edges of his body felt numb. His palms were sweating, his heart galloped. He had no weapon but his pocketknife and he really didn't want to set down his soogan and the little cotton sack Mrs. Parker had filled for him; he didn't want to draw that. He thought of Celia walking across a grassy lawn to her classes. The buildings, she said, were made of stone that changed colors according to the light. He pictured a rainbow, but the ones she named were hardly colors at all: charcoal, gray, brown like a mule's back. Maybe Mr. Rome would find her one day. He pictured the little man reared-back reciting the wordy love message he had prepared, and choked a laugh.

One of the boys looked at him. "You pretty bugged-up," he said.

The white boys moved away from the back wall. A dozen, fourteen, fifteen, a clenched little army. Road toughs, scared boys just looking for work, boys on the run from bad daddies, drunk mothers, no mothers, something sad in their eyes, something wild, something hateful. For a sec he wanted to stick out his hand.

Hopeless, Delvin thought, useless. But then he didn't mind.

An ache in his shoulders, a sorrowfulness like a headache. He wrapped his right hand in his bandana.

The old time—the dream time—slipping away, he thought—it was something the professor said. As if we were supposed to hold onto it.

One of the white boys flung a rotten cucumber. It hit a burly stutterer colored man in the shoulder, Coover Broadfoot. Delvin knew him from the Chat-town streets, from games of clip poker in a house around the corner from New Bethel church, from the Emporium, from his auntie's funeral, from Coover's teariness, from the set of his head like a little soot-headed lamb's.

Then somebody yelled and, their eyes slitted and wild, the white boys rushed among them, flailing and whipping their sticks.

The africano boys bunched up and all at once sprang at them, fought back hard and cunningly, striking the white boys across their faces, kicking at their knees.

Delvin caught a glancing blow against his upper arm but he didn't feel it.

A big africano man, somebody he'd never seen before, picked up a medium-sized white boy with blond hair thick as a pelt and threw him against the side of the car. The boy landed on hands and feet, crumpled into a heap, slowly gathered himself, crawled a few steps and ran up against another africano boy, somebody called Rollie, a ruthless man missing his front teeth, who kicked him in the side. The white boy rolled like a stumplog rolling down a hill.

Delvin punched somebody, cracked somebody across the eyes with the side of his wrapped fist. Somebody whapped him in the back of the head and somebody else caught him with what felt like a firebrand across his lower back. It was a tall boy hitting him with a section of bamboo cane. He staggered away, knocked against another white boy who punched him to his knees. How did he get in this? He saw a blue-colored band of light weaving in among the roiling shapes. He was suddenly off to the side.

All the while the white women shrieked hatefully, their voices, especially the voice of the big woman with the piano legs standing foursquare grasping in her thick chalky hands a piece of broomstick, brandishing it—condemning, excusing nothing. She saw him and shook the stick at him and seemed about to come for him.

Somebody pulled him to his feet and he jammed himself back into the fray. At its densest it was a big pulsing congery of boys, a wild patch. He banged on somebody's back. Somebody slugged him on the side of the head and he saw red bursts, flares. He was shoved against the wall that gave and bounced him back. The boards smelled of sweat and faintly of piss. He edged away and crouched, sprang up and hit a skinny white boy straight in the nose. The boy reeled backwards into another white boy who hit him and knocked him down. Delvin laughed.

The africano boys pushed the white boys steadily back until all but a few were huddled at the front of the car weakly brandishing their sticks and splintered cane poles. One africano boy whom no one knew, gripping his piece of broomstick like a baseball bat, kept hitting a stocky brutish-looking white boy who all the time kept shouting at him like he wasn't being hit at all. The strikes made hollow sounds against his shoulders. Finally the africano boy threw down the stick and tried with his fists but the white boy knocked him on his ass with one blow. Two africano boys piled into the white boy and forced him back into the pack. Everybody was shouting, nobody coming around to the other's point of view, nobody offering anything but slurs and insults, nobody in his heart giving in, or maybe only a few.

And then as suddenly as it had begun the fighting stopped. Everybody just quit. They could hear the train, *clanka clanka clanka*. It was as if some greater force had called out halt, or nothing had, or some strange interval timing, clockwork none realized he was party to but nonetheless faithfully followed, had crunched down to the last second of martial time and let them go.

They stood, or knelt, or sat on their aching butts scrunched against the wall, panting. None really cared to look directly into the faces of his opponents. Most'd had enough and didn't stare. Eye contact slid and dissolved and some were crying and some were gasping in and out of a hatred and a sullen despicable remorse and others were dazed and some were silently praying and others were whispering to the blank places in their souls about what had happened and what had not.

Delvin drew breaths from way down in his body. Each one hurt a little and made him remotely dizzy but he knew he was okay. He had fought with strength and will to some degree. This surprised him slightly.

No one said much. A single epithet from one of the girls—"coon fucktards!" she yelled—but somebody, a white boy, made a harsh noise, just a cry, that shut her up, and that was it. The panting mixed with the clack of the train wheels.

Suddenly the smell of corn. Delvin looked out the door. They were passing a huge field of yellowing corn. Corn as far as he could see. The season rich with the sharp silky smell of it, rich already with the early yellows and reds. The tall sumac in the road ditches going red, the shaggy flowers like spires of imperial acknowledgment, the yellow goldenrod in big bunches thickly flowering so he wanted for a second to throw himself out onto it, soft bed of gold, and the smell of corn like a natural dust, ancient and soothing.

• • •

At Klaudio, just up the line, somebody jumped off the train—Cornell Butler, the papers said later—and ran to the police. Assault by negroes on white boys. And on two white girls. Rape? Yeah, yeah—something like that. You don't even have to say it. A breeze picked lightly through the narrow leaves of a butternut tree just outside the sheriff's office, as if looking for one special leaf.

The first accuser Butler was sweating and shaking, and he had the look about him of somebody who had suffered a great tragedy.

He looked heartbroke, the chief testified later. *Just plain heartbroke.*

It took one call to the stationmaster at Kollersburg. Then another to the Cumbly county sheriff. In a matter of minutes men in cars and pickups were on the road, racing to catch the train. A line of cars filled with outraged, murderous, bloody-minded, vengeful—and all the other dark indemnities—men. It wasn't only the excitement. The men hurt in their hearts. *Beat the boys and raped the women for christ's sake.*

Carrying guns and tobacco sticks and ax handles picked up at Burns' Hardware on Harris street, they rushed toward Kollersburg. Some had experience with this sort of thing, a few were klansmen, others just attendees of lynchings and other routs and ambuscades, most were money-stretched citizens, hurled by this atrocity into sudden stumbling pellmell motion.

A breeze played in the tops of the long grove of red cedars just beyond the town limits they passed going as fast as they could, jangling and seething. Torn-looking bottom-heavy clouds were banked in the west. Art Luger ran over a something he later swore was a six-foot-long rattlesnake. Some men felt anguished with pain for the poor girls and for those ambushed boys, others felt only a satisfying urgency. Hard times had stiffened their souls.

In the boxcar things had quieted down. No one was hurt badly, though Coover Broadfoot, one of the negro men from C-town, had been struck just above the eye and was now getting a bad headache.

Others had cuts, big pear- and plum-colored bruises, welts along the back and side. Davie Considine's jaw—he was a white boy with, so the papers said, a dream to open a watch repair shop—where a negro boy (Bonette Collins) had whacked him with a piece of stovewood, ached. Several had stinging sensations where they'd been hit with limber pieces of bamboo, or numbness. Nobody was sure where the bamboo came from, but both colored and white now had it.

The girls were telling their story of how the nigra boys had over-powered them, over in an empty grain car—and some of them in *this* car—*before yall got here,* they said. *They done their ugly business.*

The fat one did the talking. She was a hurt woman, unloved, mocked, mistreated since birth, no feature in her face anything but forgettable except her mouth, full, creased at the edges as if relent-lessly gnawed, able to hold a sneer for years and back it with ener-gized profanity, a girl, young woman of twenty-two, the adrenaline gushed alternately through like rancid gouts of factuality soothing a terrifying emptiness until she had come to believe or for seconds at a time was sure she believed or what did it fucking matter she didn't have to believe a single goddamn thing about these crapface shines, it was time to stop this, stop *some goddamn thing,* by God.

In the car, sitting across from Delvin, a big negro man in overalls with a red-and-white-check lining was grinning like he had found true happiness. A sharp red line ran along the part in a man's hair. A man tried to reach way down his back and another man, trembling as he did so, scratched the place for him. Another kept stretching out his arm and pulling it back. His crew was mostly smiling and talking fast. They had won. A man called Butter gripped himself in both arms as he leaned against the back, honey-colored wall. Beside him a small boy pronounced the name Bonette over and over, or maybe he was saying *bone it,* holding up a thumb that had blood—maybe not his—on it. Another man kept shooting out his fist, punching air. Others held their heads and smiled out the open door at the world that had noticed none of this. They had beat the white boys at their own game. They had been quicker and stronger and they had more heart. They hadn't backed down. It felt good to be who they were.

We feel like we could run up a mountain and dance on the top, Delvin thought. He pulled out his notebook and wrote: *One man keeps shaking his hands and jumping up and down on his toes like a boxer*, but his fingers were aching too much for him to continue.

All of a sudden he wanted to cry. He wasn't the only one. Carl Crawford, Rollie Gregory—they looked like they wanted to cry too. Not for happiness. Some hard grief pressing down. He climbed up on top of the boxcar.

The train rolled along through grain fields, then woods, then clearings, then, out of nowhere—he'd seen this no place before—they passed the old country zoo outside Kollersburg. Under skimpy oak cages on stilts, chickenwire enclosures, sheds with open, wired-over doors. Animals, creatures from the woods, raccoons, porcupines, held prisoner inside. "Look a'yonder," somebody said. Strange but familiar sharp-eyed creatures drawn up close so you could get a good look at them. Detainees, the unredeemable. Sun caught in the fur of a mangy bobcat, what fur there was, bristling the hairs, a peacock screamed and screamed again in the late daylight as if he didn't care about anything but screaming, a bear—that must of been a bear— lay curled up like a dog, a camel bleated; and then they were gone.

The train rounded a long curve past a field of seeding sorghum. The dark gold knobby tops shook and gave in a nicking breeze. The train began to slow down. What's that coming? Delvin thought. Not just the curve. Off across the grain field he could see the wind shake the tops of some beech trees, flicking the leaves over on their white sides, flicking them back. He wanted to leap up and jump off the train. Something said to, but he couldn't make himself do it.

They were approaching the junction at Kollersburg. The train slowed. He got to his feet, danced a slow little step to get the feeling back in his legs. He climbed down through the trap into the car. The women were shouting again. Crows squawking. You get scared to the point you can't turn it off. At the edge of their group a large man with blood crusted on his knuckles. He had a dazed look. Delvin thought he would like to speak to this man, but the train was coming to a stop. He heard angry voices above the clattering and squealing of metal. Shouts. Men were running. The sound of horses. The train creaking to a stop.

He saw four white men race past the door, men carrying shot-guns, one in a bow tie and a brown vest—like a lawyer, he thought, or a doctor—but he was carrying a double-barreled shotgun. And then the runners saw the men on the train and stopped and wheeled in a fury of shouts and spit popping from their lips and cried for *you niggers* (they shrieked the word) to come down out of there, trotting beside the open door, not waiting for the train to fully stop before they were giving orders.

"You get down or by God and Jesus we will shoot you where you stand."

He knew what was happening, he saw it, but something off to the side, a lingering presence, said this is not so. Above the men's heads a lone blue jay sailed along, dipping and rising. What was the matter with that bird?

"Oh, don't let them kill me," the skinny, wrenched girl yelled from back in the boxcar gloom.

Both doors filled with guns, leveled on them, on the boys, men, of color. You had a front gun row, a second, third and gallery of guns, safeties off. The ones who had participated in lynchings knew what to do, but the ones who had never seen a mob before also, instinc-tively, knew as well. It was as if they had been here many times. As if this furious clumping together, this scarifying, claiming vengeance or redemption, was as natural as sunlight.

Wading through the mob came the sheriff and his deputies, men in khaki carrying shotguns all of the same make and model, Colt Busters, .12 gauge pump-action, loaded with double-aught buckshot. They walked without looking to the side or with any waywardness, as if they were marching to their destinies and they understood and welcomed it.

A sharp, dingy despair cut across Delvin's mind. He knew as if it was tattooed on the palm of his hand what was coming. But he

couldn't believe it. From among the ruck of eight africano boys left
in the car—one of them barely thirteen—he gaped at the irreversible
future taking shape under a richly blue September sky. The afternoon heat was like hot syrup stuffing every crevice, heat so strong it
was nauseating.

"Come on out of there, boys," the sheriff said in his heavy, florid
voice, Sheriff Benny Capers, born in 1880 in the Capers Park community over near Marksonville. As that Babylonian king called to
Daniel in the lions' den, the sheriff called to them. *What you doing
sitting back there in the filth and the murk, Mr. Daniel?*

"Wonder Where Is Old Daniel" was sometimes sung at funerals. Where was old Mr. Oliver? Where was Celia? Where was his
mother?

Delvin's body had become almost too heavy to move, but he
wasn't quite in his body, even as he experienced it doddering toward
the door. How natural it was to do what he was told! How far there
was to go! He was heavy but he floated. A line of tiny red ants flowed
steadily along the joining of the wall to the floor. Where you going,
ants? Where you come from?

The posse had dogs out there too, so he saw as he reached the
door, already shuffling like a man in irons—dogs: curs and shaggy
varmint-catchers and mongrel farm dogs had joined the party, yap-
ping and snarling. Somebody close by had already shit his pants.

They made them jump. Stepped back so the boys jumped onto
the hard yellow clay. Delvin banged his right knee but he wouldn't
feel it for hours. Not until the culprits, the lazy fools and black hooligans, had exited and been grabbed and rope-tied and hooded with
flour sacks did they call for the women to come out. One by one the
defiled were lifted carefully, almost delicately, down, the men trying
their best not to injure these destroyed ladies any further. The big
one still shouting.

The africano boys—some stoical, some dumbly distant, some
crying under the hoods that smelled of biscuits, one yelling *It's them
white boys* and pointing blindly and catching a blow, one shaking
like he'd break—are slapped and prodded and loaded into the back

of Mr. Sandal Morgan's slat-sided cattle truck and at the head of a convoy of trucks and cars hauled to the castle-like granite county jail in Klaudio.

Deputies, unable to conceal their disgust, march the boys through the jail and up the stone stairs to a windowless blind aerie at the top, unlock it with a flat brass key, and hustle them in to a complete blackness. Black on black, one says. They don't bother to take the ropes off and they leave the negroes looped together by another knotted rope in the hot dark. A few of the men, blind and re-destined, are scared to untie the rope, but Delvin finds himself speaking up to say they will be better off without any ropes at all, mentioning this almost as an aside, the misery that has come on him during the roundup unabated, stinking and stuck against his brain, a fresh damp gray endlessness stretching in all directions, his voice inside it hollow, creaking, faltering as if the old familiar language is no longer his, never had been. Hoods still on, in the dark, nobody can see anything. Delvin carefully pulls a little slack and works his hood off; it is still too black to see. Two of the boys cry steadily. Two others start yelling when Delvin comes down the line unlooping the rope. They don't want to be cut loose. Somebody elbows Delvin in the side, another jerks up a fist that catches him in the right temple, a lucky blow that knocks him silly on his feet. For a moment he is dancing among leaves in the street outside the funeral home. Celia twirls in a yellow dress under the big sweet gum trees. Two seconds later he is back in the cell. A monstrous, unavoidable despair reaches through time and blackness and finds him. He smells a stink he can't entirely place— pork grease, shit, sweat, and something else, reptilian and indelible.

Man by man he goes on retrieving the rope, picking the knots loose and coiling the rope over his elbow and through his cupped left hand. The darkness, filled with heat and a mucosal moistness, presses on him. From the dark a voice that comes from no one says: *We will smother you.* He goes on, slowly, retrieving the raw manila rope.

BOOK THREE

Bam! it went, bam! in his head like a pile driver sinking cypress logs into heavy Aufuskie bay mud for the new highway bridge, the actual driver and the other in his head almost the same but not quite—this other bam! that went on in his head some days until it seemed anchored not in memory but in his soul, bam! of doors closing and days ending and of time itself like a heavy hammer banging down hard on his head. He lay dreaming on his bunk in Acheron State Prison infirmary, bunk you could call it that was nothing but a few sticks of cypress wood bound together with grass rope and covered with a pile of cotton matting that he lay on, sick, the doctor said, with malaria—ague, cold plague—the red dog, they called it in the barracks—lying on his back with a headache like the sound of those pile drivers, the ones inside his head and the ones outside, lay thinking of the cold black waters of the river he had escaped into last winter and gotten maybe two chilled miles farther down before he was fished out with a mullet net by the sheriff of Alderson county, cast naked onto the raw bank and beaten across the back with a rope until he couldn't get to his feet when ordered to. He lay dreaming of the white piano in the Emporium his mother used to nod off to in the big red parlor after a long night's work, and slept for forty hours in the grassrope bunk, waking only to sip a little water from the tin cup Milo had placed beside his bed. Dreaming of the big snake that had lived with him and the mosquitoes that bit him and the deer flies stabbing his chest and tiny gnats settling into his ears and supping at the corners of his eyes, making themselves at home, but even in the dream he did not mind any of these creatures because he was dreaming of a white bed in a big house that opened along one side onto an airport where planes with big round propellors landed and took off and sailed away with him riding in the forward cockpit in a shiny leather helmet and a yellow silk scarf that trailed behind like a running streak engraved on the blue sky, flying to the sound of piano music.

1

"Well, what else can you call it," Billy Gammon, young lawyer, says to his colleague, assistant and investigator Baco Bates, "what do you think of when you consider it, this *prison*—not theory now for these wandering boys, but fact? *General erasure* comes to mind, among other terms, *bottomless pit, universal solvent, comprehensive alimentary chute, maw of hell.* I know there are others. *Barathrum.* Into which everything they have is thrown—hopes, plans, memories of Mama mashing scuppernongs for the juice, of riding in a little square-nosed boat through the lily pads, of cutting the fool in church—you name it—memories of festiveness and of sobering up on well water and of usefulness and of that early unfortunate marriage to the sweetest girl you ever saw . . . you name it . . . *everything's* got to go."

He stops to look out the big picture window of the Shawl House restaurant across the square where the young men, known far and wide as the KO Boys, are just now passing hidden from view inside a big black panel van on their way the two blocks from the county jail to the courthouse. "Think of it," Billy says, drunk at eight thirty in the morning, hardly ever undrunk these days and what of it, he would say, smiling at you as if you are his best friend once removed and the easiest person to believe in he has seen in a while, "think of the singular and well nigh mythological power of prison, Baco, of how no matter how strong or seemingly permanent that hard little flint representation, icy diamond of hopefulness or chagrin might be, that soul, I mean, you throw it through the doors of a prison and it is gone forever, dissolved into the dust and grease and sweat and the long black mordancy of that place. It makes me shudder just to think about it."

The panel van, traveling as slowly as a hearse, rounds the corner at Cooper street, passing the Red Rooster café where several of the older men in the community sit at the back table having breakfast, the shadows of the sycamores passing soft hands over the top and sides of the van from which, if you are a small boy sneaked away from school to watch this, you would not have heard a single sound emanating, as if the truck carried not eight negro youths to what you could call their *job*, calling, life's work really, or fate, over at the gray granite stone courthouse, but a load of silent ghosts.

"Jesus, Mohammed, old Confucius—you name it, Baco—truest of true loves, filial pieties of all kinds and duration, that time you stole granddaddy's watch and sold it for passage to the Orient—"

"That wadn't me," Baco, a tall, bony man so skinny you thought he might crack in a big enough wind, fold in two, break apart and blow in sections away, says. "I stole a jewelry box, but I didn't steal nary watch."

"It doesn't matter," Billy says. "It could be a watch or a pair of patent leather dancing shoes or a celluloid collar you picked up off the street that had a bloodstain on it that was a clue to solving the crime of the century, or a crust of, I don't know, of grease picked off the axle of the tumbrel carrying Marie Antoinette to the guillotine—it passes through that prison gate and disappears, gone to oblivion. Forever lost. Those boys' lives and everything they got inside em, good or bad, is forever lost."

As usual he has spoken too much. Baco looks with pity at him. He looks at Billy in the face, in his own face a mix of aggravation and fondness, and says, "You gon show up over there?"

"I suppose I might," Billy says. "Sometimes I feel like I could stick my hand inside those gates and it would just disappear. I'd draw back a stump. Or I could walk right on in and I'd draw back . . . nothing. It gives me a curious relief to let my mind circulate among such thoughts."

These are the early days of the trial, and it is time to get moving. A big man with an untrained shock of hair the color of iron rust, he hoists himself up and begins to make his way to the courthouse.

• • •

He knew nothing about working on a farm but they said that's all right boy we will teach you. They handed him a hoe and sent him into the fields. He learned the short clipped swing and chopped cotton for twelve hours a day and returned to the barracks so tired he hardly cared about eating. "I'll sleep this one out," he said to Marcus Millens, and Marcus just smiled a weary smile and turned to his rack. In dreams he wandered in a wide plain that he was sure one day he would get to the other side of but in the dream never did. In the morning when it was cool he felt like a man come to a new life not this one. He scribbled in his notebook sometimes but often he forgot to. He liked to stand up in the middle of the field and let the breeze play off him. Scatterings of birds passed over and he liked to send something of himself along with them, a word or a thought. It was a way to hook himself to the living world, the world that wasn't chained down in a prison. I will be loose from here by and by, he said. He had a curious smile sometimes that the other convicts remarked on. One or two tried to beat it off of him but they weren't successful. He didn't know he had the smile until they made it clear. I guess I got some feeling even I don't know about. And he believed this after a while. He would get caught up in the smells. The crotty smell of the dirt and the limber woody smell of the cotton plants, the sweet stink of bug poison, the smell of his own body and the smells that sailed over the fields, little pickets of smells, of turnips and spicy wild berries and once in a while the smell of some creature, blood even, as if down the way some ferret or quail had met its end. The prison world was one of elimination and spareness and he tried to press against this. Sometimes by holding his own wrist and just staring at the ground he thought he could get loose, or smelling his shit that he dropped behind a bush he could approach another world, but even his surging, side-stepping thoughts became thoughts of this world and his shit smelled of the field peas and sidemeat they fed him here. Still there were times, seconds like an ace in the hole, that stirred another existence in him, some ghost of times that had not been in this world but were familiar. He felt sometimes as if he was on the edge of something great. He liked to listen to the sound the wind made. Clouds like separate countries drifted from their absent worlds. He could smell Arabia or the Mongol steppes. He walked to the truck dragging his hoe to make signs in the dirt that might on their own mean something. He thought about the people he knew but this was hard on him and he tried not to do it. Cotton flowers were separately yellow or white as if there was a disagreement among them. The world was full of parts that barely fit and only fit for a little while. People turned aside, became memories or ghosts. In a split cotton boll the gray seeds lay twined in white fur. Everything would some day be far from here. He liked to taste the elements in the water he drank.

Baco is the one who'd accompany Billy down to the Shawl House where the big girl, Lucille Blaine, is staying, and according to the ruling of the judge—or close to it—she has to talk with him present at her deposition about what happened in the hours between four in the afternoon and six thirty o'clock on September 8, 1931, but of course she doesn't want to talk or if she does what she has to say is that those *nigras*, especially *that one, that main one* who is so talkative, *that Delvin Walker,* he is the one who did the most damage to her, the one who was first—and last—on the scene, he is the one ripped up her secret self like he was tearing flesh off the inner bones of her body . . .

"Lord," she says, "that pinched little monster wouldn't quit til I could smell the blood from my own body burning in my nose. Such pain as no human woman should have to experience was my pain"—*pain for life* possibly, Dr. Kates said in the deposition—"and still that black beast whanged away at me like I was the satisfaction to his Hell's own fires . . ."

He has all this down in his notes, and more, and Billy has read it and laughed, turned the page around on the big wood table so it faced Baco and, laughing, said, "Maybe she would be happier on the Elizabethan stage than here among us," pointing at her words that as she had spoken them were soaked, weighted with a malice that he wished sometimes he could get across to those reading them.

But why worry about that, he thinks, because she is right here in front of them now, in the hot courtroom, testifying as to what happened on that hot day when the leaves on the tulip trees were just starting to speckle with fall. "Yeah," she is saying, this Lucille who must weigh two hundred and fifty pounds (let's see, two hundred and fifty-eight to be exact, according to Dr. Kates's report), "oh yeah, that one over there was the first, and then the other with the big eye was next, and another, and then after that I kinder lost track, but I do remember those other three and maybe that last one too, the one, if he's the one who walks with a limp.

"He stutters, too," she turns to the judge and says. "I recollect that quite clearly. You ffffff-fat bbbb-bitch, that's what he called me. He had a little old pecker like . . ."

And the judge, who looks half asleep, is taking notes as she says this—he's not asleep, it's just been his manner since grade school, Judge Montclair Harris—and raises his white head that still shows the nap mark mashed on the back and says, "That's rich enough on the verbiage, thank you, dear."

And Lucille looks at him as if she has caught him too in a lie and sits back satisfied as she always seems to be, and is these days, for the first time in her life, satisfied and abounding and content with herself and with life on this wretched earth that stinks in her nostrils like burning feathers off the peacocks on her granddaddy's farm that her daddy shot out of hatred for his own daddy when he was drunk and burned their beautiful feathers in a yard fire—a world that every day attempts to reconvince her she is no good and shouldn't have been the hell born anyway. *What a sad world*, a little voice under her breastbone says. The lower part of her face twitches. *What a sad, ruined world.* Some nights she sits in one of the big floral chairs in her room over at the hotel with her legs crossed like a man, rubbing the hem of her shift between her fingers, and cries until she thinks her heart will break. Well. It already *is* broken—that was accomplished years ago when her daddy shot the peacocks and bent her over his knee after she cried and beat her until her bottom broke. She will never forget that, by God, or none of the other beatings either and his was just the first.

Rising sometimes from the handsome oakwood chair as she speaks, she speaks all afternoon and well into the next day about how these eight boys, "and others too, I might mention, boys who must have flown away from that train on wings because I don't see them here—yall couldn't catch em?—how these eight and them, them two I mean in particular, raped me like stabbing knives into my most private parts and wouldn't quit until I bled like that's all they wanted me for was the bleedin'."

Her hard plain broad face like a piece of cold raw field raised up, half molded and animated, and a bitterness in her eyes the world has distilled there, hatred whipped up stiff in her, durable as henge stone.

"Like I said, it was them two . . . and then them others."

But Baco knows she is lying even if he doesn't especially care one way or the other and has no love for nigras that is sure, inconstant loafers, vexatious to one like him who can be depended on in the worst conditions, hurricane or fire, etc., to do what he is supposed to do. Let em learn to get the job done first, he thinks. But this too isn't accurate and he knows it. He was brought up in the care of a negro man who could repair watches or stoves or automobiles or any form of working device, and he was the most intensified man he has ever known, Harwell Sims over to Taxus county, where Baco is from. There were others, smart and dumb; it was mixed as everything is. And besides, as Billy says, anybody'd move slow when backbreaking work is all he is ever headed to.

This is beside the point because Baco is still the one who stood in the hotel room behind the lawyers with the fat girl who seemed as if her blood had been drained out and replaced with shop poison and then she'd been set back on her feet and propelled by this streaming toxicant into the world to bring havoc to these eight boys. Well, you couldn't do much about any of it. She had a way of speaking so filled with spite that you knew it was the spite itself she loved, the making of it and the stacking of it as high as she could get it, like a wall between her and what hurt her, stuff she didn't talk about despite the ugliness she had no trouble revealing. And it didn't matter because in a way everything she said was true. *She had been defiled.* All her life really. And she was a white woman who claimed that eight colored boys had raped her, and of course the doctor said *somebody—some* somebody—had recently enjoyed her favors. She also had a second on her motion. Hazel Fran. A scrawny duplicitous girl unable to read or write, a scatterbrained person hardly more capable than a child, if a child could have been as distracted and meager and without connection to human sociability as Hazel was. She clung to Lucille like a monkey to its mama. But he could see in her eyes the gray color of road dust that she was not telling the truth. Like a daunted child, it hurt her to lie. So he talked to her in a mild way, offering her bits of ginger candy from a little paper sack and speaking offhandedly of Jesus who was of course keeping a merciful eye on the proceedings, and he could tell she picked up on it. She liked the candy. But she too claimed that these boys had committed sexual battery. With thumb and two fingers she pulled down hard on her long nose like she wanted to pull it off, squeezing it at the end, and said, "You bet they went at it. Like some devil was gaining on them every second. It burned like fire."

The red dog has him by the throat and swims him deep into the dark waters and it is as if the sides and boundaries of his body flop open and pour out his being like hot syrup, mingling it with the juices of the world until he experiences his spirit thinning out to a film and himself at the same time bobbing and cuffed by foul breeze and without the ability to gather himself. Plus a headache like an infernal hammering. In thick serpentine dreams he flies to Chattanooga and lies in the shed chuckling at the Ghost as the Ghost feeds iron filings to Old

Bob the lead horse, listening to Mr. O talk about his boyhood escapades as a gandy dancer in a Birmingham yard. Then a jump to a recount of the misery of Mr. O's actual Klaudio jailhouse visit. How, accompanied by insults and taunts and by somebody smearing yellow plum jelly from a jelly and butter sandwich on the back of his suit coat, he entered the narrow room where Delvin sat shackled at a scratched and spit-sticky table. How he strode with a full resolve of dignity up to the table as if he was about to walk right through it to embrace Delvin, but before he was all the way there his strength gave out and he stumbled and staggered against the heavy table, crying out Delvin's name, and then stood slumped and overcome until Delvin despite the guards yelling at him and his own shackled state climbed over the table and on the other side pressed his body against his benefactor's, nudging him and poking at him with the edge of his wrist until the guards beat him down to his knees, picked him up and flung him back over the table into the big square chair he had leapt out of.

"God help us," Mr. Oliver said over and over and sobbed. "God help us." Tears running down his face like water.

In his delirium Delvin cries out these words. God help us. *But no* God *does. As the professor said, the gods are gone from the earth.*

The malaria is a sickness that even the dead must feel. His head in a vise. A pain like needles coming up out of the backs of his eyes. Even the sweetest smells become the stink of shit. A freeze inside and out, chilling the mettle out of you, clamped so hard you couldn't breathe, couldn't scream. You lie under old running claws, and shiver, your bones stabbing hard-frozen flesh until you know your bones will any minute snap. You cry for blankets, for the house to be burned down on top of you, for your body to be thrown into the mouth of a spewing volcano—or would if you could cry out, if you weren't so frazzled. You're so cold every whimper's iced. And then it turns hot again. Fire claims everything. And nothing fits.

At this time he would confess any crime. Any deepest secret or falsity that could be shoveled into the light. But nobody asks. There is nothing he could reveal or explain that matters in the least to any of them. Let the shine rave. The disease ran him over like a pulpwood

truck. *His head crushed on the stones. His bones cracked open and hot
lead poured into the marrow. Day after day the same, the rank pecu-
liarities, the ugly sporting propositions, the malicious conversations
played out interminably in his head until he tries with all his sapped
might to give back whatever they want. I have stolen and killed. I have
raped and degraded. He confesses himself hoarse or would have if he
was actually speaking. Sorting the wind was all it is. A seepage.*

    Anyway, it is too late for spurious confessions. He is already gaveled.

*Slowly the dog moves through him. Out the high screened windows he
can see the shadows of live oak leaves shifting in the breeze. He hears
the shouts of the men. The world, tapping, hawking and shuffling,
returns. He hears voices he recognizes, familiar convict voices explain-
ing or evading or shifting the dices. He hears the rats moving around
underneath the floor at night and arguing amongst themselves. Gradually his dreams become less filthy. Less often he hears the sound of
horses running down the hard road. Less often he hears the big black
scorpions sharpening their claws in the dust.*

    *Finally he is able to get up and shuffle around. First thing he stag-
gers over to Conrad's bunk and stands looking into the wasted gray
face. He feels his heart pour out of his body.* And over there Little
Buster, twentysome now and the property of Danny Crakes, Little
Buster, thirteen years old when they were dragged off the train in
Klaudio, a rapist without a hair on his balls. Danny Crakes with his
bodyguards Roscoe and Bluebelle stood over Little Buster's bed weeping noisy tears. "Hey, he aint going to die," Delvin, in between chills,
raised up on his bed and said. He didn't know whether he was or not
but he couldn't help himself speaking out against those malefactious
tears. It was a sign he was getting better. Danny Crakes didn't even
bother to look at him. Bluebelle, huge, with a head like a torpedo, shot
him a glance through tear-webbed lashes. He shook an incidental fist.
A former africano cotton-bale-lifting champion, he could hardly raise
his hands above his head. Crakes, though he was not a Catholic or
known to practice any form of religion, licked his finger and made the

*sign of the cross on Little Buster's forehead. He later made his body-
guards memorize a short prayer of his own devising and with him
prompting the words he made them recite it in whispery voices to the
sleeping boy.*

*Little Buster had not understood what was happening to the eight
KO Boys. He knew they were jerked from the train, but he didn't know
what for and had no idea what was coming. "That is to say," Delvin
had told Gammon, "beyond the common understanding that they are
in a country run by white folks for white folks, so nigger get out of the
way." Fire flashed in Gammon's eyes and subsided. How fast that fire
subsided was a gauge you measured the next blow by. Something bad
was coming for the colored man caught napping—who didn't know
that? "Tell me what really happened," Gammon said.*

*Delvin looks over at the boy, at his narrow forehead with the
slightly raised ridge running down it, at the eyes that are black as shoe
polish—and helplessly friendly back then when he first saw him on the
train sucking on a lemon as he sat on a flatcar—at the soft mouth, still
untorn. And now he is a surly galboy with nothing to hold on to except
these brutes. They say DC uses these boys and when he is tired of them
drowns them with his own hands in the swamp.*

*And the sick days wobble by, right on to the last one. Sunlight streams
through the high windows, painting the old brown walls a rich dark
color unlike themselves. Delvin walks all the way to the porch and sits
down on a milk crate. Tomorrow they will put him back to work hauling
water to the cotton fields. A breeze blows the florid, analgesic smell of
the fields to him. The smell of cotton lathered with the smells of the big
garden over behind the dining hall and the smell of the chicken house
and the croaky smell of the hogs in their pen under the apple trees and
the pasture smells of bunchgrass, pigweed and sorrel, and the smell of
pine and the drifty, dry sharp smell of corn accented with mule manure
and human shit—the mix so pungent he feels sometimes as if he could
drown himself in the reek of it as under an ether and sleep the rest of his
life away. The smell is stronger now after the sickness. His shoulders
ache. And his hands, where he gripped the hardwood sides of his bed, are
bent and achy in the joints.*

Soldier Murphy comes up beside him and the two of them shift to seats on the plank bench set against the wall and look out into the sunlight strained by screen wire. It is hard to look at the light. Escaper, he is picking his way across the big field and into the swamp where from an old deep pool he would raise the submerged bateau from where it lay on the bottom, weighted with chunks of hoarded limestone quarried from the big white hole over at Talcotville and hauled by mule to build the warden's house. He left a stash of pea meal, matches and a length of coiled rope wrapped in oilcloth, stowed in a croakersack and buried under a pecan tree. He hoped the raccoons hadn't dug it up. These provisions like a hunter's hope in the books of his youth, like the boat now, long gone. But not the hope. Please contact Mr. Cornelius Oliver in Chattanooga Tennessee or Mr. Marcus Garvey in Harlem New York or Mr. Alexander Crumwell in Chicago Illinois or Mr. WEB Du Bois in Princeton New Jersey and ask one or all of them to help us. We are caught here in a net not of our own devising. And signed his name and given his address. That was the message he stuck in a syrup bottle plugged with a cob and threw in the river—stuck in several. No one wrote or came, and the captains won't let him write common letters. What you doing claiming you can write? Well, sir, I can. He hardly knows what to call these people. It is as if they flew down from space and scooped up africanos and carried them back to this alien planet. He'd had only two or three conversations with a white man in his life before this happened, these space creatures, moon men.

The smell of the fields blows up against the screen and spreads its sweet tonnage over him. Running after something is about as happy as things get in this place. There is always, as Ralph had pointed out, some of that. Even if it is only stew beans and a chunk of hard cornbread. He knew from the first that they were done for. It is like a disease, like polio or a sudden cancer that you don't know when it is going to catch you but you know it will, like the red dog. One day you wake up with it sitting like a fat ugly dog on your chest. Yet even in the dark of that first night in Klaudio with Little Buster crying and Rollie Gregory moaning from where they had beat him across the backs of his legs with a plowline and some of the others making hurt noises

*in their sleep—night (you could tell) in the black room because they
had shoved what they thought was supper (cold peas and cornbread)
in to them—he felt something crank down in him, some new figura-
tion of time that he sank into, and after the first scarifying moments
when he thrashed, fighting the suffocation of it, he relaxed and began
to breathe.*

It was like breathing air without time in it.

*Far off down the dark lanes of that first night in dreams he saw
Celia standing in a trashy field, cartons and tin cans and pieces of
rusted equipment around her, Celia looking lost. He called to her, but
she couldn't hear him; his voice wasn't strong enough. He wished with
all his might that he hadn't left her letters on that low wall in Chattanooga. An emptiness then blowing through him, hollowing him. A
dustiness and a picture in his mind, a memory really, of furniture
and family items strewn around an old house he came on once standing in the middle of a cotton field. The knee-high cotton surrounded
the house, running right up to the porch and windows, and the house
deserted. He climbed the steps and looked in. Inside everything was
still there, the clothes and the filigreed spread on the bed and an upright piano with its face broken in against the wall. All covered with
dust. Undisturbed for how long—you couldn't tell. He didn't go in,
though he saw a basket and a little box like a jewelry box sitting on a
dresser that he could use—didn't because he sensed he was not supposed
to disturb the dust. In his chest then too a hollowness. Now he saw his
old life drying and flaking away. He had to make himself stop. But
when he stopped, the crackling, stinky blackness returned. He pressed
his eyes with his fingertips until he saw stars, white stars and flashes
of purple light and little quivery yellow dashes. Around him that night
in the dark the moaning the crying the calling out as if from eroded
patches in black space.*

You could say they hadn't quit on themselves. They were still
breathing. It wasn't because they were strong or brave. Certainly not
noble. They would have sold each other out. Carl tried. Rollie tried.
But they had nothing to offer. The white man didn't even need confes-

sions. *It was as if the method was the only thing that mattered. Get that right. And they had nothing to do with that. They hadn't quit because there wadn't any way to and there wadn't anything to quit in a universe of endless effort. No quit, boys. Unless you just slacked down until you died. But even that wadn't allowed. Carl—after he tried the other—had tried that, tried rolling up against the wall and not moving, not eating, not drinking, but with a work-gloved hand they slapped him in the face until he changed his mind. Come on back to us, boy. Then they slapped him because of the trouble he'd caused them.*

And here I sit, he thinks, feeling the hard board infirmary porch seat against the bottom of his spine, resting before a journey. He laughs a little and looks across the yard at Milo Macraw, his young boy, the one who sleeps beside him at night, and a tenderness enters him, surprising him as it does sometimes, making him stop, say, under the big sycamore with half its limbs lightning-shrunk, and look up into the living branches in a kind of wonderment. Milo wants to go with him all the time. After the last escape they put him, put Delvin, in the Bake House, threw him in among the ants and ground wasps and the doodlebugs and hoppergrasses and the big black scorpions clacking their swords. He lay among them thinking of the creatures that lived so close to the earth they felt the vibration of every step and smelled every smell and sensed in the cold or heat seeping into the grains of sand what was coming and going in this world, like they had to know, like this knowledge was so important to them that, like the professor said, they had evolved—evoluted he'd called it before he met the professor—until they were able to crouch so low to the ground they missed nothing. And he wondered: What do they need all this information for? Were they waiting for some hint of something? The coming of some Bug Redeemer?

He lay among them flat on the earth studying what it was like in the bug universe, and he was lying there when the big cottonmouth slid over his belly and curled up on his chest. Its tongue flicked his chin and then it flicked his lips, and then it flicked his eyes he'd squeezed shut

and he could feel the snake's cold breath and he knew it was drink-
ing from the little balls of sweat at the corners. With its tiny delicate
tongue it licked his ears clean and his nose and the corners of his eyes
and his lips, and he could feel the snake's heart beating like the covered
drum of a distant tribe, speaking in the dark of the world of light. He
could smell the odor of the snake like the smell of garbage and he lay
still in the dark with the weight of the snake on him because the smell
told him the snake was afraid. It was hard to breathe and he thought
well I am being suffocated by a damn poison snake and then he felt
the snake's breath in his mouth, the slow, you couldn't call it pulsa-
tion, but a slithering of expelled breath from the snake's broad nostrils
making a regular susurration coming into his own mouth.

For how many days he couldn't be sure he lived with the snake lying
upon his body. Sometimes it left him but soon enough it returned.
During the periods of its absence he found no need to get up and piss
or shit or even to teethe the hard cornbread or take a sip of water.
Once they opened the door to look in on him, but seeing the big olive-
colored, cross-hatched snake coiled on his chest the guard, a small mus-
cular man named William Burden, cried out "Help me, Jesus!" and
slammed the door shut, leaving him from then on undisturbed. He
heard the LT say to let him go until they smelled him begin to rot. But
he didn't rot.

He drifted on a sea of time. And one day the snake slipped away
and didn't return, but Delvin didn't notice.

When they came eventually for his body he was asleep on the floor,
alone except for the bugs, and on that Sunday afternoon in October
he was dreaming of riding up front in the professor's van through the
north Mississippi countryside where the leaves of hickory trees lay like
yellow footprints on the red clay road and somewhere up ahead, but
not yet, the Fall of Man was walking back into history. The sky was
coral blue and the clouds were outlined in black ink that made them
stand out.

The guards banged on the tin sides of the shed to scare the snake,
but they were too late.

"Look at this crafty nigger with a grin on his face," he heard the

guard *Jim Karnes* say to another guard as they carried him out of the
Bake House. He was sick near to death with malaria. They dumped
him on the little porch outside the infirmary and left him for the
medico to find.

Well, I'm better now, he thinks, watching Milo raise his long leg
slightly to scratch along his thigh, better than I was.

2

Billy Gammon, boy lawyer, studied the notes Baco had prepared and then he walked out into the hot fall day where leaves twirled up and lay back down as a breeze smelling of cotton fields passed through the square. I better just make something up, he thought. Those boys are headed in one direction only. And he wondered if life seemed shorter to those who only moved along a single, fixed road. He nodded as he passed the townsfolk, but many didn't nod back. Nor did many in the Red Rooster, where he had dinner with Davis Pullen.

"What you think?" he asked Pullen, one of the lead lawyers, a chatty, florid man who had come in last in his law school class at the university but was in no way hampered by this, practicewise or mouthwise.

Davis chewed the edge of a yellow biscuit, put the biscuit down on his plate of soupy rice and chicken gravy and looked Billy in the face. This was Davis's big courtroom trick, the straight-in-the-face look. He had such a wide simple face that sometimes the juries, taken aback by the foolish openness displayed before them, forgot what it was they wanted to do and signed off on a not-guilty verdict. Davis had a good reputation as a lawyer who could get a man off.

"I don't know what you mean," he said.

This was one of his stock courtroom responses.

"Well, you know how most of us when somebody says we did something we can say hey man I didn't do that and then we can show how we didn't and we get to turn around and go back the way we came? I mean not just legally, but say if we get involved with a woman and then want to quit it, we can—"

"Maybe you," Davis, a twice-divorced man, said.

"Ah, yes," Billy said and ducked his head. "Or we buy something down here at Cohen's department store and old Mr. Cohen will take it back if we get home and decide it don't suit us. Or you can turn away from your sins—that's the big one, I guess—and become a sanctified man."

"You always sniping at the church," Davis said.

"Well, I know we can ask for forgiveness and start over and all. But I wonder."

"What is it you wonder, for Christ's sake?" Davis pressed his finger to a spot of mustard on the tabletop and touched his finger to his tongue, tapping his tongue with yellow.

"If life is shorter for those who can't get the use of any of these means."

"Means to what?"

"Oh, never mind. I was just daydreaming."

"You need to learn to pay closer attention to the matters at hand, little Billy," Davis said, grimacing and spitting into his soiled napkin.

They'd sat with Baco while he went over his findings. They were lucky those two women had talked so much. Or maybe not. Maybe the prosecutors wanted to make it clear how good a case they had. The colored boys denied the charges. It was clear, or almost clear, that half of them had never even seen those two white women. It was all about a fight, the lawyers knew that. Even Mr. Lopellier Harris from New York could see that. Harris wanted to make the trial about race, but nobody was going to win in Dixie building a defense on race. Nobody was going to win this trial anyway, nobody on the defense side.

Sitting in the window of the Red Rooster—PLUSH & TASTY, so the sign said—a new restaurant that boasted the largest coffeepot in town (HOME OF THE BOTTOMLESS CUP, according to the printed menu, another innovation), Billy looked out at maple leaves fluttering along in breeze like little redwing birds. Four of the boys didn't even know what they were charged with. The other four knew, and three of them could read, but only one of them, that Delvin Walker, the one raised at a undertaker's—always the richest householder in the colored community, the one who showed up at the mayor's office asking for favors, the representative of his people, who, like some african chief, was supposed to be able to keep peace with the natives, as it were—that boy Walker . . . he knew something was up.

Billy, looking out the window half dreaming of her, caught sight of Miss Ellen Bayride crossing the square, holding her flimsy blue hat on with one hand while trying to keep her armload of books from falling. "Just a minute," he said to Davis, got up, dashed out to the square and caught up with her.

"Snatchy weather," he said and suddenly almost forgot his own name. He had been waiting for days, ever since he saw her poking at a barking dog with her umbrella on the first day she got to town, to get a chance to speak to her. She worked for the big paper in the capital, brought in here because there were women involved. It was her job to get close to these women and pamper them and get them to give special admissions to her.

"Well, Mr. Gammon, you are a speedy fellow, aren't you," she said now.

"I was hoping I could help you out, here."

"Do I look like I need helping?"

She spoke lightly, teasing him. Confusion overtook him, but he fought through this, thinking it's this confusion and the going on anyway that makes these women so valuable to us—and us realizing we're willing to do it—every man in the world knows that. And, smiling all the time, knowing how stupid he looked, flushed, about to tip over, reaching for the books she now had under control, the woman laughing at him, her little blue hat cocked in a delightful way over one gray eye, he delighted in everything about her.

"Goodness," she said, stopping at the curb under one of the big oaks. The leaves in the crown of the oak shifted slowly, mightily, from the pressure of the slow breeze. "I think I have them now."

"Shoot, I thought I was timely," Billy said, smiling, almost laughing, he felt so lighthearted. "What are those books? Can I take them for you?"

"Like in school?'

"No, just a natural cordiality on my part, here on a windy summer day."

"Fall day," she said.

"Can't tell the difference in these parts, not really. Not til the heat finally breaks."

"And when is that?'"

"Some years it seems like never."

It was a dream—small, indistinct—to both of them just then, the words like dream words they were not so much making up as snatching from the air, a happiness overtaking them like a sweet scent riding on the warm dry wind. The breeze touched their faces and felt to each like the gentle fingers of the other. Ellen blushed. Billy saw the color filling her cheeks just under the smooth raised bone as a sign sent especially for him. Each sensed what the other experienced. The woman—usually private, unembellished, strict with herself—bent slightly toward him, and he slid slightly sideways as if angling for a quieter, more private spot, both of them understanding. They walked quietly along beside each other. At the door of the Shawl House, the only hotel in town and, like so many of the hotels in these rural county seats, a monumental affair, built in this case of rough granite, its windows recessed like the windows of a medieval castle, they stopped. The confederate battle flag billowed beside the state flag above the front entrance; no federal flag flew anywhere in this town, not even in front of the post office.

He smiled at her—calm, complicitous—and she smiled back, so faintly that she could have denied it in any court, and he caught it. Despite this, he felt at their parting a mournfulness like the fading of a fine day, but he knew too this was a parting that contained a promise. He put his hand over his heart. It was a gesture, a gimmick, but he could feel his heart knocking.

"Yes," he said to the question both of them held in mind.

She smiled, a gentling smile, the way a girl would smile at a pony. "Yes," she said, "I guess . . ."

And turned and pushed through the big glass, brassfooted doors held open for her by an africano man in a forest-green embraided suit.

Crossing the square back to the little office they had rented in the Cotton Exchange building, his thoughts like birds returning crankily to the rookery of the trial, he considered that all they could do in this so-called legal case was present a clean recitation—that's all it was really—of the events: a line of execution—sure, execution—for those boys to hold on to, all eight of them headed straight to the hangman's noose. Most those boys could hope for was for Billy and crew to get them life sentences at Burning Mountain.

That evening in the jail with Harris and Pullen and all eight of the boys lined up on the long bench across from them, fielding questions, some of them without reason or any connection whatsoever to the situation at hand, Gammon experienced again the exhilaration of his afternoon walk. I need something to buoy me up, he thought, but she is better than something. Ellen. Don't call the woman you love she. One of the boys was asking when he could go home. "I'm wore out sitting in this place," he said, Arthur Bony Bates, a boy of fifteen with a pudgy, smooth-skinned dark face and slow, cloudy eyes.

"We are working on that, my boy," Lopellier Harris—called Larry—said affably.

"I'll say I slapped one of those white boys, and I *did* too," Carl Crawford said, "but that's the most I'll say, I tell you *that*."

"It's violating those two women they got us on the hook for," Delvin Walker said. He was a smallish, very dark-skinned boy, eighteen, the case file said, with broad shoulders and a quick, lively look in his hazel eyes.

"I didn't violate nobody," Butter Beecham said, a man in his twenties, a laborer for life, unable to read and write. "Nobody," Butter reiterated.

"All right," Larry Harris said.

Davis Pullen looked toward the windows that were painted over with whitewash. During the day, light came through the wash, but at night they were dull and blank. Under the table he made two fists on his knees—made them and slowly let them go. The dog lines in his face deepened.

Harris carefully questioned each boy. He had arrived from New York by train three days ago and had hit the ground running, as Davis put it. "Running straight into a brick wall," he'd added, cackling. The facts as the boys experienced them were straightforward and dire. One of those white boys, identified as Carl Willis, had stepped on the hand of Delvin Walker, and from this incident a fight had started.

"Did you hit him?" Harris asked.

"Eventually I did," Delvin said. He wore a look of profound sadness. He knew what this was, this court assembly.

"Eventually?"

"He kicked me and nearly knocked me off the hopper."

That was a kind of open railroad car, Harris knew, a barrel cut lengthwise and soldered open side up onto a frame, called a gondola. He had represented tramps and itinerants, connivers and confidence men, the beat down and humbled—and the beat and unhumbled— the working men whose particular plight he was touched by and whose coming rise he believed in or at least hoped for as most favorable to his own needs, a sometime house lawyer for the WOW and the *Daily Worker*. People down here looked at him as if they thought he might any minute burst into flames.

"I caught up with him in the fight that ensued," Delvin said evenly.

"Okay, fellows," Harris said. Three of the men or boys had started picking at each other. "Walker. All right, son."

He began to ask the necessary useless questions about the fight.

"It was like a gladiatorial combat," Delvin said. "Us in a ring with those white boys snarling at us."

"A ring?"

"The boxcar. It was right next door."

"So you fought—how many was it?"

"A dozen, fifteen."

"And you held your own."

"Held it and pushed back with it."

He had teeth so white they seemed made of some substance other than enamel. Made from whiteness itself, Harris thought. "The fight was quite like a contest," he said.

"Yessuh. Except it was just more of the same from those white boys."

"In what way?"

"They always been throwing colored folks off the trains," Butter Beecham piped up. "Can you use that against em?"

"They have thrown you off the trains before?"

"They always do that."

"Yeah, yessir, you bet," someone else cried, and for a few minutes there was a clamor as the boys expressed their outrage at the treatment from the whites, something scared and wheedling, something like a stark rage, underneath, just a rumor of it, unexpressed. Delvin remained silent.

When they got the boys quieted down Davis Pullen asked Delvin, "Did you know any of those white boys?"

"No. But they all got a tendency—or most of them do."

"What is that?" Davis asked, but he knew the answer. Some darky complaint. They were always fussing.

This question would not be settled here, Harris thought. Might as well not bring it up. "What we need to stick close to here," he said, "is the facts of the situation."

"We held our own against them," another boy said. A man actually, Coover Broadfoot also a partly educated man, the other negro who knew what was going on here.

"And then some," somebody else said.

Harris's assistant Sid Krim sat in a chair a few paces back from the table, taking notes. So silent, so perfect, no one even noticed him. Before bedtime tonight he would have a record typed up by one of the stenographers Gammon had hired from the capital. He would not get the slang right, or even what some of the boys considered proper english.

"They are saying you raped these women," Billy Gammon said.

Several of the black boys laughed. Bony Bates began to cry. Delvin Walker looked scared and angry.

"They always *gon* say that, mister," Bonette Collins, a fleshy-faced man, said. "They can't hold a trial if they not saying that."

"Were any of you close enough to those women to cause a problem?" In front of Harris, Billy didn't quite know how to phrase it.

"Problem?" Rollie Gregory said. He was older, a slow-moving, hefty man from an apple farm outside Chattanooga, he'd said. Orchard, wasn't it—not farm? "Problem?"

"Did any of you have sexual knowledge of this . . . of these two women?" and he gave their names.

"I don't under—"

"Did you jelly em, boy?" Pullen said.

Gregory looked abashed, sick even.

"Lord, no."

But some of the other boys had, or they might have, it wasn't clear—might have taken a roll, paid for or offered free. They all denied it, though that young boy Arthur Bates, Bony, fourteen or fifteen, he looked sick about something. Probably he had gone with one of the women. But raped them?

"These women say you forced them."

"You mean like tied em up?"

Rollie Gregory giggled. "They too hincty for that," he said.

Gammon ignored him.

"Force can be that, yes," Pullen said, "but it can also be threats. Menacing looks. Expectation of harm on the woman's part."

"They was whores," Bonette Collins said. He was a short, nearly square man, Little Wall by Wall he was called, a carpenter, he said, not even part of the group—if you could call them that—traveling out of Chattanooga. Billy thought of the families of these boys, the eight boys, how back home the word would go around the community—rape—of white women. The awfulest crime. Lengths of knotted manila rope rolled out from such accusations. *We sit here among the dead.* Two boys leaned on their hands, others had their hands on the table turned up like offerings, a couple clutched themselves in their arms; Walker patted one fist on top of the other. Everything for them was changed for good. They might as well have not gotten up, not drawn breath that morning. Back at home everybody would downface it. You couldn't tell what the truth was. But he had found that juries seemed often able to choose between truth and falsehood. At least in the little trials for theft and robbery or threats or fraud. Except with negroes. Rarely did a negro get off. No matter how innocent he was. And now we have rape and murder—no, just rape. We'll handle the murder.

He smiled at Davis Pullen, who was busily questioning Bonette as to where he was exactly at the time of the rapes.

"They have to establish a time for these occurrences," Davis said. "We can refute em on that point. Anybody own a watch?" he said, and chuckled. Nobody did.

Harris listened without seeming to. He gazed around the room. These bleak, sullied rooms never bothered him. The facts in these cases were where the power was. The facts like stones set into a wall. The power in the wall and what was behind it, in the lives lived in the grease and stink of poverty pressing forward through time. The power was in the weight of these lives laid against the wall, and for him the subtraction of life breath by breath leading all the way back to the beginning of time, something more powerful than anything else he knew, a weight of reason and choices, a strength right now implacable from some toothless oldtimer long ago reaching out his hand for the piece of pre-masticated meat a child put into it, the look in the old man's eyes meeting the look in the child's eyes, and over there the breeze touching an old woman's face, engendering an irresistible thought, and that man over there listening for the cry of a baby in the other room where his wife lay sick on a pallet on the floor, something hard and inescapable coming for him. He dismissed none of what he loved about these scenes, the million-year history of people roughed up and knocked down by the ones slightly stronger. He never talked about this, hardly brought it into his own mind, but he felt the weight of a righteousness laid against him, pressing into his days and into his sleep.

And, too, he was a man, wearing a suit snagged with a hook from a sidewalk wire outside a haberdasher's on Orchard street, who wanted people to know who he was. And as the people he was hired to help wished they could do, he gathered influence like a golden grain.

The facts of the case, so these lawyers thought, were chits on a string, gaps here and there, adding up to not much. Delvin looked into their self-regarding, lurid faces, at the ructating misery that had not settled, sensing the complex lies they told themselves so they would not—so they thought—bring trouble down on their children, the way each was an official of this great empiric power they thought they were the checkers and refusers of, these freightless carriers and silly boys, these men with tickets, who would never suffer, or if they did, the suffering would be in passing, some condition or reversal that would consume a few days or years of their lives and then drop them and wander off in another direction. None of them lived in a state of fear or tyranny. He saw this, and as he saw he heard inside his head the voices saying that for these people Delvin and his compadres were only troublesome beasts caught momentarily in the chute. We are good-hearted and for fame and money we will get you cattle turned around the right way. Thank you, suh. But he was not cut off from his own heart by, or even from, his interceders, he was not yet disattached—that wasn't the word—nor was he threaded through or aligned with them, none of that, he was only inseparable from the *curiosity* he felt looking at them, that was where the life was, his curiosity, and he knew this. What was it they were up to? Besides rattling along in their own peculiar version of a train ride?

It just wont right, was what they said in Red Row back in Chattanooga. That was closer to the truth of things than anything he could come up with.

Suddenly he was scared to death. His bowels loosened and he bent over, gripping himself.

"You all right, boy?" Pullen said.

"I got to go to the little house."

"You can do that in a minute."

"I mean right now. Suh." But as he said the words his insides tightened up and he was all right.

Harris started to signal the guard but Delvin stopped him. "Thank you, suh, I guess I'm fine."

"You trying to game us, boy?" Pullen said.

"No, suh. I felt a flash of sickness is all. I'm better now."

"Well. That's okay," Harris said. "Now—"

"Yes suh," Delvin said quickly, "I was in the fight, but I never saw either of those two women. Not til the end."

"*None* of you boys did," said Pullen.

The stirring in Delvin's bowels returned but he fought it down. He looked Pullen in the eyes. These white folks thought they had escaped the restrictions law and custom had placed on black skin. They were the new model human—an advance on the old dark model—built for politics and money. No stoop labor. Masterminds who were also generous, so they saw themselves. *Why, if you keep to your place we will pat you on the head and give you a soup bone. And a kick to keep you honest.* Well. Best to steer clear of crazy people like that. Just go widely around them in this alien land. But, once in a while, a misstep. Or a misstepped upon. And a door opened onto misery, anger, terror, watchfulness, confusion, ricky-tick submitting, echoes of overheard jokestering, wild wandering figments and destitutions of the spirit, thumps of excruciation and succorless moaning, strutting, argufying, testification, and power and regret and wondering and a rattling panic—all these in his eyes looking straight into lawyer Pullen's.

In Pullen's eyes under a moist filigree of power churned an unsorted mess of helpless degradation, hope, dishevelment, spite, useless muttering asides picked up from relatives and the stupidity of his kinfolk over in New Hall, endurance and pluck and delight in the quick free-heartedness of his children, boredom and a weasely shrewdness brimming—the combo—rocking in a sea of rage plastered over with a foolish smile quirky as a circus poster on the side of a burning barn.

The man despised him, Delvin could see this.

3

He stands on the low infirmary porch swaying faintly to a rhythm that has risen up from the earth and overtaken him. All these boys here with their necessary arrangements. Solomon over there working a yard broom, ready to run any errand. Little Croak, who wore a pink verbena blossom in his hair to please Winky Raffin. And Winky, who got down on his knees to please the LT, those stormy nights when Delvin watched him cross the yard in the rain to enter the LT's pineboard shack. Carl Crawford, one of the boys from the train, stands waiting for him. He has a scrap of straw hat that he saved for when Delvin would come out of the infirmary and he gives it to him now.

"What's next, Mr. Del?" he asks, a muscular boy, not a boy now after four trials and all these years in the white man's penitentiaries. Even in the penitentiary the races are kept separate. A white man isn't going to eat off a plate he sees a black man eat from. Nor put a black man's spoon in his mouth, no matter how well washed it is. Lord, they wouldn't breathe the same air as us if they didn't have to. Off to the west is the river that runs along the edge of the swamp, but no one ever escaped that way. Patrols and outposts and towns in either direction, hamlets, solitary farmhouses—it would be like running a gantlet, each fouler armed and ready to shoot. That is the policy. Local folks might shoot escapees on sight and nobody would mind. One less mouth for the state to feed.

He puts the hat on and sticks his head out into the sunlight that hits him like fire flung from the roof. His body bends and his vision clouds and a dizziness spins up from the ground and envelops him; his insubstantial strength gurgles away and he sags. Though Carl tries with both arms to hold him, the two of them fall to their knees. Carl bounces up and begins to drag him to his feet.

"It'll be all right, Mr. Del," he says, ducking his head under Del-vin's arm.

They struggle up, and stand blank and unsure in the porch shade.

"They be watching us, Mr. Del," Little Carl says. Carl is thick-bodied and strong as a bull and despite the battering he has taken still somewhat kindly. He nods toward the stilt tower cornered into the fence. Two guards equipped with pump-action scatter guns, 30.06 bolt-action Winchesters and a Thompson submachine gun gaze at them, not fondly. Delvin can see them talking, the words, he thinks, like doughy little thoughts with stones inside them. His mind drifts and he is again picturing Celia (or somebody he called Celia, some ragdoll fragment) floating through a field of march flowers. His knees are bloody. He raises his knees and does a little slow-motion dance stomp and almost tips over backwards. The two guards laugh. He waves, the wave an eloquent mix of woofing and bouncy-in-his-deuce-of-benders. It is one of the many hand gestures for dealing with white folks. Every hand carries danger. White folks prefer vocal salaams, bent backs. Any movement of the hand by a black man can become threatening. But the gestures of looniness, of imbecility, of fealty—are tolerated.

This is his fourth prison. He described (in earlier notebooks) the concrete floors at Burning Mountain, the red dirt floors at Uniball, the stone at Columbia, now the packed blue-clay floors at Acheron. Here when it rains, the floors became so slick you can hardly stand on them. In each prison he placed himself in this or that nook, in fields, under roof, walking across a dusty yard, standing under a graybeard tree looking out at rain pouring down in bright sunlight, squatting in a cotton field or tucked in his own deck address and darkest corner, and looked out at the world and wrote it down. They took the notebooks away, but he got more, bought more, that is, from whoever was selling them. He paid in whatever coin he could muster. Load-humping, errand work, decoying, the wealth accumulated at three cents a day from chopping cotton or picking vegetables, trade or capital turned over at the store. One of those, he would tell the clerk,

*one just like that one you're scribbling into. The clerk each time had
to be talked into it, sometimes paid extra or traded. But this was
easy. No one can hold out against anything in prison, that is prison's
secret. No bit of information, no treasure secreted away, no practice,
no escape plan or ruinous bit of felony behavior was secure. It is impossible to protect these safes and mental cashboxes. What held fast
out in the world unraveled and fumed away in prison. Everybody
walks around with fluxed, soggy insides. It's okay. It is simply what
you have to live with. No friend will protect you, no believer, no hard
ass. They can't even protect themselves. And it isn't the various holes,
pits, cabinets, closets, unheated tin sheds, Bake Houses and hotboxes
the butchers stick reluctant or rowdy prisoners into. It isn't beatings
or starvation or forced labor in the killing sun. It is hopelessness.
Delvin's own sense of it, the crude stalled massing in his gut, comes
back. This time not just in here. By now the disease has spread like a
personal plague into all the corners of his mind. The world itself has
in this way become infected. The long gray dirt road out there, slick
as a gullet, running for miles through the sloppy, beat-down fields,
the ragged (free) men they pass standing in ditches pushing gobs of
clay into their mouths to quell hunger and for the minerals in it,
the little boys shitting grease in the thin grass, the skinny, lacerated
women not even turning to look at the truck passing. You see a griffe
squinting into the sun and realize he isn't seeing anything. One man
has a goiter on his neck the size of a citron. He has to rip his shirts
to be able to wear them. Country women humpbacked with rheumatism, children bowlegged with rickets and red-faced and slimy from
pellagra, wasting from hookworm. Nobody has the money to fix anything that can make life endurable. Hammer toes and bunions and
busted elbows and broken wrists and stomachaches that eventually
turn out to be cancer except nobody learns that is the name for it
because nobody calls the doctor and even if they did he would be the
negro doctor just now dying himself of tuberculosis over in the little
negro clinic in Sharpsburg; he'd be dead before they could piece together where it was you lived. In the whole prison no africano man*

*who has ever lived on a street or a road that has a sign on it saying
its name. Down these streets the drag-footed go.*

*And you lie on your back in the dawnlight pulled like a gray washrag
up out of dumps and poisoned dews, listening to the little hermit
thrushes and the killdeer and the meadow lark's wakeful remarks, a
man with a pure knowledge of himself like the philosophers and the
alienists wish they could somehow come by, a knowledge gained not
through manipulation and secondhand tittering but through means
of the simple quest each of these imprisoned men is on, the standard
issue of jail life: you are, in the end, only men: in the end you break:
in the end you will not be able to hold out against even the least of it.*

Here, now, as he moves from the infirmary porch out into the tire-
less sunshine, Delvin feels the truth of himself like a surplus malaria
settling in. It is not all right but it is all right. Now Milo taking his
hand—Carl has drifted away—pressing his forefinger down the row
of knuckles sweetly and back as is his way, patting the fleshy place at
the bottom of his palm. Except for scattered lumps of aching bone he
can barely feel his hands, barely feel his arms; his feet have a life of
their own and a great delicacy. He wants to lie down in the dust and
roll slowly in it. Across the way at House Number 2, from the sterile
shade of the overhang, Shorty Willis gazes at him. He'd have come out
to knock him to the ground, if he didn't have the dog. The cons think it
is catching. They think all ailments are contagious and shrink from
them, wounds, cripplings, maimings as well. In the dining hall they
yelp from distant tables that the place ought to be cleared of these infect
rats. In the barracks he will generally find his rack in an island of its
own, the others shoved away from a teeming nobody wants to touch.
Maybe find it in the yard.

Yet there are those who relish disease. The crazy boys and some of
the lap nuzzlers will cozy up to him, asking if there is anything they
can do. One, Dizzy Placer, will lick your sores if you have any to spare.

Years ago the doctor cautioned him. "Don't go letting any of these yardboys out here apply their treatments," old Dr. Willy told him. Dr. Willy died of a busted ulcer none of the white doctors around Covington wanted to treat, groaning and calling out the name of a woman nobody had heard of—so Donell Brakage told him three years ago when he was resting up from an earlier malaria attack with the other kings of misguidance in Columbia penitentiary. That was before the last trial that let all but Delvin and Carl and Bony and Little Buster go free, pardoned for their crimes. Other lawyers reaped the crop the first lawyers sowed.

The sun is getting cozy on his neck, kittenish. He leans his head forward so the beam can find more flesh. Ripe sunlight a treasure beyond counting. So bright you have to look through your lashes to see. The heat seeps under his clothes, spreading along his back like a feather cape. In November they ride in wagons on top of the cotton to the gin. He always burrows in deep, loving the encasement and, if it was possible without being torn to pieces, would let himself be lifted up into the suction tube and tossed through the machinery to come out the other end mashed in the press inside a bale. Lying there like a caterpillar in his cocoon, waiting for some chinaman across the sea to jack the bale open and lookee here what I found. Oh knit me back up. He hasn't started sweating yet.

Milo works his little trad on his knuckles. Delvin can smell the lime stink of the latrines. Last week it rained all week, but three days of sun this week has brought up the dust. A week of straight sun, and dust will whirl up in clouds the size of a county, wind-hauled a hundred miles to set an inch of topsoil down on top of some other county's dirt.

He still thinks of Celia, but she is a cattercorner, endways Celia now. And why shouldn't she be? Once he raged and spit on the ground and beat his hands into the dirt as his insides crumbled and splintered to bone in his chest. He moaned like a dog, and far out in the Babylon field at Burning Mountain he hollered his sorrow into the wind that blew everything lost into the black pine woods. At Uniball he got down on his knees and pushed his face into the streaked dirt. Loss become unified grief breathed in the dirt until he was swimming down through the richness of soil and drifting among the big lime-stone plates and the secret caves of pure water that washed him clean of everything but his humanness. You could lose your mind, lose your soul, lose your day count, but you couldn't lose that. He had cuts on his forearms from trying to. In Uniball he slashed his own face with the heated edge of a file and the cuts had ridged up so tight his face for a year felt pulled to one side. Somewhere he picked up a limp. He limped into the courtroom for the last trial; the limp hadn't changed anything.

For a while Celia wrote him and then the letters fell off. He pictured words like leaves sailing in a chill fall breeze. "What has become of you?" he asked. Asked the last address he had for her. The letters came back stamped in red: ADDRESSEE UNKNOWN. Oh but, Mr. Postman, she is known. "I know her," he cried. "I know her better than she knows I know her." He built her from the scraps available. Scraps was all they were. Curls and shreds and discards. But enough. Her five foot six of blueblack body. A sheen on her like the dew on a butternut bush. Her hair crisp and shining, catching the light so the blackness turned into a coppery gleam like the gleam of the world in its earliest days. Her eyes black as pieces of the night saved uncut for the day. Quick-mindedness. A quietude about her. Wondering at the world. Feeling around. A jump-upness. She smiled and he held this smile in an enterprise of the heart that was ever growing. Now gone. He wrote her family but they didn't write back. PLEASE OPEN THIS, he wrote on the envelopes and underlined it, hoping in a way that somebody would open the letter, maybe a passerby who knew her, knew who she was and would answer him. Finally somebody did. Her sister, Sheila, whom she almost never mentioned. Wrote him a few words on a sheet of pink paper. "My sister was married a year ago, to a man from Shreveport, a doctor. They have a lovely little baby boy. She does not need to hear from you again." He wrote back to the sister, asking for more and thought maybe I will leapfrog over her to Celia and knew this could not be. He lay down under a big hickory tree and cried until his throat was sore. For a while he continued to write letters but one day he stopped. He started a letter and quit in the middle. He sat at the edge of Big Egypt field *waiting for Tulip to bring up the mules. The stub of pencil was worn down so small he could hardly grip it. He wrote: "I watched a big old redwing hawk take a pigeon in the air . . ." and stopped. He decided nothing, he only quit. Since then not a missive word on paper.*

But still, fading as they go, the words come to him. He writes stories about her now. Stories about some woman, some slipping-away woman, who runs barefoot into a sliding surf and laughs until she makes herself sick.

Up ahead the round, stuccoed and whitewashed well with its crosstree and six buckets on separate ropes. Once at Burning Mountain he tried to escape by jumping into the well. Those were his crazy years.

Not that the escapements have stopped. He has a list: fires set in the drying corn of fall, bullfrogs thrown into the supposedly electrified fence to short-circuit it, tunnels sworn to lead to open fields of sweet grass beyond the woods; he hid under mounds of green peppers and piles of cotton seeds, crouched in garbage, jumped off the back of trucks, lit out across fields, faked sick, attempted to bribe guards, simply turned away from the group crowded around the captain and ran for it.

But the well. That is legend. He tried to swim his way out through tunnels Bennie Combers swore were there. A great underground river Bennie said that would take him quickly to the big river. Plenty of room to draw breath. But there was no river, no room for breath. He got turned around and nearly lost his life, swimming downward in the dark. They hauled him out with a scrap of net he was barely able to crawl into.

No, well, no, not today, he thinks, the sunlight like warm cream on his bare arms. Not today a swim into the dark.

He wore himself out on those early escapades, wore out the craziness. He got a reputation, and cognomen, as a willful, uncooperative prisoner, UNC in capital letters on the yellow manila folder that goes with him as he makes his way around the state prison system. The sun is sticky on his face. He could wipe it off like sap from his arms and hands and clean it from his face but he doesn't want to. The light and heat soak into his body. He unbuttons his shirt, pulls it away from his chest. The spray of scanty corkscrewed hair soaked in sunlight. You can take your shirt off if you want to, but nobody with any sense takes his shirt off under a sun like this. A black man burns just like a white one. He pulls the blue-and-gray-striped cloth away from his chest. He smells his body odor, sour as oakwood and comforting. Just working a button through a buttonhole gives him a sense of freedom. So does walking across the yard with nowhere the white man told him to go, returning by his own will to the barracks.

He steps along to the well. Milo lets go his arm, grabs one of the long galvanized buckets and lowers it. Delvin listens to the bucket clank hollowly against the sides. He feels a generation older than the boy who jumped into that other well. He leans over the parapet far enough to dip his face into the column of cool air the bucket stirs up. Leaning slightly to the side he can see the sky reflected in the black water. He jumped not toward that pinned-down blue but toward the stars. When you bring the water up it is neither blue or black, it is clear as crystal. They say it tastes of sulfur, but the taste is more like the mold on a old piece of hoop cheese.

Milo pulls steadily on the rope. The bucket, spilling water as it comes, reaches the top.

Delvin presses his hand and then his face against the chilly wet galvanized metal. The feel of it sends him back into his dreams. Celia speaking to him from the rainwet front steps of her friend's house. She is telling him to read—who was it? Douglas? No. Freeman. This goes by in a zip. He hasn't thought of Freeman for years, has forgotten him. A writer first mentioned by the professor. Well, these books, these volumes written to prove the black man deserves his freedom, are all right. They make you, while you read them, free. Books come in packed in sacks of rice, sacks of salt. They are directed to particular inmates but the included instructions are ignored. Once in a while the inmates get visitors, wives and mamas and shamed weeping daddies gathered in the fenced-off portion of the yard under a big live oak. You can socialize. In gunny sacks they bring pies and apples and kumquats and pieces of molasses candy wrapped in a wax paper twist. These bits of food are all that is allowed in. No books, no hardware, no toiletries, not even soap. There are no chairs, people sit on the ground or squat on their heels, men who will be back to work Monday morning in sharecropped cotton fields, women who will be cooking for a dozen or stooping with the men in the fields hoeing cotton or picking it or in summer cropping tobacco. They bring fresh-squeezed cane juice in glass jars, blue jars children hold to the light to see the colors in.

He dips both hands in the bucket—forbidden, but he's forgotten this rule, for now—and splashes water on his face. He holds his face up to the sunlight and feels the cool burning as the sun takes the water back.

With Milo's help he tips the bucket and pours the well water over himself. He wears the sulfurous shirt and pants and coarse heavily washed canvas underwear issued to all those who survive a stay in the breakdown ward. The water will leave its residue of sulfur stink but sweat will soon enough wash that out. The old yearning flares again, a piece of it, the edging of the spirit toward freedom that in prison you have to nub off short, most men have to. It roots in him like a sweet potato raised in a glass jar. He feels himself listing. His joints ache and he has a headache, but the crushing chills are gone. They piled gunny sacks on him. He begged them to lie on top of him, but they wouldn't. In his mind a big bearskin black and stinking of bear lay on him, but later when he asked after it nobody knew what he was talking about.

From the well a spokeway of paths radiates. In some past now lost prisoners were required to walk a certain line to the well. Now these paths each barely a foot wide are sunk in the clay; everybody naturally follows them. "A lesson for you and me," he says to Milo, pointing this out to him.

"You don tol me," Milo says, grinning.

"That's okay," he says. "I forget what the lesson was."

Milo places the empty bucket back in its little wooden slot at the foot of the well and they proceed on their way. They take the slightly curv-

ing path he named Lope. He named all the paths. Chicago, New York, Bright Leaf Trail, Dixie Highway, Salvation; he keeps the names to himself. Shielding his eyes, he looks at the nearest tin-sheathed tower. One of the guards, Hammersmith, idly watches him. He is the one brought his last letter, one of the four he has received in the last six years (since he left from Uniball), from his old train riding friend Frank. The letter was stamped Oak Park, Illinois, a suburb of Chicago. Patches, long rectangular strips, were cut out of the pages. The religious fervor of our time is, *then blank, a hole letting the air in. Must have been some fiery words. Then the sentence:* Apples are America's most loved fruit, *then more air. Then:* but what can we know of another's anguish? *then air, then the words:* anyone whose suffering is one grain worse than our own is one we can't, *then more air. The words the heat of them, and then Frank's fervor and cool distancing sliced away. Five other pages were similarly rejigged. The pages looked like paper cutouts. Here and there a partial sentence* (in our own selves we have to find . . . ; confused and broke we embrace . . . ; cancer for . . . ; a tenderness most . . .) *scraps of words, a litter really, somebody's fresh trash. He had memorized every bit, even the odd words* (reddish, conservationist, river's, unoffered) *they were like gates, buckles, fasteners, letting life in, or out; there were dozens of them. He dug a hole in the clay under his bunk and hid the letter there, wrapped in a scrap of oilcloth. It would be all right if it wasn't there the next time he looked. Frank was trying to tell him something important; the guards saw that. There was no return address: that too was turned into an air hole, escape vent.*

He leans heavily on Milo's thin strong arm. They roll as they walk, pals airing it out. Milo chatters about breakouts, about the new man, a gingercake named Arthur Fowler who, so Milo says, has tattooed a portrait of his superior court judge on his chest in an attempt to get a mistrial.

"I love the way courtrooms smell," Milo says.

Two years ago Milo was thrown by a guard into a pyracantha bush and one of the thorns pierced his left eyeball. He can see light and shadow with that eye—enough in this world, he says, to tell what's what. An escape attempt carried him to the bush. "Got to get me some wings," he says now when asked about it.

Both of them crossed miles of marsh and desert and cleft mountain track and leagues of wintry windswept fields to reach this spot. In the exact center of his body Delvin sways like a stem of billygoat grass. His body held up now by a boy. You can say he loves the boy. He pictures the slips and strips of yellow paper from Frank's letter fluttering on the breeze. The suffering of those not ourselves. *Milo's narrow ridged forehead. The broad, mashed-in nose with the elegantly flaring nostrils. The thin lips with the encircling perimeter line like something chiseled into flesh. The cheeks broad and flat and the eyes set under their ridges of fine bone gleaming like lamps. Shine me home.*

In the sky to the south a yellow biplane tats its way west. The small stiff steadily fading sound is beautiful. As are all sounds connected to the outside. Despite the fitful delirium of four hundred men you get used to the noise until the prison seems a quiet place. There are the clatters from the kitchen, the scrape of feet moving over hard clay, the shouts of the guards, the clank of chains, the cries from the dreams of low crawling sleepers, the guzzle of water from the shower tank, these familiar dead-end sounds. But there are also the sounds of rain clattering on the barracks' tin roofs, the drips onto clay, the rush of wind, the pattering of dust along the walkways, the keen up-piping of killdeer and mourning doves from the fields, the distant bombilation of the gin machinery, trucks gearing down on the rise through the cotton fields and the whisper of breeze passing over the cotton on its way from faraway to here—ordinary, fadeaway sounds to those not held down behind wire but to him treasures ladled secretly out, hoarded and prized. Some nights they can hear the radio from the warden's quarters, playing live music from the Roosevelt Hotel in New Orleans. White man's music: a thin, bobbing line of melody from which are hung chicken feathers and costume jewelry. Even the old square-jawed mountain music is better, the dancing rhythms scooting along like they are on their way somewhere not here.

When somebody escapes—tempted by the free airs outside, some-

body who has something to do out there, or somebody to meet, or a contemptible crisis, a hurt, a face laughing in a dream, life itself he has to flee—the duty guard cranks the handle of a big silver round-mouthed siren. The crank is as big as a pump handle and hard to turn unless you are strong, and they are strong. From the horn spews a metallic whine like a castaway mimic of the olden times when the gods and the earth itself spoke to human beings . . . but now is only a mockery, a falseness and scorn pounded into the brain, screeching proof of how far from dignity and brotherhood they have fallen. You want to crawl under a rock and hide. Men hunch their shoulders, muttering or staring mutely into the distance. Some cover their ears, others try to go on as if nothing is happening. But Delvin—and a few compadres— use the occasion to scream as loudly as possible. A wild vehemence, a whirling, jarring power breaks loose from him with these shouts. And a joy, if he can call it that. The guards know they scream, he and Muster and Calvin Schuler and Willie P from Hattiesburg and a few others—lifting their singalong, repealing lies and broken connections and loss—and sometimes they yell back. Maybe one or two filling the air with his own despair and loneliness. But soon the quiet returns. The low hum of prison whispering that makes up the regulation silence, carrying the iniquitous sound of guile and slander that passes for air in this place. So they lean back in their bunks or stoop low to pluck a burst cotton boll, or stretch their arms out in the dark, or crouch in the latrine over a febrile shit—listening for the woodsy, row crop silence of breeze rustling the three-pointed cotton leaves, scraping among pine needles in the dark woods; listening for the barn owls in the sycamores asking their questions of the field mice and voles and half-grown rabbits; for crows winging across the open expanse of fields the prison sits in the center of, crows croaking naw naw, *as if testing their voices to make sure they still have them.*

Across his path now steps Lionel Ansley, a gaunt man, a preacher who holds one of the services on Sunday mornings. He's been after Delvin for a while to quit his escape attempts. He is impatient with his unwillingness to attend church. Lionel visited him in the infirmary and Delvin appreciated his not visibly gloating over his condition.

The preacher told him his running ways would get him into trouble and Delvin knows that as far as Lionel is concerned the red dog has come on as a result of his jumpiness. He isn't the only one tired of his scampering; the guards, who like to make the whole prison pay for one man's flight, are getting worn out too.

The preacher nods at him, smiling, his bony head bobbing like a chicken's. Despite his narrow-mindedness he is a kindly man. You never can tell where kindness will come from. The preacher with his little commentaries never goes too far into damnation. Delvin appreciates this.

"Come on, boy," he says now, "come on over to the one place you can let what's balled up in you go."

He doesn't stop walking as he says this.

Delvin nods at his back. The preacher's abruptness makes him think of his shock when the jury foreman back in Klaudio, Elmer Suggs, said he was guilty. It had been as if Suggs himself—druggist, father of a girl with a polio-crippled leg, a stranger—had simply stood up from a passing crowd and for no reason on earth but meanness had announced in his slightly elevated voice that he, Delvin Walker, common-law son of Cornelius Oliver and Professor Clemens John Carmel, diverted lover of Miss Celia Cumberland, was guilty of raping two white women. Even after the four weeks of testimony (and thirty minutes of deliberation) he couldn't believe his ears. Surprise didn't cover it. Shock didn't. For a second he had ceased to exist. A short circuit of being in which not only body and mind vanished but all record of his having been on this earth as well, leaving a vacuum that held the shape of a human being. It was quicker than a rifle shot. He was sure none else (outside his cohorts in loss and betrayal, though he never polled them to find out) experienced this or noticed.

But he'd returned in that moment from wherever it was he'd gone (not heaven or hell, not some other planet or system of whirling rocks and gas)—nonexistence was all he knew—to a world that was subtly and completely changed. Every person, every animal, every object in it had been replaced by a duplicate, facsimile so cleverly contrived that the replaced would never suspect what had happened. He too had been replaced. The Delvin Walker who sat on an oakwood bench wearing a white cotton shirt and khaki trousers provided by the Song of Ruth AME church over on Suches street in the Congo Quarter (same for the other boys) was not the same Delvin Walker of a moment before. The boy he had been, the young man who, like his mother—so they told him—could whistle through his slightly gapped front teeth, who had begun reading Shakespeare as a boy of six and knew everything there was to know about laying out a body and getting it respectfully into the ground, a man sweet on Celia Cumberland, a partaker of life in an alien land, quick to laugh, slow to take offense, curious about every-thing, note-taker, writer of things down, adventurer by railroad and foot and hitched ride, lover of vistas and the sour fruit of the quince bush, museum keeper, this boy/man was gone.

He had stood up and started to walk out of the courtroom. A shout arose and some guard, some man he didn't even know, had clubbed him in the ear. He still had a little cauliflowering from the blow. With the blow (it had been as if) his mind had been knocked out of his body into the street two floors down. He couldn't believe it—that was put-ting it mildly.

All these years later he has come to believe it. His mind has filtered on through that.

This man, Preacher Ansley, who himself stuck a knife in the giz-zard of some man he thought cheated him, wants him to believe in some alien god. Well, he will get to that when he has finished with this other project, thanks.

He watches the preacher as he walks, swinging lightly a spring of sorrel grass against his leg, and enters the shade of the barracks. Each barracks has two lanterns. There is no real protection against night life. Men lie awake in the dark listening to the mosquitoes whine and the little house lizards chirp. His own steps are lighter now, but not from happiness. Or not only from that. He has told the doc he is better. The doc has made it clear that he isn't cured but he's accepted his claim to feeling well enough to get out. Delvin wants to be free of this extra imprisonment. At least he can escape from the infirmary. His clothes smell of sulfur and citronella. He stood in the shade on the eastern side of the infirmary shaking the outdoor smell into his shirt. But he can still smell the pesthouse on his body.

His step is trivial and untrustworthy, the step of a sick man. He wants to lie down in the dust. He stops walking and Milo offers another drink from the tin cup he carries, an act of love since he too thinks the malaria is contagious. The blood sluices in Delvin's veins; he can feel it washing back and forth, a heatedness picking up speed. The top of his back feels as if a hot board is pressing against it. He staggers; it takes both of them to catch him up. Steadies, he pauses and takes the cup. The sip of water brings with it a yearning for mountain air, for water that tastes of granite, of iron. Often these delicacies of his past revisited. At first he thought they might be helpful in sustaining his drive to escape but they aren't. He tries to avoid them, but sometimes, as now, they come unbidden.

Up ahead, on the wooden bench encircling the big water oak, Bulky Dunning sits weaving a length of grass rope. Bulky never weaves lengths longer than two or three feet. Any longer and the guards will confiscate it. Some of these lengths he is able to secrete in various cubbyholes around the prison. He plans to go over the wire using one of the joined-together ropes. Delvin knows all about this. Bulky offered to take him with him and Delvin is glad to see that during his period of incapacitation he hasn't run off. They met at Delvin's second day at Uniball, when Bulky asked if he was familiar with the negro writer Zora Hurston. No, he said, he wasn't. "How do you spell that," he asked. Bulky carefully spelled the name. "Never met anybody named Zora," Delvin said. "Oh," Bulky, a bright-eyed little man with a thin mustache, said, "I know several. Down in Florida where I come from they're all over." The remark made Delvin laugh. Bulky went on to describe her work, light-footed stories that caught the flavor of negritude without its being stained with white folks' life. "Some kind of dream?" Delvin had asked. "Better," Bulky had answered. " 'I do not belong to that sobbing school of Negrohood who hold that nature has somehow given them a lowdown dirty deal.' That's her." Delvin had let out a

low whistle. "Well, no wonder I never heard of that woman." "Yeah,"
Bulky said. "Spoken by somebody who's found a way out of the general
disrespectfulness." Delvin laughed again. The words had pricked him;
he experienced a sulky, sullen shame that evaporated as quickly as it
came. "I want to read one of her books." But Bulky didn't have one and
he couldn't remember any of the titles.

   He looks up now from plaiting his eternal rope. He stretches the
rope through his fingers and flicks the tail of it, smiling calmly at
Delvin he gets up and enters the barracks. He wanted that first day,
or the day after, to slide into Delvin's bed, but Delvin shooed him out.
"I'm spoke for," he whispered, which was what he said from the begin-
ning though it hadn't always worked; he hadn't always wanted it to;
Sandy Suber up at Uniball he loved like he'd never loved a man before,
but Sandy died of diphtheria, moaning and blind and crying for his
sister. Crouching beside his bed in the dark, Bulky said he didn't really
mind and appeared not to. They talked occasionally when their paths
crossed out in the fields and sometimes after supper Bulky would sit
with Delvin on the steps behind the kitchen and talk about his boyhood
in Florida. He had swum in the Gulf of Mexico, the first colored person
Delvin had met who'd done that, and he'd raked oysters and fished for
speckled trout with his uncle who owned a boat. These stories charged
Delvin up. He wanted to dive into that big blue water even though he
hardly knew how to swim. Delvin knows where Bulky keeps his rope.
It is coiled in a little rack under the floor of one of the old deserted
barracks where it juts over a latrine. The fit is tight and smelly. The
officers never poke up there and the prisoners they send feeling around
come back saying there wont nothing but black widow spiders. Bulky
won't speak about what is or isn't under the floor.

   As Delvin counts it this is the night Bulky plans to make the slip;
thus the occasion of his early release from the infirmary. Bulky isn't
afraid of the red dog, but he is worried about taking along a sick man.
He visited Delvin in the infirmary and though no words were spoken
on the subject, Delvin understood Bulky to be giving him the high sign
on the decampment.

   Delvin straightens up. He can bring himself to bear in whatever way is needed—this is what he always tells himself even though it isn't always true. But now the sweet lift of floating, of drifting through the hot afternoon, calls him. He nods at Bulky and with Milo supporting him makes his way along a path that curves around behind the barracks. Milo directs him into a wide turn toward the barracks door. The shade is no cooler than the sunlight and this pleases him. He squeezes Milo's arm to make him stop. Over beyond the next barracks, in a chokecherry tree that still has a few black berries in it, before Delvin was hauled off to the pesthouse, a mockingbird took up early morning residence. Bird won't be there now, but he wants to make sure. The tree is the tallest of three skinny chokecherries just beyond the barracks. The mockingbird lit each morning in the highest branches of the tallest tree, the one on the right. Mockingbirds always like to be as high as they can get. Early, just after the gray light was split open by the morning's first coloring, the bird took up its trill and its rising and falling forays, imitations of robins and bobwhites and the old brown thrasher bird, cats and even the screek of squirrels. Each morning on the way to breakfast Delvin stopped to listen. The bird is gone now. Maybe Milo'd noticed him, but he doesn't want to be told the bird no longer comes around. Looking, staring really—no sir.

"No, sir," the boy says as if he heard, "I aint seen him."

And they stand gazing like communicants at the empty trees.

After the fight, the ruinous fight, all those years ago now—twelve years by today's count—he climbed up on top of the boxcar, a blue Tweetsy car, and sat on the catwalk looking at the country. He felt strong and alive, he felt like singing outloud. Off beyond the tailing run of a big grain field the train had passed a small zoo. The zoo had a camel and a bear and a stringy panther cat, some raccoons and possums. He had seen it before on this run. The camel had two humps, one of which flopped over like a half-empty sack. The bear looked dazed. As the train passed the bear rose up on its hind legs and holding to the cage wire gazed at the train. He looked like he knew all about the fight. Delvin felt sad for the bear locked up in a cage and he remembered how the sadness mingled with the satisfaction and easy fatigue from the fight. Then it seemed, just at that moment, as if something was about to be explained, or fall into place, as if he and the bear and everything else living in the world suddenly knew about it and expected it and would be glad when it happened, but the moment slipped by like the zoo slipping by around the long bend and a salient of dark green pines.

"I missed that mockingbird," Delvin says.

He feels all of a sudden cast down, burned through by the sun, broken up and scattered. Fool loneliness, that's what it is, and what is he doing thinking about that?

In another minute they are in the barracks and Milo is trying to help him into bed.

"I don't need none," Delvin says. He wants to look strong.

He does a couple of jumps just to make Bulky, sitting on his rack three bunks away, think he is a springy character. Is Bulky paying attention? He can't tell; maybe he is looking at him through his private mosquito net.

Delvin lets himself down again, leans back and after telling Milo to wake him in an hour goes to sleep.

Two hours later he wakes with Milo shaking him and telling him to come to supper. Bulky passes the bed as Delvin is getting up. He leans down without fully stopping, or only stopping for a second—Delvin drowsy still, hot and sweaty—and says "I'll catch you on the right side," and passes on smiling in that sideways way he has so he is actually smiling at something off to the other direction.

After supper and after a walk around the compound in the Sunday dusk that smells of green pecans, after a few short conversations with this or that wise or feckless one, he heads back to his bed. The sheet still smells faintly of his body. Milo squats next to him.

"We'll wake you," Delvin says.

The boy's eyes shine. He lets his hand fall on the boy's; the pull of his flesh that always smells faintly of wood smoke is strong; he grips the two middle fingers and lets go. He wants to grab the boy's shirt collar and pull him down, smash his face right into his own. The boy's fine soft lips are sweet. He wants everything in him, wants the weight of flesh on him, wants to feel his hands, the ingenious fingers, the energy that leaps into him from Milo's touch. But he is too tired. He wants to *sleep and he wants to be alone even more than he wants the boy. He wants to escape into oblivion. His shoulders ache deep in the sockets.*

Milo runs his hand over Delvin's knuckles.

"You feel like you coming back to life," he says. "I like that."

He grins. Around them others are getting ready for their night's endeavors, alone or with a friend. The bell rings for lights out. Little Boy Dunlap blows out the lanterns. He makes a little funny squealing sound after he blows out the last one. Sam Brown, Little Boy's protector, laughs as he always does. The prisoners can hear guards out in the yards talking. They will be walking around all night. They have a routine not difficult to keep track of. Delvin lies listening to the footfalls. He recognizes Blubber Watts's heavy step. Blubber will beat you to death if you give him half a reason. Or no reason at all, Delvin thinks just before he vanishes into sleep.

4

There was plenty of room in the jail, but for safety's sake they were kept now in two holding cells at the courthouse. Deputies, sweating in the heat, brought them up the back stairs to the third floor and through a side door into another holding cell, this a large room with benches around the walls and, screwed into blocks set into the walls, steel rings heavy chains ran through. The negroes—become the KO boys—were cuffed to these chains. Their legs were shackled. Nobody'd told Little Buster or Butter Beecham about working the cloth of their pants under the shackles, so they had sores now around their ankles. These sores that were beginning to ulcerate kept them awake at night. Delvin listened to them moaning and crying in the bunks across from him. He had gotten up to see to them but there was nothing he could do; he regretted forgetting to tell them about the tuck-in. He mentioned the problem to Billy Gammon and Gammon told the deputies, but the deputies didn't care. His words bounced off their impervious eyeballs and lay withered and derelict on the floor. He thought maybe if I keep talking I'll build a pile of words that'll bury them, but he knew there weren't enough words.

Gammon told the deputies that the doc said they'd have to delay the trial if the boys got sick or hurt and he'd heard the sheriff complaining already about how much the damn trial was costing the county; he tried that.

"You the ones costing the county," Deputy Fred Wirkle said with a slapped-on smirk. "You ought to plead those jigs out and let us get on to frying em."

Gammon gave a weak smile. "We were gon do that, but if we did these New York slickers would just start the appeals and then we would really be in a mess."

"You the one's a mess, Billy boy," Deputy Bee Banks said.

He lived now in the hotel and liked being there in his little room that looked out on the alley. When it rained, water ran down the alley, carrying bits of grass and twigs and chunks of crumbling yellow dirt in a foamy stream that gurgled as it ran. It was as if he was living in a forest and not right in the middle of town. A maid came in every week to change the sheets and towels. He called his mother a couple times a week and they talked about how things were out on the farm. He had attended the state university and then the law school and she had made him promise to come back to Big Cumber county after that. He planned to leave as soon as the trial was over. Those two youngest boys didn't understand yet that they were being *tried*. "But, mister," fifteen-year-old Bony Bates said, "I aint done nothing. Tell em I aint done nothing." The youngest, thirteen-year-old Little Buster Wayfield liked to play with a piece of string one of the deputies had given him. He made a cat's cradle and swung a little acorn baby in it. He couldn't concentrate enough to make out the charges. He smiled at whatever was said to him and reckoned, so he said, that the white mens were going to do what they needed to. Yes, Little Buster, they were. The boy didn't seem to mind being in jail. He was a skinny child who had never gotten enough to eat and figured he was doing pretty well now. Most of the others couldn't read or write. The one who understood best was the one who had started it all when he talked back to Carl Willis. Willis looked like a Sunday school boy. Walker was as black as Africa. Even among the colored folks he was considered low class. He had too much smartness in his eyes. But he was young too and Billy could see how scared he was. "How you going to get me free of this, Mr. Gammon?" he had asked. "What you going to do?"

It was obvious those girls were lying. One of them, the skinny one, looked like all she wanted to do was sneak off and forget the whole thing. Billy had talked to her about the Lord, His stand on deceit. She had gotten a sick look on her face when he told her that sending them to the electric chair on a lie was the same as murdering them. But she didn't change her story. You got locked in, he knew

that. Fear—and pride, the old devil. Marcus Worley, the county at-
torney, had told him if he ever came near those girls again he would
have him disbarred. People talked like that, but they all had to live
with each other down here. After these boys—white and colored—
were gone the rest of us would have to go on living together side by
side. It wasn't like up north where people didn't live together like we
do down here. When you're close, you got to have an assigned sac-
rificial lamb. Local version. "Hell, I aint hardly *barred* as it is," he'd
told Marcus, and they'd both laughed.

He'd grown tired of legal work, but it didn't matter, still the years
rolled on. His spirit had taken the shape of the suit the profession fit
him for.

"Lord, don't you let these crackers run me to the electric chair
over some false testimony by women I don't even know." These
words from Walker made sweat break out. The tone, the word
crackers, made Billy want to slap the little seal's face. Pullen had
got to his feet and leaned over the table and said, "You better start
practicing your manners if you want to come out of this alive, boy."
He was as bad as the prosecutors. Only Harris had been silent.
Watching the exchange with a bemused expression on his hawkish face. He thought he was above all this. Thought he was smart
enough to figure a way around a Dixie judge and jury. He'd find
out on that one.

The trial jounced on like a runaway wagon. The big girl, Lucille
Blaine, could talk all day. She sneered even at the prosecutor. She
wore a dark blue crepe dress with white leather belt and white
shoes and you could hear her stockings sizzle like searing meat as
she walked from the rear of the courtroom. In the high-backed rail
chair she had the confidence of the unreachable. Poking from her
bland extruded face you could see the ridges of stony refusal, the
uncomplicitous aggrievement and hatred. The world has come to
this, Billy thought. It was decaying to stone before our eyes but we
took no notice. He had no love for these black fellows but sometimes

he wanted to go into a small quiet room and weep there. Wrath, he thought, like the Bible turned inside out.

What had been done to this woman could not be undone and this scared him.

"I wouldn't have no truck with a nigra," she said. "Who would? They got diseases and, well, it would make me sick to my death."

She showed her big shiny teeth to the jury and the jury shrunk back. She would eat the ones who disagreed. The courtroom smelled of gravy sandwiches and grease. "*This* one here, and those *other ones*," she said, "came at me in that train car like I was a chicken they was trying to cut its head off with a ax. They was all laughing and they had a fire in their eyes. They pushed me down in this old messy straw. The straw dust got up my nose and made me sneeze. I couldn't stop sneezing even when they threw my dress up over my head and went at me. I was crying and sneezing at the same time. And yelling to Jesus. That's how I got the big bruise on my face. One of them—I think—and I think—and I think—" and Pullen stopped her because the judge wouldn't and in his most affable manner asked the judge to explain to the young lady that she could only testify to what she had seen—not speculated. The judge smiled at the woman whom he would never have in his house, or even in his yard—or his street or his town that had a rose-twined arch under which travelers passed as they entered from the western environs—if he could help it, and reminded her of the rules. But when the traveler did it again, saying that she thought (*and thought and thought and thought*) it was— stopped by Pullen—the judge frowned at the lawyer and told him to quit harassing the witness. The traveler shed a smile like a bitter cry and plunged on, wielding her heavy knives and cannon and sorrow.

So she can't let on, Billy thought—not anywhere on earth or in heaven—that she, a white woman, had let a black man have his way with her. (*Somebody* had—so the doctor said—but that somebody had probably paid and got his favor before she even left the rail yards up in Chattanooga. That was what she was doing on the train— working.) Even if the nigra paid, she had still let him. If she told the truth, the bottom might fall out of the bucket. Like everybody here,

he thought—each one of us fighting and dodging and swinging whatever weapon we can lift—she was trying to fend off the shame of it.

"I was scared they was gon kill me," Lucille said, Miss Blaine.
"The way they threw me around."

A tittering at this due to Miss Blaine's massivity. She glared at
the assembled, swung a glare at the lawyers and the judge. "A man
is strong," she said. "Too strong. If any of you was a woman you'd
know that."

Her face was bright pink, and grainy like watermelon, and she
was crying now, tiny round dark tears like birdshot rolling down her
cheeks. Billy thinking this. For a moment he hated her. Even though
he knew if what she was saying wasn't true *now*, it was probably true
sometime, somewhere for her.

"They scratched me, and that one there"—she pointed at either
Delvin Walker or Rollie Gregory, the largest and the oldest of the
accused—"beat on me with his fist. Beat me like I was heaven's gate
locked against him. *Hell's* gate."

On she went, casting her net of hatred and fury. She swayed and
lurched in her seat like a woman blown by storm—or like a woman,
Pullen had said, dodging a whip. The white observers, leaning forward, their legs stiff, their hands working handkerchiefs, their faces
rigid or slack-jawed with attention—that ripe individual over there
sprawled in his chair like Caiphus or that old woman with her thin
rouged lips lifted off her dog teeth or that young bailiff pressing with
his fist a red mark into his forehead or the spiffy little judge with eyes
squinched up into his bushy brows—all absorbing this, filling up
with the befouled words, the words giving them something like life,
but better.

And what was that? he thought. What was better than life? And
what about the colored folk up in the balcony. They looked on with
subreption and woe like a dullness and thinned-out hope in their faces.

But Billy didn't have time to answer.

The big woman leaned back in her chair, settling her prayer-
meeting dress around her. "I never stop feeling the hurt of it," she
said. Her cheeks glowed with suffering virtue.

She is trading her immortal soul, Billy thought, for a moment of irreproachable righteousness. It didn't matter that she was lying. How could it? A moment like this was probably never coming again for a woman like this. It didn't matter what the truth was. What mattered was filling head and heart with righteousness, for once finding something she could put her soul into. Like everybody, whether sorting through their own meagerness or fossicking their children's lives for talents they didn't have or stacking up cargo in the back room or abetting what they thought of as goodness—some something they could get behind with all they had. And the preacher, speaking from the rolled-down window of his Cadillac, saying, "Pass it on to the Lord, sinner."

These thoughts zipped by and were gone.

Poor woman, he thought.

As they walked out last night from the hotel room they worked in now, Harris had said to him: "She's going to have to stay mad all her life." He was chuckling quietly as he said this, in wonder, a familiar wonder. Billy saw now what he meant. She was lying like a little boy saying it was trolls knocked him down and got his Sunday clothes dirty. Well, maybe it *was* trolls. And maybe this woman had been raped. Sure she had. She'd been raped and beaten and purely deceived, right from the set-out probably—this was what Harris had said as they sat out on the hotel's second-floor porch, the old man smoking a cigarillo and drinking Spanish brandy from a tiny snifter—"misused and punished for things she didn't do and lied to probably by every man she met. And now she has her chance to correct all that. These boys are the ones elected to pay the price for all those other boys who got away."

"What can we do?" Billy had asked, as if he didn't already know what the old man told him, or what was coming.

"Well, we will see," Harris had said, tipping the snifter in his short pudgy fingers so the brandy almost but not quite spilled.

Now in the airy courtroom the old man from the *Daily Worker*'s legal auxiliary got to his feet. He began to ask the woman, Miss Blaine, questions about the details. What were the men wearing?

Did she notice anything special about any of them? If they had pulled her dress over her head, how could she identify who had done what? Why was it she had not gotten blood on her? Walker and the others were cut in the fight and they were wearing clothes splashed with blood. Why was it that none of the white boys had at first mentioned that a rape had occurred? What about her history? Did she not work regularly as a prostitute on the Richmond & Hattiesburg freight lines? Wasn't prostitution her regular means of employment?

The judge stopped this line of questioning. "We are here," he said tapping the bench top with his forefinger, "to find out what happened on the afternoon of September eight."

"Why were you on that train?" Harris asked.

"I heard about jobs in Memphis."

"What jobs were those, Miss Blaine?"

"Housework, cleaning."

"Have you done much housework, Miss Blaine?"

"My share."

"Could you tell us the names of some of your employers?"

Miss Blaine had forgotten their names.

Harris asked about the treatments for gonorrhea, in Chattanooga and Roanoke, Virginia.

The judge stopped him again.

Harris picked away at her story through the warm fall afternoon. The courtroom smelled of sweat and overly saturated perfume. Delvin could smell from somewhere nearby the slightly sour odor of cow manure somebody'd tracked in. It was all he could do not to leap from his chair to argue with the white woman. "Tell me one true thing about me—ME!" he wanted to shout. He knew she wouldn't be able to say one thing. She was like a locustwood knot, nothing to her but sap and hardheadedness. Mr. Oliver used to call him hardheaded. Well he should come see hardheadedness now. He looked around the courtroom, but there was no Mr. Oliver. He had left after their meeting in the jail and Delvin had not heard from him since.

People had written him—Celia's letters were the ones he cherished—and the Ghost had been in town for two weeks. Delvin had seen him standing outside the jail and waved to him. The Ghost acted like he didn't know it was him waving. But the next day he showed up again, taking the same spot as the day before, next to the boiled peanuts stand. The steam from the boiler blew over Winston, alternately concealing and revealing him. He was as skinny as ever. Delvin had waved, but again the Ghost hadn't acknowledged him. He was in the same spot most days of the two weeks and he never indicated that he had seen Delvin. He was in the courtroom too, on the second day, but Delvin had not seen him since.

He put his hands under the table because they had started to shake. He tried with all his will to make them stop, but they kept trembling. His flesh seemed to have come loose from his skin. The thought made him wince so he looked as if he was hearing the unpalatable truth, which the jury noticed. He was so vexed it was all he could do not to leap up and run. He was going to run. If he wasn't in too many pieces and he found a way. Big hollows inside his body, gaps, cut-through places, like in the hills where one hill fell off and another hadn't hardly got started. And always these days a chill wind circulating, dipping icy fingers into troughs and low, damp spots. Sometimes he was as still as a thing that had never lived. Sometimes he trembled like a bent motor. Sometimes frozen, sometimes hot as a steam iron. The boys had begun to look to him to speak for them but he didn't think he could. He could talk, and he could understand what the lawyers were saying, but he could hardly keep from busting into tears—from running. He was *going* to run.

Mr. Pullen had laid out the case, and though he said it was clear as day that the men hadn't committed the crime, Delvin couldn't see one good thing about what was coming. Even Little Buster, a child who didn't know how to read and had to count on his fingers, saw that the joke was on the africano boys. "Might as well get to training for jail," he'd said. "That is if they don't light us up." "We in that training now, fool," Carl Crawford told him. But two of the boys were so ignorant they hardly realized they were in jail.

In his bed at night Delvin lay on his belly pushing his face into the cotton pallet, coughing up tears until his stomach cramped. *My everyday path a road of fire.* He jammed his fist into his mouth and bit down so hard the pain made him shiver and cry out. "That you, Delvin?" Bonette Collins called out. Delvin didn't answer, but then when he saw in the dark that Bonette was getting out of his bunk he told him to stay where he was. "I's all right," he said. He tried not to let them see him crying, but they could each see the dismals in the others' faces, the torment. They looked like their best friend had died. Or more, as if something promised—so ordinary and inevitable and such a sure thing they didn't have to give it a thought—had suddenly been taken away. Something—slide of blood in the veins, the world's itinerant sweetness—that you didn't even know could be taken away, something you hardly even knew you had. *But, gone* . . . you were broken and scattered. The white folks made you feel small, sure. They made you feel you were wrong to be . . . yeah, *to be.* But this that was snatched away now was none of that. This was something else. "It's like we was walking along," Coover Broadfoot said, "and a mule fell out of the sky and hit us." "I know which mule it was, too," Bonette Collins said and the others laughed; they all knew. When you thought about what was happening—what was going to happen—you got so scared you couldn't think straight.

This is grief, Delvin thought. We're in mourning.

He wrote some of this down in the little notebook Gammon had told the jailer he needed for the case—not really a notebook but one somebody'd torn crossways in half; enough to write on. It had a mud stain on it and the pages were hooped where they'd gotten wet and dried out. *You want to run right through the walls. Sometimes you can hardly draw breath; sometimes you can't get any air in your breath. Carl said he thought he was drowning. We all think we are drowning. But we aren't drowning and we have to breathe and we can't* . . . He tried to stick to what was going on right this minute. *I am chewing a piece of hard yellow cornbread,* he wrote, *one chew, two, three . . . my fingernails are turning brown* . . . and on he went, but his mind wouldn't stay on bread chewing or his nails—or walking up and down or staring at the tin-sheathed wall where a window ought to be.

The town was full of spectators. Sports and the bedeviled, thrill-seekers, the estranged and crippled, common people, farmers drifted in on market days, old men riding in weathered wagons and children walking along beside, women in poke bonnets carrying tied-up packages by the string, aficionados of death row, reporters, profiteers, the falsely cunning and bereft. Some few of the africano women tried to bring them gifts. Food in wicker hampers or stacked in plates tied with a cotton cloth. Men wanted to look at them and the deputies brought a few of them back to the cell, white men, most of whom tried to look casual or tough—or maybe they *were* tough—leaning against one of the stone posts thumbing their galluses and leering. Some were calm, others stiff. Some had been walking around for weeks with a numbness on their skin, with a burning in closed places, with a sorrow so old and ugly they took a doctor's pills to make it subside and stood on the back porch tossing bits of skillet bread to the dog or waked after midnight and went out in the dewy grass and called a name they hadn't spoken since they were youngsters, parents of children who shuddered at their prayers and were losing weight and husbands of women who locked themselves in their rooms and sat on the bed fiddling with their rings—they had come here to see the living dead. More than one with his face like it was shellacked. Most sweating, some angry, some laughing. Most able to go on with their lives, even the man on a crutch the varnish was worn off of, or the fat man in a striped shirt eating a tamale from a piece of waxed paper. The fat man wiped his mouth with his bare wrist, leaving a streak of red juice on his cheek. A bouncy little man couldn't stop grinning. A preacher dwelt in pentecostal gloom. Most—even those troubled in their spirit—were appreciative, relieved of the burden of chasing down these miscreants, of handling their black flesh or staring into their eyes in the last moments of their freedom, of being the ones sweating and running to catch up; they enjoyed now the blood surge that grew in strength as they walked the crooked jailhouse corridors toward the cell. Some experienced this episode as nothing more than a rectifying revenge—and Delvin thought, *That is what it is: revenge by murder,* and he had turned away and gotten sick in the slop bucket. They don't know me, he thought. And behind him, outside the bars, hearts ticking, breath entering lungs and blood circulating through bodies, deep into the indwellings of the brain, clattering and banging out the news: *Not me, not this time—not me.*

Carl's mother had come and Bonette's and Little Buster's, but they weren't allowed back to the cell. The prisoners could hear people calling to them from the street. At night the voices were clear even in the heavy air. Men saying, *We going to hang yu, jigs. We gon get yu tucked into hell. Gon slip up there and cut yu up. Burn yu.* Women called too. *Ha ha,* they said, *ha ha ha.* A deputy would have to go out and tell them to be quiet. *You run back in, Horton, and play with yo coons,* somebody yelled and the crowd laughed. They were marginal folk, long dispossessed of love for themselves, mostly. Cunning but not smart. They wrapped themselves in the ragged tails of night. Somebody broke into song. Crooked hymn singing. From a hymnal nobody in the cell had ever read. The voices quoted scriptures of damnation and pestilence. None with green pastures in them. None with still waters. New scriptures, hot off the presses. *Lo, from this place you will exit burning. Oh ye of the jig rind crisping. Yo body become ashes cast on the wind. Where you will dwell forever.*

He paced the cell back and forth until he was tired or one of the other boys told him to please, dammit, quit. Or somebody with a problem, some ordinary problem, some ailment or fabrication, some Bonette with a blister where he'd rubbed his thumb against his bunk or Carl with a knee that hurt or Butter whose throat always ached from all the crying in his sleep, took his attention. Delvin would dip the tail of his shirt in the water bucket and press it against the back of Buster's neck while the slim boy clutched his hand. He could feel Buster's pulse through the cloth. "I'm about to buster out of my skin," Buster said, and laughed at his only joke. Delvin sat up with Carl, who liked to pray. With Rollie, who lied about everything. Rollie's long, up-curled lip made him look like he was about to say something important, but he never did. He had the training for these ministrations and he knew they would help ease his own panic. He was the one called most often to confer with the lawyers, especially by Gammon, the young man from down the road in Tuxer. Gammon seemed not so scared of him. In the courtroom at the two tables pushed together in an L shape Gammon sat beside him and often scratched notes to him on the large pale brown sheets he carried into the courtroom. *It's going to be all right,* he wrote; foolishly, Delvin thought. *Things are going to work out. No, they aint,* Delvin had written back. *Things have already been busted to pieces. Beyond fixing.* That was the point, wadn't it? But the words, written down, scared him. When Gammon scribbled his note on the same slip of paper and passed it to him, Delvin scratched his own words out.

It was from the Klaudio courthouse that he tried his first escape. During a recess in which the prisoners were taken out of the courtroom to an unoccupied office belonging to the state farm agency in the company of the lawyers and a burly jailer who spit tobacco juice into a white ceramic mug he carried everywhere, Delvin made his first jump. They were on the third floor and looked out of three tall windows cracked to let a little air into the room. They had taken the chains and shackles off because the accused were supposed to be sufficiently cowed. Gammon was talking to him about his love of football when the bailiff stepped out to get a fresh chaw of tobacco. Brown's Mule. He hadn't thought about escaping, or not in the way he was used to thinking. A pressure—was that it?—had built up. Something, a scraping in him, low distant rasping he hardly noticed, and this worrisome discomposing in his body—this jumpiness: they had built up. Azalea bushes planted around the courthouse were not in bloom, but they were thick with gray-green leaves. Which meant the ground underneath them after these late rains would probably be soggy.

This was the sixth time they'd been in the room. This was the first time the bailiff had stepped out.

He was ready, but still, after the door closed behind the bailiff, he hesitated. Maybe the man was coming right back. Maybe the punishment for trying to escape was too severe. Maybe they would beat him. Maybe the lawyers, these rectifying white men, would desert him. Maybe he would be hurt in the fall.

Carl Crawford, carrying a strange formal quality, his face pimply with ingrown hairs, leaned toward Rollie Gregory, twirling his long fingers; Rollie laughed his crackly, misbelieving laugh. Little Buster Wayfield stared at the ceiling, moving his mouth like he was talking. Gammon was just telling him about Jim Thorpe, an Indian hero, an athlete, a performer for white men, who had been humiliated on a football field down in Florida a few years back by Red Grange and his team of NFL brutes, white men still paying the Indians back for Custer.

Then, *click*: he simply moved. A dart toward the window. He caught the look of surprise on Gammon's face. Coover and Bony looked at him and Bony in a quiet voice that sounded to Delvin like a scream, cried, "Where you going?" Everything else, even the broad day outside and the whole fraudulent enterprise they were mired in, went quiet. The window was heavy but with a hard shove of one hand he forced it fully open and before anybody moved he was out into the air. He fell twenty feet. After the first four or five the fall seemed like flying. A sense of terrifying weightlessness filled him just before he crashed ass first into the azalea bushes. A branch tore through his pants and cut a deep scratch into the side of his leg. But he wasn't hurt.

He rolled out of the bush, scrambled to his feet—the sight of the long red scratch under the khaki cloth almost made him sick—and began to run across the wide mushy lawn. A large woman in a pink dress stared at him with her mouth open. A man on the cement walk skipped a step as if he was getting out of Delvin's way though he wasn't anywhere near him. A voice cried out from the courthouse porch. "That's one of them nigras." Shouts went up, the noise beating against his body like hard rain out of the blue sky, but he was running, fleet, the town moving past him in a blur of little specks of life jumping—the squirrel hanging upside down from a catalpa branch, a little boy pop-eyed and grinning, a woman waving a yellow scarf in front of her face—all additions, subtracting as they went by, as he went by, plunging into space as he ran, each step a fall, each a bungle and bluster and a soaring, each carrying him nowhere and everywhere, and he was running, running . . .

He made it to the corner, dashed across the street, turned right and headed down past a big furniture store. There were three brown leather armchairs in the picture window, arranged looking out, empty—lonely, he thought. An outside staircase led up the side of the gray brick building across the street. He liked outdoor staircases. He was running hard. Up ahead the picture show had Joan Crawford and Clark Gable on the marquee. He had never seen either of them. There looked to be an empty lot on the other side of the theater and beyond it a large white frame building with bushes around it and past that a big yard and past that a little copse of mulberry trees. He thought he could make it to the trees and be gone. He smelled boiled peanuts. The sky was stripped of clouds.

Just then, without warning, a man tackled him. Delvin went sprawling onto his chest on the pavement. He tried to get up but the man held him. In a second another man was on him and then another. He could smell tobacco and raw vinegary sweat and corn whiskey. The men—white men—were cursing him. He writhed against the rough load of bodies—white bodies closer than any white bodies had ever been: hands, fingers gouging, elbows knocking, feet kicking and stomping and knees hitting him in the back and between the legs and an unshaven cheek scraping against his and he could hear somebody's soft panting like the panting of a dog and somebody's scratchy breath whistled in his ear and he almost laughed because the whistle seemed like the first bars of that song, what was the one? He made a whimpering sound that he had not known was in him. A woman somewhere close by was screaming. He kicked out with his feet, or tried to, but he couldn't get traction, couldn't reach any step or ledge to prise himself free.

It was no use. A silence like a gathering poison filled him.

The power that keeps the world spinning turned and stooped to him and the power behind this power bent down too and the others in the endless line and these powers looked at him and didn't say anything or do anything and then they went on and he lay still.

"Ah me," he whispered, "ah me."

5

Judge said, Everything that happened to those boys happened for cause.

But Gammon said, That's not true, Your Honor. We wouldn't be back here arguing about it for the tenth time—

Fourth, the judge said.

Fourth time, Your Honor—if we were just lying.

Not just, the judge said. You're also using up my life and my patience.

I'm sorry Your Honor feels that way. But there've been other judges. Not only you, Sir.

Because you wore them into early graves, the judge said and gazed bleakly out the window as if he saw death riding by on a horse out there.

Bulky pinches his toe but that doesn't wake him and then Milo comes up close and blows softly into his face and Delvin smells his earthy breath and begins the long swim up from a grassy bottom and breaks the surface what seems hours later with his head aching and a dizziness in the quick of his eyes.

At first he doesn't think he can move. He is too heavy to rise into the world. Milo squeezes his shoulder and the pressure begins to pump life into him.

"That's fine," he whispers, "I'm right on it."

Halfway and leftover, crumpled and spread back out, sheared into pieces weighted with stone, concentrated as a chunk of quartz. He rolls over and falls from the bunk and is caught by the men, the escape artists, around him.

"I'm fit for it," he whispers.

None but themselves are awake—there are seven of them—or only those like Dumpy Links who lies hours on his back looking up at the board underside of the barracks roof. Or Morcell Jackson who tortures himself with sexual memories of the common-law wife he strangled over in Hattiesburg. Maybe another couple kept awake by fear or rage. Cul Sampson who cries all night. None of these, according to the report, see anything. They know better than to ask Bulky if they can come, though Dumpy is on his feet naked and crouched down, ready to scurry out the door, before Bulky with a look sends him back.

It is a warm, moonless night. The Milky Way lies sloshed-over and frothing. They can see fine. They follow Bulky to the forge and wait while he crawls under the raised floor to get the rope. He comes out covered in dust and grinning.

"Fucking spiders all over me," he whispers, and he is telling the truth. Milo brushes them off, little black widows that never really sleep. The men are all barefoot. The coiled rope as big as a sheep carcass thrown over his shoulder. "All right," he whispers, his voice tight with the effort.

They head around the shed to the big sweet gum whose star-stretched shadow almost reaches the fence and crouch at its base. In the dimness a distant guard seems to move in slow motion along the side of the machine shop. Another, the bruiser, Jock Anglin, standing in the door of the guard shack, thrusts his potbelly into the night. He is just close enough for Delvin to make out the quart milk bottle in his left hand, horsemint tea he sips through the damp nights. Even this far away they can smell the citronella from the lit coil inside the shack. The oily, fruity aroma and then the smell of the river breezing up through the woods. They have no boat to travel that way (Delvin's is long gone) and there are towns both up and downstream, heartless sheriff's deputies patrolling. The laws promise the citizenry that there will be no trouble from villainous africanos and they mean it, sending men on patrols that take them into darkened alleys and along river branches

*and into shadowy parks and down the sleeping or insomniac streets.
Forty miles south the river becomes tidal, smelling of the Gulf and
freedom, but that is a long way and scary in its own right.*

*Delvin shivers in the almost cool of the almost dark night. Off in the
woods raccoons make thin yipping sounds, probably debating over a
scrap of food. A widow bird lets loose its bit of vocal material. Crickets
saw their instruments. The fence gleams like a silver net, ragged at the
top with coils of rusty barbed wire that look like shriveled nests. How
you going to work the rope? Delvin asked. The fence is fifteen feet high,
eighteen maybe with the barbed wire. They kneel in the dark under
the tree, waiting. The sickness sways in Delvin like an ancient fern-
ery, heavy and moist. If he lets himself lean back, and let go, he will
be asleep before he hits the ground. He wonders if his father is alive,
imagines him getting up from a poker game maybe, out in Abilene or
El Paso, a man who can speak Spanish and has a passel of half mexican children. Sometimes he pictures him in a straw boater, dancing
on a stage in scuffed white shoes. His anger rises. He crabs forward to
Bulky who crouches in the deepest shade by the bench peering out.*

*"How you plan to do this?" he says. His face is hot and the pain in
his shoulders has increased. Milo beside him slaps softly at mosquitoes.
Delvin feels a familiar despair. The malaria brings with it an evoca-
tion of many kinds of dumb woe and he is caught now in some of the
dumbest. "Jesus damn christ," he whispers.*

*Milo looks expectantly at him. This is a frolic for him, and Delvin
can tell he is experiencing a run of freshened life.*

*Over at the pens the hogs snuffle and one lets out a short squeal.
Bulky has the rope on his shoulder. He measures out half of it and
bunches this up with the other half. The grass rope is lightweight, but
Bulky has woven so much of it that the bundle is heavy. Delvin asks
again what he is going to do but Bulky ignores him.*

*"Ah, nah," Delvin says his voice not really audible. He is begin-
ning to feel foolish, not just beginning; but what does it matter, they
are already in a prison. He begins to chuckle, low, the sounds more like
quiet coughing.*

Bulky looks back at him, vexed. He is crouched low.

Milo lets his hand rest on Bulky's shoulder. Delvin thinks he must have something already worked out with the smaller man. Bulky has moved farther forward, followed by Milo, until the two of them make a single block under the tree. Together they ease to the edge of the big tree's midnight shade. Delvin thinks he can hear the chatter and clicking of the raccoons. Together Bulky and Milo rise.

Delvin says softly, "Yall don't," but Milo is on his feet running behind Bulky who has the rope looped out and his arm back to throw it. At the fence, holding to the ends of the rope, he throws it as a man would throw a big lifesaving ring. The coils unloose like a card trick. The body of the rope catches in the top of the wire among the barbed jumble and hangs. Bulky pulls down hard and the fence bends toward him. He and Milo stand right up against the wire pulling on the free ends of the rope. The big fence bends where the rope catches it. Bulky scampers up the two strands of rope with Milo right behind him.

Their bare toes hook in the wire as they go up.

Delvin drags himself up against the tree's grooved bark. He knows he can't make it. He is sick to his stomach.

The men reach the top and Bulky first and then Milo rolls over the rope covering the tangle of barbed wire and drops to the grass on other side. Bulky hits on his tailbone, Milo on his feet and knees; they are both in an instant up and running, Bulky with a limp. They are followed by two others and then two more moving fast after that, men scrambling and wavering like visions in the dim light.

A crumpling in Delvin's chest is weighted with a sudden heavy-heartedness. Heavy-bodiedness. He shifts his leg, his aching hip, but his hand doesn't leave the tree.

The first two suddenly free men run hard across the short space of open ground between the fence and the fields. They reach the sprawling, knee-high cotton and drop down into it. The others follow and Delvin can see their shapes moving like shadows through the cotton. Shouts break out from the camp. From the nearest tower shots are fired. The mixed reports of several guns. The siren begins to roll out its call, stretching and building up speed, louder and louder like it is climbing right up the side of the world.

Delvin throws himself down and presses his hands against his ears. His heart beats into his cupped palms. He pants. It is as if the rope still dangling from the mashed wire is attached to his body. It tugs at him, not in a steady surge but in looping fits, jerking him. He presses himself hopelessly into the damp ground and he knows this feeling as he knows the hard lifeless ground you try to become part of and make a life on in the lightless shacks and Bake Houses and reform sheds.

Armed men are out in the yard, each with something special to do. The guards shout orders at the prisoners who want to come out too. Cries rise from the barracks, yells, hoorahs and yips. The guards shout instructions at each other. Their precious stock is getting away. Some scurry about in undershirts and partly buttoned trousers, rifles or scatterguns or crankers in hand. Frank Miles runs from the guard shed in the red longhandles he wears in all seasons and Lonnie Batts skips as he runs, slapping at his chest.

Delvin can't figure why so many are on duty and then he thinks he can and worries crazily about it. In a few minutes they will have the dogs working. Delvin can hear them baying over in their compound near the mule barn. He tries to get up but he can't. He wants now to run for the rope but he knows he won't do that. He turns on his side, grasps the trunk and pulls himself up, sitting, half lying with his back to the tree. Arnold Anderson, a short, round-faced guard from Tennessee, comes around the side of the big gum.

"Whoa," he cries and raises his shotgun at him. "Here's one of em got too scared to go," he yells. He is laughing and sweating and jumpy with juice. Escapes scare most of the guards half to death. Going after these villains isn't like hunting quail or rabbits. It is dangerous. Anderson waves the gun at Delvin.

"Get down on the ground, pancake."

He knows Delvin by name but Delvin can see he isn't going to know him right now. He slides to the ground and presses his face into the dirt. My home. He smells something sweet and his mind flies to a field of grain he and the professor'd passed one late afternoon in Arkansas when the sun looked like it was sinking right down into the yellow

*wheat. He is sleepy. He wishes he could lie with his face in the dirt and
sleep his life away.*

They had to put them on the stand because there was nothing else to
do. The two doctors said the women had been raped (at least they'd
had sexual relations, Your Honor) and four of the white boys who'd
been in the fight said they'd seen the negroes with the women and the
women said they'd been held down and raped and nobody, white or
colored, stood up and said the boys didn't do it and God wasn't up to
testifying on this one so of course they had to put them on the stand.

Two of them couldn't follow the simplest question.

They don't even goddamn know they're being tried for anything, Pullen said. He had just gotten a haircut and his hair gleamed
like the procedure included a fresh shellacking and he smelled of a
musky scalp rub. He laughed when he said this. They were sitting
in the front room of their hotel office with the supper dishes stacked
around them on the big cypresswood table covered with a stained
white tablecloth.

You're correct there, Davis, Gammon said. He had taken to calling Pullen by his first name though he knew he didn't like it.

Four of the boys wouldn't have much to say except they didn't
do it.

Hell, Pullen said picking with his fingernail at the rind of beef
fat that still had the blue slaughterhouse stamp on it, half of em can't
even remember what it is they are charged with.

Well, long as you can remember, Davis, Billy Gammon said.

Har, har, Pullen gusted, a look of malevolence in his large narrowed gray eyes.

They had to put *all* of them on the stand, there was no way around it.
Every dogged man has to have his day. Even Coover Broadfoot who
offended everybody with his uppity manner and his buckteeth and
his twitchy way and question asking. *What was that and what do you*

mean by that and I wish you could tell me, he said to the judge, *exactly what they mean by that.* The judge looked at him like somehow a big black creepycrawler had gotten into his witness chair and he wanted to reach over the high desk of righteousness and swat this idiotic fool right back to Africa, but all he said was Take your time there, boy, and get it just as right as you can. The judge was free to ask questions and he did, questions that generally made it hard for anybody to wonder which side he was on, but he didn't really care, he knew what had to be done here and the truth was just whatever got dug deepest into, it didn't matter what the lawyers or the witnesses or even the parties concerned thought. Dig deep enough and *everybody* was guilty. Only the law kept them all out of jail.

Well, boy, he said, you just let yourself settle down. Have a drink of water (from the glass with a little piece of paper gummed to it with the word COLORED printed in ink on it) and then sit back in that chair and take a deep breath, take two, and go on with your story.

That was what Broadfoot did, stuttering and biting his words, hurling the undeniable—so he appeared to think—facts around the room, into the faces of the jury made up of white men who wouldn't have allowed him to set foot in their yards even if he offered to rake up all the pine straw for nothing. It was em *white* boys, he said, who jumped on em girls. If any colored boy got on em they's way back in the line and it be purely because those women called em to do it. I wadn't even close to any of that. I got a gal back in Eubanks, Tennessee, that I plan to marry as soon as I can get back to her. I wouldn't have no other woman and I certainly wouldn't want no white woman.

He went on and on placing himself and several others outside the range of these occurrences, sorting through the names and the events with the skill of one whose intelligence pressed him from all sides, sneering as he did so and panting and staring the jury in the face like he dared them not to believe him, dared them even to think he was guilty. By the time he got off the stand the jury, all twelve of the men who had never seen this young man before the trial, were happy they were not going to see him again after it was over.

And so it went.

Delvin, his turn come upon him, rose from his seat with his coarse white and blue jail trousers (he'd gone back to wearing the issue) sweat-sticking to his butt and the backs of his legs, swaying nearly to a faint, but able still, rising as man or creature swum continually for miles might rise from the depths of the swamp of being, gasping and looking wild-eyed around the place that was filled with townsfolk and reporters and maybe one or two people who had known him before this calamity flew upon him, or were drawn to him by his own behavior (he pondered this daily and hadn't yet decided; some blamed him outright, Rollie Gregory among them). Was that the Ghost up in the balcony? The professor? *Was that Celia?* He stopped in his tracks, experiencing for only the second or third time in his life the sensation of his heart catching fire. His mind went blank. The four tall windows looked like paintings filled with blue. No black man with blue eyes. No Celia either. For a second he didn't know where he was. He came to himself walking to the big wooden witness chair, a copy a guard had told him of the electric chair at Markusville. The judge was looking at him as if he knew him well and was sick and tired of his face. He could hear breathing behind him. It sounded like the bellows in the blacksmith shop over on Florida street in Chattanooga. He would never see that place again. His body felt brittle, waffled through by termites and other hurtbugs until he was eaten with holes and corridors and little bug byways and all dried up. He could hear himself creak as he sat down, or was that the chair about to collapse under him?

Pullen with an insubstantial flourish introduced him to the assembled and left him to himself. If Pullen didn't ask questions or direct him, then the prosecution couldn't either. He was alone with what he knew to be so.

He sat then in the trailing silence, waiting for some other voice besides his own to begin to speak. He needed to hear somebody else, some speaker he could respond to or hook up with in a call and shout. But there was no one. He leaned back in the chair. A half-scary man, they had taken the cuffs off but not the shackles. It was embarrassing to have to walk in front of people wearing that gear. His escape attempt had made it harder on the others. The guards jostled and poked them, drew their armatures tighter. His fellow transgressors cursed him. He coughed, and a slipperiness went down his throat. He lifted his face and felt on his skin the burning of a blow, some hit from long ago, still afire.

He said, I never did a thing but what any man wouldn't do.

He told of sitting on the steel crossbar under the hopper and reaching to steady himself when a man, a white boy, stepped on his hand. He had barked at him, barked, he said—"so quick I didn't even know it was me—or him." The white boy had cursed him for a nigger. One thing led to another and after a while in the empty boxcar that smelled of rotten peaches there had been a fight the colored boys clearly won. Yes, and on from there to his riding on top of a blue boxcar after the fight, sitting with a couple of boys as the train passed a little farm zoo under some big trees. The zoo had an old ratty camel in it and the camel had two humps and one of the humps was folded over and he had wondered if this was because it needed water to pump it back up. The zoo had donkeys and a bear, maybe it was a bear, and several raccoons and a fox or two panting in their cages under the big droopy trees, but then the train went on around this long bend headed toward Haverhill and he sat there wondering about the camel. About what life was for such a beast in a country with no sand dunes and all that. It wasn't till the train stopped in Kollersburg and the deputies called them down and rounded everybody up that he realized anything was wrong. He had never seen those two white women before he saw them at the jail. He started to say he felt sorry for them, but at that moment it was an actual lie because right then he hated those women though he also pitied them and wondered what made them the way they were, and then he caught himself again for a liar because he knew very well what made them like that because it was the same thing that made anybody mean, just too many whippings, he had seen it with dogs and bindlestiffs and even children, and sure there were those with a natural brokenness inside them too and they were the ones who at seven years old set fire to the school and all, but what it was most of the time was from the meanness they'd suffered, which there was a sufficiency of in the world, and he had sat in his borrowed courtroom chair over there looking those women in the face and seen the print of the striking hand on their faces and recognized it and wanted to stand up then and say, I know about all this, it's all right, but he didn't, as he didn't now, said no word at all about those women or what he knew, he simply stopped talking and let the communal breathing and a rustly little humid breeze fill up the silence, thinking where was I and what was I saying, oh Lord.

"Those sheriffs must have mistaken me for another person," he said. "I promised myself to somebody else—a long time ago I did that."

He scanned the balcony, but whoever might have been Celia was not there. A white boy with bronze ringlets leaned on the balcony rail picking his nose. A white woman in a smart red dress adjusted a yellow cloth flower on her shoulder. A white man in overalls fanned himself with a crushed straw hat. Jakes and Blarneys and cordial bug shifters. Too much going on to keep track of it all. Anything he might say was nothing to what he knew. The lawyers had told him to hang his story on a string of time. One occurrence after another until he was taken away by the sheriffs. They—the sheriffs at the train station—had sweated through their shirts, Delvin remembered. The stocks of their shotguns were slick with sweat. A colored boy in a bright red shirt sat on a wagon seat in front of a store. It was a hardware store and had a box of bright copper piping on the front porch; the boy had ducked down and hid behind the wagon seat. The high sheriff wore a black broadcloth suit and carried a scuffed derby in his hand. His knuckles too were scuffed. In the window of a white house across the dirt street a small white cake rested. I would like a piece of that cake, he had thought.

He wanted to tell them how scared he was, how scared he had been all along. *We all been scared. We been scared to death over here for the last three hundred years. All day every day.* Like when somebody you didn't see jumps out a door at you.

He said, "I can't tell you I have done wrong when I haven't, not the wrong you all are accusing me of."

His voice soft and plain, hardly a negro's voice at all. Billy Gammon thought he sounded like a white man. And Pullen wondered for a furious second if the boy was mocking them. I'll kill him myself, he thought.

"If I had violated either of those white women," Delvin said, "I would have jumped off that train long before it got to Kollersburg. Any of us would. We were born knowing what the penalty for business such as that is. But we didn't jump off. We didn't run. Anybody who saw us when the train pulled into that town would know we didn't suspect a thing. We were not guilty men. Not a one of us—"

He would have gone on, but he saw how they were looking at him. For a moment everything lost its name. He noticed a couple of yellowed leaves lying on the wooden floor between the judge's bench and the defendants' tables. The wind must have blown them in through the tall open windows. As he stared at the leaves—they were tulip poplar, black-speckled yellow—he realized he had forgotten the names of his fellow prisoners, and forgotten the names of the lawyers and the judge, of the women, and of everyone he knew or had known. That morning the light in the courtroom had been suffused with green, as if the sunlight coming through the windows had soaked up green from the trees and deposited it here, but now, in the late afternoon, the light in the courtroom was red, as if a storm was descending in the west and the sun had picked this up too and spread it around the room. He did not know who he was or what was happening here—everyone, everything, was strange—he only knew, and it was all he knew, where each of them was going, but this did not frighten him; it seemed only as it should be. A sweetness, a radiancy, filled him, and his weariness slipped away. I am . . . , he thought and then he couldn't think, and it didn't matter. Their eyes had glazed over. Or else they were looking at him like they were about to jump up and slap him. He wanted suddenly to reach out and pinch their noses. Chuck them under the chin, thump them on the chest. Come on, we just joking here, aint we? He felt a chill so strong the thin coiled hairs on his arms stood up. He saw himself loitering on the edge of a hobo creek tossing crabapples into the water. He looked up from the witness chair and saw for the first time a woman with deep black skin and a sharp pretty face. For a second like an eternity he knew this woman for his mama, come to fetch him out of this. But no, not his mama. That was just a dream.

6

They sling a chain through the gyves and drag him naked across the yard and throw him into the former root cellar beside the warden's house. A plank door set in the ground over eight wooden steps leading down to a square dirt room. A little light comes through the joining of the planks but not much. As he is dragged past the warden's house he sees through the kitchen window the warden's wife, a fat woman who wears a gray shapeless housedress around the clock, set a pan of cornbread to cool on the windowsill. "Wait," he cries, "I think that white woman wants to give us some of that crackling bread." Why would she be baking at night? The guard closest to him, Flimsy Plutter, jaundiced and twitchy, swats him across the face with the grommet-speckled work glove he carries for just such occasions. A fingertip cuts Delvin under the eye, making him yelp with pain. The woman looks out the window with no expression in her wide freckled face. On the radio in her kitchen Ethel Merman sings "You're the Top." On the little porch in back a calendar with a picture of the snow-covered Rockies is tacked to a post. I could be cartwheeling down that icy mountain, he thinks.

They don't bother to pull him to his feet. They simply fold the door back and fling him down the steps.

The red dog has every joint bone in his body already hurting so he hardly feels it when he hits the ground on his face and chest, though the cut from the glove keeps stinging for the three days he lies in the dark mostly sleeping or re-stuporized by the malaria. Snakes, come out of some phantom place, crawl over him like the times before, but like the times before they don't bite. They like the warmth of his body. To him they seem clean and pure, as if the ugliness and dirt of the underworld never touches them. There is no grime, no dust, nothing alien on their long bodies that are cool and dry, and the scales under his fingertips,

snugly fastened and hard, flexing as the snake stretches out its length,
fascinate him.

"We got no reason to spite each other," he says to them, dark writh-
ers in the stinky dark. They keep the rats away.

The bugs keep up their poking and probing. He rubs dirt on his
body to keep the mosquitoes at bay, and when he feels the thin sharp
scuttle of a scorpion he stays as still as possible. They never bite him
either.

Only the doodlebugs are unimpressed by his efforts or his stature, if
that is what it is, as a god among the vermin.

"Chief of the itty-bits," he says to himself like he is five years old.

The snappish little front-loaded doodlebugs have a tendency to clamp
their jaws shut on whatever living things they come in contact with.

"Yi lord," he cries softly, holding his position so the four-foot
swamp rattler lying in the crook of his elbow won't be disturbed.

He dreams of his mother. She had curly toes with brown nails that
had a shine to them. She smelled like he knew heaven smelled. She
liked to jump up and down and sing so loud Mr. Culver from next door
would send a child over to tell her to stop. She couldn't read well but
she could get anything that was in a picture. She carried photographs
around with her of people she didn't know, given to her by people she
didn't know. My sweets, she called them. She got angry like an animal
would get angry, wild and quick and lunging. He never minded being
hit by her—not afterwards—he was a child, how could he mind? She
looked at him sometimes like she would eat him up with a great relish.
He likes that when he thinks about it. In the dreams she runs like the
wind, her pale heels flashing.

In his black cabinet under the ground he feels himself jump. His
body twitches, not sharply, but in a long slow undulation like a fish
moving just under the surface of a dark pond. The snake coiled in his
elbow rustles and the stubby rattle purrs. A couple of scorpions nestled
against his chest probe with their claws. Centipedes feather their dry
legs. "Yi lord," he says softly. He can sense himself about to fly.

On the fourth night as he lies on his back resting, not so tired, the
dog slunk back for now into its cave, he watches as the lid of his cabinet

begins slowly to creak upward. He thinks for a second it is the sky itself tipping away and almost hollers out. But it is only Bill Francis, a convict machinist from Carmichael, Louisiana, raising the door. The door was locked with a nail stuck through the hasp.

Delvin hears the whistle of breath. "My God, what a stink," a whispering voice says.

Moonlight shines into the hole. The lid drops and is caught. "Sweet Jesus," another voice says.

"Come out," the first voice says, like King Darius calling to Daniel, calling to the subterranean one.

Delvin tries his voice. It still works though it croaks and rasps. "Let me say my farewells," he whispers.

"Yall step back," Bill Francis says.

Delvin detaches himself carefully from his companions of the pit. It takes a short while but he moves steadily until he can get to his knees and then to his feet. It is difficult but not impossible to climb the eight steps. The air rich with cleaned-off life. The bosky smell of the trees. The undergirded reek of the fields. A freshly birthed world. It makes him modest.

"Come on, boon," Bill says, taking him by the wrist. The man gives him a long look. "We thought you might be swole up and bit by now, but you got a special way."

What are they doing here, these convicts? They are all convicts. It is too complicated to ask. They're raising me, he thinks. Gon do some running? I expect so.

He follows as best he can as they make their way behind the work sheds and into the old barn where the mules were formerly kept and to the back where the old privies are. Bill and his crew have been working on a tunnel that has its entrance in the dried shit pit, and they are now finished with it. He has told Delvin that if he is still on the premises he will have a place in the string of folks going out. They have a rope ladder under the second seat—it is an eight-holer—that lets down through the old crumbled, desiccated shit. The tunnel runs horizontally forty feet to the other side of the back wire. It comes up behind the new barns and is only a few steps from the woods.

There are twelve of them and in a matter of six or seven minutes they are all out and running—through wild fennel and rabbit tobacco and bristleweed and goose grass and oxalis and copperleaf and paspalum and pigweed and poke—into the rustling cotton field.

It makes Delvin feel foolish. Just—what was it?—four nights, or weeks, maybe it was weeks, ago, he was trying to make up his mind to climb Bulky's rope. He misses Milo. He tries to ask if anybody's heard about Bulky, but Macky Bird, a light timer, shakes him off. He hopes Milo is out there somewhere waiting. It is another little dream. He smells of modified shit and dirt and snake musk and of sweat and animal excretions and of his own piss that spilled back on him when he peed. Webfoot Bilkins is the only one of the escapees besides Bill that he knows well. Most are boys from the machine shop and the planing mill.

They run in a straggle line to the woods and when they reach the trees they slip gradually to a scattering. They are headed to the river which is the way escapees know not to go. The only way out is through the swamp—so he thought. But maybe they have something planned, something fixed. The guards haven't come after them, not yet anyway. Maybe Bill Francis paid in some way for a clear path and maybe the way downriver is open. Maybe a miracle has occurred. The moon shines through leafy trees spattering white on the ground. A large bird lifts from a branch and flaps ponderously away. It looks like no bird Delvin has ever seem, larger than a hawk or an owl. Maybe an eagle, he thinks. He is barefooted but nothing he steps on bothers him.

After a while he comes to the riverbank. Some of the men are just putting out in a little snub-nose boat. When he tries to get in, they push him away.

"We got too many already," a voice says, he thinks it comes from Artus Manigalt, one of the mill workers, a man from up north somewhere.

A large hand shoves him in the chest and he slips and falls into the water. The water feels good but he is suddenly—oddly—afraid of snakes. He almost laughs at this but the fear is real like a knife rasping on his skin. He ducks his head under to clear his thinking and to get a start on some cleanness and maybe to make himself all right about being scared; when he comes up the boat is sliding out into the current. One of the men has a paddle and he is trying to get one of the others to use it. The other man turns his face away and the first man hits him in the back of the head. Others grab him and there is a brief mute struggle and then somebody says, "You cotched him," and then there is quiet and then comes the soft, heavy splashing of a body let go of, and then paddling begins. Delvin's hand half rises, issuing a farewell, and suddenly it is like it was all those years before when the white boy cried out in the woods and he thought they had killed someone, how suddenly alone he'd felt. That was what they always wanted you to feel. And here it is with them now, with him—and he twirls around, reaching for something, a handhold he forgot he needed, and he feels a slick root and for a second it is the body of a snake and he prays as one would pray to an estranged brother on the road of darkness in the middle of the night—yes, he says, yes, it's all right, and he looks down into the water that purls softly against his legs, looks at moving blackness, and then he begins to move.

He makes his way stumbling along the riverbank through reeds and low bushes. Once again he's gotten himself into a futile situation, is what it looks like. But then it is where—for right now—he wants to be, not in futility but on the run from that black hole in the middle of a black hole. He sloshes through spindly maidencane and bulrushes and comes on a piece of forked log resting in the grass. He pushes this out into the river and climbs on top of it and lies down and paddles out into the current, and, scared and thinking how fine it is to be out beneath the star-spattered sky, guides it downstream.

Up ahead he sees the snub boat and then he loses it in the night haze and distance and rides quietly until maybe four or five miles on as they come down on the town he sees the boat again far ahead amid lights and what appear to be a string of boats. The boats have motors attached and when the white men in them see the little boat coming toward them they rev up and head toward it. The boys in the over-loaded escape boat try to paddle to shore but they don't have the power for it. The white men begin shooting even before they are close to the boat. By time they have gotten to it one of them shouts back that there aint anything in here to shoot at cause these niggers is all dead already.

Delvin comes right down on the guard boats. Before he gets there he slides off and stays low in the water, just touching the log enough to keep hold of it, and in this way drifts by the picket line of jailers and sheriff's deputies and local men both hired and freely come for action. For several minutes they are all around him, heavy shapes in dark clothes. One small boatload pushed by a little motor pokes at the log but Delvin has gone under and though he keeps his grip on the mossy skin they do not see him in the dark and the log turns in the current and is away downstream. Somebody fires a shot anyway and Delvin feels the bullet slap the heavy wood.

Then he is free of the boats and free of the lights and he travels along holding on to the log, trying to keep from falling asleep. He wants to let go and drift away but he catches himself. A barge stacked with cotton bales, pushed by a squat tug, chugs past and he hears the white men on it shouting at each other. It sounds as if they are having a fight. They curse, making threats; it is like hobo life, and thinking this his spirit wakens or shifts in a new way, or an old way recalled, and a sadness cuts into him. But there is happiness mixed with it, a sense of life going on in a world he is part of, not this world of battering and futility but the other—pinched as it is—smelling of churned water and living things moving through the air. It's natural to him and he realizes this, the world that can't really be taken away from him, no matter the prison they put him in. He watches the stacked bales disappear ahead and listens to the voices, rich with unimprisoned life—anger edging into sorrow and bafflement and an exculpatory meekness that touches him through his skin—fade into the night.

Lights, solitary and feeble, come and go along the black ribbon of the distant bank. Mostly the dark, entering into every crevice and over-

looked spot. All those wandering around by themselves in the dark, lying down in it in rooms and on riverbanks and in woods where the big brown owls speak their solemn questions. The professor said that entering each small town was like the Israelites coming out of the wilderness. It's not your light sets you free, he said, it's all those others. He decides to get in to shore. He is too tired to stay out in the water. But he doesn't have the strength to paddle in. All he can do is get up on the log. He does this and crams himself in the sunder and rides along on his back watching the stars as they wheel grandly down into the earth and then he slips into sleep and rides along dreaming lightly of a woman, whose name escapes him, holding in her hands a skein of flowering vine, and turns in sleep and slides into the water.

The cool water wakes him.

Already it is dawn. The river has widened out.

He is near the east bank, approaching a line of willow trees that drag their long slim fingers in the river. He paddles that way and catches onto the spindly trailing branches. Working hand by hand downstream he comes to an opening and pulls himself in to the bank. A stand of mallow bushes in full red bloom behind the willows. His heart beats hard and he raises his eyes and looks at the sky that is the color of blue-eyed grass. He eases off the log onto his knees and the ground seems to sag under him but maybe that is only him and he gets to his feet and at first hunched over then upright puts his footprints into slick black earth and staggers ashore. He stands there looking around and he doesn't know what to do next. The complicated green bushes all filled in, the red, loose-petaled flowers like gifts he maybe is supposed to take into his hands. I don't know. Then something comes to him. He backtracks and drags the log up the bank over the prints just in case he finds no place for himself on that side of the continent. Then he crawls up through the mallows to the grassy edge of a field spotted here and there with tall purple pokeweed and stands up, eyeballing the terrain: a fleshed-out hacked and vine-strewn world with no sign of a special prison other than the one that is everywhere. Hilly fields like bosoms lifting into the distance. He pushes back into the

mallow bushes, squirrels a place among the sour-smelling leaves, lies
down and falls asleep.

There was a time, the professor said—we all remember it in our bones
and in the stories we tell—when the gods spoke to human beings. When
God's voice came from bushes and streams and rocks and told human
beings what was so in the world and in themselves. Everybody was
able to hear and the gods spoke about this and that and maybe they
spoke too much and embarrassed themselves or maybe people just got
bored hearing some rock or snatch of poke salad yammering endlessly
about love trouble or tactics or what to eat for supper, but anyway the
gods began to go silent. One by one they dropped off until there was
no more talking from the celestial quarter. Then we felt our alone-
ness in the world. Then we got scared and started building forts and
piling up money and inventing artillery and we started shooting at
our neighbors and we were scared of anybody who didn't look like us
or act like us. It was time to call on the gods but when we did nobody
answered. We were on our own in a way that made expulsion from the
Garden look like a dropped piece of bubble gum. And it aint changed.
The silence—and you can believe it—is rock solid. The gods have de-
parted to other lands. We been left to make our own way to glory. And
truth is, few can do it. But that don't mean, the professor said, that we
got cause enough to stop trying.

Later in the day a small africano boy fishing the river for shell bass
comes on him but he is afraid to wake the ragged man and he runs
home to tell his folks. An hour or two later three africano men shaking
the bushes find him and after a short parley bring him to the home of
the little boy. A man in the four-room slabboard house is drunk and
laid out in the back room with pneumonia. He tried to treat himself
with jick whiskey bought for a half dollar over in Munn City and the
combo of the pneumonia and the whiskey is killing him. His brother,
who lives with the family, and his wife, who is the mother of one of

the brother's children, offer Delvin a seat at the table and they try to feed him but he is so worn out—he doesn't think he is really sick any-more, just tired to the bone—that he can hardly keep his head up. The brother offers him a drink of elderberry wine and he takes a sip to be polite but he doesn't want any of that really. He lips the glass vaguely and puts it down. The wine is purple and has black specks floating in it.

"If I could lay down," he says. They fix him a bed out on the screened-off half of the back porch and he lies down on an alfalfa-stuffed mattress and thinks This smells like the shed back home, and it isn't only that but he can't remember right then what it is and falls asleep. He dreams of fish thrashing feebly in a poke (but maybe it isn't fish), and of a white man in a leaf-strewn alley entrance making hobo signs (the double diamond of Keep Quiet; the two straight bars of Sky's the Limit; the triple thatch of Jail) and grinning in a scornful way. He is overtaken by a sobbing that seems wholly part of the dream until it wakes him and his cheeks are wet. He lies in the shade of the roof overhang, coming back mostly to himself. The little boy comes out to look at him. The boy smells of raisins and Delvin remembers sitting on the pantry floor at Mr. O's as a child eating raisins from a cloth sack with the picture of a raised-up circus elephant stamped on it. "My name," the boy says and points above his head at the wall. Scratched into the chinking mud are misspelled words, unintelligible signs—Morus, maybe that is a name. "Morris," Delvin says, and the boy smiles, whirls and runs back into the house. He feels slow and dodgy, without intent, saturated and feebly draining, raveled at the edges, parts coupled and strewn about, wayward. The air is coarse and lively against his skin. Raisins, he thinks. He used to pick them one at a time from the sack, eat them slowly, dreaming of life out in the wild mountains.

He stays with the family for a week until he feels the red dog loosen its grip and then he decides to leave because he wants to get down to the coast. The state men have poked around looking for him but when they

came by the folks hid him out in a canebrake under a tarp soaked in
tar wine vinegar and even the dogs missed him.

"No reason to go that way," the brother, a stringy man with a
small face flat like a cat's, tells him. "Aint nobody down that way looking to shelter a black man."

But Delvin wants to go. He has heard the surf crashing in his
dreams and in them he sits beside a great blue sea.

After much calling on the holy trinity and the blowing of milk
smoke into his mouth by a man who never saw his father, the placing
in his ear of a lock of hair from a child the same color as the sufferer,
the forcing of a cup of hot boiled and strained mule manure tea down
his throat, his chest painted with turpentine, and a bag of asafetida
from the mountains tied around his neck, the sick man dies choking
from the pneumonia. When Delvin looks in from the door he sees the
man's gray pinched cheeks and his nose like a stob and his eyes already sunk into the sockets like ball bearings dropped in mud and he
thinks here is something familiar but he doesn't go into the room. The
next morning they bury the man in a little africano cemetery down
the sand road a mile from the house. The cemetery is set off by itself
inside a low twisted stake fence at the edge of a pasture that has a
half dozen stringy cows in it. Delvin never mentions that he knows
something about preparing the dead. He doesn't mind fiddling with a
corpse but he doesn't anymore care for sticking himself into anybody's
grief. A stubbornness in his soul, a disheartened doggedness, maybe
a divination, some shaky repudiation of the former life, has taken
him. The wasted man drowned in his own spit, coughing and gasping
and squinting into corners for God or the devil or who knows what—
Jacob's ladder maybe to climb him out of that sticky place—and an
abrupt wild panic had come erasing the squint and then a blankness
erasing that and no god came.

The burying is on a sweltry day with a dampness attached
that makes him feel as if his blood is running hot in his veins. Everybody feels feverish. The body in its raw pine coffin held together
with nailed-on baffles stinks of the fever. Oscar is the man's name.
Somebody cries it out from the back of the small crowd, a woman no

one admits he knows. A bird in a maple tree makes little pip-pip-pip *noises. His brother, Oscar's brother, cries like a baby. Delvin has been on burial details at Acheron, silent pilgrimages where nobody spoke up about anything. A chaplain tossed a handful of dry words in after the deceased, this nonentity it was clear the Lord cared nothing about. The preacher here, a small man who smells like he has been drinking, says the Lord is already holding brother Oscar in his arms. "Not too tight," the man next to Delvin says. "It's hot where he is." Delvin shivers and wants to shut the man up but he says nothing. Not outloud. Farewell, brother, he says silently, God be with you, have a good . . . —and then the words drop off as if he's come to a cliff. But it aint no cliff. It is a dam. Behind which a slowly pulsing body of words is backed up, a lifetime—twenty lifetimes—of words and everything else. Somebody throws a bouquet of tea olive in the hole. Delvin can smell it above the stink of the corpse, a sweet drifting scent of the world going down into the ground with him. Tears come to his eyes and the woman next to him, wife of the brother, looks strangely at him, as if she has just realized who he is.*

Back at the house he tells them he needs to get farther south.

The brother—his name is Willie Drover—says, "Aint too much farther south you can get," and even one or two of the grieving women laugh at this.

"I got some business down on the Gulf," he says, thinking as he speaks the words that he is half lying because he doesn't really have any place to get to except away and that isn't a place unless every place not a state prison is.

But he doesn't mind being made fun of. He is rich—or half-rich—in his spirit on this side of life even if he is slow to rise and suspicious. He favors this walk-around and jump-down, linger-on-the-porch, eat-at-a-table-with-the-children-and-the-women, nobody-hanging-around-with-a-whip side of things. Let me stand and shiver and nobody but somebody worried momently for him might say anything. How you feeling? Well, I'm just fine. Even the big chinaberry tree out the window looks filled with a special life, the big clusters of purple flowers exuding sweet scent you could walk up and put your face in. The sunlight on the gray dirt road out the window seems to shine with a manifold potency. No whipping on that road, no pits to lie down in. He tells some of this to John Paul, Oscar's almost-grown son. John Paul says he doesn't know anybody who don't have a whipping in his future.

"Not like the kind I mean," Delvin says.

They sit beside a little feeder stream peeling birch twigs and looking at the tiny swirls the water makes where it catches against branches and bits of trailing leafage. The air smells of pine and some moldering bit of animal flesh that hasn't quite finished curing. The plan for a journey has come to Delvin. He wants to get out to the ocean and travel on it. "I'm going to make a big circle," he says.

"And come right back here?"

"Someday maybe, but that's not what I mean. A circle with a chunk left out of it. Or a squinched circle."

John Paul spreads one of his big hands. His knuckles look like scuff marks. "You gon be a traveling man?"

"For a while."

He wants to tell him about his plans for writing a book, but he hesitates. To say the words—he is afraid they'll curdle it. And hell—a book—he is just talking, just dreaming on his feet.

"I want to see something I hadn't ever seen before."

"You can see that right here. We just had a display there in the house."

"I'm sorry about that. I know how a passing can cut deep."

"Not too deep—not this one."

"Yeah, and I know you got a promising life here and all, but I'm thinking of my personal plans."

"Sure you are. I got plans too. Sometimes I can see em right out in front of me. At least up to a point."

That point being, so Delvin knew, the one where you give up because you have to admit to yourself that every day is going to be like the one you just finished. It is why things around here like weather and holidays and births and deaths and the mysteries of religion are so important. Harmless fun. Constant pressure from the white folks until you got to bust out. So you rob a store or kill somebody and here you go down into the hole. Big Broadus back at Burning Mountain said he ought to just settle down and do his time. Well, that is what everybody with sense or asleep out here is doing too. In him is something scratchy and moving. Good or bad he doesn't know. Something clucking at night or whispering to him or pleading. Maybe that is the way the gods have come back. The professor said conscience is as close as we get anymore to the gods. But in prison his conscience has become strained and elaborated with unusual amendments and declarations. He doesn't know anymore what kind of voice speaks to him. He can hardly sit here now with this farm boy talking. He wants to leap up and run off, just keep running.

"I think I want to move around for my whole life."

"I was in New Orleans once," John Paul says, "but it knocked me down and trampled on me. I was lucky to get back here with any hide left on my body."

"You didn't uncover anything you liked?"

"Sholly I did. That's what got me runned over." He scratches his temple with the end of a twig. "I guess after you sit in the jailhouse for a while even a section of dirt road with nobody on it starts to look good."

"I reckon."

"I don't want to get into no jailhouse."

"No you don't."

He doesn't either want to get in a jailhouse and feels the press and cluster of an excisement only partial, ragged in his body as he moves about the homestead. He is shy of the porch and the steps and the rooms filled with the smell of fatback and corn mush and the smells of women and he is shy in the yard where they have set out wild rose bushes in buckets and shy too even in the backhouse where an old Sears & Roebuck catalogue serves as paper. He sidles away, drifting along a line of diminishing notification, and finds a little spot among myrtle bushes back behind the house where he feels most safe and sits on the grass there thinking. He can think about anything and so he thinks of the Gulf and the wide world beyond it and he's done this before even *though the cons told him not to but this time it seems close enough to touch almost. Space. That's where they keep it. So get down to the Gulf. His heart beats faster than usual and he knows already his loneliness has extended out into the world, following him like a dog. It is still there. I am a common man, he thinks, and on this day I am free to walk around loose but I am still lonely and maybe there is no cure for it. He wonders what Milo is doing, if he is alive, and Ralph Curry and Peaches and Still Run Siems and Bony and Carl and the preacher and his minions. He leans over his knees with his hands gripped together as the worshippers do and says a few words about the wideness of the world and finding a place in it, just general commentary and wondering. He is still tired but a new energy has poked up in him like a fresh growth. He is tapping along like a blind man, looking for a way to open up. The sun streaks his shoulders with a softening light. He begins to cry and he lets himself go with this until he hears himself making noise and stops. He leans over his knees and presses his hands flat on the grass and holds them there like he is holding the world down. Or gripping it by the handle. Nobody comes along and tells him to move on.*

Two days later he catches a ride on a wagon heading down to Salt Town to pick up a load of oysters and fish. Every so often this run is made and the seafood brought back under croaker sacks piled with cracked ice to sell in the communities, white folks first. The bed of the wagon gleams with fish scales. The man who carries him, Billy Foster, wears a pair of washed-out overalls and a patched gray shirt buttoned at the wrist and all the way to the Gulf he talks mournfully about his wife who has recently taken up with another man. There are fish scales on his cracked boots and his small flat fingernails gleam like scales. He seems at every minute about to cry but he doesn't.

"You can't make em do what they won't," he says glumly, clucking at the hammer-headed mule over the cotton plowline he uses for reins.

The sky is cloudy for the ten miles down and as they arrive in Salt Town it begins softly to rain. Delvin bids the man farewell and walks along the sandy main road out to the beach that is gray and littered with pine straw and forbidden to a person of color and stands under the tall longleaf pines looking out at the chopped-up gray Gulf. The water seems to be moving steadily toward him and this bothers him and he retreats farther back among the trees. Three or four short roads run in from the main road to the water. A few white men are standing out in the low brown surf working a long net. He walks back closer to the waves, but not far, not even out from under the pines. He doesn't like the shaky look of the water, doesn't like how big and empty it is, and the white men spook him. Getting out into that world of salt and waves and white men pulling on nets like they think they are back on the shores of Galilee or someplace; it is too much for him. He'll just stand a while under these whishing pine trees, he thinks, and enjoy being a free man.

7

Gammon entered the visiting room that was only a squared-off bit of an old holding cell that had bars over a single taped-over window with one little corner scraped away so if you put your eye to it you could see across the street the corner of the Miller Finery sign and the screen-door entrance to the Collins Bakery and a set of cement steps leading where you couldn't tell, and told Delvin that he had found the woman he saw in the gallery and she said she was not his mother.

"Maybe she is lying to protect herself—and me."

"Maybe that is true," Gammon said, "but she says it isn't—I asked that too—and says that she dudn't want to come to the jail."

"Maybe I will just have to go see her," Delvin said and laughed a dry laugh. He could feel a mercilessness rising in his soul. Soul, he thought, I don't know what that is.

Gammon looked at him with mixed compassion and and aggravation and said he didn't think things were going very well.

"I thought it was your job to keep everything hopeful."

"Yes, that is what I am supposed to do and I am sorry I have failed."

"Don't worry your head with it," Delvin said. "I won't be long for this place whatever you do."

"I hope that dudn't mean you are going to try to escape."

"You are a foolish person," Delvin said without heat. He felt things flattening out, sliding away. He knew his mother was gone, but just one little (maybe) glimpse and it was as if she was back. Something peeled off in his heart. He grimaced.

"It's not cause of you," Gammon said.

"What's that?" Delvin said, startled.

"The trial."

"I sho didn't help the truth along though."

"Truth's a stone these folks don't want to swallow."

"It was just so clear to me that we done nothing. And before I could say a word the bottom fell out."

"Nothing you could do really."

"I might as well have just got up and danced and capered."

He wanted the boy to shut up, stop talking so much.

"The truth," he said, "no matter what they do with it, is now in the court record. That's a good thing."

"Yeah. For the historians."

The boy was smart and he knew the story but he hadn't been able to tell it. Like all of them he didn't believe what was happening to him. Three hundred years of teaching, and they still didn't get it.

"We'll do all right."

"Yes, a foolish person," Delvin said, smiling a plain, uninflected smile. In his mind he said *Let them be brought before me: I will deny every one*. He didn't know what this meant or where the words came from. Back in his cell later he whispered the words again: *I will deny every one of them*.

Billy Gammon returned to his three-dollar-a-night hotel room and lay on his bed. He had spoken to Miss Ellen Bayride from Birmingham that night and she had looked at him as if he had got some black on him. That was what happened to lawyers who put up a rigorous defense for negro men. Such negro men as this. Well, that part of it was all right. But he was sorry she felt that way, disappointed, and dismal. He pictured her walking to her house where she stayed with her aunt, Mrs. Walter Shrove, after sending her story by wire to the paper in the capital. She would sit in the kitchen eating supper and talking about the WCU with her aunt. Her aunt was a big wheel in the WCU, the Baptist women were the ones, so they claimed, who really ran the state. This was probably true, he thought. They are the ones who want most to keep the colored folks from getting ahead. Ahead they turn around and start rustling the women. Would they think that was bad or secretly good? Jesus, he thought, sat up and poured himself a drink. He wished he was a man of heroic character. He was not, he knew that. If you put your heart into it you are going to get a chance to see what you are really made of. So said his uncle Henry who had contributed to his raising, overcontributed. He had stood outside the telegraph office looking at her through the dusty picture window as she sent her story off to the capital. In the dust with his finger he wrote *I am what you don't think I am* and she had turned around and seen the words—written backwards in the white dust—and acted as if she didn't see them and went back to speaking to the clerk and after a while he had walked away.

Slippery, bendable stuff, that's me, he thought, and plumped his pillow and lay looking up at the ceiling.

Delvin sat all night on the floor of the holding cell pressing his back against the tin-sheathed wall, falling asleep and waking in a start, coming out of sleep like coming out of a fit, only quieter. He imagined he could press right through the metal and timber and brick and bust out into the night. *Everything's already moved off and left me*, he thought. And he thought *I got one dip and that's it,* and a heavy pain entered his body and he lay on his side thinking where are they?—who are they and where are they?—remembering the time in Jackson, Mississippi, when he rode in a cab for the only time in his life, hurrying to the hospital where the professor had gone when he thought he was having a heart attack. He wasn't but they had him in bed in the colored ward and he was sitting up looking out the window. Just now, he said, I saw a man try to hand a sandwich to a squirrel. He was smiling and the smile was held close to himself, a personal smile he had for his own private joys. *I got to get me one of those smiles*, Delvin had thought. He told the professor about riding in the cab that smelled of hair preparation and the window handle didn't work but was choice anyway, but the professor wasn't paying attention. *I couldn't get my story across to him then either.* The professor had a better one. But he knew he had stories inside him that were like silver fish swimming in fresh cool water. I got to keep em alive, he thought. Don't let time to come chisel down and take em. Maybe, he thought, maybe he could do that, maybe not. Bonette and Little Buster Wayfield whimpered in their bunks. That was all right. Carl slept soundly, emitting little puffy snores that sounded like rain falling softly on the plank floor. These boys he didn't even know really. Chattanooga boys he would probably never even have talked to, n'ar would they have talked to him. He leaned his head back and pictured riding on a train to Celia's house. His mother was there waiting for him too. And maybe his father who he couldn't picture from life but looked, so his mother had told him once, like a photograph of John Wilkes Booth, except he was colored. He had been embarrassed to tell anybody that his father looked like President Lincoln's assassin. But he would write it down in his book. The night lay its hand on him like an ordination, he didn't know for what salvation, and pressed him down into sleep. In a dream he saw his father, and his father was bending down to look at his face in the smooth surface of a stream, only there was no reflection. He tried to get out of the dream and thought he woke but he didn't, not yet, but he didn't remember what came after except it was too dark.

As he settled onto the board seat in the enclosed back of the state truck carrying them to Burning Mountain penitentiary, Delvin tried to picture what he was missing out on that day but he got only as far as rice pudding and the copy of Joe Bakerfield's Boston speeches that he'd left in the professor's truck.

I'm just a sweetback, he told himself, which was what they called those just sampling the hobo life, passing by on the cob.

His first escape attempt would not be his last; he had promised himself that.

Beside him Bony wept steadily, like a tiny seep. He had cried all night in his sleep and he was crying when he woke up. He leaned against Delvin and from time to time Delvin put his hand on his shoulder. Bony had pissed his pants when the pharmacy clerk jury

foreman Bivins, with the warrant held up in both bony hands, had
read the verdict in his cramped and wheezy voice.

*All you bastards, you menless men, you hopeless negroes, are sen-
tenced to forced familiarity and slave labor and a stab in the eye. You
are all condemned to hell.*

So this is where you keep it, Delvin thought when he heard the
man read the sentence. He hadn't expected anything different but
still he was shocked. You think somebody's going to wake up, some
bit of religion or hope or human reason or kindness is going to kick
in, but then it doesn't and you stop thinking that. His knees had
wobbled. He'd thought he was going to vomit and he swallowed back
down a mouthful of bitter juice. Rollie had cried out and behind
them in the balcony reserved for colored a few women had shouted
out—not his mother—and a few had called for Jesus or Mary or
Elijah. The judge told them to shut up. He had no kindness in him,
this judge. "We will appeal," Billy Gammon had whispered to him.
"Don't worry."

But then the road of your life forked and you were being dragged
down the dark one. For the rest of my life I'm going to be trying
to get out of something. Everybody had lied. The white boys, the
women, the doctors, even two of the boys in his gang. It wasn't a
gang, but two of them, Bony and Little Buster, had begun to believe
they had assaulted the women. On the stand, squirming in the big
brown chair, they had said they might have broke in—Little Buster
said it and Bony confirmed—on those two women.

Suddenly the whirlwind dips down, picks you up and throws
you against the rocks. No wonder all those women cry out in church.
Where do you turn then?

Well, you sit down here and you start thinking how you are going
to get loose.

Running is all he thinks about. He thought about it on the truck
ride carrying him fully sentenced into the heart—no, the liver, no,
the excremental bowels—of Dixie, and he thinks about it as the gray-

suited guards walk them through the wire gantlet to the back of the
Burning Mountain prison where there is a cleared space behind the
big mess hall that stinks of stew beans and carbolic acid and march
them up a flight of steel steps and in through a door above which
is a sign that says WELCOME TO YOUR BURNING MOUNTAIN HOME
and lock them inside where the concrete walls have sweated through
and the place clangs and bellows with blows flung against metal and
stone and they are welcomed by no one. And he thinks about it when
they make them strip and place their hands against the wet stone wall
and spread their legs and he feels the probe of a round-headed stick
up his ass and then they make them shuffle into the dip pool where
a mixture smelling of kerosene and sulfur and some other foul substance kills the lice and and all traces of civilized life so they come
out burning with their new skin (that is still black) and are hustled
to the showers where the water stings like acid—even then, among
the piercing proofs of grief, he thinks of how to break free; and he
thinks of jumping as he walks to the holding tank, where Butter gets
in a fight with Rollie Gregory and almost chokes him to death; and
later on that afternoon in his cell, which holds three men who are not
happy to see him though they are curious and they touch and pat
him and pump his muscles like stringy lions testing the new calf—
they consider him a fool and causer of trouble for negroes in general
because he raped those white women; and he thinks about it the first
night as he crams the end of his wool blanket into his mouth to stifle
his cries.

Every day in Burning Mountain prison he thinks of how to get
out and joins a group that fashions shanks of sufficient quality and
plans to perforate the guards—as Ricey Fleming put it—and flee
from the cotton fields into Big Panther woods. He never has a shank
in his hand but when the time comes he runs as hard as he can, a fleet
boy with thin hard calves and narrow hips, and reaches the woods
where he wanders around for four days before they find him hiding
in an earth cave below a big chestnut tree blown down in a cyclone
the year before. He is dirty and hungry and bitten by deerflies and
after they keep him for a day and a half chained to an iron hoop

jammed into the red dirt in front of the metal shop he is thrown into and left lying on his belly in the Wire Room which is a cage out in the exercise yard open to weather and to the gaze and taunts of the inmates. He remains there for a month like a half-habitated carcass under fall storms and drying spells swirled about with the rich alluvial dust of the fields and environs, crouched for a time like a cat waiting to spring away, then sprawling, attempting to tell himself stories that he half makes up about traveling into a strange country by boxcar train. *The woods a distant slum of leaves*, he says, *untended quarter of loneliness and peril.* He dreams of banditries worked on his close person and aches in the dreams for the touch of a woman whom he never knows, never can even see—she isn't Celia—but one who speaks in the hollow, coughing voices of animals penned up for life. On the afternoon they come to get him again he is standing like a soldier facing the wire, seeing if he can with his mind lift himself to the other side of the prison wall. "Thought I'd go get a Orange Crush," he says when somebody asks him about it.

They put him with the death row prisoners and he doesn't get off his cellblock again for two years, except for the afternoon escape trial conducted at the prison where ten years are added to his life sentence, until he goes before a judge—a new one—for a new (same old rape) trial in which the witnesses are a little more shaky this time and the prosecutors just a little more tired.

Like leaves falling from the tree of knowledge, the group, the old KO Boys, sheds members. The years knead them, cuff them, crease their backs, spit into the open pit of their skulls, and let them go. Bonette and Butter Beecham are released—called too incapacious to perform the acts they were accused of. They weep with their faces on the table. When Butter raises his head, Delvin sees a man blind with joy and relief, and he thinks he will be sick from despair. The letter he gets from Butter (penned by his aunt in florid, looping script) thanking him for his care of him during their time together is like a trick that nearly drives him to kill himself. Placer Wilkes gives him a little triangular piece of glass in the exercise yard to do it with. The shard is cloudy green like runoff water and brings back the memory of Jim's Gully in Chattanooga, the one separating the negro life of Red Row from the whites. The only private prisonwise place is his bed, and late in October he lies in the half light under the thin covers, drawing the glass across his throat. Humped under the blanket like a jackoff artist sunk in a dim wretchedness and ignorance, he feels like a fool. A shaky, choked, exasperated laugh catches in his mouth. He wants to explain himself. A fly has gotten in under the blanket with him. He can feel it crawling on his back. Explain? *It's a burning palsy*, he says silently. He probes with the glass. Where does this instrument come from? From under the earth maybe, incised by an ocean turning and forgetting. He can smell the water in the stone walls. He can hear distant cries, men calling out under the weight of smothering dreams. He curls up tight and a little at a time lets himself go into tears, stopping and starting, catching himself each time just before falling over the brink. For a second he loses hold, grabs himself back, jabbing the point of the glass against his forehead. This scares him, but not badly, not enough to change how he thinks. There are tears on his face. He scrapes them off with the flat of the glass. Slowly he comes back around. The fly has crawled down to his waist and he tries to trap it there but it gets away.

The next day he returns the shard to Placer who loses it in a game of two punch to a man who breaks it against a bone in his hip trying to stab a vein. "He never meant to go tits up either," Placer says, disgusted.

On a sunny morning in late September when the cattails in the road ditches are starting to fray Delvin and three of the leftover KO Boys are shipped to Uniball, a brick and wire stronghold out in the western part of the state, and there, a month later, Delvin is raped for the first time. The rapist, a metal worker from Missouri named Big Cordell Owlsley, decided Delvin was his kind of boy, and one afternoon in bleak weather he shoves him against a stack of wet lumber and holds him there while Delvin tries to knock his hand away and can't. God save me, he silently says. They are in the shadows in back of the carpentry shop where nobody can see them except those who could spy on them from the slit windows of their cells. It is a show. The lumber has a sour smell. My stage, Delvin thinks, pitying himself and angry. Cordell spins him around and pins him against the raw boards and holds him until he stops squirming. The big man wants first to get across to him that Delvin is not strong or able and he does this. He pulls Delvin's stripes down, and as he does so Delvin recalls somebody doing this years ago when he was a child in the foundling home and he feels now as he did then, helpless and brokenhearted. It is near dark, fall going on wintertime, and cold on his bare ass and the wood is wet against his thighs and he thinks *I got to dry off* and he says this like a prayer but the man pays no mind. Big C's stiff wrinkled penis bangs against him, knocking on the door that he forces open, lifting as he does so. He's smeared grease on himself that he got from a thick streak on the leg of his uniform. Searing pain skeets up into Delvin's chest and down his legs and then, like a wave, slackens and he can feel it rolling back in a slow decline that becomes more fantastical and sustaining as it goes. He leans forward against the wood and the hardness and sourness of the logs do not bother him so much. A humid disgust rolls sloppily through him. Then he presses back hard against the man's belly that he can feel jamming his spine and this is fantastical too, impossible to believe and some-how encouraging, and for a second he feels safe and without much to care about and then the humiliation and the shame build a putrid radiance and he knows himself hopeless and desolate like a child hurled down into muddy water, except more helpless and smaller than a child, and he wishes the man would go ahead and kill him.

In a few seconds Big Cordell is through. He turns Delvin around and embraces him and leans with him against the sour lumber so their two bodies are heaped together like spillage left over from a botched organic process, some feral disaster and murderous unox-idized carnage, something done now for good, and then as Cordell gets his strength back he cuffs him in the temple with the heel of his hand and tells him he is lucky not to be dead.

"Yeah, dead," Delvin wheezes and Big C cuffs him again.

Everybody who didn't see it says he did and they are all for it, or close to all because they knew what was up when they saw it. The three KO boys who came with him to Uniball look pityingly at him, scared near witless, he thinks, and one, Carl Crawford, mocks him to his face. For three days he walks with a limp and then for some reason extends it in duration until he becomes known for his limp, a made-up thing, something private to himself no one else knows the truth of. Shame turns his face at first and he knows he is hurt deep and this shakes him but in prison each day is the same, you can count on that and he begins to merge with the sameness, the eat and sleep and work of it and the walk and the muttering and the lights on all the time and nobody your brother but everybody your kin and he returns slowly to himself despite the shame. Nobody cares how he feels about it and he waits for that time to come for him too.

The curtain raiser rape is the initiation. Tidal, hurried at first then less so, the ushering frenzy never quite gone from it, the drear and loneliness underneath it not ever quite obscured, the sense he gets not of endearment or even of partnership maintained like a necessary toll, the distancing, the forsaken man standing in rain at the edge of a muddy field part of it, a regular feature, still times come when he reaches back and strokes the man's sleek body. Occasionally Big C pulls him around so he faces him. He holds his forearm over Delvin's eyes. "Got me some," he says, maybe those words or others drowned in the corrosions of his own energy, but mostly there are no features at all beyond the squeak and slap of flesh and his greedy eyes looking. "You get out of here," Big C says when it is over and pulls him back and kisses him sloppily on the mouth and then half throws him away. He wants Delvin ripely and keeps him handy like a ripped-away branch stuck in a bucket of water, until one day Delvin, grown stronger, sprouts, coming into himself fully despite delays, more steely in his mind, and without caring much about what happens, turns suddenly in the big man's arms and batters his skull half in with a piece of angle iron.

He leaves him lying evermore only partially alive, in a pile of wooden boxes used to ship the fruitcakes the prison bakery is famous for.

Everybody sees that too.

And he knows after they don't come for him that he'll be left alone now to walk the halls and climb and descend the steel stairs and go out the big double doors to the trucks and ride to the fields and bend his back over a hoe or drag a sack or pile the cotton in the cotton house or into the wagons for the mules to haul to the gin and he will get to eat his meals in peace and sit on his bunk scribbling into his little torn notebook (*sky like a dense gray blanket*; *somebody left a scrap of pink ribbon tied to a gallberry branch*; *for ten days the water has tasted of sulfur*) and time with him in it will pass until he can run again.

It isn't long before he finds a sweet boy of his own. Gal boy. Frankie Overstreet, from Caning Bay, Louisiana, a strong boy who is steady and can take direction. Together they work on the next escape, which means nothing more than on Juneteenth afternoon while the cicadas shrill in the hard maple trees the two of them walk away from the work gang sent out in the aftermath of the Tull river flood. They are cutting brush and pulling it away from a two-story house that floated off its foundation and across a field into a slough behind the Mercantile Appliance factory outside Covington when Delvin, followed by Frankie, steps off a thigh-sized maple limb into a second-floor bedroom, walks through the open bedroom doorway, along the hall and down the stairs, through the living room and out an unwatched west-facing window on the other side and slips into the woods.

He is gone this time for three days shy of a month. During this time Frankie leaves on a truck hauling oysters to Texas.

In New Orleans a waitress he meets puts him up in her cottage in the sixth ward, where he gets a job washing dishes at the Empire restaurant, famous for redfish stew and an étouffée made with six kinds of seafood all caught locally. It is there that a vacationing prison guard named Elder Watkins spots him. Watkins doesn't at first recognize Delvin, but then on his way back to town, where his wife and brother wait in a French Quarter hotel, he becomes convinced that the scowling boy he glimpsed through the open kitchen door was none other than the escapee Delvin Walker, had to be. He stops in a rain squall with water dripping down his neck to use a police call box on Charles street that his brother, a New Orleans cop on furlough for taking kickbacks from restaurants such as the Empire, has lent him his key to and asks for help.

The nearest station house sends two cars and the cops capture Delvin who has not noticed Watkins; he is sitting on the steps out back, eating a bowl of crab stew and drinking from a bottle of Cuban rum with some of the busboys and the waitress Corleen Bell, who's been soaking the male influence out of his body for the past two weeks, and he thinks he is, if not safe, free, and is beginning to feel comfortable at Corleen's house, where as soon as he gets a little ahead he is planning to start his book of factual experience that he is calling at this time *Layaway Dixie*.

The cops come trotting down the fly space between the restaurant and the Pearl Box Factory fence on the other side and scoop Delvin up before he hardly knows what is happening. As they begin to beat him, he says calmly, "I am all right about going with you." He says this three or four times before they knock him senseless.

Concussed, his left arm (the stronger one) broken, he is carried across state lines back to Uniball, where the arm is splinted using untreated pine flats and he is ushered into the disposal cell, one of several rooms in the basement under the former gymnasium from when Uniball was a private school for the wayward sons of rich planters. These rooms that were once storage bins have been enclosed and set with stout cross-braced metal doors, new this year, painted yellow.

Delvin is flung into the second bin from the right as you look down the hall. The throw half unsets his arm, a problem he is forced to correct on his own, which he does with his right hand pushing his back hard against the mortar wall to try to counterbalance the stabbing pain.

He screams, but then who, thrown battered and broken-armed

into moldy darkness, does not scream from time to time? The guards ignore him.

It is here he discovers that his spirit has the kind of amplification and reaching toward far places that allows him to lie still while snakes crawl over him.

Ginny Galled, you might say—a negro name, Ginny Gall, for the hell beyond hell, hell's hell—he begins to tell himself his book.

. . . born on the back steps of a sporting girl's house in Chattanooga and from there travels a crooked way through the cobbled streets of that town and into the woods and back to the visiting circus and then to the undertaker's house where as a six-year-old boy he liked to sit on the back of the hairy-footed dray horse Old Bob. The horse was so wide he believed he could sleep on his back, get a mattress and blanket and move onto him. He asked Mr. Oliver if he could and Mr. O laughed his high sweet laugh and said why sholy you can my boy and it wasn't until they caught him dragging the mattress from his little sleigh bed out the back door that he was stopped from trying. "But you told me," he said to Mr. O as tears streamed down his face. "Yes, I did, and I was wrong to tell you you could do something that I couldn't really let you do." Mr. O was tangled up. "I'll have to keep an eye on myself from now on," he said. "I'll keep an eye on you too," the little boy said. Mr. O said, "I'm sorry, Slip," which was what he was called around the house in those days.

When the trap in his cell door opens and his two pails are handed out to the guard and in a minute the door opens again and in are shoved two fresh buckets, one an empty slop pail and the other his week's worth of what the underground population calls cinder soup, with a chunk of cornbread so hard it has sunk to the bottom without soaking any juice in, he is barely interrupted, even in his thoughts, or especially in his thoughts.

He continues his story. In it he lists the different local bugs and green fruits he ate as a child, including red and black ants, doodlebugs, bees, dirt dobbers, beetles of various kinds, four types of grasshoppers, worms, all raw; among the fruits he ate: green plums, blackberries and raspberries, cherries, apples, grapes, quinces and figs. He lies quietly on his wood bunk trying to think of others. He sees his name written high on the wall of his bedroom where he climbed up a stepladder to scrawl it, using one of Mr. O's mascara pens from the preparation room down in the basement.

The story goes uninterruptedly on.

He begins to say parts of it over to himself until they fill his memory.

The first line of the book is *I waked to the sight of a woman wildly dancing.* He says this sentence over to himself, and all the sentences that follow, until they are carved into his brain sentence after sentence and he has memorized a first chapter. The work is both exhilarating and tedious, and there begin to be times when what he says outloud is not strictly true. He didn't really chase Jack Elbert down the alley and leg-swipe him so he fell into the barrel of an old washing machine and broke his left ankle. It didn't happen like that. Nor did old Mr. Anse Carter say he, Delvin, was bound for the hangman's noose. He said the Ghost was.

He goes over these parts of the story and corrects them and then changes them again, just slightly. He can't stay away from the little changes that seem to brighten things.

He grows confused and loses his place.

He stops telling the book for a day and lies on his back, sleeping and thinking and listening to the scurrying of the rats, and realizes finally that something is breaking apart inside him. He begins to weep. For a week he cries, waking each day in the slush of himself and turning on his side and weeping, letting the tears run down his face and drop onto the packed dirt.

He thinks, well, I can maybe get to the other side of this bawling, but then his thoughts cut back to his mother and his phantom father and Mr. O and the professor in his truck and Celia—and Celia—everything becomes elaborated and tricked out with grief.

When the tears finally stop he is not redeemed or relieved or free in any way he can figure, he is only exhausted.

Above his head the heavy wooden floorboards of the kitchen creak as the cooks walk back and forth. "Yall need to go off and take *lessons*," he cries. A muffled curse comes back. A guard he doesn't know unlocks the door, steps in and punches him in the face. "You think that hurt?" Delvin says and licks the blood off his lips. The guard has already stepped back out into the corridor.

Sometimes in his dreams he smells horses. Sometimes in his dreams his mother squats alone beside a small night fire in woods so vast all the sound is lost in them. He wakes crying.

Noises are coming out of his mouth. The noises are unfamiliar and have a grouchy, splintery quality that scares him. It is as if some old man with bad intentions is speaking from his head. He turns on his side and tries to remember the time Mr. Oliver took him fishing. They both slipped on a blue clay bank and fell into the little pond out on Hazel Burch's farm and scared the ducks, and a big drake came after them and scared them both. The noises are wheezing and snorting now, and he thinks, well I am a madman. He loses track after that of how things are with him, but one day the door opens wide and two men drag him out and he is carried to the infirmary and flung down onto a bed.

This is his first bout with malaria; the red dog nearly kills him.

He shakes and rattles all the way down to his most minor bones and hallucinates that he is boarding a big silver airplane bound for the rice paddies of China and he shouts out against this because he knows this is a white man's trick to sell him back into slavery. Celia speaks from out of a pink silk scarf wrapped like a burnoose around her face and says he will never get to the woods. He cries in his bed and it takes another ten days to come back to himself and when he does he is chastened and meek and unpitied by anyone.

When he is returned to his rack on Block 5 he finds his notebooks have been confiscated.

He is put on kitchen duty washing pots, and though the hot sink is extra hot in the heat of summer he is glad to be able to feel this double accumulation and begins to get well in spirit. He has never minded washing things. In sinks or creeks or road ditches or big-bellied washing machines that danced around the floor, him gripping the handle of the mangle, wringing water out of some blue shirt or pair of stempipe trousers, he has never minded the work of getting what was dirty clean. From time to time he stomps on the floor to let whoever is down below know that he is not alone. "We done cotched ye," he says out loud, his voice taking on the phraseology of a blackness he never practiced back at the Home.

It is thirteen months before he escapes again, and this time he unscrews the chain traces off his mule and gallops him across a mile of cotton fields and down into Regret Swamp where, exhausted and oddly fretful, he is taken in by a couple of poachers who after he falls asleep in a foul-smelling birchwood bed turn him in for the standard reward of twenty dollars a head for escaped prisoners.

He is on his way back to the underground bin at the same time his lawyers, Gammon and his crew, get him another trial, and he is transferred to the capital, where his trial takes place starting on May 2, 1937. The lies are flaking from the stories, but there are many stories and they have been told by every white person connected with the accusations and so take some time to shuck off.

This particular go-round the slight woman Hazel Fran, grown more slight since 1931, is unsure if she was actually raped and is now unable to identify the attackers except for Delvin and Carl Crawford who she still thinks might have assaulted her, *I'm not absolutely sure, Judge, Your Honor, but I think they were there at the time.* The other woman, Lucille Blaine, whom everyone in the courtroom—including such juried-up Kluxers as Clifford Bumper, Carlton Fuchs, Brother Wren and two others who have participated in lynchings plural and attended half a dozen more, all of which they considered justified, necessary, even righteous—know to be a liar, sticks to her story. She is an indissoluble lump of solid rage, in person.

The doctor, Mills, has a shamed look on his face as he once again sets out the medical proof of male violation.

Gammon presents a witness who says he had sex with Miss Blaine the morning before she was supposedly raped in the afternoon.

Miss Blaine sits at the prosecution table, heavy and menacing, her tongue stuck half out of her mouth. She flings curses at the defense witnesses. The judge, a middle-sized man with a homely, unoffending face, has to admonish her. She accuses the judge of being a nigger lover and has to be escorted briefly from the courtroom and taken to a windowless waiting room where a woman bailiff smirkingly tells her she doesn't want to go to jail herself for something it's only a nigra's doing, honey.

Everybody senses the sadness and despair fuming around her like a cloud of bottleflies as she passes by but nobody calls it that.

Every human being, so the story goes, has to find something to believe in, to base his ridiculous hopes on, and she has found this.

Delvin does not account particularly well for himself. Already bearer of an extended sentence (escape fiend), he has lapses during which he forgets the order of things and thinks this is the second trial and then for a sec thinks he is sitting in the cab of the van, debating with the professor the true facts of the slave revolt in Haiti, and then suddenly he is snatched up by a rage that according to the *Capital City Observer* seems to fill him like a gust of hot wind fills a sail and he lets loose with a gusher of vituperation aimed at the state judicial system and the state itself ("impoverished, derelict agency of numbskullery and perversion"), including every soul in said state, though those accusing him of these crimes, so the paper points out, are all natives of other states, including not only the accused's home state of Tennessee but such northern states as Ohio and New York. Gammon has allowed him to be put up for cross-examination and he does no better, really, at the hands of the state prosecutor. He does get across to the jury that he believes himself to be falsely accused, but that is pretty much the limit of it.

• • •

By this time the state is becoming embarrassed by the whole confabulation. The first two trials were hot topics in the national media.
The state, which already considers itself put upon and misused as
all get-out, is now presented in an even more unfavorable light. The
nativeborn, who think of themselves—white folk, that is—as among
the most accommodating and generous human beings on earth, are
scalded by the adverse publicity. Dolts, bigots, murderers, inces-
ters, juicers, addled row runners, slew-footed cretins and nutcases,
nightcrawlers, dusters, general miscreants and shovel-faced fools,
showoffs, clods, shitheads—utter assholes—are some of the terms
used against them.

But if they have never grown used to such, they are prepared.
Ever since things first began to go badly with the cheap labor business, the locals learned to fling back what was flung at them. They
are beginning in this instance to grow tired of the acidic innuendoes
and outright slanders. This crazy nigra and all those other crazy
nigras have caused them more trouble really than they are worth,
or than standing them straight up by way of a profound lesson in
how to behave is. Men lying in their beds under window fans sucking in the scents of yellow jasmine, fertilizer, spun cotton and Bull
Durham tobacco smoke feel in their deepest recesses the faint but
insistent pressure of a misused people rising. The powers of custom
and church-sponsored reason are all that hold back a tide of despair
that otherwise would swamp these men and drive them to wild futile
acts. But they—like everybody—have to find a way to go on without
befouling themselves, or at least without making it look as if they did.

Out beyond the tiny zone of actuality, the meaty core of fact from
which they receive their instructions to do what is necessary to stay
alive on earth (no matter what), pressed and marbled with the sweet
fat of love for those children whose lives are being cut down at the
root by falseness, beyond this supersaturated mix of divisible reali-
ties, they experience, as always, the need to hold to a position that is
imperishable. Only such a position will allow them to take a break

and start to get some fun out of life. That's what, goddammit, this routine with these grassy coons is about, they say.

"Everybody down here thinks he is right," Gammon says, pulling on his cigar. "He is too scared not to think it.

"Movement, that is the sine qua non of this universe," Gammon says. "Keep it moving." He has developed motes in his right eye and though the doctor assures him they are harmless, they scare him. "What is wrong with this malefactorous boys of Klaudio, this KO Boys thing, is it has stopped moving. Everything living that can still twitch is bailing out of that ratless grounded ship." He has haplessly married a game-legged woman from the capital whose family owns a string of peanut mills in four states and who wants him to give up the law and go traveling with her. "The prosecutors want to live happily. The juries, the judges, the defense lawyers, the uncoddled and spiritually mutilated accused—they want to live happily. Even the white boys who got their asses kicked. Even the two *violated* women. Or even one of them." He has promised his wife he will retire from the law in the spring. "There is still a woman," he says, "this adiposal Cypriot from Chattanooga, Tennessee, and points north and south, who holds to her story that Delvin Walker and Carl Crawford and Little Buster Wayfield, among others, committed the crime of rape on her body and must be punished for it."

He looks heavily at his listeners, a couple of beat reporters plus loafers and afternoon drinkers and ex-preachers—the common habitues of the Constitution Bar on State street. He wishes he was singing Schubert lieder in a choir. He signals the barkeep for another.

"The exasperated gents sitting at their restaurant tables ordering without menu or leaning back in Adirondack chairs under the scuppernong arbor drowsy with the heavy wine of ripe grapes and the soothing hum of honeybees, or jumping from a third-story window to escape the Meredith Hotel fire on Custom street, or sitting on a doughnut cushion to ease their hemorrhoids at the Melody mule and horse auction in Loris, or watching their young daughters dive from the ten-foot board into the clear green waters of Aucilla Springs, or walking or fighting or sleeping or arguing with an associate or straining on the crapper or praying or whining or crying out to God or cursing the day they were born—these men, who by circumstance or personal effort have become embroiled in this calamity, cannot quite get this dear woman, lying snoring on her back, I expect, as we speak, through the balmy hours of a late spring Saturday morning, say—have not been able to prevail, or suggest with enough persuasiveness, or lean against with appropriate gesturing, or outwait or outwit, to retrieve from her a recantation that would set them free.

"This is a true story," he says, sipping assertively from his iced whiskey. "Of course it is human nature to buy into positions that claim the means to solve problems of assault against the well-being of the one buying. So there are those deeply disposed to carry the hurt forth and onward."

His listeners have mostly turned away.

Gammon knows that later in the afternoon about dusk, even drunk, he will begin to wish he was dead. It is something he has almost grown used to.

These are some of the factors Delvin struggles against at this time.

The latest trial, its facts rubbed, squeezed and twisted to produce enough juice to quench the mortal thirst of its participants, lurches wheezing to its end. Coover Broadfoot's sentence is reduced to three more years, to be served in the restful conditions of Burning Mountain prison. Bony, who has shanked his cellmate, and Delvin Walker, the chosen, will go on as if these extra trials haven't happened. Delvin is not however returned to Uniball, where he would be thrust back into his punishment conditions, but sent onward like a dupe in a prank to the next skookum house on the list of houses for Uniball troublemakers, down on the Salt Plateau in the middle of the state.

After a few years in the soppy heat—after another trial in which the by-now-wobbling parties, as the day fades to sunset, fight like weary and desperate, numbed and baffled dogs—he is shunted on to Acheron, a raw spot in the woods in the southern regions.

From there he has just now escaped.

He sits hunched against his knees, looking out at the slowly flopping meager surf. The inshore water is the color of weak coffee and the combs of the surf too are stained a faded brown. Down the beach the blackened stumps of stubbed-off trees protrude from the gray sand. Through a thin rain he can see woody islands out in the bay. He looks up at the tops of the tall pines stirring faintly in breeze. The rain falls softly. It is mild, soothing; weather without malice. A freeboard rain. He has come a long way and he has a long way to go. But for this moment there is nothing but easily drawn breaths. He wishes Mr. Oliver was here and the Ghost and Polly and Elmer the assistant and Mrs. Parker and everybody from those days. Wherever they are, pressed down by life or sweating over some difficult task or running for their lives in a dream, let them step aside for a time and come sit on this sandy beach and rest.

He pushes up to his feet and takes a few small steps. He feels like a child, a lopsided novice, manhandled into the world. They said back in Chat-town that he was a zigzag baby. Zigzag by way of his irregular birth, by way of his wayward mother, needing all the luck he could get from the caul. They would say now that the zag had put him in prison and sent his life off into the briars. But here he is. For a moment he is here, free under these big pine trees. The wind soughs and shudders, a mild wind bringing with it hints and foretelling. He dances a few steps, swinging his shoulders, bending down, straightening his back as he moves. Under the hard hand a life moves. *Somebody wrote those words and he read them. Words come all the way from some room in some city up north, some dreamer sitting alone at a table, who drew them off the reels of mystery and power in himself.*

He scoops up a handful of beach sand, lets it pour through his fin-

gers. *The sand is soft, mixed in its coloring like something halfway between dirt and sand. With his gritty fingers he dabs his forehead. He knows he no longer looks as young as he is. He's seen men in prison who look like Methuselah. A sadness, his own, the one he located early, pushes in among the hopefulness. A mournfulness—the miseries they call it in Chattanooga. Chat-town. Where people come and go. He wants to go back there, slip through like a will o' the wisp, touch down here and there. Then he'll see.*

He lies back and listens to the surf lightly flop and sizzle, the brown Gulf water sliding up and sinking back again.

BOOK FOUR

1

He walked east on the Old Spanish Trail, sinking to his ankles in the soft gray sand, and getting rides from africano folk passing in mule-pulled wagons. The road was paved in stretches now (and in those spots marked with small signs with the number 90 and the words DIXIE HIGHWAY stamped on them in black lettering), and among the wagons, flatbed trucks and a few autos made their way under mossy live oaks and through the pine barrens between the little board-and-brick towns. He stole a two-dollar bill out of a church basket in Chipley and was caught by the preacher's nineteen-year-old son who was home from the war Delvin had barely known was going on, but the preacher took pity on him and let him keep the money and fed him at the kitchen table and gave him fresh clothes to replace the tatters he had been given by the Drovers off their own washline back on the banks of Aufuskie river and with the money and resurrected feelings a full belly gave him he bought fishline and hooks and a cane pole and fished his way across Florida in ditch creeks, branches and rivers, pulling in croakers and bream and roasting them on fires he built off the road among the circulating night creatures and bugs. Carrying the fishing pole fed him and made him inconspicuous, a colored man with a harmless purpose trudging the highway.

In August he was in Jacksonville, living with three other men in a dirt-floored cabin on the river where he idled on his plans and worked shifting sacks in a coffee warehouse and one early morning without discussing anything with himself or saying goodbye caught a freight headed to Atlanta. The passenger compartments were crowded, but the rods were emptier than he remembered except for the old men and the crazy boys running from imaginary pursuers and he pretended to be one of the lost and blubbering crazy ones, telling a story of wild men from the west riding huge machines that chased after him.

"Hell, boy," an old cross-eyed white man who claimed to have once been manager of a streetcar company in Long Beach, California, said, "you just been seeing them tanks."

He knew vaguely what a tank was but he knew little else about down-to-date life in the fall of 1943, but that didn't matter because he was playing crazy. Around him in the car men talked of war and of mighty personages and of great battles fought with big guns and these matters got into his nap dream and tore loose big chunks of space from the sky and from cities that loomed like vast archipelagos over his tiny sleeping body and in his sleep he shuddered and whimpered and cried out and the men mocked him. In the Atlanta yards a white man wanted to fight him but he knocked him down with a single backhanded punch to the face and he felt a surge of killingness shoot up inside him and he could sense himself losing dominion and he staggered sideways and anybody who looked into his eyes would think he was looking into the eyes of a hellion. The experience frightened him. It was caused by the accumulation of poisons acquired in the penitentiary, he figured, but he was not sure how to make the poisons go away and he sat in the tall sooty grass thinking until he had to get up and go because another man, a stranger with marcelled hair, had come up to him and said he knew him. He ran away from this man as fast as he could.

Later he found himself in an area of the hilly city where those of his own kind lived in shanties beside dusty red clay streets and he met a woman there and lived with her for a couple of months. At night this woman washed vegetables and ran the pea sheller at the big farmers market out on Airline Road, and in the mornings she would slide into the big bed in her pleasant back bedroom and they would make love and she would talk a little about the night's work before going to sleep. He would get up and sit on the back steps looking at the goldenrod flowering down by the back fence and at the big hooped-over tomato plants in the garden filled with ripe fruit and the corn stalks just streaking brown and watch the little red-throated hummingbirds buzz around the statice bushes and he would think he had come into a kind of heaven. The woman wanted him to marry her but he didn't want to do that. It was no longer because of Celia, but he didn't want to stay in Atlanta and he couldn't bring himself to ask this woman, Minnie May Layfield by name, to come with him. He wanted to get out of the Southland entirely. That is, after he had visited Chattanooga one more time.

He told her a little about his life, eliminating the prison part, speaking of his time on the cotton plantation and his years on the rails before that and his travels with the professor and a little about his life in the funeral home in a small city he didn't name. Minnie May loved him and didn't mind his falsifying—she knew it for what it was—but she thought he was foolish not to marry her and told him so.

"We are supposed to enjoy the bounty that is offered us," she said as they sat in the afternoon on the back steps sipping iced tea with a piece of lemon in it she had brought home from the market, his first lemon since he was a child. His teeth were loose in his head (like seeds in a gourd, he said) and his bones ached from the residual malaria but he was delighted to receive the bounty of these small touches, ice and citrus fruit, and he told her so.

"I mean some of the larger style bounties that have come your way."

"I am also happy to have received the gift of your hospitality in much greater ways, I can promise you that," he said, and rubbed along her strong smooth thigh. "I don't mean just this either, though I do enjoy it."

"Where in Ginny Gall'd you learn to talk like that?" Minnie said, looking off into the sweet gum that was beginning to soak up yellow.

He blushed in his deep black skin, and the blushing was new, or new again, and ran his knuckles lightly over her up-turned palm that was pink and hard as a workingman's.

He found a woman's body—this woman's body—to be voluminous

and swampy, massive, without end, a colossal force that threatened to sweep him away, that crammed against him, making him think of the Gulf that time off Sunny Point and of dreams and of the strange rolling affections that came on the darkest of prison nights. Touching her set off alarms that the touches themselves quieted.

"Well," she said, "what *do* you mean?"

A flight of fast airplanes moved across the sky to the south, headed toward the big military airfield out that way. He counted them with his finger: eight. Nearer, half a dozen crows circled something interesting. A breeze picked at the leaves of a yard maple where she said redbirds had nested in the spring before blue jays stole the chicks.

He said he didn't know what he meant, but she had more to say and he listened and then his mind drifted off to the early years with Mr. Oliver out on the side porch as Mr. O made up names for the constellations, fashioned from the speckling stars the constellations themselves, and told stories about these chariots and kings. They were always stories of fortunes lost and found and long journeys hauling the remains of heroes. Never love stories. Delvin's favorite was the story of the invisible leopard. A giant cat that leapt from hiding to eat passersby in the upland jungles of old Africa. No one could kill this leopard. One day a man claimed he had captured the beast. He produced a large cage in which he said he had the leopard. He charged people a quarter to view the big cat, and many paid to see the leopard that was in fact not there. Some people said the exhibit was a hoax, but many other people came away satisfied. One day a young boy, a brave boy from a nearby village, said he didn't believe the leopard was in the cage. Nobody ever hears it roar, he said. The man said it was a silent leopard, everybody knew that. Silent my eye, the boy said. He said he would go into the cage to prove it was empty. Fine, the man said, but you got to pay a quarter like everybody else. Here it is, the boy said. The man said, I'm sorry, but I can't let you get in the cage. I couldn't live with myself if that leopard tore you to pieces. It's all right, the boy said, I was getting nervous about it anyway. They became friends and after a long time the man admitted to the boy that there was no leopard. The boy said, I knew you was lying. And I'm gon tell everybody. Then he threw open the cage door and leapt in. The leopard ate him up.

That was a great story, Delvin thought, very scary, and he wished he could hear Mr. O tell it again. But this woman was talking.

"Gettin what?" he said. "Married?"

"Why, you aint even listening."

"Yes I am, I just got caught in a dream. It's a ailment I have."

"You don't have no ailment, you just wont paying attention."

"I'm sorry," he said. "Everything out here in the busy world catches hold of me sometimes and I forget what is happening."

She gave him a long look. He had told her about the red dog and she believed him, but in Atlanta at that time there were few such cases and she knew only two people, a machinist and a peach sorter, who had caught the disease and it didn't seem too much of a bother—if it was the same thing he was talking about—for either of them. She was sad because she knew she couldn't keep him around. Sooner or later she asked each of the boys she took in to marry her and they always turned her down. She was not pretty and she had a rough temperament but she knew herself to have a tender heart if they could just stay around long enough to find it. It was easy to find.

"Well, dreamer," she said, "I'll give you the rest of the week to make up your mind and then you got to go—or if you—you know . . ."

"About the marrying?"

"What you think I'm talking about?"

She got up and went back into the house.

Delvin sat on the steps, unsure of what had just happened. She had wanted him to say how pleased he was but there was this other and it had scared him. He sensed her plans, her configurations of desire underneath her simple demands and he had shied. But he had crossed this woman's threshold, eaten her baked bread and frolicked in early morning recreation in her big bed, and even simplified it was too much for him. He had known many men who thrived in prison

because prison asked so little of them. But he didn't think he was one
of those men or if he did he thought still he was the boy—the man
now, thirty years old—he had always been. He was finding out this
wasn't so. A redbird hung half upside down in the little chinese elm
at the side of the yard. Life was coming steadily back to him. Often
it hurt. He had watched the natty mockingbirds hopping around on
the grassy margins outside the prison wire and he had thought about
how easy it was for those birds to go anywhere they wanted. Birds,
rats, toads, bugs, even skeeters, could dash away free creatures
beyond the fence. And now he had dashed away and was skittering
around loose in the so-called free territory. But each step or shake of
the wrist baffled him. And he hadn't thought it would hurt so much
to be free, at least loose.

He walked over to Willie Feveril's place and sat out in the backyard listening to him talk about the war. Willie, a tall man with a
craggy face and a look in his eye as if he was warding off blows, had
been kept out of the war by his clubfoot.

"I darsent go anyhow," he said, sipping from a beer bottle filled
with screech liquor. "It aint my business what these white folks get
stirred up about. None of em like each other much and every so often
the not liking spills over into the killing." He spit between his feet.
They were sitting on an unpainted bench under a big butternut tree.
"When they gets they fill of killing they go back to the not liking. Not
one damn thing changes."

The Atlanta streets were full of soldiers and he had to be careful
he was not stopped to produce a paper saying why he was not in
uniform. Word had gotten around that a man was living at Minnie
May's house and yesterday a frog-faced fellow with a heavy limp
had stopped by the house to say they were talking down at the store
about he was a deserter. Delvin thought the man might be lying but
now he was scared. He thought of stealing Feveril's card or paper or
whatever it was but he didn't have the strength for it right now. This
world out here was a mystery to him; he was shadowed by a fragile
and dessicate past and bewildered by the rackety present. It was best
to keep his mouth shut and just watch carefully.

He'd bought a notebook and a pencil out of the two dollars Minnie gave him each week and started keeping a record of what had happened to him in prison; he could remember that. He was scared to write openly about prison life, scared of getting caught that way, so wrote in a squinched script. He read some of the childhood parts to Feveril who said they brought back his own raising in Atlanta. " 'Cept I didn't have no mama who killed a man. Why'd she do that?"

"Man tried to shame her."

"They wont nothin else?"

"Something mysterious." He didn't want to say more, he never did. The old man she killed had been her regular Saturday-night date for years. That's what he had heard over at the Emporium. But there was more. An unavoidable dark hand stretching forth unsuspected by her in a world where a black person had to stay alert at all times. He carried not only the shame of her crime, but the surprise, and the dread of its perplexing circumstance. "Got stretched out past what she could take," he said.

Feveril had a job sweeping at the Jeep plant over in Riverdale, but he was bad about missing work. "I got a sister," he said when Delvin asked about this, "and she brings me goodins in from the country when she comes. I aint going to serve in no army I can tell you."

Delvin enjoyed Feveril's stories about his sister, about farm folks and the long country days, and he thought of heading out that way, but he had a journey to make to Chattanooga and then it was on from there to the northland. This had fixed in his mind by now. But he was taking his time about getting started. He liked living with Minnie May. He enjoyed cleaning house for her and cooking and hoeing in the garden out back and rolling in the bed with her, and that wasn't all. Maybe he *would* marry her. She had a frightful temper. She was always blowing up about little things, things Delvin didn't even see. It was like she had magnifying eyes. Feveril said she'd been that way since she was a little girl.

"I think she's mad about being so plain—excuse me," he said in deference to Delvin's situation.

"I aint missed that part," Delvin said. "She's got other good qualities."

"I know she do."

"How you know?"

"I've knowed her all my life and she's a big woman—you can't miss em."

"Hmm."

Delvin didn't think homeliness was what was bothering her—or not the only thing. "She just hadn't fulfilled her purpose," he said.

"Depends on what it is, I guess."

"That's right."

When Feveril went in to pour himself another from from his kitchen jug, Delvin wandered out of his yard. On Lester street on his way to Minnie's he heard the strains of a song he was familiar with, "Der Stürmische Morgen," coming from the little one-man barbershop. He peeked in as he passed by and saw the barber, Mr. Eulis, sitting in his tipped-back porcelain chair listening to the Victrola with his eyes closed and moving one finger the way Mr. Oliver did when he played the same Schubert song on the wind-up machine in his bedroom. Down the street outside Leary's grocery a tan dog stood on its hind legs trying to lick one of the hams Mr. Leary had hanging from the porch eave. A little boy dressed in white stumped slowly on crutches back and forth along the walk in front of a house on Bee way. A large man wearing pressed overalls without a shirt sat in a tree swing staring at the soft dust under his feet. Delvin wished the man would look up so he could hail him and smile. He'd started hanging a smile on his face since he left prison, making himself appear friendly. Wherever he got a chance and figured he could *take* a chance. Stella Burkle, a fine-looking woman but crazy, walked along on the other side of the street, swinging her big white patent leather pocketbook. If you spoke to her she would hit you with it.

Maybe a limp, he thought, maybe I ought to go back to that—throw the marshals off. But it was too late. People knew he had been sick, but that was all they'd heard of that might exclude him from military service. The penitentiary would keep you out. 'Cept they were probably putting prisoners now on work gangs for the good of the country. Well, the country needed cotton and the prisons he'd been in were good at producing that. The war was one more fright jabbing at men in prison. Negro men locked up in a lost corner of the white man's world. What's gon become of you? Who are you? Who you be? And here comes Mr. Billy Camp and his goat cart. The old man, walking beside his two-wheel cart pulled by two billies and accompanied by half a dozen outwalker goats, passed by going the other way. He gave Delvin a friendly wave with his leafy mulberry stick and Delvin waved back. Maybe he could join up with him, see the country at goat speed, pass as a friendly colored crazy man. Back at Minnie May's white cottage home he sat on the back steps wearing a stained derby with a hole in the back the size of a peach, a hat he had picked out of the trash in Jacksonville. The warden at Burning Mountain had worn a derby with two scuffed marks on the front like the white eyes of a ghost. He had picked up his notebook on the way through the bedroom. The little slip of blue paper he put in it to mark his place was gone; Minnie May had looked through it. So now she knew he was an escapee—probably. But why had he left it for her to easily find? In the book he had taken note of the tin washtub hung on the shed wall, the beans coiled around their strings in the garden. A leaf on a spicebush that spun crazily in no wind he could feel, white as the wing of a cabbage butterfly. He'd studied the soft slim prints of Minnie May's bare feet in the dust by the back steps, prints that reminded him of his mother's. First thing his mama did when she came home was to take off her shoes. Walked around all day in her bare feet, leaving tracks he'd followed like a detective. He didn't think about her as much as he used to. But still in dreams she came to him, laughing or crying, mute and determined, one time yelling at him with her thin arm raised like he was a dog she was bound to beat on.

Sitting now on the back steps, tracing with one finger his mother's name, Cappie, looking at Minnie's footprints that might have been his mama's, he began to cry. He shaded his face and choked down the sounds, careful still of prison dangers. His body shook.

It wasn't all grief. Mingled with the pasty, durable, extenuated sadness was a happiness, a new one, a stretching out of himself, long-shanked and agile—he was, in this moment of American time, free, a misplaced man, overlooked, drifting on the breeze, a wanderer amid the garrison of interlockedness, sunk deep enough in negro life for a while not to be missed, uncounted by any census, omitted by the tax man, skipped by the army. Only the cross-Dixie skookum boys were looking for him.

He wiped his eyes.

If they were looking. Maybe they'd . . . but he knew they hadn't forgot. Couldn't down here afford to neglect for too long any unaccounted-for colored man. Colored man—the *rules* he had to follow—was the linchpin of the whole business down here. Lynch pin.

In the garden he picked a tomato and ate it sitting on the ground next to a big pepper plant. The calendar said it was fall but it might as well be summer. The sky was speckled with tiny white clouds like little checkmarks. From another yard, not far off, came the thunk of an ax. "Rooster," a woman's voice called, "come here and help me mend that winder shade." The smell of frying pork from far off, sweet smoke. He dried the tomato juice off his hands by rubbing them hard together, picked a pepper, shucked the flaky white seeds and ate that. Then he picked a few late runner beans, shelled them out into his palm and ate them. Then a small summer squash, the ring of yellow blossom a ruff around one end. I could eat myself around the world, garden to garden.

In the wash shed he cranked water into a tin basin and scrubbed his face and hands. In the piece of mirror propped on a piece of shelf he studied his face. There were deep lines running down his cheeks. He liked that; before prison he'd been a fat-faced boy, now he looked like a man who had seen trouble and lived through it. He patted his hair, mulling its length. Before he was arrested he wore his hair brushed out and squared off with a part razored on the left side, but afterwards, in the convict life, he had his hair cut short. Now, out in the world again, he'd let it grow some, and over here in Atlanta he'd gone to Mr. Eulis's and while "Laudate Dominum" played on the Victrola had him chop a part into it. He'd tried a mustache, but it looked like a black caterpillar on his lip so he shaved it off. Minnie May had a razor right here in the house, left over from the last man who lived here, and he used that, glad to come that near to having his own. He took time lathering his face, leaned in close to the mirror, examining his creased cheek, the little dents up near his ears, the stubby chin. Sometimes he'd wash the lather off and start over just for the feel of it. Minnie May often heated water in a kettle and carried it out to him; he loved it when she did that.

He took his time shaving, no rush at the moment, pausing to study his face as it reappeared out of the lather.

"What's going on in there?" he asked it. "You ever gon own up?" He touched the thin puffed scars on his left cheekbone. "I reckon not. No telling what you might have to own up *to*." In case somebody was listening he laughed a little shushing laugh to cover his embarrassment at talking to himself.

He carefully washed his face and carefully patted it dry and stared at himself in the mirror. "We'll keep you awhile longer," he said. He washed the razor, dried it on the towel, folded it and put it in his pocket.

Back in the house he shucked his clothes and slid into bed next to the sleeping Minnie May. She slept on her back, making a soft purring noise, a snore with a tiny bubbling sound at the end of it. He nestled against her and she automatically turned away but he pressed on until she turned toward him. She wore a loose gray slip washed to a softness like fresh ginned cotton. Softer than that. He slid his hand up behind and pushed the slip up her smooth body that was almost as dark as his, so smooth he felt the rough chafe of his own fingers against it and was almost ashamed to touch her. He could smell her now, smell the spicy odor of her and the fresh sweat and the verbena spice oil she poured over herself and wiped off with a cloth, smell the barley soap and the shelled butterbeans and the okra she itched from and he could smell under these other, unplotted mysteries, deeper reeks and perfumes. He contorted his body until he could put his nose close to her lower back and he inhaled the rich odor of her woman smell and sniffed all the way to her girl smell, even, so it seemed, to her original baby smell, a faint residue of it like a thin sprinkling of garden rain.

With his scarred knees he drove her legs apart and he liked the forcing, liked the resistance, the body's stiffness and her own pushing back and he kept on driving, hard work he bent to happily, the fullness of his power given to the task like turning a plow in heavy clay, forcing the big coulter with his own body, feeling as he did so the heat rising, the burning life of this slick, fumy soil. He leaned back and stared at her as he separated her from her steady opposition, uncovering her, exposing the black wallow and red pit of her. He touched her with his fingers, three, then only one, surveying, scouting the trail and found it. He slid along trough and excavation, rummaging, loosening. He had at last stopped thinking of Milo and the others. He had believed that if he kept on long enough, if he kissed deeper and held her tighter and stayed close to her and drew her perfumes and funks to him, listened to her and rubbed against her and spoke to her of her desires and longings and of his hunger, spinning a new life from smells and touches and sight and words, conjuring the bed and the house and the streets and the ungovernable city into shape around them, that he could sink into it, into *her*, and he would forget. And that was happening.

She had started moaning even before he entered her and when he did she stopped. He held himself still, waiting. In the silence he could hear a redbird whistling. Down the row a woman called. "Frankie," she said. "Frankie, come on over here." As he shanked into her, waxy leaves of pain slid off. He was raw and charged, alight. He started slow and picked up speed. She began to whimper, or was that him? He was cast forth in long looping lines swinging out over deceptively calm waters. Then she bucked back against him and surged forward, attempting to pull his body on a rope. He followed, shoved her down and jammed her back into the earth, crushing the juice out of her. She clucked and sputtered and banged against his side with her fist. Knocking, knocking, he thought—*come on in*—and abruptly he cut loose from what held him back and thrust himself hard through his own body, driving into her. But he was too strong to collapse.

"Not yet," he said. "Not yet."

She shoved and underbowed her back hard as if she was going to break bone.

Something ran through their bodies slamming door after door. *Catch me, catch me.* He did, and even as he did so he was aware that this confabulation was only a promissory note and appeal to the greater desire that was lodged, had been lodged, all his life deep inside him. What it was he didn't know exactly but there were times, and they were not in a bedroom or bunk, when he almost caught a glimpse of what it was, what he really wanted, but then it shied, like a dragonfly catching the breeze, and he couldn't say. In the meantime there was this. He pounded his way in and moved softly among the simple treasures he found.

After a while he got up, went into the kitchen, pumped water over a fresh rag, wrung it and brought it back to the bed and cleaned her.

They lay uncovered in the warm curtained air without talking, touching a little here and there, and then they fell asleep. He dreamed of cotton fields, of stopping at the end of a long row to take a drink from a bucket handed to him by a man whose face he couldn't make out. As he held the dipper to his mouth he saw over its rim a fish-shaped cloud high in the east. The water tasted better than any water he'd ever drunk. Something was about to come clear, something he'd forgotten about until now but had always longed to recall. He had to remember it, but he couldn't stop looking at the fish-shaped cloud or tasting the water. I've never tasted water in a dream, he thought and waked.

Minnie was gone but she'd left supper for him in the safe. A note written in her big looping hand, misspelled and hard to make out, said she loved him and would be back late because she had to go see her mother. He ate the butterbeans and picked the meat off the ham hock and gnawed her crumbly, agreeably sour cornbread and then he got dressed and went out to Longley's Beer Bar and stood around drinking with a man he knew who had been in prison down in Florida and liked to talk about the life there. He didn't mention that he too had been in prison but he listened to the man's stories. He had a hard unforgiving nature familiar to Delvin. After a while he grew tired of listening and played a game of pool with a man who said his name was George Butters, a sawed-off, tan-skinned man with white patches of vitiligo on his face, and beat him handily.

About midnight the place was raided by the police looking for a draft cheat who'd supposedly robbed Calhoun's grocery down the street. Delvin slipped out the back and ran down to the river where a man in a thin raincoat told him about a big freight forming up for St. Louis by way of Chattanooga and Memphis. Without deciding anything particularly he caught a ride on a jitney over to west Atlanta and walked six blocks to the rail yards, climbed aboard the freight and as the hundred-car lineup racked and creaked out of the yard he lay on top of a red boxcar watching the moon come up over the crown of the Mosley Hotel and Bathhouse, thinking of Mr. Oliver and the Ghost.

2

In Chattanooga, just off Wildmon street, he leapt from the train neat as a cat and slipped through the moody early morning foglicked streets into Red Row and across town and up hill to the old familiar corner of Columbia street and Arvy road, to find, instead of the comfortable, viney, outstretching old house and funeral home, a green and white Sinclair gas station. He stood out in the now paved street looking at this piggish oddity with wonder and sorrow. He couldn't believe it. Magic had whisked the old place out of sight in some trickery that in a merciful blink would reveal the wide front steps and the big crape myrtle at the edge of the porch and the high white facade that always looked raked back. He became so shaky he staggered and backed up against a big cow oak across the street from this dwarfish foolery. A smooth, damp breeze slid along, touching this or that tree. The leaves of a large tulip poplar he recognized were already burned by fall. He wanted to embrace the familiar tree, pump it with questions foolishly, pump somebody.

He loitered on the sidewalk, squatting on his haunches, letting the facts push amazement and grief through his body. A man in gray coveralls drove up in a shiny blue Chevrolet car, parked by the station, crossed the paved court and unlocked the door. Delvin walked up to the man and with a sound in his throat stopped him.

"I'll have her ready in a minute," the man said, a white man with a half ring of white close-cropped hair fringe around his tanned freckled head. "Car run out of gas?" he said.

Delvin couldn't speak.

"You need a container of some kind?" the man asked as Delvin followed him into the station that smelled not of corn mush and formaldehyde and Mr. O's exuberant cologne but of used motor oil.

From a narrow metal locker he unlocked with a small key the man got a broom and started back out to the front.

"You not looking for a job, are ye?"

Delvin said nothing.

"Well, you can start by sweeping off that concrete out there if you aint too fancy for it."

Delvin took the broom from him and began to sweep off the little sidewalk and forecourt. Across Arvy road where the old circus grounds used to be was a line of low red, tarpaper-roofed warehouses. He recognized a mimosa bush under the unlit corner streetlight or told himself he did. He kept sweeping, afraid to ask the white man what had happened here. His head began to hurt and he thought his malaria was coming back. It couldn't be that. His mind was like a closed door. He stood outside of it sweeping steadily.

After a while he leaned the broom against one of the two gas pumps, went inside and asked the man about Mr. Oliver.

"Old man Oliver?"

Delvin felt his spirit fall into a hole. "Is he still alive?"

"Last I heard."

A stuttery joy filled him.

"He's living over yonder, somewhere over in the Row, I think. Maybe it's that old preacher woman's house over by the . . . Exhilaration Church, I think they call it."

"Thank you," Delvin said. He was still so discombobulated he went out, got the broom and started to walk off with it before he remembered and turned back and handed it to the man who'd followed him out. "I don't guess I need a job right now.'"

"Okay," the man said, handed him a fifty-cent piece and took up sweeping himself.

Delvin walked around back of the station. Everything was gone there too, except for one of the garage sheds. Parked in it now was a dusty stake truck.

He walked then ran down the alley toward the Row, but soon he slowed down and dawdled some, stopping occasionally to catch his breath that was heavy and hot in his chest. Now that he knew Mr. Oliver was alive he had doubts about going to see him. He didn't want to upset him, didn't want him carrying guilty knowledge; mostly he was afraid of being turned away by him. But he kept walking.

On the Row the first person he saw that he knew was Libby Holmes, a now retired domestic who remembered him as the delinquent boy who stole apples from the box in front of the old Heberson market. She looked at him as if she was taking down details for her report to the police. He smiled and nodded and asked how she was doing and inquired as to where he might find the present residence of Mr. Cornelius Oliver.

"Aint you supposed to be in jail?" she said, and he thought, I am going to be in a car heading back to Acheron before lunchtime.

"Well, I was, but they let me out when I finished my time, thank you Miz Libby for inquiring."

She sniffed and shifted her blue taffeta parasol and said, "That good man is staying over here to Miz Corrine Cutler's house I believe."

He thanked her twice and went that way through the unpaved streets under the big leafy trees that seemed even more now to be roomy hideouts and past the barbershop and grocery and the insurance agency and the Knicknack Art Shop and the hardware store with barrels of nails and digging tools out front and past the other stores that were mixed among houses that looked no more prosperous now than when he left. Over all a blue sky with puffed rafts of white cloud a child might dream he could float away on. Few young men were about except for a couple in army uniforms. One boy with a garrison cap pulled low sat on the front steps of the old Vereen house, turning something small in his hands. He looked lonely. Delvin felt a surge that made him want to run up and shake hands with everybody he saw, but then, almost as powerfully, he wanted to slink back into the alleys and under the big shady trees so nobody'd see him. It'd been several months now since he'd been locked up, but who he was, who he'd become in prison—the shallow, scornful

vigilance, the fear like a lacing in his brain, the edges everywhere—
kept hanging with him, making him nervous.

He found Mr. Oliver sitting out on the porch of the Cutler house
sipping a cup of boneset tea. Delvin climbed the steps not knowing
what he would do or what unhappy surprise might come next, but
when he saw the old man—he had become an old man—he began to
weep and he threw his arms around his shrunken body and hugged
him or would have except Mr. O who was crying too said the cancer
had made his skin kind of touchy and he had to be careful. "Just
better lightly pat me," he said.

They bleared at each other and Delvin sat down on the porch
floor and asked how he was—"How are you, dear"—the man gray
in the face and contrived into old age by his body's struggle with an
indefatigable disease. Delvin could see clearly what the facts at issue
were. He asked nothing about the funeral home but quietly just told
the old man he was free now and doing fine and listened.

"One day life just bucked me off," Mr. Oliver said.

He had come down with the cancer five years ago—"I lost my
regularity, that was the sign of it, and couldn't get it back no matter
what Mrs. Parker tried—she's still in the world, over here cooking
for the Sunderson family, in Wildwood I believe"—and he thought at
first he could fight it off but that became a full-time job so he sold the
funeral home and traveled around the country trying to get cured.
Wound up spending his money in phony clinics and wonder working joints. He'd even gone down to Mexico—"By Pan American
airplane"—where he ate mashed peach pits—"I could have gotten
my fill of them right here"—and drank bovine gall and other bitter
liquids that no human should ever put to their lips, and nothing had
worked. He had returned to Chattanooga six months ago on the bus
from New Orleans, broke—"and spent, you might say"—and was
now waiting for death to take him like a man would wait to return to
a home he had never been happy in but had to go to because there
was nowhere else.

"Least I can be assured of a place to lay my head," he said and laughed a creaking, mucosal laugh.

Small peaked sores dotted Mr. Oliver's face. He was missing teeth, which he tried to conceal with a palsied hand. He had an old blue silk quilt wrapped loosely around him and he wore a maroon knit wool cap and matching scarf puddled under his throat.

Casey Boy was nowhere around. He'd took off, Mr. O said, and joined the army. "Fool thing to do," Mr. Oliver said and waved a flimsy hand.

Mrs. Cutler's son stepped out directly and asked Delvin if he wanted to come in for breakfast.

Delvin thanked him and said he'd as soon sit out on the porch with Mr. Oliver.

The son, large, wide, with a small close-cropped head, smiled in a friendly way and said he would bring food out to the porch.

Delvin asked about Polly and Elmer and George and the Ghost, and Mr. O said he had given them legacy gifts and let them go. He didn't know where they were now.

The breeze had dried out. It creaked in the spindly branches of a sycamore next to the house. The mountain sky was a translucent, unhindered blue.

"I could sit out here for years," Mr. Oliver said, "I've come to like it very much." He said this as if Delvin had asked him a question. He didn't inquire about prison. They didn't talk about the war.

A few negro men in uniform walked on the streets, a couple of them passing in front of the house, swinging their arms as they went by. One of them was the Ghost, traipsing back and forth like he was on misshapen guard duty, a peculiar askew figure in dirty army khakis and a crumpled garrison cap. Delvin hailed him from the porch. The Ghost came angling up, walking half sideways like a dog, his head held slightly to the side, the freckles on his cheeks pinker than ever. He gravely shook Delvin's hand and spoke cheerily to Mr. Oliver who didn't seem to recognize him. "I'm home on leave," he said.

"Leave?" Delvin said. "You look like *you* got left. That a army uniform?"

"I help out with the soldiers. With the cooking."

"Cooking?"

He was glad to see the Ghost, but something about him, his peculiar listing manner, his off-speaking and the way his pale eyes darted—he wanted to throw him off the porch too.

"So they finally let you out," the Ghost said, studying Delvin's face.

"It took some doing," Delvin said. The news about his escape had scattered like spilled leaves; he'd overheard some people in Jacksonville say every newspaper in the country had written it up. He read about himself first in a paper somebody had used to wrap onions, sitting behind a barbershop with some other men eating fish stew the barber's wife had prepared for passing tramps. All the assembled had heard about his jump and he had hidden his face in the shade of a droopy magnolia and then cut quietly out of the yard before he got his fill of stew. In C-town they must have been patrolling the streets with shotguns.

"We all figured they would give up trying to trickerate you sooner or later."

He said it like it was a joke and strung a little frolicky cutup kind of patter together and after a few minutes said he had to be on his way. He bowed to Mr. Oliver and grinned at Delvin and skipped down the steps, the tail of his gray army-style shirt flapping.

Delvin caught up with him out in the street across from a large white oak that had the word GIT carved into its trunk. A large man wearing a shirt made of rainbow patches walked by carrying a sign that said BARLOW BAR-B-Q.

"Where you headed?" Delvin wanted to know. He was afraid the Ghost would try to get him picked up and wondered why this was and wanted to get him to say.

"I'm on my way over to the Emp," the Ghost said in a finicky, snubbing manner.

"I thought you were done with that place."

"I don't believe I ever said anything like that."

"I was probably given false information," Delvin said, thinking of his mother gone from there for a quarter of a century now. "I mean—" He couldn't get the words out straight. He wanted to cry— lord, that was most of what he'd wanted to do since he got out—but he couldn't do that here, now, not in front of the Ghost.

"I got me a friend over there," the Ghost said, "a white woman."

"They got white women at the Emporium?" Times had changed.

"It's almost fifty-fifty," the Ghost said. "I'm gon get her to marry me and we gon have white children."

Delvin turned his head, galled. He started to say something, to tell the Ghost that no kind of mustafina child would be white—no way to wash a black man enough times to make him white—and why would he want that anyway, but he was tired of such arguments even before they started. The world bulged with information, with a full baggage of crumbled-up bits and pieces and you could grab out as big a handful as you wanted and make whatever suited you out of it. Half-facts and letters of intent and unspoken questions and rumors and whispers of vanished lives and snubbed-off growing things that would never be spoken of again. 'Cept you couldn't make yourself white. Maybe he couldn't make himself free. He stuck his hand out and took the Ghost's small pink fingers in his thick flat black ones and shook. His broad hand had softened over the last couple of traveling months but there was still a hardness under the softness that he could tell the Ghost felt. He could recall everything from years ago that included them both, but he didn't mention any of it. He looked him straight in the eyes and in the pale colorless eyes that couldn't bear sunlight and shied from whoever was looking at him but looked back at Delvin now, sly but bashful too, scared, too, and worshipping, he saw that the Ghost loved him. And the Ghost could tell he saw. Winston, *he* could tell. Delvin wanted to say, *Don't betray me*, but he couldn't bring himself to, and hoped it wasn't necessary. It flashed through his mind to threaten the Ghost—just for good measure, penitentiary style—but he didn't do that either. You could do anything, you could do everything, but what did it matter? That was something else he'd picked up prison, in the local philosophy class: *nothing's worth fighting for*. Was that where he was living now? For a moment he had lost his strength. It was like a hand on his chest held him back. *Don't . . .* , he wanted to say, or, *I'll kill you*, or, *Please*, or, *Remember how I saved you*, but he didn't say any of these things. He couldn't. Even when he felt the hand relax. Maybe it was love held him back, maybe something else.

He smiled at the Ghost who was only half looking at him now. The Ghost's eyes were like a kind of crystal. "Maybe I'll catch up with you over there," he said, and he was smiling, in as friendly a way as a man who'd just skipped on twelve years in the penitentiary could.

After he walked back to Mrs. Cutler's and talked some more with Mr. Oliver and sat with him as he slept in his chair on the shady porch while the breeze pried at a chinaberry tree by the eave and shook the little bunchy leaves that hadn't yet turned, he thought about where he was headed—as far north as he could get before Canada (or maybe on into Canada)—and pictured a grassy yard and a house among trees and him out on the porch in a rocking chair under a blanket like Mr. Oliver, working on a book, and he felt a sadness sliding along, sloshing along with the thoughts and the little quivers of knowledge that came along too, the ones that confirmed that he would never be sitting on a porch in this town again, that he was a ghost himself come back briefly to haunt the old venues. Again the tears rose, but again he didn't cry them.

In his padded rocker Mr. Oliver snored loudly.

Delvin got up and kissed him on the forehead and stood looking down at him. His old smell was gone, replaced by a sour mucky stench not quite overpowered by the odor of wintergreen. People got so they didn't want to visit somebody who was dying, but they loved to show up to look at a corpse. So the old man had told him years ago as they sat on the side porch watching a thunderstorm come in over the mountains. Mr. Oliver had ridden the train from Alabama to this place and made a life out of nothing but his clever self and hard work. And now he was sleeping his way toward death on an old christian lady's porch. Well, all right. On the Gulf shore he had walked into the ocean and stood up to his waist in salt water that had never been swum in by africano people. Only africano ones ever in it were those bodies swabbies had rolled off the decks of the slave ships crossing from Africa. He had pushed his face into that salt water. A white woman walking with a big brown dog had called for him to get out of there, but he ignored her. At least until she walked off. Then he high-footed it out of the pale, lank surf and ran for his life.

He wanted to stop people on the street and say that once he left here he'd never be back. Yall come too, he wanted to say—cry out— all of you, you're free now.

He touched the pitted back of Mr. Oliver's hand, still a little plump but now ashy and showing red under the knuckles. He didn't want to leave *him*. He wanted to go back to the funeral home and get some supper and sit out on a cutblock in the alley and listen to old Mr. Starling from next door tell stories about dances and frights back in the slave times. But no, he didn't really want that. He wanted these living to go on living, that was the most he wanted. It hurt him to see this battered man here, snoring, a spit bubble like a tiny crystal ball on his lip, hurt to see death crept up so close to him. But that too wasn't enough to come back for. From the minute he had slipped away from Acheron prison he had felt the exhilaration of freedom. At first it had been so powerful he thought it would be enough to make him happy in the world. But that sense of things had dimmed. It was wearing out. He was nearly back to being a black man in a white man's kingdom. But not quite. Before the last of that bounteous sense faded away he wanted to stand again in the streets of the town he was born in. Let me see what I feel in Red Row on the dusty street in front of Heberson's store or standing on the porch of the Home or sitting down to eat in the kitchen. But all those places were gone. He hadn't counted on that. Well, he should have. Everything was on its way out, handed off into some other configuration, some past you could think about if you wanted to or had to, turned over like soil in a new field in spring to show its bright, glistening other side. Now he had to go. Or would soon. He was older but he was part of the new. And he wanted to tell this to somebody.

He spent the morning sleeping in a back bedroom at Mrs. Cutler's house and then in the afternoon up the gully in a little pinestraw nest he fashioned under some rhododendron bushes, sleeping some more and writing in his notebook. Mostly notes. Fragments of nothing much, signs painted on the sides of barns saying HERE IT IS in some form or other, extra tall men craning to see over a board fence, a woman washing her hair in a tub out behind a poultry yard. A big dark hemlock by a stream had jolted him. He wanted to jolt people. Touch them in a secret place. That was all right. He'd seen army men in full packs marching down a dusty road that went nowhere. "What you think of that?" he'd asked the man standing beside him in the boxcar door. "A clown parade," the man had said and spit out the door. "I got the cure for loneliness!" shouted a man peering from a lit window in Jacksonville, but he'd ducked back in before Delvin could ask what it was. Standing under a church window in Monroeville he listened to a choir director correct the same bright-eyed girl six times before she burst into tears. Six, ten, twenty-seven times—whatever it takes, they'll get you. A man stood so long on a trestle bridge showing off a string of croakers with the train coming he'd had to jump for it into the river. He'd come up without his pole or his fish. Once the professor'd laughed so hard he cut a fart that busted the seat out of his britches. "Could have been worse," he said and they both laughed until their bellies hurt. "I got it," a man in faded longhandles rose in an empty fertilizer car to say, "but I don't know where I put it." A big woman who said she was from Alaska had slung her wispy girlfriend so far through the boxcar door she landed in a field of golden wheat. And jumped up yelling. "I got to go," he would say, and he would go, make his break for freedom, no matter how foolishly. *That was me*, he wrote, *the one missing at the head count*. His mama had to flee because she killed a man after white folks beat her five-year-old boy for stealing a fake jewel attached to a dress in the window of a shop in Chattanooga. The jewel was yellow like a cat's eye and he had to have it. *That was me*, he wrote. And the old, ever-denied guilt licked about his heart. From his leafy hideout he looked back down the long slope to a field grown up in Joe Pye weed. The flimsy tops of the weeds, strangled by fall, nodded and gave in a breeze that didn't reach up to where he was. "I am that boy," he said.

After a while he walked back to the house to check on Mr. Oliver but he was sleeping. He used a brush he'd found in the bathroom to brush off his clothes. He sat out on the porch a while and then he started to the Emporium. A couple of old men he thought he recognized sat on the short green bench in front of the overly clean white-man's store that had replaced Heberson's. He and the Ghost had stolen whips of licorice from the old store; the candy'd turned their palms brown. "Now I'm full colored," the Ghost had said, and Delvin had asked him if he was sure that's what he wanted to be. Looked like now he'd found another satisfaction. From behind the building came the sound of somebody chopping wood. That man there putting a crate of cabbages in a car trunk—we buried his wife out of the funeral home twenty years ago. She was a tiny scaredy woman killed when a bakery wagon knocked her down and backed over her. He remembered Culver joking that they ought to cut a casket down for her and save Mr.—what was his name?—some money but nobody had laughed. The old man—Hunt, that was his name—looked up from his conversation and stared at Delvin. I guess he recognizes me. A chain had started to form. From moving identityless through the world—some essential signifier rubbed so thin that not only was he walking through a foreign land but he was walking through it nameless—he had begun his return to substance, to palpable life in the minds of his former townspeople. Judgments might be made, conclusions drawn, plans of action or gossip take shape. It was scary, yet he wanted to experience this, have it once more: somebody in the so-called free world thinking of him. Minnie May was thinking of him—maybe she was—but that was in Atlanta and he'd left her behind; he wanted more, or wanted it here, in the town he was born in, right now.

He didn't make a fool of himself as he walked under the big rustling trees, didn't when the half dozen young men pulled up in their green Olds convertible to the front door of the Hopalong Fancy Room and as they jumped out gave him a quick and not-so-quick lookover, one or two trying to place him in the sultry early fall twilight on Red Row—didn't exchange witticisms or offer challenges or dares or start in on the dozens, he merely walked calmly on. One boy, who had a piece of yellow satin ribbon tied around his waist, nodded at him, a squarish man with a face black and polished as a shoeshine.

Hell, I'm like one of these Sunday showoffs, these fancy boys strutting. But he wasn't really showing off. He was joining again. He didn't want to wait until he got up north and found a place in some town not so fearful of africano folk, some mixed neighborhood in Ypsilanti or Pontiac or Toronto where he would settle in and accept a stipend from the Brotherhood of Africa Aid Society to write his autobiography; he wanted in on things now.

The wanting had come on him like an attack of some kind. Or an understanding that appears from nowhere and catches you eating a muffin or sitting on the toilet or shouting out a piece of homemade verse in a hobo camp. This was after all his hometown. On that corner there, Ellenton and Bunker Hill, he had paid a dime for a big sack of scuppernong grapes, bought from Shorty Youngblood, whose sister was said to be the prettiest girl on Red Row. He had hoped buying the grapes would ingratiate him with her but it didn't. His footprints were all over that corner. He had skipped, run, walked, danced across it, stopped at a shout, laughed, railed against foolishness, his own included, passed by as if he was on his way to glory, or shame, halted in his tracks to tell Mosley Wilkins that he, Delvin, would one day marry Miss Estelle Franks, convey to Arthur Turnbill that it was not possible, as it was claimed in the story about Fleet Willie Barnes, to run a hundred miles nonstop. Over there, in the right now of time, Mrs. Arthur Coventry, standing in her yard futilely raging, just like she used to, swung her cane at a big mullein plant. She called him by name—"You, Delvin Walker!"—asking what sorriness he was up to now. To her, prison or no, he was still just an impertinent boy. She shook the cane at him. A few strands of green matter clung to the tip. He could smell cornbread baking and maybe gingerbread. At Sammy Wolper's down the street they baked bread every day in a big pig-iron oven, still did apparently, maybe they would forever.

But mostly the street was empty of people he knew. The big round-fendered cars were shiny from the rain earlier in the day. He had lain on the narrow floral-smelling bed in Mrs. Cutler's house listening to the light, hesitant rain peck at the tin roof, half counting the drops, half coming to know each one, half marking where each hit, which pile of dobber dust, which leaf or cheek, which shingle or board laid aside and forgotten. Forgotten! That was the conjur. That was the evil word. In each place, each comfy corner, each sideboard with its special teapot or trencher, its little carved doodad brought back from campground, he was forgotten; every porch had grown used to his absence, each room and kettle and heart. He had passed, still living, into the realm of ghosts. It was enough to take the heart out of a man. But oddly—and this was odd to him—he felt not an emptiness but a gathering, a sweetness and an openness that he had not expected. He wanted to run forth like a child, singing some snappy song.

He cut along the alley behind Suber's Hardware, headed toward the Emporium, walking fast under the big skinned sycamores, on his way to someplace with a name. But then for no reason he stopped at the little auto repair garage Jimmy Dandes operated behind his house and stood in shadow under a monkeypaw tree listening to a couple boys playing guitars. He had stopped in this place when he was a child to listen to these boys' father play ragtime tunes on his banjo. The two boys, twins, he remembered, looked nothing like each other and their playing too strained against harmony. They stood in the alley on each side of a small fire that as far as Delvin could tell had no reason for being except maybe somebody just liked little fires.

Then a young woman in a light, flower-colored dress covered

with a white apron came out of the house carrying a big platter of fresh fish. The men quit playing and began to help her. One of them set a four-legged wire grill over the fire, laid a skillet on top and filled the skillet with lard from a tin bucket. The lard crackled and spit and the men stood looking at the fire. One of the boys ran to the house and came back carrying a small table and some plates and a sack of cornmeal. He looked across the alley and saw Delvin standing under the droopy-leafed tree.

"Do we know you?" he said in a friendly way. He was the brother with the lopsided face.

"I'm not sure," Delvin said, taking a step forward. "I hadn't been around here for a while."

"Didn't you use to work over to the Riverlight cotton warehouse?" the other said.

"No, that wadn't me."

"You play ball for the Negro Pioneers?" the first asked. His name, Delvin remembered, was Harley.

"No, I never played ball."

"You from Chattanooga?" the other with the round face said. Delvin couldn't remember his name.

"Born and raised."

The woman was dredging the fish (they looked like bream) in cornmeal and laying them aside on the table. The closer boy—young man—the one whose face seemed to slant too far down on one side, asked if he would like to join them for dinner. Delvin without thinking said he would be happy to.

He helped them fry the fish and then he carried the platter of crackly, steaming bream back into the yard where the young woman directed him to put it down on a long trestle table that had a dark cloth laid on it. Lanterns were lit, citronella lamps set out on two chairs and then, helped by a couple of young girls, an older couple came out—Delvin recognized the father, now grown grizzled, with thin sunken cheeks—and took places in fat armchairs at either end of the table set up under a maple that was still, so he could see in the light, mostly green.

The boys explained to their father that Delvin was raised in Chattanooga and had just returned from several years away. The old man asked who his folks were and Delvin said he had found that they had passed on years ago.

"They would be who now?" the old woman, a sharp-eyed person with puffy cheeks and a light cloud of almost pure white hair, asked.

"Walker," Delvin said.

"I don't believe I recollect them," the old man said. "They live over this way?"

"Long time ago," Delvin said, "but they moved out toward Shipley Station, died out there."

"Well, I'm sorry to hear they've passed," the old woman said, eyeing him rigorously.

Delvin thanked her. The first bite of fish had burned the roof of his mouth, a problem with hot food he had picked up on the prison circuit. He juggled the fish flesh with his tongue until it was cool and swallowed it down. One of the girls over by her mother giggled and mimicked him. He laughed.

"What sort of work you do?" the old man asked in a friendly way.

"I'm writing on a book," Delvin said. He took a long pull of tea. It was cooled with chunks of ice hacked off a block. He picked out a piece and pressed it to his lips.

"Burn yoself?" the old man said.

"No sir, I just like ice."

"Pass that bowl on down," the old man said to one of the boys, indicating a blue china bowl with ice chunks in it. The girl, slim with a broad mirthful face and quick black eyes, bobbed her head at him. She made big chomping motions.

Delvin said, "I used to cut down through the alley back there looking for my friend Buster Moran."

"The Morans, sho," one of the boys said. "They moved away."

"Old Moran was a pipefitter, I believe," said the old man. "Out here to Cranley's. On the colored shift."

"I believe he was," Delvin said.

Mr. Dandes talked about his farm out toward Scooterville,

passed down in his family since it was deeded to them just after the Civil War.

"We been out there all summer," the lively girl said. "That's all we do in the summer—just farm, farm, farm."

"Whoo, you don't do nothing," the older boy said, Harley. He had a riotous bush of shiny hair. "And sit under the arbor writing letters."

The girl blushed. Delvin could see the blush on her light skin, feel it, as if the heat traveled, on his own face.

"What kind of letters?" he asked because he wanted to know and wanted her to speak to him.

"She writes to the government," the other boy said.

"What about?' Delvin said.

"About their shortcomings and about their longcomings too. I ask them if they are trying to be as helpful as possible."

"She's a complainer," the lopsided twin said.

"I wrote the president a letter when I was a little boy," Delvin said. This was true.

"What happened?" Harley said.

"He wrote back."

"What'd he say?"

"He said he was enjoying himself—I'd asked him about that—and he hoped I was enjoying myself too."

"Were you?" the girl—more than a girl—asked.

"I was at the time."

As he spoke to her—this, what, sixteen-year-old girl, seventeen maybe—he experienced a bluster and yank of feeling, something slung onto a pile of odds and ends, an accumulation of breached and disordered living, messes and blunders and crushed years and thoughts too sullen and miserable to do anything about, packed against clotted falsities, outright lies, hopes packed hard into sprung joints—useless dumb hopes—stuffed with the knotted eccentric sadness of the jailbird; slather of meanness and repudiation and scarcity. He hurt in his gut and the ache like a fresh malarial sickness sucked into his bones and filled his mind with confusion. He wanted to lash these ignorant people with sarcasm and bitterness, to humiliate them and leave them with pictures in their minds that would haunt and hurt them.

Excusing himself—forcing the polite words out of his mouth—he got up and walked away from the table.

He made his way out into the alley and stood in the ample dark, letting pain rush unhindered through him. He was not here, but he was not any other place either. He sat down, unlaced and took off his boots, removed his socks, stood up and walked half a dozen steps in the soft sand that covered the alley. He stretched out his hands like a man sleepwalking in a cartoon. He reached for the air and for whatever was in the air or might be soon. He could smell the hot lard. He could smell the smoke from the fire, birch wood and chestnut, he recognized them, still did. The chestnut trees were dying all over the country, a blight, come from where nobody knew, no way to cure it, the trees just died. He could smell something else, apples, yes, cut apples, a sweetness, unrevisable. Some said *that doesn't ring a bell*, but for him everything did. Bole and bunch, dry squeak of old runner carpet, a cracked vase painted blue, a white shirt on a hanger hooked on a bedroom wire, smell of liver frying in the morning. The world a checklist of old favorites. He turned and walked slowly back, running his toes through the sand, taking his time. He smelled the roses on runner loops hanging over a fence. He went over and stood close to them. The blossoms were white and flat-faced and sweet. He touched a flower along the back of its face, feeling the swell of the bud it came from.

"It's a cherokee rose," a girl's voice said from behind him.

He turned. The young, dark-eyed girl stood there. She too was barefoot.

He made a tiny sound, as hard to hear as a dog whistle.

The girl moved up and stood silently beside him.

"Indian roses," he said. "I knew a Indian once."

"We are part Indian ourselves—at least that's what Daddy says. But he likes to make things up."

She laughed a small, crackling, unrueful laugh, a slender girl with high-flown wiry hair.

"Would you like to take a walk?" he said.

"All right."

They walked past quiet houses, secret lives alit in windows or concealed by the dark. In one yard a tire swing, the tire painted white. In another an old car up on a homemade lift, doorless, hood up, wheels like tilted snaggle teeth. At the next, on a back porch, two women sitting at a round table whispered furiously. They looked up and the whispering stopped, started again as they passed. Leftover summer frogs made clicking sounds. A nightbird issued the early version of its song. The two of them, man and girl, man and woman, boy and woman, boy and girl, walking, not touching, Delvin still barefoot carrying his boots, feeling sand and leaf, a stick, grass, round pebbles, a flat slab of rock under his feet, the girl close beside him, barefoot too; neither speaking.

They reached the end of the alley and stood in the opening that spilled a fan of pale sand like a little river mouth into the faintly lighted street. A tall shuttered house that had belonged to a traveling preacher reared just across quiet Silver road. The night was warm but Delvin could feel the coolness underneath, a coolness that carried winter in its arms. Other nights, feeling this, he might shudder for what was coming, but not now. The warmth was strong enough to keep them safe, for a little while. The silence extended between them until Delvin didn't know how to break it or if he could. Just then she spoke. She asked him who he really was.

"I'm uneasy about answering that," he said.

"I guess that's an answer."

He sensed that already she was trying to catch something that eluded her, catch her footing. He sensed a sadness in her and an energy that was not all straightforward, and a roughed-up gaiety. Her hands were long-fingered, strong-looking, almost as large as his.

"Are you timid?" she said.

"Vigilant."

"What are you looking out for?"

He figured that she knew. "Goblins."

"Plenty of them around this place."

He was silent. With Minnie he had been let alone to grope his way; both of them groped. Now he sensed he was in another confabulation. He didn't think he could keep up. Maybe it wouldn't matter.

"I feel like asking you a hundred questions," she said.

"Cause I'm a puzzle to you?"

"Yes—but everybody's that—just some people you want to go ahead and put the questions to them, get on through the whatever it is keeps them off to themselves."

"Lots of situations'll do that."

"Lots of reasons to build hideouts."

"Sholy."

"But they don't matter."

"How come?"

"Cause if you got to ask the questions anyway, you ask them. And then the other one, the one you asking the questions to, why, he has to decide for himself whether he's going to answer them or not."

"Maybe he can't."

"If he can't, then maybe that's the answer to all of them."

"That's a lot of weight," he said.

"I don't think so."

"Let me ask you something. Why do you want to know so much about me?"

"I can't help it."

The world seemed to have gone off in all directions. Every day he'd been free had been painful to him. It hurt to decide things. Soon as he could he'd latched on to a woman, Minnie May, sturdy and forbearing, owner of her own house, a small house on a quiet street, a woman away much of the time, grateful for what he might give her. Let her decide things. But what she decided scared him. And it scared him that Mr. Oliver was feeble—dying, he could see that, the future drying like a bubble of spit on his long lower lip. Out here everything was important, everything was too much: flake of soap on your wrist, smell of a bakery, somebody asking the time—like asking if you had the answer to their secret dilemma. It was all he could do not to turn himself in. Not to flee into some kind of drunkenness.

Some other accelerating dark. But he had somewhere to go. Something to do. He had to hold on to that.

He looked at the girl. Her face turned in profile and she seemed to be minding business of her own.

He said, "I like windy rain. I like salad beds—mustard and turnip greens mostly. I like cattle at night. Piney woods in a mountain distance. I like to see winter wheat growing in a big field."

She snapped her fingers, looked at him sideways under her brows, said, "I like riding in trucks. I like smelling things, anything that has a strong smell to it, even a stink. I like those birds with feathers that change from black to green according to how they take the light. I like stomping my feet in the dust."

He said, "I like seeing how far I can make a thought go in my mind before I lose track of it."

She said, "I like gritty cornbread and books about smart women."

They fell silent again.

Above the houses, above the continuation of the alley behind the houses in front of them, three stars, faint blurred bits, ceaselessly changing entities, hung above the smear of city brightness.

"Where were you on the way to when we shanghaied you?"

"The Emporium."

She took a half step back. "You one of those it's important to go over there?"

"Yes. I'm looking for somebody." He hadn't let this simple thought come forth before now but it was true.

"I'd like to go over that way."

"You want to gawk?"

"I guess I do—or no, I just want to see what that life's like."

"Like any other, I guess."

"I don't mean that."

"What do you mean?"

"Don't get mad."

"I'm not."

"I want to see what folks over there . . . are featuring . . . in themselves. I think people can't help but be curious."

"That's rightly so," he said.

"Will you take me?"

"Okay." He blurted this out but a second later it felt like a mistake. He was weighing himself down, whichever way he moved. But then he guessed he was bound to make mistakes.

A thin breeze angled in off the street, cooling their skin. A depressed feeling came over him. He wanted to ask at the bedhouse about his mother. He wanted to be alone with what he felt about that. "You know," he said, "I don't think . . ."

"It's all right," she said. "You don't have to take me."

"It's not that."

"No," she said, turning away.

She had a fading, falling quality to her, a weight of promises and needs that troubled him. Every knock at the door felt like all the pressers come to get him. He said, "I want to see if anybody there has heard anything about my mother."

She looked at him, paying out the line of kindness. "Some odd girl's not what you need at this time," she said.

"I've come a long way," he said, "just to take a look-see."

"These nights lately," she said, scanning the high parts of the sky, "since the big storm, have had such a deep blue to them. They say the blue only goes up for a few miles but it makes me feel good that we're wrapped up in it."

"Buttered in blue," he said, smiling.

She smiled back at him. Her broad face was open and friendly, without guile.

"I'm going to shade off this way," he said, indicating the direction—right, east—with his thumb.

"Born and raised in Chattanooga," she said, still smiling. "Shouldn't be hard to find your way back this way."

"Maybe I'll slip by . . ."

She seemed to be fading into the dark, but it was just a cloud passing over. The moon hadn't come up yet. He moved off. When he looked back he couldn't see her, wasn't exactly sure where she'd been standing.

3

The Emporium was lit like an ordinary house. Soft lamplight in the windows, a single lightbulb in a large lantern above the big white double front doors. He went around the side through the arched wooden gate to the back that had been partially paved with bricks and set up with a barbecue grill and tables under colored lights on strings swept up into two of the big fruitless mulberry trees. A couple of white men were sitting in mission chairs drinking beer. An africano woman sat on a bench near them. They looked up when he came through the garden area. He nodded to them, and exchanged pleasantries. He was bound up with nervousness. He asked for Miss Ellereen, the proprietress he remembered, but the woman told him she had died six years before.

"Ate herself to death," she said, grinning easily.

"Who is the principal these days?" Delvin said.

"Miz Corona," she said. "You selling something?"

"Not at the moment."

One of the men was giving him a long, studious look. "You got a familiar face," he said.

"Everybody says that."

"Yourn, boy, has a peculiar aspect."

Two white men, secured by alcohol. They had pudgy, half-collapsed faces, that rucked, white-person skin. They were wearing parts of army uniforms; lost soldiers maybe.

"How you ge'men doing?" Delvin said remembering the protocol, more important, and lasting, than the army's.

"Especially fine," one, the slightly fatter, said.

He was thinking how strange it was to speak to white men out in the world. In prison or out he had to call them mister.

"You a fighting man?" the other white man asked.

"Nosir. Cause of my bad leg."

"You a lucky boy." He elbowed his partner. "Aint he a lucky boy, Snell."

"Luckiest boy I seen today," the other, a red-haired man, said.

"Who you looking for?" the first man asked.

"I was looking for Miss Ellereen, but the lady says she died."

"I don't remember her. You must be from around here."

"Yessir, I is."

"You a Red Row boy?"

"Born and bred."

The girl was studying him too. "What's your name?" she said.

"William," he told her. "Mind if I step in the kitchen to see after Miz Corona?"

"Sho, it's all right," said the girl, just a farm girl skidded this far and no farther.

"Thank you. If you ge'men will excuse me."

"Oh yeah, Poke, go on, go on," said the bigger man, waving his wide fish-belly hand at him.

In the kitchen he came on Ostella Baker who had been a helper here years ago. She didn't seem to remember him. He asked about his mother—he couldn't keep from it—and every word of asking sounded foolish, backward in his mouth, but still necessary, still a kindness he could do for her. He felt exhausted just trying to keep up.

Everywhere thought extending itself into objects; he could feel the minds percolating around him, a gadgetry of ideas, comeuppances, answers for every problem. The smallest thing, that piece of equipment on the counter, the one with steel protrusions like round combs at the end of stalks . . . he didn't have time to ask about it.

"She worked here years ago," he said, "but she got accused of killing a man and she had to leave town."

The girl, woman now, with her hair shoved under a blue turban, cocked her head and said yes, she thought she remembered. "But I believe she's passed on," she said.

His knees went wobbly. A lightness filled his head and a pain pressed into his left temple. I shouldn't have asked, he thought. He looked hard into her light brown eyes.

"There was somebody like that . . . right here. I don't recollect," the woman said, flustered.

"Anybody around who'd know?"

"Miss Maylene. She helps out Miz Corona. And Miz Corona would know."

He found Miss Maylene in the large first-floor bedroom converted to office use. It had another small room behind it that looked out on the garden. A tall woman in a yellow tulle dress, Maylene from Dalton, Tennessee, stood at the wide shiny desk, sliding wax paper in between layers of blue blouses. The room smelled of camphor. The woman waved her fingers, picked up a glass atomizer, and sprayed the air in front of her. Behind her, outside the window, somebody turned on a red light. The woman straightened herself and stood stiffly with one hand out in front of her as if holding off the atomizer spray, or feeling her way. She didn't seem to know him, not at first.

"Yes," she said, "I remember Cappie. She came back here several years ago. You work for the police, don't you?"

"No mam, I never been associated with that outfit."

She gave him a long birdlike look, cocking her narrow face to one side. Her wrists were spindly.

"Are you an army man?"

"Not anymore. They sent me home because of my leg." He had scars on his legs—where he'd been lashed—if she wanted to check his story. "I'm Miss Cappie's son—one of em."

"Not the one that went to prison."

"No, mam, I'm his older brother."

"I see the resemblance. Well," she said sitting down at the desk, "I am sorry about your mother. Sit down," she said. Her arm like a relic. "That chair."

He took the pink plush-bottomed reed chair in front of the desk and sank down until he could hardly see over it.

"That's my mercy chair," she said, smiling.

He propped himself on the edge. "I hadn't seen her since I was a boy," he said. After the first shock he felt calm.

"She was sick when she came here. A couple of people remembered her. It was just after the time that Miss Ellereen died. You remember her?"

"Yes'm, I do."

"She got a wasting disease, cancer, or something, and we had to keep her in one of the little houses out back. She got it down in her testines and it was a little . . . stinky, you might say." She smiled in a funny way.

"Miss Ellereen?"

"You remember how big she was. Won't nothing left of her when she died." She smiled more brightly. "Then right after that your mother showed up. She arrived in a cab. She was wearing a leather dress, like a Indian squaw. What's that called—"

"Buckskin?"

"Like she was a squaw . . . or a cowboy woman—Annie Oakley or somebody. From out west."

"I understand."

"She was skinny as a bird. She had a flat white hat with little red cloth balls on a fringe around the edges. She was shaking so bad the little balls shook. I believe Miss Corona had just taken over, maybe it was that same week—I believe Miss Corona was afraid at first to let her in. But then a couple of the other women recognized her, or recognized her name. The girls, except for me and Miss Corona, were all too young to remember her. I believe Buster—the workman—he remembered her too. He was a friend I believe of your brother's when he was living over here at Mr. Oliver's—the funeral home?"

"Yes."

"He was the one went up and gave her a hug. He reminded them of who she was—told them, I mean, like they was waiting for a explanation."

"She was sick?"

"Sick? Did I say sick?" She glanced into her open palm as if the answer was written there. "She was run down and dog-tired.

She didn't say if there was anything else wrong with her. She just seemed real tired, wore out. They had to near carry her up the stairs. She made it all the way up to the third floor. They put her in one of the little rooms up there. She seemed stronger for a couple of days. She even came downstairs and sat out in the back over by the garden."

Just then the door opened and a large tawny-skin woman, ample in all her parts, spilt here and there from her pale blue gown covered partially by a green satin wrapper, entered the room. Delvin got up. He recognized her too: Miz Corona. Miss Maylene introduced him and explained what they were doing. Miz Corona—broad-faced with flesh across the bridge of her nose and filling her cheeks, dark, sharp eyes, a thin mouth heavily rouged—studied him, passed over without seeming to recognize him, and spoke to Miss Maylene about a plumbing problem, overflow on the other side of the house.

"Your mother was a funny lady," she said to Delvin. "Even there at the last she was making jokes."

"Do you know what was wrong with her?"

"Weary, like so many. Worked to death. I spect the running didn't help. She liked to sit in the garden. Right out in the middle of it among the squash and the butterbeans and such. Didn't like the flowers much, just the old fuzzy yellow squash fruit and the little butterbeans and all. Said where she'd been living she couldn't get vegetables like that to grow. She would lift the tomatoes—not pick em, just weigh them in her hand, put her face down among the squash leaves—dip way down, almost fall out of her chair." She glanced at the door. "Then one day," she said quickly, as if she was already passing like time itself to other things, "she couldn't get out of bed. You remember that, May."

"She was right upstairs."

"That's right. Tired on top of tired. The next morning when the girl went in to wake her she had passed over."

Delvin felt a stillness in him, as if a little boat had stopped rocking. "Who buried her?"

"We did," Miss Maylene said. "Miz Corona had us pay for the funeral right out of the operating money. We keep a fund for the girls—emergencies . . ."

"I mean, which funeral home?"

"Oh. Mr. Oliver's." Maylene patted her own wrist. "He's on his way out, too, I hear."

"Notice is taken, May," said Miz Corona.

Delvin experienced a small sadness propped on another, greater, sadness. He was sweating, just slightly, and felt a little cold at the same time. There were pictures on the wall, mountainscapes, tall gray peaks with tiny people standing around at the bottom. He had a feeling that everything was about to bust loose. He wanted to lie down somewhere.

"Could I see the room where my mother died?"

The two women glanced at each other and he saw the look of exasperation pass over Miz Corona's face.

"You can if you want to," Miss Maylene said. She called out the name Desiree.

Miz Corona stuck her hand out, palm down—did she want him to kiss it?—and Delvin took it, shook the bulging flesh carefully as he thanked her for her help.

A door on the side opened and the Ghost, wearing khaki army pants and a pink shirt, came in. "Desiree's busy," he said. He stared straight at Delvin and Delvin could see surprise hit his face like a shot. His eyes brightened and he pursed his orange lips. But he didn't say anything. Neither did Delvin.

In the twitchy second or two as they gazed at each other, seconds Maylene spoke into, telling the Ghost to take this man up to the Mockingbird room, he saw his life aimed at this spot like an arrow shot years before, launched into the darktown sky on the July day he was born, anniversary of the futile Union victory at Gettysburg, and fallen here, in a cathouse on Red Row. An ache like an old terrible wound began to throb in his side. Heat flooded his chest and into his face. He steadied himself on the fat yellow arm of the couch he stood beside. He wanted to scream—blast all the crusted-over tears from his body.

"You all right?" Miss Maylene said. "Get him some water, Caroline," she said to a woman who had come silently in.

They got him a glass of water, sat him down on the couch. From a small silver flask Maylene poured a shot of colorless liquid. "Local heaven," she said in smiling indication. Miz Corona had left the room. The Ghost just stood there, thin as a wraith, yellow and pink, avid.

In a minute Delvin was better. He smiled at them. His first feelings were strange to him, something not quite right, as if he had planned them. They played off into silence now like notes run by a single hand along piano keys. A sadness held steady. And relief. In his body a looseness, a calm. He got slowly, carefully, to his feet and thanked the women. His gratitude was as strong as his sadness.

In a minute he and the Ghost were climbing the back stairs. The stairs smelled of old washings, of liniment and spicy perfume and several combos of urine and rotten vegetables and pepper sauce. Neither spoke. They crossed the third-floor landing and entered a narrow hallway. The walls were covered in an old-fashioned rose paper down to a muddy brown wainscoting; dim electric bulbs burned in wall sconces stained with verdigris. A narrow strip of featureless dark green carpeting covered the floor. He'd not been in this part of the house before. Doors, liverish repaints crusted into whorls and random patterning, lined the hallway, a few of them open partway. Halfway down a woman's quavery voice sang, *"If you can catch me you can keep me,"* from a song he remembered hearing playing on the checkout deputy's radio as he was being loaded onto the truck for the ride to Acheron penitentiary.

Just beyond a partially opened door and an oblong of drowsy yellow on the floor was his mother's door, as indicated by the Ghost. He didn't have any need to come see the room beyond his suddenly wanting to. You take a step, he thought, and the one step leads to another. He felt like he was moving deeper into the dark. But maybe that wasn't it, maybe he was moving toward the light—or to nothing special.

The Ghost held up one hand for him to stop, took a big ring off his belt, deftly located the key, unlocked the door and held it open.

"You the first bellhop I ever met," Delvin said.

"You the first on-the-loose jailbird *I* ever met." He smiled and stuck out his hand. It was slightly greasy but he held on to Delvin as if he didn't want to let go. "How you doin, really, Del?" he said. "I am sure sorry about Mr. Oliver. I couldn't talk much about anything out at Miz Cutler's."

"I know. I spect I'm doing pretty well, now that I can walk around unfenced." He surprised himself how tightly he gripped the Ghost's hand.

"I'm sorry about your mama." He still looked nervous.

The room was small, only a bed with a coarse gray wool blanket and uncased square pillow and a little white table beside it with an unlit tin kerosene lamp on the table. A narrow wooden clothespress. A small dormer window looked out on the backyard. He could hear laughter down there.

"I'll step out here a minute," the Ghost said and closed the door behind him, leaving Delvin in the dark but for a washed-out light coming in the window. Delvin started to call him back but then he didn't. He stood in the kerosene-smelling room and then he sat down on the bed and then he lay down on it full length. He curled up on his left side and put his head on the pillow. You'd think time could twist in such a way that the old dried-out moment might come back to life in the present one. What others—what girls, what men passing through, maybe dark horses like the Ghost—had lain on this bed since his mother had slept those few nights here and died? Maybe no one had. Maybe her old festive being still traced itself here. He squeezed his eyes shut. No. It didn't matter.

He was tired, a graininess in his mind, sand in his eyes; he drifted off to sleep.

How long it was later he wasn't sure, and in the darkness he wasn't sure where he was, or if he was somewhere else beside his sling bed at Acheron—or was it Columbia? Strange—he had almost stopped waking in those places. The Ghost's hand was lightly shaking him as no hand would in prison. He did not come up panicked or fighting. He came up dizzy, as if he was drugged and swimming through layers of drizzle.

"It's you right on," he said, swung his legs out and sat up. "I mean it's me."

The Ghost stood near enough to grab him. "You need to get a move on," he said.

Delvin was almost alert. "Somebody call the police?"

"They will soon."

"Damn. Those old women figure me out?"

"Somebody will if somebody hadn't awreafter."

"What you being mysterious about?"

"You just better come on. Time to move yo hocks."

Again he could hear singing, a low rough female voice, singing the same song; he must have been asleep only a minute.

"No way I could spend the night here, hunh?"

"You wouldn't want to do that."

"Lord, I'm swackered."

"You on the run already, aint you?"

"I'm on furlough."

"Like one of them army boys."

"How come you aint hitched up?"

"Weak heart. How come they didn't put you in?"

Was he crazy? "They gave me a pass on the whole shebang."

"Well, come on. It's time for the civilians to air out."

On their way, moving slowly, Delvin half alert and memorizing as he went, walls and floor, the hall doors like a cascade in his mind, the faint lights like a lost measure of something grim and unforgivable, half a dozen steps down the passage the Ghost reached to close a door that stood open. "I thought I told you to keep this door shut," he said into the room.

"You don't run me," a woman's voice said. It was the singer's voice and a voice he had heard before.

The knob was jerked out of the Ghost's grasp and the door pulled open. Framed in the doorway, heavier than the last time he saw her, was Lucille Blaine, the woman who'd put him in prison. His mind churred in a white heat. He experienced a weightlessness and he felt as if he could fly—as if he would. He choked and quickly cleared his throat. His chest burned.

The woman looked straight at him and with the tensity that accompanies great acts he waited for what was coming—murder, sorrow, hanging—but then he saw she didn't seem to recognize him. She had not even appeared at the last trial, and in the one before that her story had sounded so slurred and disembodied the judge laughed outright at her, but still they had not let him go.

He shivered and glanced down at his left hand that seemed to be rattling at the end of his sleeve. He felt as if he was shaking out of his skin but his hand was barely trembling. The woman stared at him. She gave no sign that she knew him. Had he changed so much?

Then she grinned, showing missing teeth—number one on the right, number two on the left—a grin offered like a bag of tarnished jewelry to whatever in the world showed up.

"Looks like you found a fresh fish," she said to the Ghost.

She winked at Delvin and grinned.

"Come on," the Ghost said to him in a flat voice. The words seemed to come from far away. "You got to be back at the camp."

"You an army boy, hunh?" the woman said.

Delvin grunted.

"Mr. Go-Slow the GI Joe," she said, elaborating on the grin.

Without wanting to—never once in the years having meant to—he saw the fear in her eyes, the lifetime of it. Fear, yes, cultured by hate, but not absolved. And he saw the marks on her skin from the grinding stones that crushed her in the dark and saw the streaks and creases where the burning waters had rolled over her and saw the gouges where the knives had flensed her and saw the pasty cadaverous leftover skin where the vampires of false witness had sucked her blood. A revulsion rose in him at this, a spurning, distant yet collapsible, showered over by his own hate and the hard blows of an old raised hammer. Seconds collected like specie, legal tender for all debts public and private. He had beat the ground with fists, feet, hoe, shovel, cap, with his own bony head, banging the life out of her by proxy. He had screamed in a cell until they threw cold water on him, dragged him out and slung him still screaming into the dark closets of punishment. He had sobbed until his throat was raked raw, until his body ached in every acheable part. He could make a list. This cut, this scrape, this sprain, this blow from the shovel-faced guard, this unloosing of tendon, ganglia and fasciae, this cough, this wheeze, this shiver, this itch, this scar—this breath— issued him by Lucille Blaine of Chat-town, Tennessee.

Yet he continued to stand there in the dim yellow light. On a radio down the hall Mr. Jack Benny, another white man, mock-argued about a restaurant bill. The studio audience—gentle people, wizards, unapprehended malefactors, old ladies in itchy undergar-ments, girls with fever sores, men smelling of licorice schnapps— ignorant white people—laughed, as they say, fit to bust. Out there, among the passing audience of uncharged felons and saints and col-lectors of trash and the rustled and fractured losers and freakish lay-abouts and all the good people of the earth, among the tedious miles of the great republic, war-spooked and weary, in the elaborating dusk, these two, jailbird and slattern, doing their best to keep their feet as the cold ball rolled on through endless space, gazed at each other, eyes light-brown-gone-to-green peering into eyes dark-almost-to-black, and, as if nudged or prodded or slipped, or in frazzlement fallen, shifted the final micro measure that separates nothing from something.

Delvin began to turn away, but she called him back.

"Hey," she said, "I'm sorry, soldier boy. Why don't you come in." There was a softening in the rasp of her voice, quiet, not quite kindness, almost a plea. "Hey," she said, "you come a long way to get here, I bet, so why don't you sit a while with me."

She began to make room for him on the bed, swept soiled un-dergarments, pages torn from movie magazines, broken nail files, crumbs of misery, off the pale blue cotton cover.

"Come on," she said.

She was trying, a little, to make up for her harsh manner just now, he could see this. He could see she still didn't recollect who he was.

"I get to shooting off my mouth," she said, "no telling what's going to come out. You want some pop—or some gin? I got a little gin. Pete," she said, speaking to the Ghost, "go down and get us a bucket of ice. And another bottle."

Delvin looked into the Ghost's pale eyes, into the eyes of this man who knew him. "It's all right," he said.

"Don't take my foolishness to heart," she said, smiling crookedly.

Delvin saw the brokenness, the faltering about to spill into help-lessness. He thought of his mother and he could hardly remember her and this had been the truth of it for years. This woman's unlucky hair, like wire rusted on her head, her pudgy graceless fingers reaching to grasp the lid of a jar of cold cream smeared at the rim with a streak of rouge, the yellow warty elbow showing from under the loose sleeve of her brownish, sweat-streaked wrapper, reminded him of something that had nothing to do with this place and time. Not his mother, and not anyone he recalled, but another world, faltering as it passed.

The Ghost was standing just out in the hall in the sight line of both people, waiting for Delvin to come along, waiting for the moment representing reason and hope for the future and the house's wish for no disorder among the help to take hold.

"Where you from, soldier boy?" the woman asked, and even though she sounded as if she was reading from a paper Delvin could hear the restless appeal in her words.

She screwed the pale pink lid on the jar, set the jar aside on a table from which half-dollar-sized flakes of yellow paint had peeled and slopped gin into a squat glass she first wiped with a grime-gray handkerchief. A wire strung under the corner ceiling held a couple of fake-fancy dresses on hangers. She offered the glass to him.

This was a moment of great import. Did he take the glass that would in some sense extend forgiveness, if only in the most cursory way, to her? Or did he refuse? Did he in refusing dash the glass to the floor? Or did he take the glass and smash her across the face with it? Was this a trick? Had she recognized him after all and was only playing along—coldly or stiff with terror—until she could signal for Winston to get the laws up here?

He accepted the glass and set it on the low dresser that was close by, close enough to make it easy—appropriate even—to set the glass down; as if the universe had colluded with direction and destiny. He set the fluted cloudy glass down, just snagging it with his little finger and almost but not quite tipping it so she made a barely perceptible move toward it, the two of them leaning closer. She smiled in an unhappy, self-regarding way.

"Yes," she said, "a drink might not be what you need just now." She dipped her finger in the metallic-shiny gin and licked the liquor off it. "You must be from around here."

"I can't stay," he said as one might to an unmarried older relative, sad solitary person without recourse or hope for fun, blurting the words like a rube or a boy. *But I must be on my way. The living—the freshly escaped—have to be on their way.*

"I can make love come down around us," she said. "I got tricks. I got conjures."

She flopped back down on the bed, staying just upright enough not to be defenselessly collapsing or offering, and smiled foolishly. He could see that her hand wanted to come up and hide her snaggle mouth. He wondered if she was drunk. The room had a faint medicinal smell.

"Well," he said, half turning away.

"Wait," she cried, leaned forward and pulled out the top drawer. "I'm famous."

In the drawer were packets of newspaper clippings tied with red cotton string, half a dozen of them. She started to draw a fat packet from the drawer but he stopped her with his hand on top of hers. He could feel her soggy skin, the soft reddish hairs. His fingers were damp.

"I been in the news," she said, "all over the country. Ask that boy there, he'll tell you." The Ghost had become ghostlike, silent, staring, the fingers of one hand twitching in the palm of the other. "Aint that true, boy."

"Yes . . . m," the Ghost said, the final syllable or smear of syllable, the *m* or *mam*, still faintly snugged against the *s*, almost erased. The woman heard in this sound, so stifled it could hardly be caught by God himself, the disrespect, but she was infused with a thin solution of yearning—for kindness, for a tenderness that existed only in faint early morning dreams, themselves fading. The sound was like a distant bell tolling out the days of her life. Delvin saw her for what she was. He saw the unerasable sadness and the hate and the bitterness she couldn't quite contain and the cravenness and beggary she couldn't contain either; he knew the back precincts of near worthlessness she long ago had stopped trying to crawl out of—yearning even so for a little fanciness, a respite, a cool spot on a hot day—he had learned all about this yearning in prison and was an agent of it himself and he knew this too, and he had tried out the lame and careless usages of it that led nowhere except into deeper pain.

His eye twitched, once, twice, and he covered it with his hand. Out in the hall the Ghost shifted his feet. Delvin heard the rubber soles of his house shoes scull on the dry carpet. He removed his hand from hers.

"It's sufficing," he said.

He meant she didn't have to sell him anything, leastwise not reports of his own life's catastrophe.

"You ought to read some of these," Lucille Blaine said. "It was me that saved the day on this one."

Her voice faltered as she spoke.

In her voice—accent of ridgeback Tennessee, one of the castdown—he heard a river winding, dark, shining river of life descending the falls and granite steps from the high mountains to the valley, running onward through the hay fields to the plains and the sea. Was it simply too dim in this room for her to make him out? Had he changed that much? She'd never seen him anyway, really, not close. Maybe she had not even paid attention. The single long-necked bulb was shaded on the window side with a sheet of yellow paper taped to it. He could smell the hot paper. He could smell too the sumpy odor of female blood and, wearing at the sharp blade of it, the odor

of a familiar perfume, elixir of the bordello, all-purpose solvent con-
cocted of middle eastern fossil life soaked in essence of decompos-
ing lilies, Heaven's Night—Whore's Holy Water, it was familiarly
called—shipped out of Detroit City by the tankcar load throughout
whoredom, perfume she was at that moment even as she continued
to clutch their two lives in beggarly embrace atomizing into the air
between them; his mother's perfume.

For a second rage filled him. It flashed like a hot white light, like
something alive and so strong its grip hurt him to feel it. But it was
passing through—he knew this, felt it give and start to swirl away just
as the Ghost, who had snuck up close, hit him from behind.

He lurched into the woman who with surprising agility shoved
him away. He fell onto his face on the bed with the Ghost's knee
standing in his back. Against his throat he felt the sharp edge of a
razor. "You collect that, don't you?" the Ghost said. "You collect
what that is?"

Delvin said nothing. The woman in a swirl of garments and perfume had scrambled to her feet away from him. His head was turned
to the side and he could see her standing against the wall staring
shock-eyed at him, as if he was—not the the devil, but worse, and
she recognized him. All right. He waved at her as once in a moment
of hopeless hilarity he had waved in a courtroom at her, and before
the Ghost could cut him reared and knocked the razor away. The
woman sprang on him but he too was quick and he slipped under her
flailing and away and as she fell hard on the bed he cracked her in the
side of the head with his fist. She slumped senseless into the pillow.
He too had a razor. The Ghost was scrambling around after his on
the floor. He came up with it, a short cutter with a pearl handle, and
saw what Delvin was holding.

"You better get out of here," the Ghost said.

Delvin looked hard into his eyes.

"I got to preserve order here," the Ghost said.

"Think you can?"

"I don't know, but I got to."

The woman on the bed looked asleep.

"Jou kill her?" the Ghost said.

"Naw, boon. I knocked her out."

"Well, you better hightail it."

He didn't want this man telling him what to do. But he knew he had to go.

"Stand away from the door. "

The Ghost edged away, closer to the woman on the bed. She was snoring.

"Don't come after me. Don't call anybody."

"I won't."

Delvin grinned at him. "It's all yours," he said.

"Has been—is—will be."

"Sho."

He turned and dashed out into the hall, bounded down the stairs and then, walking calmly, quietly, left the house.

Over the mountains to the west the stars were up, little white parings. He headed that way, the woods weren't far. In his mind he was already gone, riding a freight north. As he ran, the train faded and was replaced by a small, spare room . . . in Ypsilanti maybe . . . or Toronto. He was in the little kitchen making himself a pot of chinese tea. On his desk a fresh page poked up from the typewriter. In it he was running through a field of blossoming sorghum, escaping from Uniball prison. He ran toward the blue bristling escarpment of leafed-out mountains. As the first cries started up behind him he entered the dark woods of his freedom.

ACKNOWLEDGMENTS

Thanks to Michael Signorelli, PJ Mark, and Cal Morgan for their help in carrying the load, and to Buzz Wagner, Anne Sunkel, Michael Block, Lawrence Joseph, Stan Brent, Robert Morris, and Jack Eppler, and thanks to the folks on Tuesday nights at St. Mary's and to my fellow travelers at the Chinatown Y, and thanks to Marcia Markland who stood up for the book, and a special thanks to Arlo Haskell, Miles Frieden, and the trustees of the Key West Literary Seminar for making possible several lengthy stays in KW that were revitalizing and essential to the work I did during those years, and most of all thanks and love top to bottom, front, sides, in around under and behind the house of this fiction to Daniela.

ABOUT THE AUTHOR

Charlie Smith is the author of eight novels, eight books of poetry, and a book of novellas. He has won numerous awards, grants, and fellowships, including the Aga Khan Prize, the Levinson Prize, the J. Howard and Barbara Wood Prize, a Guggenheim Fellowship, and a grant from the National Endowment for the Arts. The *New York Times* has selected three of his books as Notable Books of the Year and two as Editors' Choices. His writing has appeared in numerous publications, including the *New Yorker*, the *Paris Review*, and the *New York Times*. He lives in New York City.

ALSO BY CHARLIE SMITH

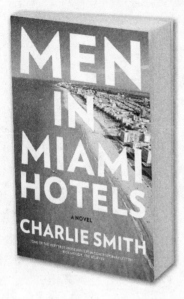

MEN IN MIAMI HOTELS
A Novel
Available in Paperback and E-book

The story of Cot Sims, a Miami gangster who returns to Key West aiming to—among other things—save his mother from homelessness after a recent hurricane. For love, for cash, and for the hell of it, he snatches a trove of emeralds that his boss, the relentlessly vicious Albertson, keeps hidden on a small island. And then trouble, coiling around him for years like a snake, bites.

THREE DELAYS
A Novel
Available in Paperback and E-book

"*Three Delays* is so stunningly composed, so wildly, implausibly, excessively written, that it makes the entire shelf of novels from the last generation superfluous.... This book consists almost entirely of the incantatory, rebel-angel prose that has made Charlie Smith a consummate outsider, and also one of the very best prose writers in contemporary letters."
— Rick Moody, *The Believer*

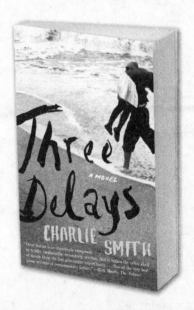